BROKEN SILENCE

Danielle Ramsay is a proud Scot living in a small seaside town in the north-east of England. Always a storyteller, it was only after initially following an academic career lecturing in literature that she found her place in life and began to write creatively full-time. After much hard graft her work was short-listed for the CWA Debut Dagger in 2009. Always on the go, always passionate in what she is doing, Danielle fills her days with horse-riding, running and murder by proxy.

DANIELLE RAMSAY

Broken Silence

AVON

AVON

A division of HarperCollins*Publishers*
77–85 Fulham Palace Road,
London W6 8JB

www.harpercollins.co.uk

A Paperback Original 2010

First published in Great Britain by
HarperCollins*Publishers* 2010

Copyright © Danielle Ramsay 2010

Danielle Ramsay asserts the moral right to
be identified as the author of this work

A catalogue record for this book is
available from the British Library

ISBN-13: 978-1-84756-229-6

2

Set in Minion by Palimpsest Book Production Limited,
Falkirk, Stirlingshire

Printed and bound in Great Britain by
Clays Ltd, St Ives plc

Acknowledgements

I would first like to thank all my family and friends for their invaluable support. Thanks especially to Francesca, Charlotte, Gabriel and Ruby, without whom I would never have started the book, let alone completed it. The four of you are my raison d'etre. Thanks to Janette Youngson and Paula Youngson for their constant encouragement, and to Mark Burrell. Particular thanks to Vicki Walton, Kaaren Turner, Victoria Cox, Patricia Savage, Suzanne Forsten, Pamela Letham and Gill Richards for being there when I needed them. Thanks to my long-standing friends, Dr Barry Lewis for his sound advice, and a heartfelt thanks to Eliane Wilson and Professor Peter Wilson to whom I am heavily indebted to for their kindness and constant support.

I am eternally grateful to my literary agent, Jenny Brown. Thank you for believing. Thanks also, to all at Avon, for being so wonderful, and in particular Kate Bradley for being such an incredible, inspiring person to work with – no writer could have a greater editor.

And finally, thanks to my horse, Tico who in all the stress of writing kept me firmly grounded – at times literally!

For Elizabeth Ramsay and John Ramsay – you are my inspiration.

Chapter One

She felt sick, really sick.

She moaned as the ground started to swirl in front of her.

'Oh fuck!' she slurred as she drunkenly collapsed onto her hands and knees.

Trembling, she waited for the nausea to pass.

Finally certain that she wasn't going to puke she pulled her long blonde hair back from her face and looked around, but it was too dark to make sense of the rubble and half-fallen walls of the abandoned farmhouse. She suddenly realised that she was alone.

'You fucking shit!' she yelled out, angry that he had just left her there in the middle of nowhere.

She waited, but there was no response. The surrounding trees and bushes conspired against her, rustling and creaking, fooling her into believing that someone else was there.

'Fuck you and your fucking attitude! I hate you! You hear me? I fucking hate you!' she screamed defiantly. 'You're the one with the problem, not me!'

She slumped back onto her knees and stared up at the black starless sky. Everything seemed so pointless. She hated him. She hated him for using her and then just throwing her to one side. She would have to be stupid not to notice that he wasn't into her any more. She had heard the rumours. Who hadn't? She knew there were other girls, but she'd hoped that she had meant something to him. She had foolishly believed that he could take her away from her crap life; that he could somehow save her. But now that he had got what he had wanted, he wasn't interested any more.

She felt a cold wetness on her face and realised she was crying. She wiped her damp cheeks aggressively, angry with herself for feeling like this. Angry that she had let him get to her.

'I don't fucking care what you say. I'll tell whoever I want to about what you've done to me. Then you'll be sorry! You hear me? You'll be the fucking sorry one, you bastard!' she threatened, ignoring the tears as they continued to fall.

Exhausted, she attempted to get to her feet. Certain that she could stand she pulled out her mobile phone from the front pocket of her short black denim skirt. She tried to make out whether she had any new messages or calls.

'Bastard!' she muttered when she realised she didn't.

She started to scroll through her phone book looking for his number.

Suddenly she heard footsteps coming up behind her. She smiled, relieved that he'd come back.

She froze as the smile faded from her lips.

'I . . . I . . . didn't mean the things I said . . . yeah? I was just really mad with you, that's all . . .' she stuttered as she shook her head.

It took her a second to register what was about to happen. Shocked, she dropped her phone as she numbly staggered backwards as she tried to get away.

In her panic she tripped over and fell to the ground. She grabbed her scarf which was lying beside her and rolled over onto her knees as she attempted to get up. But a hard kick to her back winded her, forcing her down again.

Suddenly the scarf was pulled from her hand.

'Ahh!' she cried out as her head was yanked back by her hair.

She felt something being slipped around her throat. She couldn't understand what was happening. And by the time she did, it was too late. The scarf was already securely knotted around her neck. She screamed as she clawed at the material. But the harder she fought, the tighter the scarf was twisted, silencing her.

She frantically tore at the scarf, desperate to breathe but she couldn't loosen its hold over her. Panicking, she scratched at her neck ferociously as the burning pain in her lungs intensified. Finally, she collapsed forward, unconscious of what was about to follow.

Chapter Two

The phone was ringing. It had to be bad. He could feel his heart pounding. He turned over and buried his head into the pillow but the ringing continued. He tried to ignore it but it was pointless. He opened his eyes and lay there for a moment drenched in sweat.

It was dark, still night. He looked down at the cluttered floor gingerly and squinted at the alarm clock, his head exploding with the effort. It took a few seconds before he could make out it was only 4.30 am. And another couple of seconds before he realised the phone was still ringing. He stretched out his trembling hand and groped around on the floor.

'Yeah?' he mumbled hoarsely.

'Detective Inspector Brady?'

Without answering, he disconnected the call and dropped the phone to the floor. His head was thumping. He had the mother of all hangovers, which wasn't surprising considering he'd been on a suicidal bender for the past couple of weeks. He had been downing a toxic mixture of whisky and beer to forget his wrecked life and block out the recurring nightmare he had had for as long as he could remember. But lately nothing seemed to work. Even when he sank into a drunken sleep he always woke up sweating, heart racing.

He tried to recall the previous night. All he could remember was drinking too much and then . . .

He felt sick at the thought. He winced as the knot in his stomach tightened. He turned his pounding head tentatively. A young woman lay asleep on her stomach beside him, naked from the waist up, the duvet discreetly covering the rest of her body. Her thick, dark, shoulder-length hair was spread out over the pillow. He watched as she gently breathed in and out. He couldn't even recall her name let alone what she did for a living.

He swallowed hard, trying to dislodge the sour taste in his mouth. Never before had he plummeted to such a nadir. There hadn't been anyone since Claudia, his wife, had left. And now here he was with some young woman who he didn't even recognise lying naked beside him.

The drinking was supposed to distract him from who he was, not make him feel even worse about himself. He thought about getting some painkillers and decided that he couldn't be bothered to get up and rummage around in the dark. The last thing he wanted to do was wake up Sleeping Beauty.

The phone started to ring again. He froze as she started in her sleep.

'Fuck!' he muttered.

He stretched his right hand out and blindly searched amongst the months of debris scattered on the floor.

'What?' he answered in a thick Geordie voice, silencing the shrill ring.

5

He watched as she stirred briefly before slipping back into a restless slumber.

'Brady?' questioned a low, deep voice.

'Who wants to know?'

'DCI Gates.'

'Sir?' questioned Brady, thrown.

'You're a hard man to get hold of, Jack,' continued the dispassionate voice.

'With all due respect, sir, I'm not expected back until Monday.'

He regretted the words as soon as he had spoken them. Gates wasn't the kind of man that you wanted as an enemy.

'You have half an hour to get it together.'

'But . . .' he objected.

'I'll have a car waiting for you. Make sure you're ready,' Gates ordered, leaving him no choice.

By the time he had thought of a response the line was dead.

He stared blankly at the phone trying to figure out what was going on.

Moments later he was roused from his musings by a dull, heavy pain in the pit of his stomach. He needed to piss. He pulled the duvet back and swung his legs onto the floor.

A searing pain shot through his left inner thigh. He instinctively pressed down hard with both hands onto the knotted wound and held them there as he waited for the pain to subside.

He didn't know who he hated more; the bastard who had tried to blow his balls away or Claudia for leaving him while he lay fighting for his life. Admittedly he had given her a good enough reason, but even he hadn't expected to come round from surgery to the unwelcome news that she'd had enough. Not only had she left him, she had left the area. It didn't take him long to find out that she had gone to London and had no intention of coming back to the North East.

He hated his life, hated what he'd become without her. Not a single day had gone by since she'd left him when he hadn't considered finishing what the bastard who had shot him had intended. But that was over six months ago, and here he was, still drunk, still bitterly alive.

He could feel a clammy sweat building up on his forehead and wasn't sure whether it was because of the pain in his leg or alcohol poisoning.

He looked at the clock. 4.54 am, he thought, sighing heavily. He stood up shakily and waited a few moments, unsure of whether he was too drunk to stand. Finally certain that he could stay on his feet he slowly limped over to the bedroom door.

'Where . . . where are you going?' murmured a sleepy voice.

He paused.

What could he say? Sorry, I don't even remember fucking you last night, let alone your name?

He shook his head.

'Go back to sleep,' he muttered.

He watched her mumble her consent and turn over. He stood for a moment wishing that his life were that simple.

*

Bleary-eyed he blinked back at his reflection and ran his fingers through his long dark hair pulling it back from

7

his face. He'd been meaning to get it cut but hadn't got around to doing it. He stared at his heavy hooded, dark brown bloodshot eyes.

He was six feet two and slender with some muscle. He was attractive; at least that's what his soon to be ex-wife had told him. Not that he could see it. But he knew there was something about him that women liked. Sleeping Beauty lying in his bed was testimony to that.

But throughout the five years he had been married he had never fooled around. Not once, not until that fateful night. And even then it was over before it had even started. But it was enough for Claudia to bail. He knew it was a convenient out for her. After months of Claudia working long hours in a blatant attempt to avoid him, Brady drunkenly and pitifully fell into the arms of a seductive new colleague – Detective Constable Simone Henderson. Claudia had walked in on them without Brady knowing. It wasn't until the following night when his balls were nearly blown away on an undercover drugs bust that he realised that Claudia knew about his indiscretion. She had rushed to the hospital as soon as she heard he had been shot, wanting the reassurance he was still breathing so she could have the satisfaction of handing him divorce papers.

Brady lifted a wet hand and tried to wipe clean the smeared blur that was his reflection. He looked rough, too rough to crawl into work. He ran his right hand over the dark stubble that covered his chin and crept up over his cheeks. In a last ditch attempt to straighten himself out he splashed icy cold water over his face. It made no difference; he still looked half-cut. There was only one thing that would sober him up and that was a hot shower

8

followed by black, bitter coffee. He needed to at least appear sober if he was facing Gates. He knew that whatever had happened must have been serious enough for Gates to be calling.

Chapter Three

Brady heard the doorbell ring and looked at his watch: it was 5.25 am, bang on time. He dragged heavily on the cigarette in his hand before crushing it out. Already the third one of the day, he noted, acknowledging that he had failed to kick the habit before returning to work.

But at least he was starting to sober up. Add to that a shave and a change of clothes and he looked halfway decent.

Brady poured himself some hot black coffee and looked around at the chaos that had crept into the house after his wife had left. Row after row of empty Peroni bottles, half-eaten Chinese take-away cartons and empty pizza boxes pretty much summed up his life now. It stank.

He switched off the kitchen light and walked down the hallway, his heavy footsteps resonating on the wooden floor.

He looked around in disgust. A lamp was still on throwing a gloomy light over the mess his life had become. Overflowing ashtrays were scattered all over the room. Discarded whisky and beer bottles lay across the dusty wooden floor. Over six months' worth of weekend newspapers were dumped on an old leather armchair. Books lay in piles around the room, while others haphazardly lined the handmade wooden bookcases that covered two of the walls.

His office at the station, with its high, rattling windows and bulky, rust-stained, leaking radiators, felt more comfortable to him than his own home. More so now that he couldn't stomach living alone in a three-storey five-bed-roomed Victorian house. The fact that Claudia had not only moved out, but had taken every scrap of furniture that wasn't nailed down didn't help. He had volunteered to be the one to leave, but Claudia had declined his offer. The fact that she had walked in on Brady in their bed with a young colleague had been incentive enough for her to pack up and go. And to be fair, he couldn't blame her. Between them there had always been one rule, never bring work home.

They had both worked for Northumbria Police. It was his job to lock the scum up who made decent people's lives a misery and it had been Claudia's job to support the same scum by offering them legal representation; regardless of the crime. She was a lawyer and also acted as the Duty Solicitor at his station. She was damned good at her job; so good that the law firm she worked for in Newcastle were preparing to offer her a partnership.

They had met through work and somehow had survived everything it had thrown at them until now. Brady knew that even his boss, the emotionally cold and unflappable DCI Gates, had a soft spot for Claudia. Who didn't? She was strikingly beautiful with a mane of long curly reddish hair and a fiery personality to match. But Brady hadn't married her for her good looks; it was her quick wit and stunning intelligence that had seduced him. And the fact that she was everything he wasn't; middle-class, educated and compassionate. She fought injustice because she believed in civilisation. He, on the other hand, didn't believe in a better society. Brady was a realist and to him, civilisation was just another false god that idealists liked to believe in. His job was to prevent the world from becoming the dark and dangerous place he knew it to be.

Brady looked at the two empty whisky tumblers sat side by side on the tiled hearth. He recalled bitterly how he and Claudia would often share a bottle of whisky in front of the fire while Tom Waits played in the background. In the early days they had passionately argued about anything and everything from politics to literature. He felt physically sick as he thought about what he had lost. She had meant everything to him. More than even she had realised.

Wincing, he bent down to retrieve his jacket from the floor. Pulling it on he turned to see who Gates had sent.

It was Harry Conrad. He looked half-frozen. As always, his blond hair was cropped short and neat. Clean-shaven, with the look of a man who took time over his appearance, Conrad wore a conservative charcoal-grey suit with a blue shirt and dark blue tie. Over this he wore a heavy dark grey woollen overcoat.

That was Conrad for you: always clean-cut, well-dressed, polite and ready to take orders, even at five in the morning. Conrad had the makings of a Detective Chief Superintendent. He was well-liked by his superiors because he was eager and always did as he was told. That guaranteed success, something Brady had found out the hard way.

'Fuck it,' Brady said under his breath.

Gates really was trying to mess with his head. It was cold, too cold and dark to be out of bed. And too early to be dealing with this.

'Gates sent me, sir,' Conrad eventually said. He looked uncomfortable; his five feet eleven body hunched over, head down.

Brady suddenly felt old as he stood looking at his thirty-year-old deputy. Brady may have only had eight years on Conrad, but for the first time he could really feel the age difference.

'Why?' Brady asked as he narrowed his dark brown eyes.

Conrad shoved his hands in his coat pockets uneasily while Brady continued to stare at him.

'I was just ordered to pick you up, sir.'

Brady didn't reply.

Conrad uncomfortably filled in the silence.

'We've got a murder victim, sir. A young woman.'

Brady didn't know what he had expected when he started back on Monday, but it definitely didn't involve any high-profile cases. He felt uneasy, something about this didn't feel quite right.

'What details do you have?'

'I've just been called in myself, sir. All I know is that the body was found in West Monkseaton, on some abandoned farmland near the Metro line.'

'Do we have an ID?'

Conrad shook his head.

If Conrad had said North Shields or even Shiremoor Brady would have understood but not West Monkseaton. It was classed as the upmarket part of Whitley Bay. Then again any place was better than Whitley Bay; to say the small seaside resort had seen better days was an understatement. The town was a testimony to the credit crunch, most of the retailers having closed up leaving behind a trail of depressing, musty-smelling charity shops and seedy pubs.

The only thing the rundown coastal town had going for it was that it was within commuter distance of Newcastle upon Tyne; a University city with a thriving student population and Goth culture. Newcastle was also known for the Bigg Market where punters would binge drink into the early hours, women staggering in their four-inch heels, and short, strapless dresses leered at by packs of thuggish men in sleeveless shirts – regardless of the North East's all-year sub-zero temperatures.

But Brady knew from first-hand experience as a copper that the seaside resort of Whitley Bay could also hold its own when it came to binge drinking and lewd behaviour. So much so, it came as no surprise to Brady that the small, shabby, seaside town had been rated as a weekend stag party destination equal to Amsterdam.

'Gates is waiting for you at the crime scene sir,' Conrad emphasised. He was under strict orders to collect Brady and get him to Gates ASAP.

'Let me grab my keys,' answered Brady as he rummaged through the unopened mail and other objects dumped on the ornate marble mantelpiece.

Conrad looked around uncomfortably at what had become of his boss over the past two months. He had known the place when Claudia had been around and found it difficult to accept that it had degenerated into this soulless squalor. The smell of decaying food and stale alcohol clung nauseatingly in the air, as did the overwhelming feeling of despair and loneliness.

The last time Conrad had seen his boss was when he had visited Brady in hospital, shortly after surgery. Unfortunately, he had witnessed Brady losing it after Claudia had served him with divorce papers. That was over six months ago. Brady had refused to see him after what had happened. Wouldn't allow him in to visit and when he discharged himself, refused to answer his door or any of the phone or email messages Conrad had left. Conrad had been worried, but not surprised that Brady had gone to ground given his state of mind after Claudia had left him.

Clutching his keys Brady limped out to the hall. Conrad followed.

'Haven't seen you since the incident, sir,' Conrad offered, unsure whether he should mention it.

'Yeah, well I've been busy,' answered Brady.

They both knew he was a lousy liar.

Brady felt awkward. He had avoided Conrad for the past six months, deleting any messages Conrad had left without listening to them. So what? Brady thought. Conrad should be the one feeling guilty, not him. He had had word from an old colleague that Conrad was rumoured to have requested a transfer. Admittedly, it was only a rumour, but it still felt like a betrayal given everything they had been through. To make the situation worse, he had also heard that Conrad was scared that Brady would have some kind of breakdown. Even Brady had to admit that if he was in Conrad's place, the last person he'd want to be teamed up with was himself. Not after what Conrad had witnessed.

'So, put in for a transfer yet?' As soon as the words had slipped out Brady hated himself.

Conrad was thrown.

'No, sir. Why, should I have?'

'You tell me!'

'You've lost me, sir?' replied Conrad.

Brady could hear the hurt in Conrad's voice making him feel even more like a bastard.

'Forget it . . .' he muttered. 'Forget I said anything.'

'No, if you have something to say then say it,' demanded Conrad.

Brady looked at him, mildly surprised, but impressed at Conrad's ballsy outburst.

Brady shook his head.

'It doesn't matter.'

'I disagree. The fact that you could even think I'd put in for a transfer says it all,' Conrad stated.

'All right! You want me to tell you what really pissed me off?'

Conrad looked at him, locking his steel-grey eyes on Brady's.

'You of all people knew what Claudia did destroyed me. I mean fuck it, Conrad! You were there! She didn't even respect me enough to tell me in private. She insisted you stayed in the room so you could witness my humiliation. What the hell do you think that did to me, eh?'

Conrad steadily held his gaze without saying a word.

'So why then would you go to Gates? Why go over my head to my superior and tell him that I was a liability to myself and the job?'

'Because it was the truth,' answered Conrad simply.

Brady shook his head as he looked at his deputy.

'You left me no choice,' added Conrad.

Brady turned away. He couldn't look at Conrad. He didn't want him to see the pain in his eyes. He knew that Conrad was right; he had left him no choice.

Brady knew that what Conrad had seen in the hospital that night had scared him. Brady had scared himself. But it had affected Conrad so much that he had gone to see Gates without a word to Brady. Conrad had suggested that

Brady needed a psychologist to help him get over being shot. In reality what he needed was a bloody good solicitor to help him get over his wife.

He couldn't believe it when the police psychologist casually dropped by the hospital. Brady had the feeling that Gates had been secretly hoping that he had finally lost the plot and that the psychologist would recommend he should retire early from the force on medical grounds.

It didn't take long before Brady found out that Conrad was responsible for his shrink sessions. After that he refused to see him, knowing that he would do something to Conrad that he would later regret and then really would be in need of a shrink. When he finally discharged himself from hospital he ignored the barrage of phone messages and texts left by Conrad.

'You know why I couldn't tell you,' explained Conrad. 'You were in no state to hear reason, not after . . .' His voice trailed off, reluctant to bring up Claudia's part in Brady's self-destructive meltdown.

Brady knew Conrad was right. Nothing Conrad could have said would have stopped him that night. Nothing.

His memory of exactly what had happened that night after he had come round from surgery wasn't that clear. But what he did remember was Claudia coming in and handing him divorce papers and Conrad being forced to stand there, not knowing what to do. Then Claudia turned on her high heels and left without giving him a chance to absorb what she'd done. After that, he couldn't really be sure of what followed. He vaguely recalled pulling the wires from his body as he tried to get himself out of bed to go after her. And then Conrad perilously trying to stop him. Despite his condition he came at Conrad with a strength he didn't know he possessed.

It had taken two male nurses to get him off Conrad and to forcibly hold him down until a doctor came with an injection so strong that it knocked him out for the rest of the night. Conrad had dutifully stayed by his bed for the next twenty-four hours, despite Brady having broken two of Conrad's ribs in the struggle. But Brady had no memory of Conrad's vigil. Nor did he remember repeatedly calling out for Claudia, unaware of what had happened. The days following came and went in a painful, drug-induced blur until eventually he accepted that Claudia wasn't coming back.

Not that Conrad had told him that. It was his psychologist who had shared this information. Allegedly, Conrad had refused to even tell Gates how he had sustained the injuries, despite visibly having a broken nose and stitches zigzagging over his top lip and across his eyebrow. Add to that the medical report that had been filed on Brady's sudden insanity. Even a fool would have realised that Conrad had got caught in the crossfire. But Conrad was loyal and he had done his best under the circumstances to protect Brady. And even Brady had to acknowledge that Conrad was protecting him when he went to Gates.

'Look . . . Conrad, I understand. All right?' Brady quietly conceded.

It wasn't until now with Conrad stood in front of him that he realised he wasn't angry at Conrad. He was angry with himself for putting Conrad in that situation in the first place. And he knew the real reason Conrad went to Gates wasn't because he wanted him to lose his job; it was the opposite, he wanted him to hold on to his job. And if that meant bringing in the police psychologist, then Conrad had no qualms in requesting that Gates did exactly that.

'Honestly, I understand,' he repeated.

Conrad nodded, grateful that they had finally cleared the air.

'Jack? Jack? What's going on?' interrupted a soft voice from the top of the stairs.

Brady felt as if somebody had stuck a knife in his stomach and twisted it. He'd completely forgotten about her.

They both turned and looked up. Sleeping Beauty was standing shivering in what appeared to be just her T-shirt and skimpy knickers. She pushed her dark tousled hair out of her sleepy face as she stared in bewilderment at the two men below her.

'It's nothing. Go back to bed,' Brady answered, embarrassed. His throat felt dry and tight. He didn't want anyone knowing his private business; especially Conrad.

Looking at her standing there, vulnerable and still drunk, he felt disgusted with himself. He realised in that moment that Claudia was right about him. He was a bastard. He would never change, not really. And here in front of his and Conrad's eyes was the evidence. He couldn't believe how low he had stooped. He could now see what had eluded him last night: her age. If she were twenty-one it would have surprised him.

'Come on,' he said as he turned to Conrad.

Conrad didn't say a word.

Brady knew what he would be thinking. And if he were in Conrad's shoes right now, he'd be thinking exactly the same thing; that he deserved to lose Claudia.

'Jack? Jack?' she called out in a tremulous voice.

He turned and looked up at her still standing there, shivering.

'I'll . . . I'll leave my number so you can call me about tonight . . . yeah?'

Brady nodded and then walked out into the black, empty night after Conrad. He knew for her sake the best thing to do was not call her back. Let it go and pretend it had never happened.

He could see nothing but blackness as he reached the path at the end of his long, front garden. But he could hear the thunderous crashing of the heavy waves as they beat against Brown's Bay below. He lived on Southcliff, an imposing and exclusive row of Victorian houses that lined the cliff, facing out towards the North Sea. Nestled on a tight bend between Cullercoats and Whitley Bay, Brady had never been sure whether the row of houses fell in the sought-after fishing village of Cullercoats or whether it marked the very edge of the shabby seaside resort of Whitley Bay.

Claudia had fallen in love with the place as soon as she had seen the bending cliff with its dramatic plunge to the waiting rocks below. On a good day the view from the first-floor living room and second-floor study were breathtaking; dazzling azure waters lay perfectly still as far as the eye could see. White sailing boats and small, brightly coloured fishing boats would serenely blend in against the backdrop of stunning blue. But when the sea mirrored the grey, blackening skies overhead, the brooding waves would thrash against one another as they threw themselves against the cliff, violent and furious. At times the waves would be so high they would crash against the path lining the cliff, covering the large windows of the house in a thick, salty sea spray. If one of the local fishing boats was unfortunate enough to be out collecting lobster nets during a storm, Brady would watch through the murky windows mesmerised, while the tiny boat would be mercilessly tossed from one black wave to another.

'Bugger me! It's cold!' he said as turned up his jacket collar against the cold, bitter air coming off the North Sea.

Conrad didn't reply as he made his way along the walkway towards his car parked on the tight bending road at the edge of the jutting cliff.

Brady knew Conrad wasn't impressed with what he'd seen. And Brady couldn't help but agree with him.

Chapter Four

Conrad pulled the car over, joining the ominous line of police cars and vans parked along the edge of the road.

Brady inwardly steeled himself as he looked out at the twenty or so uniformed and plain-clothes officers. It felt as if he had been gone for a lifetime, not six months.

And given that it was only six-ten on a bitter November Friday morning, he had every reason to resist getting out of the car.

'Are you sure you're up to this, sir?' Conrad asked as he turned to look at him.

'Why wouldn't I be?'

'No reason, sir,' answered Conrad uneasily.

'Do you really think Gates would have called me in if I wasn't?' Brady asked him darkly.

Without waiting for an answer he got out of the car and slammed the door. He left Conrad to find somewhere to park and headed towards the blue and white police tape flapping miserably in the biting northern wind. The tape was sealing off a cumbersome iron gate. Brady presumed that the abandoned farmland beyond it was where the victim had been discovered.

He turned back and looked at the main road. It was

deserted, blocked off by the police. A dismal, magnolia-painted Modernist building stood bleakly opposite. West Monkseaton Metro station; Brady knew it well enough. He could smell the stale piss drunkenly sprayed by passers-by against the badly-lit damp corners. He could hear the clinking of leftover bottles of cheap alcohol from the teenage kids who would travel from Shiremoor or North Shields and stand in huddled groups, shivering and laughing against the bitter night. Soon it would be swamped by early morning bleary eyed business-suited commuters clutching their latte or espresso from the local deli. They would dodge their way past the rolling, broken bottles and the pools of stinking piss trying not to breathe in the stench.

Brady shivered as he turned back to the farmland. He tried his best to walk without a limp, aiming for the two brutish officers guarding the entrance to the farmland.

'Sir,' PC Hamilton nodded. He quickly dropped his eyes and fixed them on his feet as he moved out of Brady's way.

'Inspector Brady?' queried the other younger officer.

Brady looked at him. He knew that his black jeans, black polo shirt and black leather jacket didn't adhere to the Superintendent's dress code which was how he presumed the rookie had guessed right about him being the DI. Brady's lack of suits was legendary at the station. It wasn't to say that he didn't look professional, but casual professional was how he liked to term it.

'Sir, the DCI was expecting you—' the young officer faltered, flustered.

'And?' prompted Brady irritably, aware that he was late.

'The problem is you've missed him. He left a few minutes ago,' the constable mumbled uneasily.

'Shit!'

The last thing he wanted to do was piss Gates off. Not on his first day back. If Conrad had put his foot down like Brady had said then they would have gotten here over five minutes ago.

'Do either of you have any mints?'

'Sorry, sir?' questioned the young officer, confused.

'Bloody mints! Do you have any?' replied Brady losing his patience. The knowledge that Gates had already gone had left him in a foul mood.

PC Hamilton hurriedly pulled out a packet of mints from his jacket pocket and handed them to Brady.

He would need them when he came face to face with Gates. The last thing Gates would tolerate was the smell of booze. A reformed alcoholic, Gates had led a Puritanical crusade against the vice, intolerant of any officer who came in to work oozing the telltale lingering perfume of a heavy night's drinking.

Brady pocketed the mints and bent down under the tape and walked through the open gate.

Below in the distance he could see the cold glow of lights set up over the crime scene. The constant hum of the generator to power the spotlights muffled the low talk of the officers behind him.

He walked down the dirt track that had been ravaged by weeds and long, wild grass.

'Never knew this existed,' said Conrad catching him up.

Brady nodded as he looked around. It was a dark, lonely spot; an ideal location to murder someone or dump a body. All around him thick clumps of bushes loomed threateningly, wild and overgrown, hiding a multitude of sins.

'Who do you think comes down here?' asked Conrad.

'Kids,' answered Brady. He had already noticed a couple

24

of empty, plastic cider bottles dumped in the overgrown bushes.

'It's the ideal place to come and get pissed or high. No one is going to bother you,' continued Brady as he turned his head and looked back at the unlit track leading up to the main road.

He stopped abruptly and sighed.

'Shine your torch down here, will you, Conrad?'

'Crap!' Brady cursed as he looked at the dog faeces stuck to the sole of his boot. 'There's your answer, Conrad.'

'Sir?'

'Kids and bloody dog walkers. That's who come down here,' he muttered as he tried his best to clean his boots.

*

'What the bloody hell is this? Didn't I make myself clear when I said that I don't want any more bloody footprints messing up my crime scene? You lot have already buggered up enough! Now clear off!' thundered an irate white-clad figure as he emerged fuming from the crumbling walls that would have once been a farmhouse. Behind the ruined walls spotlights coldly illuminated the crime scene.

Conrad stiffened his shoulders, his jaw rigid as he readied himself for battle with Ainsworth, the Scene of Crime Unit's senior officer; infamous for his ill-temper and obstinacy.

'Good to hear that you're still the same sour-faced old bugger!'

'Jack Brady?' spluttered Ainsworth.

'They couldn't get rid of me that easily,' answered Brady as he approached the senior SOCO. He was a short, portly man with a receding head of curly silver hair and a large, ravaged face that belied the fact that he was only in his mid-forties.

'Bloody hell! So when did you start back?' Ainsworth questioned as he shook his tired head in disbelief. 'I didn't think it would be for a while yet, not with what I heard had happened to you . . .' He paused as his small, razor-sharp eyes quickly took in Conrad who stiffly waited behind Brady.

'Yeah, well seems the boss thought I was ready to start back so here I am,' Brady answered with a wry smile.

'Well, Jack, I'll say this, you've got your work cut out here. It's a mess . . . a bloody mess . . .' Ainsworth said, shaking his large head. 'And you better tread carefully. I don't want you being replaced like that other poor bugger,' he warned.

Brady felt himself flinch as Ainsworth's words struck him. He turned to Conrad.

'Do you know about this?'

'No sir.'

Brady already had a bad feeling about this investigation without hearing from Ainsworth that he'd been called in at the last minute to replace some other poor sod who had no doubt got on the wrong side of Gates. One thing he didn't like was surprises. Not where Gates was concerned.

'Now follow my exact footsteps, and I bloody mean mine not one of the other set of bloody footprints we have all over the place here,' Ainsworth ordered. 'Like I said, Jack, it's a bloody mess.'

'So it seems,' answered Brady, feeling uneasy about what lay ahead.

Chapter Five

Brady slowly breathed out. From a distance the victim's long blonde hair hid the extent of the trauma. It was only when you got up close did you realise that her features had been horrifically smashed beyond recognition. The skin hung in shards, exposing lumps of shapeless, raw flesh and bone. Something hard and jagged had ripped and torn at what had once been her face, leaving behind a gut-wrenching, unidentifiable, gory mess.

Brady didn't want to think about the fact that the body lying there was someone's daughter. Shoving his hands deep into his pockets he looked up at the oppressive, dark sky.

Conrad attempted to clear his throat.

Brady turned to him. He stood rigid by Brady's side, his face sickly pale.

'At least she was dead before . . .' Conrad's confident, privately educated voice trailed off.

Brady nodded, he didn't feel much like talking.

He forced himself to look back down at the body. He had seen enough murder victims to know that luckily for her she was already dead before her attacker had decided to remove her face, otherwise they would have been looking at a gruesome bloodbath. The purplish, bluish marks around her neck were indicative of death by asphyxiation. Brady presumed the black scarf loosely knotted around the victim's discoloured neck had been used to strangle her first, before the frenzied attack on her face took place. He could make out desperate scratches on her neck where he presumed the victim had tried in vain to loosen the choking material.

He couldn't help but notice the short denim skirt that barely covered her mottled, greyish-blue naked thighs. Or the tight, short-cropped black T-shirt that was so low cut that her well-developed breasts and black lacy bra were on show. His eyes drifted to her navel, attracted by the sparkling gem pierced into her belly button. But something else caught his eye. He crouched down and took a closer look.

'Sir?' Conrad asked as Brady turned to him.

'Gloves?'

Conrad handed Brady a pair of latex gloves.

'What is it?' Conrad asked.

'I don't know,' muttered Brady, frowning.

He gently undid the button and zip on her hipster denim skirt revealing black see-through pants. She had no pubic hair which didn't surprise Brady. He was savvy enough to know that fashion, or more precisely the ever-expanding porn world, pressurised young women to sport Brazilian waxes, coupled with ludicrous fake boob jobs.

But what did surprise him was the striking tattoo of a fire breathing jade dragon discreetly curled below her left hip. Brady turned and looked at Conrad.

'See how red and raised the skin is?'

Conrad nodded.

'This is recent. The scab has gone but the skin's still

28

inflamed,' Brady stated. 'I reckon she got this done about four or five weeks ago.'

He didn't know much about tattoos, but even he recognised that this was a work of art.

He carefully buttoned up her skirt, covering her modesty. Not that it mattered to her now, he thought, but she was still someone's daughter.

'How did you know it was there, sir?' asked Conrad, surprised.

'Part of it caught my eye,' answered Brady as he carefully took in the rest of her body.

She was also wearing an open black jacket and tan suede Ugg boots that reached halfway up her slender, bluish calves. But the boots had nothing to do with the weather. Ugg boots were just a fashion statement; a very expensive fashion statement at that. She could have been any one of a hundred young women who would have been out drinking last night in Whitley Bay. Brady was suddenly filled with revulsion at what was going through his head; she looked no older than the girl he had taken home. He felt a deep twist of regret as he realised he knew as little about Sleeping Beauty as he did about the body lying before him. Behind him he could hear the hushed voices of the forensic officers, waiting for him to finish.

Let them wait, he thought. The SOCOs already had all the photographs they needed of the victim and the crime scene, so a few more minutes would make no difference when it came to bagging up evidence. Brady needed time to think, to breathe in the bitter reality of what had happened to this girl. He needed to understand why she had been brought here of all places. And crucially, why the murderer had chosen to kill her.

'It doesn't make sense,' he mused.

'It never does,' answered Conrad with quiet reverence.

Brady shook his head but couldn't bring himself to explain what he had meant.

He let his eyes drift over her outstretched small, fragile open hands. He could make out that her finger nails were neatly manicured but couldn't see anything else. Forensics would find something, he was sure of that. Whoever had done this to her would have left some trace behind. It was the law of averages, thought Brady.

He paused for a moment, catching his breath as his eyes were drawn back to her mutilated face; the harsh lights set up by the SOCOs sparing nothing.

'Poor bloody girl,' Brady quietly stated.

'Yes sir,' answered Conrad.

'What do you think?' Brady asked.

Conrad shrugged.

Brady wasn't offended; Conrad rarely committed himself.

'Does anything strike you as odd?' Brady continued.

'Yes, her face or what's left of it,' Conrad offered.

'No, I'm more interested in what her attacker didn't do as opposed to what he did,' answered Brady.

'She doesn't seem to have been sexually assaulted,' answered Conrad. 'If she had her clothes would either have been fully or partially removed, but there doesn't appear to have been any attempt made here, sir.'

'And, she doesn't appear to have struggled,' Brady added. 'Apart from these scratches on her throat here, Conrad,' he said pointing. 'Which suggests she fought to loosen the scarf from her neck. But that seems to be the extent of it.'

If she had struggled with her attacker he would have

expected some visible hair or tissue from the assailant to have been left in the victim's hands or under her nails. A last attempt at desperately holding on to life. He was sure her own skin tissue would be evident under her nails, but as to her attacker's, he wasn't so certain.

'Maybe she was knocked unconscious from behind first?' Conrad offered.

'But then why strangle her?'

'Perhaps she started to come round, sir? So her attacker then strangled her with her scarf?'

'Maybe . . . Let's see,' Brady said as he carefully knelt down beside the girl's body, wincing as a burst of white pain exploded in his thigh.

He breathed in shallowly for a few moments, waiting for it to pass.

'Are you all right, sir?' Conrad asked with genuine concern noticing that Brady's olive-skinned complexion had paled.

'It's nothing,' Brady lied.

The last thing he wanted was Conrad questioning his ability to work.

'Shine your torch over the back of her head for me, will you?'

Trying to ignore the searing pain he felt, Brady carefully lifted what was left of the victim's head and examined the back of it for trauma.

'Nothing, we'll just have to wait and see if any fractures are found during the post-mortem.' He had seen enough blows to the head to recognise the trademark and there didn't appear to be one there. But he could still be wrong.

'Why did he do that to her face?' Brady questioned as he shook his head.

'To make it difficult for us to ID? Or maybe it's not that

31

straightforward. Maybe the murderer is playing with us psychologically?' Conrad suggested.

'Could be,' Brady said, swallowing hard as he looked at the victim.

He had to agree, the murderer had made their job difficult, whether it was intentional, he couldn't say.

'But crucially, why spend time after she was dead doing that to her face? That says something, don't you think?' Brady said as he looked at what was left of the victim.

'You definitely think she was strangled to death rather than a blow to the head?' questioned Conrad.

Brady nodded.

Conrad stared at the telltale smudged bruising around the victim's neck. He had worked with Brady long enough to know that when he had a hunch he was rarely proved wrong.

'Her death makes no bloody sense though,' muttered Brady irritably to himself as he staggered to his feet, wincing slightly.

'No sir,' agreed Conrad.

'Come on then, let's leave this to Forensics,' he concluded.

They'd find out what he couldn't see; always did. If he was lucky Forensics would find some traces of the murderer's DNA on the victim's body, if not hopefully under her fingernails. But from where he was standing, it didn't look as if she had resisted her attacker. Which led Brady to the assumption that she had known her murderer. But before he could put together a list of potential suspects known to the victim, he needed a positive ID on the body. Only when they knew who the victim was, could they start to piece together exactly what had happened to her.

Brady took in the crime scene. Trees circled the building

adding to the dense, suffocating blackness. He dropped his gaze back to the surrounding bushes and wild bracken growing in thick clumps in between the fallen rubble and the crumbling walls of the farmhouse. The abandoned Belfast sink lying in the corner gave Brady the impression that they were standing in what would have once been the kitchen. The size of the room was at least ten feet by twelve feet, but the crumbling stone walls and old wooden rafters that lay rotting amongst the rubble and wild vegetation made the space cramped; so much so that the victim lay on a mound of grass and weeds in the centre. Brady was certain about one thing; it was the ideal location to bring someone in secret. Conrad shifted uneasily. It was clear he had had enough; the greyish hue to his face gave him away.

He'd get over it, thought Brady. Something worse would happen; it always did. It was human nature. Imagine the worst and someone's already done it; at least ten times over.

Brady hated civilisation; it gave people a false sense of security. In reality they were just animals in clothes. Animals that raped, sodomised, tortured and murdered whoever and whatever, even their own; regardless of society. He had seen it, tasted it and breathed it every day of his working life. The world was dark; the problem was people chose to ignore it and believe in a false god: civilisation.

Unfortunately for Conrad, he was still one of those poor, deluded bastards. The job would soon beat that idealism out of him, thought Brady. It had happened to him. It happened to everyone, sooner or later.

'Come on, let's get back to the station. This bloody place is depressing me,' Brady muttered.

They had their work cut out and the sooner they started the closer they would be to apprehending whoever had

Chapter Six

It was cold, still dark and had just started drizzling. Typical, thought Brady as he slammed the passenger door of Conrad's metallic silver Saab. In the distance he could hear the bleated moan of a foghorn. The air was thick with a salty dampness. Brady dragged heavily on the fading glow of his cigarette butt before throwing it into the gutter. Sixth one of the day, he thought; so much for giving up. He turned up his jacket collar as he looked up and down the hazily lit street. Cars were tightly jammed into any available space. It looked as if Gates had called in every officer, regardless of holidays or shifts. Brady limped slowly towards the heavily worn stone steps that led up to the station, kicking an empty beer can out of his path. What a dive, he thought as he watched the can crash into a smashed vodka bottle. The telltale leftovers of a Thursday night in Whitley Bay. Behind him the Saab skulked off as Conrad left in search of a parking space.

He limped over to the steps that led up to the closed wooden doors and decided to take the easy route and walk up the ramp that had recently been built as a PC suck-up to accessibility. The only time he had ever known it to be used was when a drunk in a wheelchair had been arrested for lewd and threatening behaviour. The crap that arrest had earned Gates with the press was still a standing joke at the station. Gates still hadn't found out that Brady was the one who had leaked the arrest to the press as part of a bet with a couple of other coppers from CID. Gates was ever vigilant when it came to adhering to political correctness so to be accused of being the most un-PC PC in the North East by the local press was a hard blow. If Gates had known Brady was responsible his career would have been over long ago.

He steeled himself before pushing open the heavy wooden doors that led into the station's Victorian tiled entrance. He looked at the public notice board on the wall. It was filled with the usual crap. The station was as gloomy and depressing as ever, just like the job. Brady breathed in the same acrid damp that had greeted him for too many years.

The station was housed in a dank Victorian building located in a side street leading off from Whitley Bay's small town centre. These days the town was known for one thing: binge drinking. Once famous as a seaside resort it had sunk to an all-time low. A nirvana of pubs and guesthouses lined up together, catering for every stag and hen party's wildest and crassest desires; from topless bar staff to lewd threesome live acts. Anything went now that the credit crunch had kicked in. Disposable cash was at an all-time low, so pubs and clubs were doing whatever it took to pull hard-pushed clientele in.

Brady shivered in disgust. He hated Whitley Bay; it was a shabby rundown ghost town during the day where empty, dilapidated Victorian buildings bleakly lined the sea front. But at night it became prey to the lowest of scum. Bouncers in dinner jackets and bow ties tried to maintain order as they threatened drunken punters with their small eyes and overweight, thuggish bodies. Bank holiday weekends were the worst. Scum travelled in from miles around in order to drink themselves into oblivion before ending the night by trying to get into someone's knickers. He had seen it for himself; the gorging, the vomiting and the senseless shags in the back lanes as they drunkenly waited for a taxi to take them home to their other halves. In the morning the promenade would be strewn with half-eaten kebabs and chips covered in curry sauce fought over by scavenging seagulls. Occasionally the odd, shrivelled condom would be left discarded down a side street or on the beach, as readily forgotten as the drunken, fumbling act itself.

Brady pushed open the door that led into the reception area.

'Bloody hell, Jack!' exclaimed the desk sergeant as he looked up.

Brady gave a grimace of a smile. He was more than relieved to see Turner on desk duty. He'd had quite a few drinks with the desk sergeant over the years.

'I heard you weren't due back until Monday?' Turner questioned.

'Yeah, well Gates decided that today was a better day than any,' Brady replied warmly.

Turner, a short, rotund, balding man in his early fifties, leaned towards Brady.

'I better warn you, Jack, all hell's breaking loose here,' Turner said in a conspiratorial tone.

Brady searched Charlie Turner's tiny, dark eyes hidden beneath sagging, crumpled eyelids and realised he was being serious.

'What's going on?'

'What? You must have heard about Jimmy Matthews? He was suspended earlier this morning! I expect that's why you've been called in early—' Turner stopped as the doors behind Brady swung open and then slammed closed. The heavy dull sound reverberated throughout the old building.

The knot in Brady's stomach tightened. Turner knew that he and Jimmy Matthews went way back. They had both signed up to the force the old-fashioned way and had worked hard, watching each other's back to get to where they were now: Detective Inspectors.

'I can't say any more than I've said. But, watch your step, eh? Gates is in no mood for games right now,' Turner said in a hushed voice before Conrad reached them.

'So, Harry, how's it going?' Turner asked as he nodded at Conrad.

'Fine, just fine,' answered Conrad, straightening his tie.

'It's going to be one of those days,' stated Turner as he shook his head. Murders were always bad news; especially when they landed on your doorstep.

'Sure is,' agreed Brady, wondering what the hell Matthews had done to be suspended. At least he now knew who it was he had replaced on the murder investigation. The question was why?

A sudden spasm of pain in his left thigh made him flinch.

'You sure you're all right there, Jack?' queried Turner.

'Yeah, it's nothing. It comes and goes, that's all,' lied Brady as he tried to keep his voice steady.

'Bloody bastards,' Turner said in consolation.

Brady wanted to tell Turner to save his pity. He deserved everything he'd got. Maybe if he'd had his wits about him rather than feeling guilty about the previous drunken night with DC Simone Henderson it would never have happened.

The night he had been shot he had been following some low-lifes in North Shields when he had the sudden feeling that someone was tailing him. He didn't say a word to Conrad or the three other guys in the back-up van a few streets away. He wanted to make sure first. Soon the dealers he had under surveillance were on the move. He shook the fear that he was being tailed, putting it down to paranoia, and made his way down to North Shields quayside. He had an instinct that something big was about to happen; he just hadn't realised that it was going to happen to him.

He had parked in a dark side street which led down to the quay and got out of the car and waited. He had pimped his soul for what little information he had; the news of two warring drug dealers wanting to sort out territory was enough for him. He saw movement ahead as the men he had followed got out of their car and approached another one. He radioed Conrad and told him that it was going down but before he knew what had hit him, a bullet was lodged in his thigh, too close for comfort to his balls. The shock hit first, then the pain. He felt something; a sticky warm feeling seeping from between his clenched arse cheeks. For a God-fearing moment he thought he had shit himself. Then he realised with great relief that it was blood. Thank fuck was his only thought. He didn't want anyone back at the station thinking his bowels had bailed out under pressure. Shit like that could never be lived down.

By the time he had realised what had happened it was too late. He had heard a car further up the street screeching as it tried to get away. The gun was never found. He presumed it was an unregistered piece loaned from any one of the enterprising, hardened scum that could easily be found if you looked long enough. Unsurprisingly no one witnessed the shooting. He was under no illusions. This was North Shields quayside late at night. The only witnesses that would have been around would have just as readily pulled the trigger on a plain-clothes copper as the shooter himself.

A huge investigation was ordered by his superiors. After all, one of their detectives had been shot and they had to look as if they gave a damn. His superiors put on a good show of solidarity for the media, but privately they let him know he'd crossed the line once too often and this time they held him responsible for blowing the investigation. The gunshot wound to his leg gave them the ammunition for deriding him as too much of a risk-taker; stating it had only been a matter of time before he or another officer under his command ended up injured, if not dead.

The story that he had been sprung by local drug dealers became widely accepted. As expected, nothing turned up and inevitably the case went cold. Whether his cover had been blown, Brady couldn't say. He'd crossed enough people in his life to make him realise that any one of them could have had him shot.

Brady looked up at Turner's concerned, ageing face and gave him a half-smile.

'I'm not dead yet, so don't look so happy!'

'You sure you're ready to be back?' asked Turner, unconvinced by Brady's camaraderie.

'Doctor wouldn't have passed me if I wasn't, now would he? You know what a tight-arsed bugger he can be,' replied Brady.

'Well, I can't argue with you there,' agreed Turner, smiling as he shook his head. 'Bit of advice, bonny lad,' offered Turner as he bent his head towards Brady's. 'Get some food down you while you've got the chance. It might put a bit of colour back into you.'

'Thanks, Charlie. Come on, Conrad, I don't know about you but I'm starving,' Brady said as he edged past Turner towards the wooden doors behind the reception desk.

Turner shook his head as he watched Brady disappear through the doors, followed by Conrad.

'Watch your back, Jack,' advised Turner just loud enough for Conrad to turn and catch his gaze for a few brief seconds.

Chapter Seven

'Sir?' prompted Conrad. 'The briefing will be starting soon.'

'Relax, will you?' Brady said as he pushed his empty plate away. 'You're starting to make me feel bloody edgy.'

Brady could see that Conrad would rather be anywhere else than sat in the station's basement canteen. The canteen was a depressing place at the best of times without the flickering overhead fluorescent lights adding to it. But Brady delighted in the greasy smell of fried food and cheap, bitter coffee. He felt most relaxed sat smoking at one of the many outdated sixties red, laminated tables, underneath the cracked basement windows. It always amused him that the basement windows were protected by wrought-iron bars. Who the hell would want to break into a cop shop? he wondered as he stared up at the dismal, bleak attempt at daylight outside.

Not that he could smoke by the windows any more. The new law had turned the building, as was the case with all public service buildings, into a non-smoking environment. Instead, Brady and the rest of the addicts were driven to standing in smoke-filled conspiratorial huddles outside the emergency exit door at the back of the station.

'Not turning soft on me are you?' questioned Brady as he turned his attention back to Conrad.

'No, just have no appetite,' answered Conrad pushing his uneaten fried breakfast away. The truth was he felt as sick as a dog and couldn't understand how Brady, after seeing the state of the murder victim, could have just eaten a bacon and fried egg stottie.

Brady watched him. He knew that the state the victim had been left in had gotten to Conrad as much as it had to him. But the difference was Brady had eight years on Conrad and a lifetime in the force working his way up from the bottom. And along the way he had dealt with every imaginable crime possible. This young murder victim was just another statistic. But for Conrad, an Oxbridge graduate fast-tracked through the system, brutal murder victims like this one were still a raw and disturbing experience.

'Jack!' a deep voice boomed suddenly from behind.

Brady turned round and grinned lamely.

'How are you doing?' thundered Tom Harvey as he landed a large calloused hand on Brady's shoulder.

'Great,' replied Brady.

Harvey pulled out a chair and sat down with a deep sigh.

Brady waited. Harvey wasn't the kind of Detective Sergeant to waste time with small talk. He was a man in his mid-forties who had been in the force for as long as Brady could remember. There was a time when Brady and Harvey had shared the same rank, but then Brady had been promoted. They had spent too many nights discussing a case over a pint or two to let Brady's promotion affect their friendship. Harvey was happy to admit that he was too steadfast and plodding to go higher than a DS and had added at the time that he couldn't deal with the politics that came hand-in-hand with promotion. But then again, neither could Brady which was proving to be a problem.

'I heard you were due back. But Christ! Talk about timing!' Harvey said as he caught Brady's eye. He rubbed his large hand over his clean-shaven jaw as he weighed Brady up. He noticed Conrad shoot him a disapproving look at his familiar tone with a senior officer, so for Conrad's benefit he loudly added, 'Sir.'

Brady smiled at Harvey's heavy-handedness at pretending he was something other than just plain old Jack Brady.

'What the hell happened to you while I was away?' Brady asked as he gestured towards Harvey's dark charcoal suit and dark maroon matching shirt and tie.

'Just lost a bit of weight, that's all,' answered Harvey. 'It's worked wonders for my personal life,' he added with a wink.

Brady couldn't help but smile. There was a time when Harvey wouldn't be seen in anything other than khaki chinos, an unbuttoned shirt with the sleeves rolled up and tan brogues, but since Gates had taken over as DCI things had changed.

'Dora!' Harvey thundered warmly at the short barrelled woman wiping down the table next to them. 'Be a pet and get me my usual!'

'How many times do I have to tell you? Place your order up at the till. I can't be running around all day after the likes of you,' she answered in an irate, thick Geordie accent. Her large breasts heaved as she breathed out in exasperation.

Harvey's eyes sparkled as he playfully winked at her.

Dora harrumphed, and shook her head in defeat before walking away.

'Have you seen Jimmy yet?' Harvey asked as he turned back to Brady.

Brady sat upright.

Harvey shot Conrad a look which told him that he wasn't wanted.

'I need a fresh coffee,' Conrad said, taking the not too subtle hint.

Harvey waited until Conrad had moved off before speaking.

'He's in a bad way.'

'What the fuck's going on, Tom?'

Harvey leaned forward. 'I don't know why exactly but from what I heard he lost it for a few minutes at the crime scene. He was one of the first called out and . . . Fuck! Your guess is as good as mine,' Harvey said as he shook his head. 'Bloody took his coat off and put it over the victim's body! I mean . . . fuck it! What the hell would possess him to do that?'

Brady remained silent. It just didn't sound like Matthews; he was one of the best DIs on the force and had in his time encountered worse murder scenes than this one. Brady knew that sometimes a grisly murder could send even the most hardened cops over the edge, but not Matthews. Brady had grown up fast and furious on the desperate streets of the Ridges, Matthews in war-torn Benwell, each learning to survive on instinct and fists alone. Neither believed that their work in CID could change what happened in the Ridges and the Benwells of the world, but they would do their best to contain it.

Brady had seen as many murders as any other DI during his time stationed at Wallsend and the West End of Newcastle, but as of yet, nothing had significantly thrown him. He casually put it down to the fact that he had had a tough childhood, tougher than even Matthews' thuggish upbringing; one that had prepared him well for being a copper.

45

Brady looked up at the dim, grey light squeezing through the bars of the basement window. He couldn't think straight, it just didn't make sense. Matthews was different; Brady would never make it beyond Detective Inspector, whereas Matthews had the makings of a Chief Superintendent. He was ruthless, that was all there was to it; bloody ruthless.

'Got to go,' apologised Brady as he stood up. He had to find Matthews.

His leg had stiffened again making him wince.

He turned to Harvey.

'Tell Conrad that I'll see him at the briefing.'

'Sure,' replied Harvey. 'The Incident Room is being set up in the first-floor conference room, so you've got no excuses for being late. Remember, 8.30 am sharp. That gives you fifteen minutes, even you should make it in time!'

Brady managed a faint smile despite the irritating throbbing in his leg. They both knew his time keeping was poor.

'Just so you know, we really tried to get those bastards who did that to you,' Harvey said as he glanced at Brady's leg. 'Especially Conrad. There were times during the past six months when he worked two straight shifts.'

'Yeah, he's a good bloke,' Brady acknowledged as he looked over at his deputy.

Chapter Eight

'You look like shit!' Brady said to Matthews as he entered his office.

He had expected to find Matthews waiting for him. It's exactly what he would have done in his situation. But he couldn't help being thrown. Matthews' face was sickly pale and his eyes, which watched Brady's every move, shone with a feverish madness.

Brady limped over to his desk and sat down. He could see that Matthews had already helped himself to a generous measure of the Glenfiddich he kept in his drawer for when things got too much.

'You want another?' Brady asked as he jerked his head in the direction of the malt.

Matthews nodded dejectedly.

Brady obliged him with a liberal refill. He picked up another mug off his desk and thought about pouring himself a small measure. Something about Matthews' silence told him he was going to need it. He then thought the better of it and put the malt back. The last thing he wanted to do was rile Gates more than usual and drinking on the job on his first day back wasn't a good tactic.

Brady watched as Matthews gratefully downed the malt

before letting out a low, wounded sigh. He shook his head in disbelief before lifting his eyes to meet Brady's. They had the despairing look of a rabid dog condemned to die.

'I'm in deep shit, Jack,' Matthews started, his voice quivering.

Brady waited tensely.

'I . . . I don't know where to start . . .'

Brady felt his stomach objecting to the greasy breakfast.

'I . . . I knew her . . . I fucking knew her . . .' muttered Matthews shaking his head.

'Who?' asked Brady, not wanting the answer.

'The girl . . . the one who was . . .' Matthews' voice trailed off.

'You can't have done.'

Brady cleared his throat as he waited for Matthews to agree with him.

'Jimmy? Come on, man.'

'Don't you think I'd fucking know?'

'Come on, Jimmy. You can't have known her. There was nothing left of her face to recognise.'

Matthews didn't answer.

Brady swore to himself.

'For fuck's sake, Jimmy! Do you know what you're saying?'

'What kind of question is that? Do you think I'm crazy or something?'

'Do you want the honest answer?'

Brady tried to get his head around what Matthews was saying. But it didn't make sense. None of it was making sense.

Matthews stared hard at Brady, trying to anticipate his response.

'I . . . I took her home in my car last night and—'

'You what?' Brady asked, incredulous.

48

He realised then that Matthews must have been screwing her, or at least attempting to. He tried to control the panic he could feel rising through his body.

'When I got to the crime scene ... you can't imagine what it was like,' Matthews said through trembling lips. 'When I saw her lying there ... what had been done to her ... I ... Oh Christ!'

He paused and looked at Brady with the hollow eyes of a man who had death shadowing him.

'I panicked, Jack! I fucking panicked ...'

Brady was speechless.

'That's why I covered her with my coat. Don't you think I realised that my DNA might be on her? I mean I ... fucking hell! I drove her home in my car ... and then she turns up hours later ... dead ...'

Brady could feel the knot in his stomach tightening. It explained why Ainsworth, the senior SOCO, was so pissed off when he and Conrad had arrived. He had had enough of CID literally messing up his crime scene.

'At first I thought ... I thought it was Evie ... it was her jacket ... She was wearing Evie's jacket ...'

Brady sat upright, his head buzzing.

'I ... I don't follow?'

'The long blonde hair ... the clothes. Fuck, Jack! When I first saw her I thought it was Evie! I thought it was my little girl lying there!'

It was at that moment that Brady realised that Matthews was in shock. He didn't know what he was saying. He couldn't, because it didn't add up.

'The last time I saw Evie she was still a skinny kid with pink braces. There's no way that the victim was her age,' he stated, relieved.

Matthews just stared at him as the madness slowly returned to his eyes.

'Come on, Jimmy, she looked as old as the girl I took home last night!'

Suddenly the atmosphere in the room chilled. Matthews' green eyes had dangerously narrowed to glinting slits.

'You bastard! You sick bastard!' Matthews hissed between gritted teeth.

'Whoa!' Brady said, holding his hands up as he tried his best to defuse the situation. Matthews wasn't the kind of guy that you wanted to piss off. 'She was just a kid . . . a dumb kid!'

'Come on, Jimmy! She looked at least twenty. She was no doubt out drinking and shagging last night before this happened to her,' Brady perilously insisted.

Matthews stood up, ready to lunge at him.

'What? Bloody hell, Jimmy, she had . . . you know . . . it was all there! She had tits and everything!'

'For fuck's sake, you sick bastard! She was only fifteen!'

Chapter Nine

'I can't do this, Jimmy.'

'The hell you can!'

Brady slowly shook his head.

'I can't keep quiet. If you're right then this is somebody's kid we're talking about. Somebody's fifteen-year-old kid with their face gone, for fuck's sake!'

Yet Brady knew he owed him. Owed him big time. But what Matthews was asking was the impossible. He was expecting Brady to risk going to prison for him. He picked up the bottle of Scotch and thought the better of it. Damn Matthews; all he'd wanted was to return to work quietly.

Suddenly a sharp rap at the door added to the tense atmosphere.

Matthews signalled for Brady to get rid of whoever it was.

Brady got up from his seat wincing.

A more persistent rap followed.

'I'm coming!' Brady shouted as he limped towards the door.

He yanked the door open, but not wide enough to allow a view into his office.

Conrad stood in front of him.

'Oh shit. Don't tell me it's already started?'

'Five minutes ago,' Conrad replied. 'Gates sent me to find you. He's in a foul mood, sir.'

'That's all I need. Make up an excuse for me, will you? I'll be there as soon as I can.'

'I'll do what I can, sir,' answered Conrad.

Brady breathed out slowly. He could trust Conrad. He was a good bloke, which made Brady feel even worse about the way he had treated Conrad after Claudia had walked out on him.

He shut the door and waited until Conrad's footsteps had disappeared.

'What do you want from me?' Brady asked, turning to face Matthews.

'I need your help. I need you to make sure my name doesn't come up in this investigation.'

Brady numbly stared at Matthews. He couldn't believe what he was asking. How the hell was he going to keep Matthews' name out of it? He didn't want to think about the fact that someone could have witnessed him with the girl before she was murdered.

It was impossible; he couldn't do it.

'Call it payback,' prompted Matthews.

Brady didn't move, didn't say a word. Matthews had him by the balls and he knew it. Matthews was the only person he could have gone to when he was on the verge of losing everything. Without question, Matthews dealt with it discreetly. Brady had never asked how, didn't want to know, but needless to say Matthews had made the problem go away. Now Matthews had a problem of his own. A problem that Brady somehow had to fix.

'All right,' agreed Brady unwillingly. 'But tell me you're not involved in any of this?'

'You of all people know me better than that!'

'Are you sure?'

'What the fuck's got into you, Jack?' snapped Matthews. 'Did I ask you any questions when you came to me desperate for my help?'

Matthews was right. Brady realised he had overstepped the mark. He didn't know what had got into him. Matthews needed his help now. Quid pro quo. It was that simple. The problem was it didn't feel that straightforward. Even if he didn't end up inside because of this, there was a good chance he was going to lose his job. Matthews was asking Brady to keep quiet about his involvement with a murder victim hours before she turned up brutally dead. Too much was at stake. But they both knew Brady didn't have a choice; he had rolled the die a long time ago.

'All right, I'll do what you say,' conceded Brady. 'But Jimmy, I need more than your word. You need to let me in on what the fuck is going on here.'

Matthews didn't say anything.

'For fuck's sake, Jimmy! This is me you're talking to.'

'I . . . I don't want to get you involved,' Matthews blankly stated.

'Fuck it. You come to me with the news that you knew the murder victim. Not only that, but you were with her the night she was murdered. Bloody hell, man! Tell me how I'm not involved?' demanded Brady.

Matthews sighed and cradled his head in his hands.

'You don't understand,' he muttered.

'Too right I don't understand.'

'I'm . . . I'm in trouble, Jack. Way over my head. And . . . and if I'm honest I don't even know where to begin,' Matthews said shaking his head.

Brady had never seen Matthews like this before. The man was scared shitless.

'Jimmy?'

Matthews looked up at him dejectedly.

'You didn't do it, right?'

'No . . .' mumbled Matthews.

'Then we can—'

'Shut up! Just shut the fuck up!' Matthews shouted.

He suddenly stood.

Brady watched as he started to pace the floor.

'You don't get it! No, I didn't fucking murder her. But that's the least of my problems right now.'

'So tell me what's going on.'

'I can't.'

Brady sighed. He realised that it wasn't worth talking to Matthews in the state he was in. It was better to let him get some rest first and then they'd decide what to do later.

'Go home, get some sleep and then we'll talk,' suggested Brady.

Matthews looked at him and wearily nodded before making his way to the door.

'Jimmy?' Brady questioned. 'The murdered girl, who is she?'

'Like you said, I need to go home and get my head around what's happened. After I've figured out what I'm going to do, I'll tell you anything you want to know.'

Matthews opened the door and then turned round to face Brady.

'And remember, if this gets out I'm not the only one with something to hide.'

Chapter Ten

Brady did his best to sneak in. As usual, his best wasn't good enough; at least not where Gates was concerned.

'Ah, Jack! Pleased to see that you could join us,' Gates greeted coolly.

'Bugger,' Brady muttered under his breath, feeling heads turn as he closed the door. The briefing had started at precisely 8.30 am and he was twenty minutes late; not a good thing with a boss who hated tardiness.

He thought about joining Gates at the front of the room, but as soon as he spotted DS Adamson standing there, the idea lost its appeal. He made his way to the back wall and leaned against it.

Brady caught the mocking stare of DS Robert Adamson. He held it for a second too long, forcing the uptight bugger to shift his arrogant gaze. Adamson belonged to North Shields CID and was presumably here because they needed extra bodies for the murder investigation. He was a young, arrogant man in his early thirties who typified the new breed of copper that accelerated their way through the ranks after graduating from University.

Adamson was five feet ten but his stocky build made him appear much taller. Brady hated the way his reddish blond hair was trendily gelled to look messy and tousled. His heavy-set square jaw was typically clean-shaven while his intelligent bright blue eyes lacked any subtlety or compassion. Simply put, he was out for what he could get. Unlike Brady, Adamson toed the line. His suits were always dark and imposing, with matching ties and plain white shirts. Overall Adamson reminded Brady of a politician. In other words, he couldn't be trusted.

Brady had known from the first time that he'd been introduced to Adamson that he was a bullshitter. Adamson had tried to win Brady over with his false bravado but it hadn't worked. Consequently, Adamson had since treated Brady with competitive contempt. Brady had the rank that Adamson so clearly thirsted after. But as Adamson stood beside Gates, Brady had the uncanny feeling that he was sizing up Brady's position as DI.

Brady looked about the crowded room and quickly found Conrad. He nodded at his deputy, relieved that he had Conrad by his side and not a backstabbing Iago figure like Adamson. Harvey then caught his attention, making no attempt at disguising his amusement at Brady's typical tardiness. Brady surveyed the rest of the room realising that out of the thirty or so faces before him he only recognised about twenty. He had either been gone longer than he had realised or, as Adamson's presence suggested, Gates had called in CID from other Area Commands; standard procedure with something as high profile as a murder investigation.

Brady's head was still foggy; the result of his conversation with Matthews. Consequently, it was too easy to drown out Gates' voice, focusing instead on Anna Kodovesky. She was sat directly in front of him with her long legs crossed, forcing her skirt to ride up further than she would have liked, but Brady wasn't protesting. And neither were the coppers on either side of her.

Kodovesky had made it clear from her first day at the station as a Detective Constable that she was only interested in the job. And Brady didn't complain; she was a damned good copper. But some of the guys at the station couldn't see past her legs and were laying bets on who would get into Kodovesky's knickers first. So far, no one had succeeded and the bet was now standing at a grand. Brady knew that Kodovesky was too smart to fall for any of his colleagues' lines. If he really thought she couldn't hold her own, then he might have broken up the wager. But Brady knew that if Kodovesky found out he was protecting her honour, she would have chopped his balls off.

He suddenly started as he realised that Gates was bringing the briefing to a close. He relaxed his body against the wall as he thought about what they had so far, which was effectively nothing. All they had was an unidentified murder victim. And as for motive, nine times out of ten, it was sexual, which was the line Gates was following. But Brady wasn't so sure. Nothing about the body suggested that the victim had been raped. Given the ferocity of the attack, there was one thing he was certain about; this was personal, the victim had known her murderer.

He pulled out the packet of mints from his pocket, placed one in his mouth in preparation for Gates, who he knew would be more than eager to greet him on his first day back.

'All right people, we have a job to do, so let's do it. And remember, no one, and I mean no one goes home until we have a positive ID on the murder victim. You hear me? As of now all leave is temporarily suspended and I'm expecting no less than eighteen-hour shifts from you lot. This isn't just your jobs on the line here, it's mine as well,' Gates reminded them.

Brady knew that the jibe was intended for him.

'I want to see everybody back here in four hours and by then we better be making some headway. I need something to give at the press conference this afternoon and it better be good!'

It was no secret that Gates was after the Chief Superintendent's job. O'Donnell was rumoured to be moving on and Gates didn't want anything or anyone messing up his chances of promotion. Brady decided to leave before Gates cornered him. He needed to talk to Matthews. The more he thought about it, the more he felt uneasy. Something wasn't right. He had questions that needed answering; questions he should have forced out of Matthews instead of letting him go.

'It's not like you to be in such a hurry, Jack! Something you want to tell me?'

Brady stopped. Just as he had feared, Gates. Beside him, Adamson stood erect and self-important.

'No sir,' answered Brady dutifully, trying his best not to breathe. The mint had dissolved and he was sure that his breath reeked of the past six months he'd dedicated to drinking.

Unsurprisingly, Gates didn't seem impressed with his answer.

He was roughly Brady's height but, unlike Brady, he was fit, despite being ten years older. His muscular, toned body was a testament to the hours he put in at the gym. Even his receding dark hair was cropped fashionably short, making him look younger than his age.

His dark brown eyes unnerved Brady; they belied a cold, detached intelligence. The heavily etched lines on his face spoke of a lifestyle that demanded more than most people could offer. His skin was covered in harsh, pitted acne scars, some partially hidden by a permanent five o'clock shadow, but there all the same. Overall Gates' face wore the cold hardness of his life as a DCI.

Brady couldn't help but notice Gates' large but slender hands with short, manicured nails as he irritably tugged on the sleeve of his black uniform with gold braid, exposing the cuff of his expensive white shirt.

'We need to talk. My office in ten minutes.'

'Yes sir,' answered Brady.

He still couldn't shake the feeling that Gates didn't think he was up to the job. Adamson had made it clear he was out for promotion and what worried Brady was that Gates had made it equally clear in the past that he was heading for demotion.

'You know DS Robert Adamson?' Gates asked Brady.

Adamson flashed him a hungry smile.

'We're lucky to have him on board,' continued Gates. 'Just a damned pity we can't persuade him to transfer here from North Shields.'

Yeah, damned pity, thought Brady.

'And don't be late,' instructed Gates coldly. 'There's something we need to discuss,' he added before turning on his heel.

Chapter Eleven

Gates slowly cleared his throat as he looked at Brady.

'Do you know what Lyndon Johnson said about J. Edgar Hoover?'

Brady shook his head. He wasn't sure where the hell this was going but he knew it wasn't good.

'Better to have him on the inside pissing out, than on the outside pissing in. If I had my way, you wouldn't be capable of pissing ever again. But for some unfathomable reason Chief Superintendent O'Donnell likes you. I don't know what your hold over O'Donnell is, but be warned, when he goes, you go.'

'Yes sir,' acknowledged Brady, accepting that DC Simone Henderson's transfer on personal grounds hadn't won him any favours with Gates.

He had found out from Conrad that Simone had put in for a transfer while he'd been laid up in hospital. He couldn't blame her. He would have done the same if it were possible. But with Brady's record no one would have him.

'What do you know about Matthews?'

Brady shrugged.

'Come on, Jack. I know you two go back a long way. I'm

suspecting your late arrival at the briefing was down to him. Am I right?'

Brady didn't answer him. He couldn't.

'I don't know why one of my best DIs lost his nerve but I can promise you this, I'll find out. And mark my words, if I hear that you know what's going on with him, you'll find yourself in uniform walking the streets of Blyth until the day you retire!'

'Yes sir,' dutifully answered Brady.

'Right, firstly you should know that I've called in Amelia Jenkins.'

Brady instinctively flinched. 'Sir?'

'She isn't overly keen at the prospect of seeing you again either.'

Brady refrained from replying.

'We could do with all the help we can get right now. The last thing I want is a repeat of the Megan Carter investigation. I want this turned around ASAP. Understand? And if that means you working with Jenkins then that's what you're going to do.'

'With all due respect, sir, she's a psychologist. What can she bring to a murder investigation like this?' questioned Brady.

'A hell of a lot as far as I'm concerned,' answered Gates impatiently.

He placed his elbows on his desk and leaned forward.

'If you've got a problem working with her, then just say. I can take you off this investigation and hand it over to someone else, Jack. I know for a fact that DS Adamson would be perfectly happy being partnered with Jenkins.'

'No sir, I have no problem working with Dr Jenkins. I'm sure she'll prove to be invaluable,' replied Brady, resisting the urge to tell Gates exactly what he thought.

'Good, pleased we've cleared that up. Jenkins should be arriving here in the next half hour. I'd appreciate you being around to brief her.'

'Actually sir, there's a couple of leads I need to check out as soon as possible,' Brady replied uneasily. 'I'll make sure DS Harvey is around for when she arrives.'

'If you can't do it personally then I'd rather Adamson filled in Jenkins,' replied Gates. 'No disrespect to Harvey but I believe Adamson would be a better choice.'

Brady didn't answer. He knew Gates was playing the old graduate card; as if that made Adamson a better copper. Harvey had worked his way through the force just like Brady, from the bottom up. No formal education, no favours, just long hours and hard graft.

'Obviously, this is your call,' Gates said as he waited for Brady's agreement.

Brady shifted slightly. Gates had him over a barrel. It wasn't his call, Gates had left him in no doubt.

'I'll instruct Adamson to brief Jenkins when she arrives,' conceded Brady, standing up.

'Before you go, Jack, I wondered if I could have a word with you? Off the record?' Gates asked, gesturing for Brady to sit back down.

Brady's mouth felt dry. He had no idea what was coming. Only that it had to be bad for Gates to be delivering it.

'It's about Claudia,' Gates began.

Brady waited, barely breathing.

'I'm sure you already know that O'Donnell's sanctioned Claudia's proposal?'

Brady numbly shook his head. He hadn't even realised the post had been given the go-ahead.

'O'Donnell somehow managed to get support from the

Home Office for Claudia's proposition which opened up the extra funding needed to make it viable.'

Brady felt as if Gates had punched him. He couldn't believe Claudia hadn't told him. It had taken her eighteen months, from suggesting the need for a groundbreaking new legal advisory position that would work to coordinate the activities of Northumbria Police and the UK Human Trafficking Centre in Sheffield, to getting it off the ground. Claudia had ideas of her own which ultimately included setting up a Human Trafficking Centre in Newcastle equal to Sheffield's.

This was close to her heart. At times, Brady thought too close. As a lawyer, Claudia had worked endless, unpaid hours representing women and children who were effectively human slaves illegally trafficked from Eastern Europe or Africa into the North East of England. She was interested in the legal quandary these women and children found themselves in once extricated from sex slavery; illegal immigrants fearful they would be forced back into slavery on their return home; that or murdered. She had championed a few cases so far, succeeding in securing the victims the right to seek asylum in Britain. But she had also lost more than she had won, powerless to prevent these women and children ending back up where they had begun their lives as sex slaves.

Brady gripped the sides of his chair. He couldn't believe that she couldn't bring herself to tell him. He tried to get a handle on the situation. The last thing he wanted to do was lose it in front of Gates. But the thought that he really had lost her for good was killing him.

'The only reason I'm telling you, Jack, is because Claudia is refusing to take it.'

Brady stared at Gates numbly. He knew this job had meant everything to Claudia. 'Why? Why isn't she taking it?'

He couldn't believe that she was walking away from everything she had fought so hard to achieve.

'I was hoping you could tell me.'

Brady numbly shook his head.

He knew the answer, and Gates knew that. There was nothing he could do any more, so he stood up and left.

Chapter Twelve

'Charlie, can you do me a favour?' Brady asked the desk sergeant.

'Aye, bonny lad, as long as there's a pint in it,' Turner grinned amiably.

'For you, Charlie, I'll even stretch to two,' Brady answered, smiling.

Brady's smile disappeared as he glanced around. He'd never seen the station so busy; extra uniforms and CID had been called in from across the region to cope with the murder investigation. Nothing much happened in this seedy, rundown seaside resort, at least not until now. Murders typically didn't affect the middle classes of Whitley Bay who lived far enough away from the town centre not to be affected by the pubs and clubs that had brought the seaside resort to an all-time low. They led self-satisfied, suburban lives in their exorbitantly-priced properties, completely unaware of the diseased scum that ran the streets at night. He knew of a few notorious gangsters, the local mafia, Madley being one of them, who had no qualms about disposing of a rival in the Tyne. But murders of that sort barely caused a ripple in most decent people's lives. Whitley Bay was typically known for drunken louts acting lewd and fighting amongst themselves and a few burglars who needed easy cash for drugs. But a brutal murder in tree-lined suburbia was a completely different story.

'So, what's this favour then?' Turner asked as he raised his thick, wiry eyebrows at Brady.

'I've got a hunch about something,' Brady confided. 'But I want it kept quiet.'

Brady trusted Turner. He belonged to the old school of policing, unlike the new breed who didn't have a clue about 'hunches' or 'gut feelings'. Instead the new coppers were taught to feed murder details into Holmes 2 and sit back and wait for it to spit out the answer. There was no doubt that the computer system saved invaluable time. It could sift through masses of information in seconds; information that would have once taken twelve detectives at least a week to get through. Brady had lost count of the number of times he had favoured one lead over another because of an inexplicable hunch. But he knew that this time he wasn't telling the truth. This wasn't a hunch, but rather Jimmy Matthews' troubling disclosure that the victim was only fifteen years old.

Turner had been a desk sergeant at Whitley Bay station long before Brady had joined and knew more than most of the other coppers put together. But as was the case with many of the coppers from the old days, he was rarely given any credit for it. A new breed were coming through the ranks who didn't drink, didn't compromise themselves for anyone and certainly didn't give a damn about the job; it was all about politics and getting to the top without dirtying their hands. The likes of Brady and Turner who still played by the old school ethics were slowly being phased out, replaced by a generation who had no respect for them, and worse, saw them as a walking liability.

'Go on then, bonny lad, what can I do for you?' Turner questioned.

'I need a printout of females between the ages of fifteen and eighteen reported missing in the North East over the last few weeks.'

'Give me a couple of minutes.' Turner turned his back on Brady and logged in to the computer. Minutes later he handed over three sheets of printed paper.

'Thanks,' said Brady, taking the printout. 'I owe you a pint.'

'I've lost count of how many bloody pints you owe me, bonny lad,' Turner said, shaking his head.

Brady waited until he reached his office before looking at the information. He sat down at his desk and quickly scanned over the list of names, ages and addresses.

'Naomi Edwards, 17, Wallsend,' Brady muttered as his eyes scanned down the first page of the printout.

'Shit,' Brady cursed as he turned to the next page and finally the next.

He read down the list of names until he came to the third one from the bottom.

'Sophie Washington, 15, West Monkseaton . . .' Brady faltered.

How the hell had they missed something as crucial as this? But he knew the answer; the team were looking for a missing female between eighteen to thirty. He couldn't fault them; even Brady found it difficult to believe what Matthews had told him. To Brady, the victim's body resembled that of a young woman in her late teens or early twenties, not a girl of fifteen. If it hadn't been for his conversation with Matthews, Brady wouldn't have even considered other possibilities so early into the investigation.

His eyes read the date she had been reported missing. He read the date again to make sure he wasn't mistaken: three that morning. He then double-checked the location of her parents' home: West Monkseaton.

Something like this couldn't be kept quiet. If the missing fifteen-year-old girl was the murder victim then all hell was going to break loose and that would only be the beginning of it.

Chapter Thirteen

'Shit!' cursed Brady as he disconnected the phone.

It had cut straight to Matthews' voice mail. He checked his watch; 9.47 am. He had no choice but to ring Matthews' home number.

No one answered.

He tried to ignore the fact that Matthews didn't want to talk.

He picked up his jacket and limped out of his office to meet Conrad.

*

'Come on, Conrad. What are you waiting for?' Brady questioned as he slammed the car door shut.

He was pissed off and needed someone to take it out on. Unfortunately for Conrad he was the closest target. It was Matthews he wanted to kick, but the problem was he couldn't get hold of the bugger.

'For you, sir,' answered Conrad. 'As usual.'

Brady smiled. If felt good to be back.

'Actually, Dr Jenkins has asked to join us,' Conrad stated.

'No? Shit. Why the hell would she want to come with us?'

'Because DCI Gates has assigned her to the investigation, sir,' replied Conrad carefully.

'Tell me something I don't know,' muttered Brady.

'She's just arrived and caught me as I was leaving. She was adamant about coming with us. Something about you briefing her about the investigation?'

'Shit,' cursed Brady. 'Tell you what, Conrad. Just drive, will you? I'll worry about Dr Jenkins.'

'Whatever you, say, sir,' answered Conrad. 'But she won't be happy.'

'Good, that makes two of us,' replied Brady.

'I better warn you, sir, she's not a woman who likes being messed around.'

'Tell me one who does?' asked Brady, thinking of Claudia.

'Do you mind?' he asked as he pulled out a pack of cigarettes from inside his jacket. There was no question about the fact that he needed one.

'Does it matter if I do?' Conrad asked as he buzzed down the passenger window.

'Appreciate it.'

'Just don't get any ash in the car, sir.'

Brady suddenly realised the car was new. Same model, but brand new.

'Whatever we're paying you, it's too much,' Brady replied as he gestured at the state of the art dashboard.

He lit a cigarette and inhaled deeply making a mental note not to accidentally burn the leather upholstery. He rested his head back against the seat and momentarily closed his eyes as he enjoyed the icy damp air washing over his face. He felt very tired and realised that he had only had a couple of hours' sleep, if that.

'No word yet on the victim's identity?'

'No, sir. Few maybes, but nothing concrete,' answered Conrad.

Exactly as Brady had expected.

His phone rang. Without thinking he answered it.

'DI Brady?'

'Yeah?'

'I take it I've wasted my time?'

'I'm sorry?'

'You know exactly what I mean. I turn my back for one minute and you conveniently disappear. This is typical of you to run out on me, Jack. However, this isn't one of our counselling sessions, this is a murder investigation. And it was DCI Gates who requested my expertise, not the other way around.'

'I apologise for not being there to brief you, Dr Jenkins, but I have instructed DS Adamson to show you what we've got so far,' answered Brady evenly.

'I've cancelled patients to help you with this investigation but if you're not interested in my expertise then I'd rather know about it than have you waste my time. Which it seems you're rather good at.'

'I honestly don't know what's given you that idea.'

'Cut the bullshit, Jack!'

'Got to go, but we'll catch up when I get back to the station,' Brady concluded abruptly before disconnecting the phone.

'Sounds like she's not too happy with you,' stated Conrad.

'Yeah? What makes you think that?' asked Brady as a flicker of a smile played on his lips.

'Take a right, here,' he instructed as they approached a roundabout.

'Yes sir,' answered Conrad as he swung over into the right-hand lane.

'At least she's got Adamson to keep her busy.'

'I'd be careful of Adamson, sir. He's interested in no one but himself. Let's say he's not a team player,' answered Conrad as he narrowed his steel-grey eyes. 'Word is he's after a promotion and he doesn't care how he gets it, or who he takes it from.'

'I take it you don't like him?'

'We joined at the same time so I had the misfortune of spending two years with Adamson. When the training was over, I swore I'd never work with him again.'

'That bad?'

'You don't want to know.'

Brady knew Adamson was a roach, but to have Conrad say it worried him. In all the time he'd worked with Conrad he'd rarely heard him say a bad word against anyone.

'Where to now?' Conrad asked, after taking the right turn.

Brady looked out the window and realised they were heading along Seatonville Road. Not far now, he uneasily thought.

'Fairfield Drive, West Monkseaton. Number 18.'

'Can I ask why there, sir?' Conrad ventured.

'Later. Just let me see if my hunch is right first. The less you know about this, the better,' Brady answered, not wanting to jeopardise Conrad's career, as well as his own.

Chapter Fourteen

Number 18.

He walked up the newly paved driveway carefully lined with shrubs and trees. He glanced at the one-year-old dark blue metallic BMW 5 Series saloon parked in front of the electronic white garage doors, passing it to reach the white, wooden porch.

He took a deep breath before ringing the old-fashioned doorbell. As he waited, he took in the original 1920s ornate stained glass in the front door and below it the antique polished brass lion's head knocker and letter box.

Heavy footsteps approached as a man in his late forties opened the door.

'Yes?' he curtly demanded.

Brady noted that his overall appearance may have been conservative but it made a statement. He was wearing a casual pale blue Armani jeans stripe shirt and Crombie front pleat dark grey trousers, finished off with black Kurt Geiger shoes. The man obviously liked to look good; nothing brash, but it took money to wear those clothes.

Brady held up his ID.

'I'm sorry to bother you, sir, but I need to ask you a few questions about your daughter, Sophie?' Brady began.

He seemed to deliberate over Brady's words. He may have been clean-shaven with short black hair, respectably peppered with flecks of silver, but behind his black Christian Dior spectacles his red-rimmed, bloodshot eyes told another story. Craggy lines spread out from the corners of his eyes as he suspiciously narrowed them.

Brady waited until he reluctantly held the door open for Brady to walk past him into the stained-glass vestibule. Brady made his way through into the wide hallway conscious of his feet, heavy and resonating on the polished parquet flooring. An antique writing bureau and a burgundy leather chair sat under an impressive wooden spiral staircase. Opposite it was an old oak hall table with a small stained-glass Tiffany lamp and an empty brass letter holder. Above the table, a large, imposing mirror sat, reflecting the wooden staircase as it spiralled up to the first floor.

He tried not to limp as he made his way down the hallway towards the fresh smell of ground coffee coming from the kitchen. He stopped dead as he caught sight of the forty-something, long-blonde-haired woman anxiously waiting in the kitchen doorway. She tightly pulled her black silk flower kimono around herself as she looked at him. Even though it was well after ten, she still wasn't dressed. Brady inwardly winced as her dark blue, desolate eyes searched for anything that resembled hope.

Brady fought the urge to leave. Her hair, the shape of her face seemed uncannily familiar. He deliberated apologising for wasting their time. He could hand the task to some other poor sod. But, he knew he couldn't do that. For Matthews' sake he had to see this through to the end.

*

'Here you go,' Simmons said as he thrust the photograph he had just taken off the Smeg fridge at Brady.

Brady was sat with Mrs Simmons at the large wooden table positioned in the centre of the spacious kitchen. Both had cups of black, unadulterated coffee. The only difference was Brady had politely drunk most of his, whereas Mrs Simmons' remained untouched.

'Thanks,' Brady replied as he looked at the school mugshot. 'Pretty girl.'

Simmons didn't answer. He didn't sit down either.

Brady followed Simmons' eye as he distractedly stared through the double-glazed doors that led out onto the patio area and the south-facing lawn.

When Conrad had pulled into Fairfield Drive, Brady had grimly noted that the Simmons' house backed onto the abandoned farmland. He now realised that the eight-feet-high wooden fence at the bottom of the long garden was all that separated them from what was now a crime scene.

'So, let me get this straight. Sophie left here at 5.30 pm to go to Evie Matthews' house—' Brady began.

'Didn't I already say that?' Simmons snapped as he turned and caught Brady's eye. 'For God's sake! We've already been over this, Evie is her best friend. She's always going over to the Matthews' house. Those two are inseparable.'

Brady nodded, surprised by this revelation. Matthews had failed to tell him that Sophie Washington was his daughter's best friend. What was troubling Brady was why Matthews had withheld such vital information.

He looked back at the photograph. He couldn't dispute it; the long, blonde hair exactly matched the victim's.

'What time did you try calling her mobile?'

'About 2.40 am,' Simmons answered irritably as he ran his hand through his short hair.

'That late?'

'I must have fallen asleep in front of the TV. When I woke up it was 2.30. Louise had already gone to bed and so I naturally presumed Sophie had come home. It wasn't until I went upstairs that I realised she wasn't back.'

'Is that unusual?'

'Yes,' answered Simmons quickly.

Too quickly, thought Brady, noticing that Simmons shot his wife a look to silence her.

Brady turned to Louise Simmons.

She looked up at her husband nervously and then stiffly nodded in agreement with him.

'Could she have run off then?' Brady tentatively asked.

Simmons shot Brady an exasperated look.

'What I mean is was there any reason for her to stay away? An argument say, or a disagreement about a boyfriend or something?'

'No! Sophie had no reason to run away and . . . as for boyfriends . . . Christ! She's only fifteen! She's more interested in being with her friends than boys.'

'What about staying the night at a friend's house?'

'Don't you think we'd know? We already told your people where she went and that she left there at 10 pm!'

'I am sorry about this, Mr Simmons, but these are standard questions I have to ask,' apologised Brady.

76

'Well, just hurry up and get on with it, then. The quicker you finish the sooner you can be out there looking for our daughter.'

'Of course,' Brady replied sympathetically.

'Can you tell me what Sophie was wearing last night?' Brady asked as he turned and looked at Louise Simmons.

'A black denim skirt and a T-shirt,' quietly answered Louise Simmons. 'Oh yes, and Ugg boots.'

'Anything else?' quietly questioned Brady.

She shook her head, forcing back tears.

'Are you sure?'

'Oh . . . she was wearing a black scarf . . .' she whispered, biting her lip.

Silent tears trailed down her face as she looked at the school photograph lying on the kitchen table.

Brady acknowledged uncomfortably that Sophie's clothes matched the clothes found on the victim.

'Does Sophie have any tattoos or body piercings that you know of?' Brady gently asked.

'Why do you want to know all this?' exploded Simmons suddenly.

'No particular reason. Like I said, Mr Simmons, these are standard questions,' Brady calmly replied.

He looked at Louise Simmons.

She numbly shook her head.

'No . . . no, she had nothing like that . . . she's just a fifteen-year-old girl, Detective Brady.'

Simmons turned his face away from his wife uncomfortably.

'Sir?' prompted Brady, realising that Simmons knew something.

'Sir, does Sophie have a tattoo?' Brady repeated.

Simmons avoided Brady's eyes.

'Like my wife said, she's just a fifteen-year-old schoolgirl.'

It didn't take a psychologist to know that he was lying. Brady was certain that Simmons was hiding the fact that he knew about the jade dragon tattoo and the belly button piercing. But why keep quiet?

'Are you sure, sir?' persisted Brady.

'Why? What do you know? What is it that you're not telling us?' Simmons retaliated, turning the heat back onto Brady.

'Just procedure, sir,' Brady replied as he stood up to go. 'I'll run some checks back at the station. And as soon as I have any news I'll be in touch,' he said as he turned to Louise Simmons.

Tearful, she nodded as she looked up at Brady, still hopeful that he could bring her daughter home, alive. The mascara from the day before was smeared under her dark blue eyes and her long blonde hair hung dishevelled and uncombed. Brady was uncomfortably aware of the striking similarity between mother and daughter.

He noted with interest that Simmons who was irritably waiting for him to leave was very together, especially compared to his wife.

Brady tried his best to give Louise Simmons a reassuring look before turning and leaving the kitchen.

Simmons followed and cornered Brady once he'd reached the front door.

'You know something, don't you?'

'No sir,' Brady replied evenly.

'You're lying,' Simmons hissed, not wanting his wife to overhear.

'I'm really sorry. I understand this must be very difficult for you.'

'The hell you do!'

Brady didn't answer.

'You want to tell me what's going on at Potter's Farm?'

'Sorry?' Brady questioned, trying his best not to let his unease show.

'Your lot are out there. Have been for the past few hours. The farm's been sealed off and you've got police officers crawling all over the place.'

'I'm afraid that's confidential, sir.'

'I'm not an idiot, Detective Inspector Brady. If something's happened to . . . to Sophie . . .' Simmons stopped himself short.

'Like I said, let me get back to the station and see what I can find out,' Brady offered.

Brady waited until he heard the door closing behind him before he took out his mobile to ring the station. He needed to arrange for two family liaison officers to come out after uniform had delivered the fatal blow. He was no good when it came to dealing with people's grief. He was good at causing it, according to his ex-wife, but when it came to dealing with it, he was always the first one out the door. He aggressively kicked a stone and watched as it rolled along the pavement towards the Saab.

'Tom? Yeah, it's Jack. I've got a new development regarding the murdered girl.' Brady looked back at the house.

It was a comfortable, four-bedroom semi-detached, in a quiet, respectable neighbourhood. Yet, less than a hundred metres away a horrific murder had been committed.

Brady gave the details he needed to and then cut the call. He walked over to the Saab and climbed in.

'This is connected to the murder, isn't it?' Conrad asked as he took in Brady's sallow, drawn complexion.

Brady nodded as he looked for a cigarette.

'I had a hunch that we weren't looking in the right place,' Brady said after lighting a cigarette.

Conrad shot him a questioning look.

'The victim,' answered Brady. 'I decided to drop the minimum age from eighteen down to fifteen.'

Conrad still looked puzzled.

'You know kids today, especially girls. They seem to grow up so damned fast that I decided to widen the search. And,' Brady paused as he inhaled, 'it seems my hunch was right.'

'Are you sure?'

'As sure as I can be. The parents have to identify the body first—' Brady faltered, realising what an ordeal that would be.

'How old was she?'

'Fifteen, Conrad. Fifteen years old. She was just a kid,' Brady replied quietly as he looked back at the house.

'Conrad, do me a favour and get me as far away from this bloody place as possible.'

He closed his eyes in a futile attempt to shut everything out. But there was one name he couldn't get out of his head, and that was Matthews.

Chapter Fifteen

'I just need five minutes to clear my head,' Brady said before slamming the car door shut.

In fact, he needed to make a call. One he didn't want Conrad overhearing. He walked over to the steep steps that led down to Tynemouth beach. It was deserted; the bleak, black sky and grey, solitary sea were enough to dissuade the usual dog walkers and lonely joggers. Brady stood and looked across the dark, empty vastness before him. And then he saw it; violence at its purest. There it was, brooding, blood-black violence. He stood transfixed as the thunderous waves spewed out venomous froth all over the beaten sand.

Conrad studied Brady's figure from the safety of his car, and wondered what was going through his head. He accepted that with Brady you had no chance; more so when even the police psychologist couldn't figure him out. He watched as Brady took out his mobile phone, curious about who he was calling.

'Where the fuck are you?' Brady demanded.

'It's better you don't know.'

'I'm serious. Where the fuck are you, Jimmy?' Brady repeated.

'You heard me the first time. Leave it, Jack, you don't understand.'

'Don't be a bloody fool! Let Gates sort this out before you end up losing your job,' Brady warned. 'Or worse.'

'Don't you think I already know that? I have no fucking choice.'

'For Christ's sake, Jimmy. You're talking shit. Look, you need to come in. We've identified the body. It's only a matter of time now,' Brady warned.

'Are you crazy?'

'Jimmy, let's talk this through face to face, yeah?'

'What the fuck aren't you getting here, Jack? I don't want to involve you . . . not in this . . .'

'In what for Chrissakes?'

'Fuck it, Jack! Why do you think I'm lying low?'

'Because she was a fifteen-year-old girl that you drove home on the night she was murdered. Who also happened to be your daughter's best friend! Shit, Jimmy! It'll be obvious to Gates that you recognised her.'

Matthews let out a low, maniacal laugh.

'If only that was all I had to worry about.'

'For fuck's sake, Jimmy! What's going on?'

'Madley.'

'What?'

'Yeah, I expected that response from you. Why the fuck do you think I didn't want to say anything?'

'Oh shit, Jimmy! Tell me you're not involved with Madley?'

Brady shook his head. CID had been trying to get Madley for years. But no matter how hard they tried, they just couldn't get anything on him. He was the local mafia boss, feared by all for his unforgiving nature. But, he was also revered for his drug money rumoured to run into the millions. He had a huge house on Marine Avenue, one of the many surprisingly affluent streets in Whitley Bay which would have set him back close to a million, not to mention another two-million-pound farmhouse set in one of the most stunning parts of Northumberland.

Brady had seen it for himself, a staggering eighteenth-century farmhouse with outbuildings, stables, paddocks and thirty acres of wild fields hidden behind rows and rows of trees. Once past the electronic gates, the gravelled drive was dominated by trees on either side for the mile or so it took to get to the imposing building and its original cobbled courtyard. Behind the farmhouse the Cheviots stood, proud and majestic, and to the south Northumberland National Park lay spread out for miles and miles. For a lad from the Ridges, even Brady had to admit that Madley had done well for himself.

Add to that the three nightclubs; two in the city centre and one in Whitley Bay. Brady had also heard that he had recently bought the Royal Hotel on the sea front, right next door to his nightclub, The Blue Lagoon. CID still couldn't touch him.

'Jimmy, whatever mess you're in with Madley, I can help,' Brady offered.

Matthews' silence said it all.

'You don't understand . . .' Matthews mumbled, more to himself than Brady. 'I . . . I fucked up. I . . . I owe Madley more money than I could ever pay in a lifetime. You've got no idea how much. But I thought I'd got him to trust me . . . I mean he's had me working for him for the past few months to pay off what I owe him and then I fucking blow it.'

If there was one thing Brady was certain of, that was that Madley trusted no one; not even his own mother.

'Listen, Jimmy, if you're scared, go to O'Donnell.'

'Yeah?' Matthews questioned sceptically. 'It won't do any bloody good, Jack. You'd be surprised at who's controlling Madley.'

'Go on?'

'Who does O'Donnell share drinks with after golf? And who is it that's been financing all of the Chief Superintendent's new projects?'

Brady didn't reply. He already knew the answer: Mayor Macmillan. Brady knew the recently elected Mayor was involved in all sorts of shady deals but even he was struggling to accept that Macmillan had power over someone like Madley, let alone the Chief Superintendent.

Brady had known O'Donnell for years; way back when the Chief Superintendent was just a humble DS. If it hadn't been for O'Donnell literally grabbing Brady off the war-torn streets of the Ridges, and offering him a chance at a different life, then he wouldn't be stood where he was now. Brady had been an angry adolescent, one who had every right to be pissed off with his life. And he had started to get a reputation on the streets for his suicidal 'couldn't give a fuck' attitude. If O'Donnell hadn't cornered him one night about the brutal murder of a young male from Wallsend, then he would have ended up like Madley. Somehow, O'Donnell had got through to him. Even though Brady had never talked about who had killed the kid, O'Donnell still took him on. Admittedly, it didn't happen overnight, but O'Donnell had seen something in him as a teenager, enough to put his career on the line to risk helping Brady get out, never knowing whether Brady had in fact been involved in the murder. They had an unspoken agreement never to talk about it. It was part of Brady's dark, troubled past and that was where O'Donnell had chosen to leave it. Brady had stood back and watched as O'Donnell excelled through the ranks, going on to become a boss feared by everyone, including the likes of Jimmy Matthews.

'So tell me, Jack, who the fuck's going to be able to get me out of this?' questioned Matthews.

'Gates, Jimmy. He'll sort this. You know him, he's straight. Take what you've got on Madley and Macmillan to him.'

'What evidence? I've got nothing,' Matthews hissed. 'And fuck! Do you think Gates can protect me? Shit! This is Madley we're talking about here. If he thinks I've crossed him then my career with the force is over with and . . . and I'll lose everything . . . the house . . . Kate, Evie . . .' Matthews faltered.

'Listen, they'll be fine. I'll make sure of it. All right?'

Silence.

'Jimmy? Jimmy?'

'I stole from Madley, Jack. I saw an opportunity when I was in his office last night. His safe was open and I couldn't resist . . . I . . . I . . . owe money everywhere and I . . . Shit! I thought this might give me some power back against him but . . .'

'Fuck.' There was one thing he knew about Madley, and that was he didn't tolerate anyone crossing him. He knew Madley wouldn't kill Matthews, he was a copper after all which made things messy. But as Matthews was now aware, Madley could destroy the life he had built in an instant and leave him with absolutely nothing. And for a man like Matthews, that would be a fate worse than death.

'Shit, Jimmy! What the fuck did you take?' Brady demanded, worried.

He listened to silence.

Matthews had already hung up.

'Fuck it, Jimmy!' cursed Brady as he stared at the deserted beach.

It was sublime; nature at its most beautiful. The black, thunderous North Sea raged relentlessly against the craggy, treacherous rocks. Brady looked down Tynemouth's stretching, naked sands towards the haunting Priory. Raised high on a cliff top, the ruin dominated the horizon, over-looking, as it had done for centuries, the ravaging, wild sea.

In the halcyon days, he and Claudia had spent endless weekends discovering hidden beaches from Lindisfarne down through to Alnmouth and Bamburgh. They'd discovered desperately remote beaches brutally exposed to the harsh North Sea, so remote it was easy to forget civilisation. But stood now, watching the furious waves rant and rage against the jagged cliffs and rocks, Brady knew that there was no other beach along the Northumberland coastline that could be more dramatic and breathtaking than this one.

For a second he thought about calling Claudia. He needed more than ever to hear her voice. He stood for a moment and watched the ominous black clouds close in towards him.

Before he could talk himself out of it he had already got her number up and had pressed call.

He held his breath as he waited, not sure whether she would answer. He didn't know how many messages he had left on her voice mail in that first month. But it was enough for her to think he was mad. He would find himself drinking bottle after bottle of whisky to forget her and then before he even realised what he was doing he would call her, unaware that it was three or four in the morning. She never once answered, forcing him to leave painful, awkward messages, pleading for her to just talk to him.

And then he got it. He suddenly realised that he was acting like a crazy stalker. So he quit. And for the past month he hadn't attempted to contact her. That was, until now.

'Jack?' she hesitantly answered.

He held his breath, not knowing what to say. He had waited for this moment for six months and now he was lost for words.

'Jack?' she repeated.

He could hear an edge of worry in her voice.

'Yeah, I'm here,' he replied softly, not sure what else to say.

'What do you want?' she asked, suddenly sounding cold and professional.

'I . . . just want to talk to you,' Brady answered, unsure of what it was he wanted from her.

'Don't you think we're past talking?'

Brady swallowed hard. He closed his watering eyes and covered his smooth, olive-skinned face with a trembling hand.

'I . . . I . . . just needed to hear your voice,' he answered honestly.

She didn't reply.

'I miss you,' he said impulsively.

He waited, but she said nothing.

She was making it as hard as possible for him.

'Did you hear what I said?' he asked quietly.

'I heard,' she answered.

'Don't you miss me?' he asked, feeling more vulnerable than he had ever done in his life.

'Jack, this is pointless. You screwed up, not me. So stop

turning this around. I didn't destroy our marriage, you did. And it's about time you accepted that. And as for missing me, you don't miss me. You miss the idea of me.'

'That's unfair.'

'Really?' asked Claudia.

'Yes,' answered Brady quietly.

He listened to the heavy silence and wondered what she was thinking.

'I still love you,' he said.

He heard her give out an exasperated sigh.

'It's too easy to say those words. Actions are what count, Jack.'

He dropped his shaking hand from his face and opened his eyes.

'What more can I do?'

'Until you know the answer to that, then there's nothing for us to talk about.'

'Wait, Claudia?' Brady asked, desperate for her not to hang up on him.

Silence.

'The job offer with O'Donnell?'

'What about it?' she asked, clearly not wanting to continue the conversation.

'Why aren't you taking it?' Brady asked.

'You know why,' she coolly replied.

'Claudia, look . . . can we arrange to meet up to at least talk about things?'

'I don't know if that's a good idea, do you?' she answered.

He didn't reply. He couldn't because all he wanted was another chance.

'Look, Jack, I've got to go. I'm kind of busy right now.'

'Sure, of course you are,' answered Brady inaudibly.

He heard the line click as she hung up on him without even saying goodbye.

He watched, unable to move as the waves thrashed against the rocks on the beach below him. He breathed out slowly as he tried to steady himself. He felt wounded and didn't know how to stop the actual physical pain he was feeling in his chest.

All too aware that time was getting on and that he had to get back to the station, Brady tried to get his head together. He rubbed his eyes roughly before glancing cursorily at the solitary, haunting, black outline that was the Priory. Then he turned and walked back to Conrad who was still sat with the engine idling, patiently waiting for him.

Chapter Sixteen

It was nearly midday and Brady was sat in his office going over what Matthews had said to him about Macmillan being behind Madley. Worse still, having the Chief Superintendent O'Donnell in his pocket. He knew O'Donnell and was certain that this could never be the case. Matthews must have got it wrong, that was all there was to it. He also had serious doubts about whether Madley was working for Macmillan. The other way round was more likely. Madley was a law unto himself, plain and simple.

Brady had been watching Macmillan, a corrupt politician, for the past year. He had recently been elected as Mayor. But the public didn't realise the kind of man they had representing them. The police and the press were well informed of Macmillan's dodgy past. Even Rubenfeld, a snitch for a local paper, couldn't get his razor-sharp teeth into him despite Macmillan having a burglar for a brother and a prostitute for a younger sister. Both had a drugs habit to support and consequently, both had spent time in the station's holding cells. But neither of Macmillan's siblings' illegal transgressions ever made the local paper's front page.

And as for Macmillan, Brady knew his hands were dirty; but trying to prove it was another matter. The night Brady had got shot he had been staking out a new drug dealer, who his sources had told him was working for Macmillan. But before Brady could get something on Macmillan, some bastard had blown his cover; literally.

Brady knew when to keep his mouth shut, more so after Gates had told him in no uncertain terms that he wasn't interested unless Brady had concrete evidence against the man. And that was the problem with Macmillan, he made sure he socialised with the right kind of people. Even his penchant for prostitutes, the younger the better, was never reported at the station, let alone in any of the papers.

Rubenfeld knew all about Macmillan's dirty little ways, but even he couldn't get anyone interested in exposing the Mayor.

'The greasy git has the right approach. He knows how to stop people talking. Money, Jack. Money! In the right hands you can get away with murder!' Rubenfeld had grumbled that night in the pub before knocking back his fifth whisky chaser.

Brady hadn't been able to resist counting; after all, it was his money that was loosening Rubenfeld's tongue.

Brady sighed now as he thought about it. Rubenfeld was right and he knew it; money could buy anything.

*

As soon as he opened the door to the Incident Room it hit him. Perfume. It was an intoxicating smell, one that embodied the wearer; expensive, distinctive, desirable, and equally unattainable.

An attractive, tall, dark-haired woman in her early thirties stood up. Her long, slender body was dressed in a fifties retro-style grey woollen dress. A large buckled belt accentuated her narrow waist and shapely hips, which provocatively swayed as she walked over in her three-inch designer heels.

She smiled at Brady.

'I'm surprised to see you back so soon,' Dr Amelia Jenkins coolly greeted.

Jenkins' sleek, raven-black razor-cut bob swung back from her prominent cheekbones as she turned to DS Adamson who remained seated at the long conference table.

'Robert has been an excellent replacement,' she added as she flashed him a smile.

Brady refrained from saying what was on his mind. The arrogant look on Adamson's face assured Brady that he hadn't wasted any time with Jenkins.

'He had a lot to say about you,' Jenkins continued.

'I'm sure he did,' Brady said as he looked straight at Adamson.

Brady couldn't stomach the guy and he was certain the feeling was mutual. He definitely didn't like the idea of Adamson and his ex-shrink discussing him. He wanted Adamson out of the way. He could see that Adamson was already starting to make himself quite at home. Next thing, Brady would find him setting up office in his damned room.

'Adamson, I'd like you to accompany Harvey to Rake Lane Hospital with the Simmons so they can ID the body,' Brady instructed.

'Surely I'm better off working on the investigation here rather than wasting my time acting as a chaperon?' Adamson asked disdainfully.

Brady stared at Adamson.

'You're done here,' he firmly answered. 'And Adamson?'

Adamson looked at Brady contemptuously.

'Don't ever undervalue the significance of accompanying the next of kin when identifying a murder victim. Their reaction to the victim's body will be very telling.'

'What exactly do you expect them to do given the fact that her face is unidentifiable?' sneered Adamson.

'I'm more interested in their reaction to the tattoo,' replied Brady curtly.

Brady heard Conrad shift his feet uncomfortably behind him. He couldn't help but notice that Jenkins was watching his reaction to Adamson with great interest.

Then again what else did he expect from her? She was after all the police shrink; his shrink. That was until he refused to cooperate. He had been forced by Gates to sit in front of her, hour after hour while she watched, waiting for him to break. She had tried to make a big deal of Brady's childhood but he refused to talk about it. When he did eventually talk, it wasn't to discuss what had happened, it was only to tell her that he was going to deal with his problems the old-fashioned way; with a bottle of Scotch. That had been over five months ago and he hadn't seen or heard from her since.

Brady noticed the sneer on Adamson's face at the mention of the tattoo due to its intimate location.

'Just do as I've instructed otherwise you'll find yourself removed from this investigation,' Brady ordered.

'On whose authority?' challenged Adamson as he clenched his heavy-set square jaw ready for a fight.

'On mine. This is my investigation, regardless of what you think. So either you accept your orders or you go back to North Shields.'

Adamson's bright blue eyes blazed with anger, telling Brady that this wasn't over.

'And you'll find that DCI Gates will back me up, Adamson. So don't think he'll be interested.'

Brady watched as Adamson's jaw clenched even tighter but he kept his mouth shut. Adamson straightened his tie before picking up his suit jacket. He looked at Brady.

'Anything else before I leave?'

'Tell Harvey to wait for Dr Jenkins. She'll be accompanying you.'

'Whatever you say, boss,' replied Adamson thickly.

Brady waited until Adamson had left the room before turning to Jenkins.

'Look, Jack. I really wish I could help but . . .' Jenkins stopped and apologetically shook her head. 'I don't know what good I would do by being present at an identification.'

'I need you there. I wouldn't trust Adamson answering the bloody phone, let alone accompanying the Simmons to ID their daughter,' answered Brady.

'Still . . . I don't see how me being there helps?'

'The victim was just a kid, a fifteen-year-old kid,' Brady quietly said. 'She was choked to death first. And then for some reason, whoever murdered her decided she was too pretty. So her face was bludgeoned beyond human recognition.' Brady's eyes drifted over to the explicit photographs of the victim displayed on the whiteboard on the wall in front.

'I will use every resource available to me to get whoever

did this to her. And that includes you, Dr Jenkins,' Brady said as his eyes met hers.

Jenkins didn't react but Brady knew he'd hit a nerve. It was a cheap shot but he had no choice. He needed her to be there when the Simmons identified the victim, that was all there was to it. He knew she had a background in criminal psychology. It wasn't his business to ask her why she opted out and turned to practising clinical psychology instead but he presumed something had shaken her to her core. Which was why he was so surprised that firstly Gates had asked her to be part of the investigation, and secondly, that Jenkins had agreed. He made a mental note to do some homework on Dr Amelia Jenkins to find exactly what had caused her sudden departure from criminology.

'How can you be so sure the victim is their daughter anyway?' asked Jenkins. 'Don't you think that such an elaborate tattoo is unusual for someone her age?'

Brady stood his ground calmly.

'No, it's her,' he quietly insisted. 'And yes it is unusual, but something about this tells me she wasn't your typical fifteen-year-old schoolgirl.'

Jenkins raised her eyebrows.

'Don't tell me, a hunch?'

Brady shrugged.

'Something like that.'

Brady walked over to the table and poured himself a drink of water. He slowly drank the lukewarm liquid conscious that Jenkins was watching him. Finished, he placed the glass down and looked up at her.

'I need you with them when they identify her. In particular I need you to watch Paul Simmons' reaction.'

'Why can't you do it if it's so crucial to the investigation?'

'Because the man doesn't trust me. He knows that I suspect he's hiding something. Without me there he's more likely to let his guard down. I believe he'll know it's her, but it will be the tattoo that will convince him.'

Jenkins shook her head, unsettling her raven-black, sleek bob.

'You've lost me.'

'I guarantee that Louise Simmons will not recognise the body. She will reluctantly acknowledge that the clothes and hair are similar but she will deny that it is her daughter because her daughter does not have her belly button pierced, let alone a jade dragon tattoo tucked discreetly below her navel. No one wants to accept that their child is dead. No one more so than Louise Simmons.'

'What do you mean? What makes Louise Simmons so different from any other bereaved mother?'

'Because she feels guilty, that's why. She knew something was going on in her daughter's life, something profoundly damaging. But she never did anything about it. Instead she ignored the doubts, choosing to believe that her daughter's destructive behaviour was more to do with her ex-husband's, Sophie's father's suicide over a year ago.'

'All very insightful, Jack. I'm impressed. Tell me, is this another hunch of yours?'

'No,' answered Brady. 'I just did some research on the victim's father. Alex Washington jumped off the Tyne Bridge last year. It seems he suffered from clinical depression, coupled with stress from work and whatever crap was going on in his personal life. I guarantee that Louise Simmons believed that Sophie wasn't handling her father's death that well and that was why she was so uncommunicative; staying out late and doing God knows what shit teenagers do nowadays. Including getting a tattoo.'

Jenkins smiled at him.

'You sound old.'

'I am old,' replied Brady.

Jenkins held his gaze long enough for him to briefly forget that Conrad was still in the room.

Embarrassed he cleared his throat and turned to look at the whiteboard.

'Paul Simmons will definitely know by the tattoo that the body lying in that morgue is his step-daughter,' Brady asserted.

Jenkins frowned at Brady.

'That's an odd statement. You know what you're suggesting?'

'Trust me, luring people into a false sense of security while you're actually analysing their every move is what you're good at,' he answered as he turned to face her.

She smiled at him slowly.

'Is that what you think I did to you?' she asked as she swept her hair back off her high cheekbones.

Brady smiled faintly as he shook his head, noticing for the first time her striking scarlet-coloured lips. For a moment the intense colour reminded him of Claudia's obsession with Chanel lipstick.

'I don't want to waste time talking about me while we have a murder victim turning very cold in the morgue.'

'A typical "Jack Brady" response,' Jenkins coolly answered.

Brady shrugged.

She turned and collected her things then headed for the door. She paused and looked back at Brady.

'At least I get a straight answer from DS Adamson.'

'But straight answers don't interest you, do they?'

Jenkins stared at Brady, her expression saying it all, before turning and leaving.

'Always got to have the last word, sir,' stated Conrad.

'What gives you that idea?' asked Brady.

Chapter Seventeen

Brady had asked Conrad to drive him back to the crime scene. It was after one in the afternoon and time was running out for them. But he needed to have another look around; this time in daylight.

There was something about the murder that was niggling him. He had to wait for the post-mortem report from Wolfe, but from what he had seen at the crime scene the victim hadn't appeared to have sustained sexual injuries. Instead, her murder hinted at something darker and more sinister; that she had known her killer.

His phone started to ring. For a brief moment he thought it might be Matthews.

Realising who it was, he cleared his throat before answering. 'Yes sir?'

'Any developments?' questioned Gates.

'No sir,' answered Brady.

'Damn. What about the post-mortem? Do we know if the murder victim was raped?'

'No sir, Wolfe hasn't verified that yet. As soon as I hear from him I'll let you know.'

Brady inhaled deeply on what was left of his cigarette. Without thinking he stubbed it out in the spotless ashtray.

Conrad didn't say a word, but Brady could hear his jaw grinding.

'So, are you going to tell me how you figured out the identity of the victim?'

He foolishly hadn't been expecting that question.

'I just wanted to cover every possibility, sir,' Brady lied. 'Which was why I decided to widen the search by lowering the age range.'

He realised that he was getting himself in deeper and deeper. Only a fool would believe that Matthews hadn't recognised her. Not with the way he had reacted when he saw her body. And definitely not once it became public knowledge that the victim had allegedly spent the hours leading up to her murder with Jimmy Matthews' daughter, Evie. At least that was what the Simmons believed. They were adamant Sophie had gone to Evie Matthews' home on the night she was murdered. Brady didn't even want to think about the possibility of someone having seen Matthews driving the victim home.

The last thing he wanted was Gates realising he was hiding something.

'And what about DI Matthews? Have you heard from him?'

'No sir. Why? Is there a problem?' Brady asked as casually as he could.

'You tell me.'

Brady didn't reply.

'As soon as you hear anything I want to know. Understand?'

'Yes sir,' answered Brady as he looked out at the approaching crime scene.

He put his phone away as Conrad pulled in as best he could. Cars and vans blocked the road and even the pavements. Brady looked towards the gate that led down to the crime scene and watched journalists scurrying like rats over one another to get the best shot of the farmland and the crumbling farmhouse.

To them the murder of a fifteen-year-old girl was newsworthy, meaning it earned them money. And this story was too newsworthy for Brady's liking. More so when you threw into the mix that within a twenty-five-mile radius they had fourteen hundred registered sex offenders; nineteen of whom had gone to ground. Whether their disappearance was connected to the murder was anyone's guess. They had God knows how many officers assigned to track the buggers down. But finding them was another matter.

Brady got out of the car and slammed the door. He looked up at the thundering blades overhead. A news helicopter was flying low, too low over the crime scene. Brady looked across at Conrad and gestured up at the helicopter.

Conrad nodded.

'I'll sort it, sir,' he said.

Brady's headache still hadn't gone and it now felt as if the rotating blades above were slicing through his skull.

'And can you check that they've actually started carrying out those DNA swabs? The last thing we want is a repeat of the Carter case!'

'Yes sir,' answered Conrad as he took out his mobile.

Northumbria Police had screwed up big time on the Megan Carter investigation. They may have come good eventually, but that was down to sheer dumb luck. It had nothing to do with the investigative team; their reaction had been too slow at the time and they'd paid for it. By the time they had got the resources together to take DNA swabs from male residents within a four-mile radius of where the victim's raped and strangled body had been found, the murderer had already left the area.

Gates still hadn't lived that investigation down; no one had, despite the murderer serendipitously being caught three years later. He had been arrested for drinking and driving in another part of the country and a routine DNA swab had been taken. It matched with DNA samples taken from the crime scene and finally resulted in a murder conviction.

Since then, Gates had used every investigation he had been in charge of to try to lay to rest the Carter investigation. Brady knew that Gates needed a speedy outcome with this case, one that would portray Northumbria Police in a favourable light again. If Gates succeeded in doing that, then it might just be enough to get his career rolling again.

Consequently, Brady had immediately ordered a team, which would soon include DS Adamson, to start the laborious task of taking DNA mouth swabs from all adult male residents in West Monkseaton and the surrounding areas. After Adamson had blatantly challenged the assignment Brady had given him, he wanted to remind him what policing was all about and had decided that some good old-fashioned door-to-door enquiries might just do the trick.

But more importantly, Brady needed a suspect or suspects. And if he was going to keep Matthews' name out of it, he needed it fast.

Chapter Eighteen

'Yeah, Tom? What have you got?' Brady answered as he left Conrad to sort out the helicopter.

He limped towards the group of journalists and on-lookers gathered around the sealed gate that led down to the crime scene. Crowds put him in a bad mood; especially ones filled with sleazy, shameless journalists. Worse still, he really needed a drink. He was starting to get the shakes and couldn't decide whether it was alcohol poisoning or withdrawal. Either way, he was craving a shot of malt just to settle his nerves.

'The parents have confirmed the identity of the girl. Sophie Washington. School kid, fifteen years old,' replied Harvey.

He took out a cigarette and lit it. He'd been quietly hoping it had all been a coincidence and that Matthews had been overreacting.

'I want you to find out who her friends were and interview them. We need to find out whether they know anything about a current boyfriend or any ex-boyfriends.'

'I'll get on that straight away,' answered Harvey. 'Do you want me to check out who Sophie Washington was with last night as well?'

'No . . . Conrad and I will deal with that,' replied Brady. 'I already have a good idea who it might be.'

'Yeah? Who?'

Brady didn't answer Harvey. He had other things on his mind.

'Between you and me, where do you reckon Jimmy would go if he wanted to lie low?'

He'd lost touch with Matthews since he'd been laid up with his gunshot wound and didn't know where to start looking for him.

'Shit, Jack! You know Jimmy better than I do! Where else do you think he'd be if he's not at home with the wife and kid?'

'Who is she?' asked Brady, stopping and turning his back to the crowd.

'Some tart that he met at The Blue Lagoon a few weeks back,' replied Harvey, his voice slightly distorted over the phone line.

Where else? Brady mused. It was one of Madley's nightclubs. Matthews was a hardened regular, as was Brady until he'd buggered his leg. They made their presence felt and Madley kept them drunk. It worked both ways.

'I don't suppose you know where she lives?'

'Hah! You know Jimmy. Likes to keep his private business private if you get my drift? Nah, all I know is that she was blonde with the biggest tits I've ever seen! I think her name was Tania but that's about as much as I know.'

Brady sighed inwardly.

'Jimmy hasn't got himself into any bother, has he?' asked Harvey.

'No . . . no, Jimmy's fine. Just a few problems at home.

You know the shit he gets up to, well let's just say it's finally caught up with him,' Brady answered.

'Can't say I'm surprised. I don't know how the son of a bitch managed to get away with it for so long. I mean, fuck! You remember the time that shit-hot nurse he was screwing gave him the clap? I couldn't look him in the face without laughing for a week. Especially after he'd said she specialised in highly contagious diseases. She did that all right. And then his wife had to pay a visit to the VD clinic and guess who treats her? The bloody cow that gave Jimmy the clap in the first place!'

'Yeah, that's Jimmy for you.'

'Fucking right it is! He's one hell of a guy.'

'He really is. As soon as you have anything regards boyfriends let me know, yeah?' concluded Brady. 'Oh yeah, and do me a favour, will you? Take Dr Jenkins with you. She's the right kind of person to have around when interviewing these kids. She'll know whether or not they're hiding something. May as well use her while we've got her.'

'Sounds good to me,' answered Harvey.

'And that doesn't mean you try and shag her, OK?' warned Brady.

'I knew it! Me and the lads had bets on whether you were shagging her. Seems I won. You bloody dog, Jack Brady!' laughed Harvey.

'You're one sick bastard,' replied Brady before disconnecting the call.

Brady threw his cigarette away and started walking towards the crowd.

He nodded at the short, shabby figure making his way towards him. He would recognise that ugly face anywhere.

'Things must be worse than I thought if they've had to

call you in,' Rubenfeld said in a deep, raspy voice, the result of too much booze.

Brady gave Rubenfeld a pained grin.

He couldn't remember a time when Rubenfeld hadn't been around. As far as Brady could remember Rubenfeld had always worked for *The Northern Echo*. It was the biggest-selling newspaper in the North East and a lot of its sales were down to Rubenfeld. If there was a story to uncover, Rubenfeld was guaranteed to be the first one there. Brady didn't know how he did it, but he had an uncanny knack of turning up when he was least wanted. But if Brady was honest, he needed Rubenfeld as much as Rubenfeld needed him.

'So what are you after?' Brady asked.

'Now that would be too easy!' Rubenfeld replied flashing his small, pincer teeth. He rubbed his two days' worth of dark stubble as he scrutinised Brady.

'I've heard something that might interest you,' Rubenfeld began as he lit a cigarette.

He'd caught Brady's attention.

'How about we go somewhere a bit more private?' Brady suggested.

*

'One black coffee and . . . ?' Brady called out to Rubenfeld.

'A double Scotch,' grunted Rubenfeld. 'Well, it's gone lunchtime,' he replied in response to Brady's cynical expression.

'That'll be seven pounds ten, mate,' the bartender said.

Brady handed him a tenner. He then nodded at the bleached blonde cleaner who'd been suspiciously watching him from the other side of the bar. He made a mental note to get statements taken from whoever was in the pub last night. The Beacon was literally a five-minute walk from the crime scene.

Brady picked the drinks up and limped over to Rubenfeld.

He sat down heavily on the barstool. He was feeling short-changed; always did when he ran into Rubenfeld. He watched as Rubenfeld did his usual trick and knocked it back in one, swift gulp.

'Ahh! Now, down to business,' Rubenfeld replied in a satisfied tone. 'First, I want to know what really happened,' he said, leaning in towards Brady. 'And don't feed me any of your usual bullshit, Jack.'

'What's in it for me?'

Rubenfeld locked his beady eyes on Brady's.

'Jimmy,' he whispered throatily.

It took all of Brady's willpower not to lean over the small, round table and grab Rubenfeld by his short fat neck and squeeze whatever he knew out of him. But he knew from past experience that it wouldn't work.

'Spit it out then,' rasped Rubenfeld.

'We've got a murder victim. Found in the early hours of this morning,' Brady began.

'Tell me something I don't know,' Rubenfeld replied irritably. 'Bloody hell, Jack. You know better than that.'

Brady shrugged and decided to wait it out. It failed.

Rubenfeld stood up and put his shabby black raincoat on. Regardless of the weather, or the location, Rubenfeld always wore it. Brady couldn't imagine Rubenfeld without it. Underneath it he wore a black linen suit; equally scruffy and in need of dry cleaning. Brady presumed that Rubenfeld had never quite acclimatised to the bitter North East weather after coming back from the South and had compromised on a heavy raincoat. Brady admired his pragmatism; this was the North East of England after all, where the temperature rarely rose above 60 degrees during the summer and the rest of the year was spent under a miserable, disgruntled drizzle.

So much for global warming, mused Brady.

'Yeah, all right,' he reluctantly muttered. 'But it better be worth it!'

Rubenfeld sat back down.

Brady looked over at the bartender and caught his eye. 'Same again,' he ordered as he raised Rubenfeld's empty glass.

'The victim's just a kid . . .' Brady paused as Rubenfeld raised his thick, black eyebrows.

'A fifteen-year-old schoolgirl to be precise. I've just had a positive ID,' Brady stated, dropping his voice as the bartender approached.

Brady took out another tenner and handed it to the bartender. 'Keep the change.'

Rubenfeld swiftly drained the glass and then turned his attention back to Brady.

'Cause of death?'

'Can't say until the post-mortem comes back.'

'Suspects?'

'Too early,' Brady answered.

'Where's she from?'

'Here, West Monkseaton,' Brady answered. 'Murdered literally yards from her own doorstep.'

'You'll be releasing her identity then?' fired Rubenfeld.

Brady weighed him up; he was one sleazy son of a bitch.

'Sophie Washington,' Brady conceded, barely loud enough for Rubenfeld to hear. But he heard it.

Brady had no choice; he needed Rubenfeld on his side.

Rubenfeld rubbed his coarse chin as he considered what Brady had told him.

'Well, I'm glad I'm not in your shoes just now! Or Jimmy's come to that,' he rasped.

'Why? What's going on?'

'That's what I want to know,' Rubenfeld replied. 'Jimmy's got himself into a bit of bother with Madley. Word has it he's pissed Madley off big time.'

'Why? What's he done?'

He knew then that he should have taken Matthews seriously when he said that Madley was out to get him. Brady had just assumed that Madley didn't have the balls to touch a copper; maybe he was wrong.

Rubenfeld shook his head.

'Don't fuck with me!'

'Do I look like I'm fucking with you?' Rubenfeld snapped. He nervously ran his fat fingers through his short, receding black hair.

'You know what Madley's capable of, Jack. And I for one don't want to mess with him.'

Rubenfeld checked his watch.

'I've got to run if I'm going to make this evening's edition. It's due to roll in less than an hour.' He paused, narrowing his distrustful eyes. 'Come to think of it, where is that tight-arsed bugger, Jimmy? Shouldn't it be him throwing his weight around, considering the state of your leg?'

'He's tied up,' Brady answered.

Rubenfeld didn't buy it.

'Don't get involved, Jack. Not when it concerns Madley,' Rubenfeld warned as he stood up.

But that was exactly it, thought Brady. He was involved, and had been, from the moment he'd found Matthews sat in his office.

Chapter Nineteen

Brady kept his head down and pushed his way through, ignoring the barrage of questions. The scavenging rats were willing to sink their teeth into anything that moved. With the limp, Brady was too easy a target.

'DI Brady? I thought you'd retired?' shouted out one journalist.

Brady ignored the question and bent down under the police tape. They knew him from the shooting. His story had made the headlines for three days running in the local papers. It wasn't every day that a copper got shot in an undercover drugs bust. Brady kept going. It was easy to block out the frenzied yelling behind him, he only had to think about his next task after revisiting the crime scene; re-interviewing the murdered girl's parents.

'Where's DI Matthews? Rumour has it he's been taken off the investigation and that you're his replacement. Is that right, DI Brady?' a female voice called out. 'DI Brady? Harriet Jacobs from *The Evening Chronicle* here,' she added, hoping to make an impact.

Brady didn't react even though his guts twisted with every word. He kept his back to the crowd and continued walking down the dirt track towards the crime scene.

'Why was DI Matthews suspended? Is it connected to the murder investigation?' Jacobs shouted after him. 'Did you hear what I asked you, DI Brady? Why was DI Matthews taken off this investigation?' she added in a last-ditch attempt at getting a reaction.

Brady had heard her all right. The question had cut straight through the crowd. The fact that someone had talked to the press didn't surprise him. What did surprise Brady were the questions; they were about Matthews, not the murder. It didn't make sense. Matthews was the type of guy who was liked by everyone, even Gates. But, from the question he was just asked, it was obvious that someone on the force had it in for Matthews. The question was, who? One name kept coming up. DS Adamson.

Brady just couldn't shake off his suspicions about DS Adamson. Adamson had already proven that he had no loyalty to the investigative team, let alone Brady. As Conrad had said, he was out for himself. And with Matthews conveniently out of the picture, Adamson might have a real shot at promotion. Especially given how much Gates wanted Adamson to transfer to Whitley Bay.

Brady tried to ignore the doubts he was having about Adamson. He had other things on his mind, in particular finding Jimmy Matthews before Gates became suspicious. That is, if he wasn't already.

Chapter Twenty

'I'd have thought you'd be too bloody busy to be making social calls,' Ainsworth, the senior SOCO, greeted when he spotted him.

'Wanted to get a second look,' Brady answered as he took in the ruined farmhouse.

'Different feel to it in the daylight,' Ainsworth commented following his gaze.

Brady noted that he was right. It did feel different. When he was called out early this morning it felt as if they were miles away from suburban West Monkseaton. The overgrown hedges and looming trees had added to the blanket of blackness, blinding Brady to the row of houses that backed onto either side of the farmland.

He ignored the urge to have a cigarette. Ainsworth was a good enough reason not to; this was Ainsworth's office now and even Brady wouldn't cross the line with him.

'I take it you're not here for a bloody chat. Presume you want to see where your victim was attacked?' Ainsworth asked.

Brady nodded.

'All right, but follow my exact footsteps. It's bloody difficult enough to figure out what's what down here with all the bloody onlookers we've had . . .' Ainsworth grumbled. 'If it's not your lot making my job impossible then it's the bloody public. Bloody useless, the lot of them!'

'Why do you work with people if you're such a miserable old sod then?' Brady laughed.

'I don't,' Ainsworth answered flatly. 'They're already dead so they're no bother. It just so happens that the living keep bloody interfering with what I'm trying to do.'

Brady followed Ainsworth. Someone, no doubt kids, had built a large bonfire, using some of the broken rafters and other debris left lying around. It was still smouldering. Brady wondered whether any of the kids who used the place last night could have witnessed what had happened; or even, been responsible?

Ainsworth noticed Brady taking in the piles of discarded broken bottles and used needles that littered the ground. Evidence that the place was popular with the local kids.

'Bet their parents don't know what the little bastards get up to down here.'

Brady liked Ainsworth for the same reason that everyone else couldn't stand the cantankerous old sod; he hated civilisation, or what had become of it. It didn't matter where you were; an impoverished council estate or so-called respectable suburbia; kids were kids and would find a way to get pissed and shag around. It was human nature, but without the clothes on.

Brady looked over at the area where the murder victim had been found. He then looked up at the sky overhead. It was partially obscured by trees, so at night it would be dark, too dark to see anything.

He suddenly thought of the witness who had stumbled with her torch upon what was left of Sophie Washington's face. Before he left the station he had briefly read the statement that had been taken from the witness. She was a divorcee in her early fifties, who lived alone with her dog. Every morning at four she walked her black Labrador down the track of the abandoned farmland before leaving for work at the local Sainsbury's. This was the first morning in years she had never made it to work. The state she was in when the police arrived after her 999 call was enough to convince even the most hardened cynic that she had innocently walked into a horrific crime scene. Unfortunately for the police she hadn't seen or heard anyone else before her dog found the murder victim.

'Trying to ascertain whether someone could have witnessed something?' Ainsworth asked, following Brady's gaze.

'Yeah, but given the conditions when we came out early this morning, I seriously doubt it.'

'That's not to say someone wouldn't have heard something,' Ainsworth replied.

'Maybe,' muttered Brady.

Brady looked up towards the dirt track. He could just make out the road and the traffic lights. The depressing Modernist building that was West Monkseaton Metro station loomed on the other side of the road.

'Give me a bloody minute will you?' Ainsworth suddenly barked at a SOCO standing nearby. 'Christ! They'll expect me to wipe their arses next.'

'So what have you got for me?' Brady asked, ignoring Ainsworth's outburst.

'Hah!' Ainsworth spluttered. 'Would have been a lot easier if your lot hadn't muddied the bloody water. What with Matthews pissing us around by trampling over whatever prints were there and then the idiot goes and finishes the job by covering her body with his coat. What the bloody hell is that all about then?'

Brady shrugged.

'I'll bloody strangle the useless bugger when I get my hands on him!'

Join the queue, thought Brady.

'But we did find enough blood and flesh to confirm that the murder victim's face was definitely bludgeoned in situ,' Ainsworth stated.

Brady turned to him. His gut feeling had told him that Sophie Washington's body hadn't been dumped; that this was a murder scene.

'No weapon yet. But, if it's been dumped here, we'll find it,' Ainsworth promised. 'From the mess we saw under the UV light, I reckon you could be right about the murderer using any one of the pieces of rubble lying around.'

'No sign of her mobile?' Brady asked, knowing the answer.

Ainsworth shook his head.

'No, but you'll be the first to know if we find it. However Fielding here has found something that just might interest you,' he said as he gestured towards the waiting SOCO.

Brady suddenly felt a kick of excitement; it had been a long time since he'd felt this way.

'Go on then, Fielding, what are you waiting for? A bloody round of applause or what?' barked Ainsworth.

Brady turned to ask Ainsworth something else but he was already bollocking some other poor sod.

Instead he limped after the SOCO who had started heading off towards the dirt track.

'So, how do you cope working with a miserable, old bugger like Ainsworth then?' Brady asked once he'd caught up. He threw in a smile, ignoring his throbbing leg.

'Oh, he's not so bad. You eventually get used to it,' the SOCO replied, pulling off her face mask.

'Can't breathe in these things,' she explained, smiling.

She then pulled back the suit's white hood and shook free her short, ruffled black hair.

She playfully ran her fingers through her hair as she smiled at him.

He couldn't help but stare into her bright, green eyes. They sparkled with mischief.

'So, what is it that you're supposed to be showing me?' Brady asked.

'That depends on you,' she said suggestively.

'Jack! Jack!' Ainsworth panted out from behind them.

'Damn,' she said, hearing Ainsworth's voice. 'What if you take me out for a drink and then I'll show you?' she suggested flirtatiously.

Brady felt awkward. For once he didn't know what to say. His conversation with Claudia earlier had thrown him, and he could still feel the physical pain of her rejection.

'When?' she asked with a coy smile.

'When?' Brady repeated, feeling like an idiot.

He ran his slender, long hand through his dark hair as he smiled at her, embarrassed.

She seductively returned the smile, slowly taking in his prominent cheekbones and strong, rugged chin. She then looked up at his deep, penetrating, dark brown eyes.

'When are you going to take me out for a drink?' she urged as Ainsworth's stocky figure closed in on them. 'I know now isn't exactly the best time to ask but in this job there never is a good time,' she added, lightly smiling.

'I'm a little stretched right now,' he replied apologetically.

The last thing he wanted to say was that he wasn't over his wife yet.

'Fielding, what the bloody hell are you playing at?' barked Ainsworth. 'Haven't you shown him yet?'

'No sir,' she answered.

'Bloody typical. Can't get any of you lot to do what I ask! If I want something done I have to do it myself,' Ainsworth complained. 'Go do something useful for a bloody change.'

'Yes sir,' Fielding replied. 'See you later,' she added, as she smiled at Brady before leaving.

'Don't bother, Jack!' Ainsworth threatened. 'She works for me, remember. I want her mind on the job, not you. So forget it.'

'What do you take me for?' Brady questioned as he shot Ainsworth a look.

'For the dog that you are, Jack.'

Brady didn't bother arguing. It was clear Ainsworth had heard the rumours about Claudia leaving him because of his loss of judgement when it had come to DC Simone Henderson. Brady accepted that his failed private life was common knowledge in North Tyneside.

'Right, back to business. This way,' Ainsworth brusquely added.

He followed Ainsworth feeling disgusted with himself for losing his head when it had come to a colleague; a junior one at that. It had cost him more than he could ever have imagined.

'This is what I want to show you,' Ainsworth said turning back to Brady.

He looked up and realised that Ainsworth had crossed over the dirt track and was now on a grassy bank. It was overgrown with wild bushes that partially obscured the seven-feet-high wooden fence running the length of the farm. Brady noted that the fence separated the row of semi-detached 1930s houses backing onto the farmland.

He limped over to Ainsworth's impatient figure and watched as he pulled a clump of wild branches back to reveal a significant gap in the wooden fence, large enough for even Brady to climb through. Brady knelt down and looked through it. A muddy lane led straight out onto Fairfield Drive, the street where the murder victim had lived.

'Shit,' muttered Brady.

'Footprints found here match the boots that your victim was wearing, confirming that she came in this way. And it seems that she was with someone,' Ainsworth stated. 'Whether she met them here or she came with them, I can't say. But by this point,' Ainsworth gestured to where they stood, 'she was definitely not on her own.'

Brady raised his eyebrow questioningly.

'We got a partial handprint on this side of the fence which matches another handprint we found by the body. And we found what we presume to be male footprints given the size here, identical to prints found at the crime scene,' Ainsworth explained.

Brady's phone started to ring. He pulled it out of his jacket and looked at the number.

'Sorry, I need to take this call,' Brady apologised as he stood up.

'Yeah, yeah,' muttered Ainsworth. 'Any excuse not to work.'

Brady shot him a grin before turning away to answer his phone.

'Amelia?'

'You were right about Paul Simmons,' stated Jenkins.

'Yeah?'

'He knew it was his step-daughter as soon as he saw the tattoo. Not that he admitted it. He made out he recognised her from her clothes and hair.'

'What was his reaction?' asked Brady.

'He seemed genuinely shaken.'

'You're sure about that?'

'Are you questioning my judgement?' asked Jenkins.

'No . . . yes . . . maybe,' replied Brady.

'Look, I'm sorry. I know it's not what you expected to hear.'

'On the contrary, it is exactly what I expected,' stated Brady.

Chapter Twenty-One

It was a cold, simple fact that the first suspects in any child's murder were the parents.

Brady looked at Louise Simmons. It may have only been 1.37 pm but he couldn't blame her for the stiff gin and tonic clutched between white-knuckled, trembling hands. She looked like she needed it. Her face was drawn; haggard lines etched their way from under her glazed, icy blue eyes and around her rigid, thin lips. She had cruelly aged since his first visit.

The silence hung heavily in the room. Brady fought the compulsion to get up and throw open the heavy, sumptuous red and gold leaf curtains. The glow from the large Tiffany lamp sat on the ornate antique sideboard failed to penetrate the gloom of the room. Even the coal fire which hissed and spat in the original Edwardian hearth couldn't take the chill out of the room.

Brady shifted his feet on the polished wooden floor. In front of him was a wide, old wooden chest that served as a coffee table. A heavy, hardback book on the Impressionists was neatly positioned on the chest, along with a book on contemporary art and another on Art Deco. He carefully placed his coffee on the chest, fearful of disturbing the books on display. Or the large, handmade bowl that was filled with carefully arranged, exotic fruit. Brady now knew that Louise Simmons was an art teacher at a private girls' school in Jesmond, a sought-after expensive suburb two miles out from the city centre of Newcastle and seven miles inland from Whitley Bay. It explained the books and the eclectic pieces of art work he had noticed covering the walls in the hallway and also in the spacious living room where he was now sat.

Paul Simmons was an IT manager with Sage business and software services in Newcastle. He looked the part: cold, clinical, uptight, arrogant and egotistical. Brady wondered for a moment what it was that had attracted Louise Simmons to her husband? And more to the point what exactly did they have in common? He imagined that Simmons' arrogance and attitude might have been attractive to begin with, but wondered whether it was starting to wear thin.

Brady looked up at the oil painting hanging over the fireplace, and resisted the urge to ask Louise Simmons more about it.

He suspected the painting was a stunning copy of King Edward's Bay, an oil painting by F. W. Reaveley, a Tynemouth-born artist who began painting local sea and landscapes from 1891. Brady knew the painting was owned by a private collector, but was sure that the painting above the fireplace couldn't be the original which was probably worth a small fortune by now.

Instead of asking more about the painting he turned to look at Paul Simmons who was stood in the large bay window with his hands clenched, jaw rigid, eyes resentfully narrowed as he watched every move Brady made. He did little to hide his disdain at Brady's return. He wanted Jimmy Matthews here.

'What hope do we have of you lot finding out who . . . who's responsible if you're sat here?' Simmons suddenly spat.

'We're doing everything we can, Mr Simmons,' Brady reasoned.

'Including ransacking her bedroom? Don't you think you've done enough damage?'

'I'll personally make sure everything is replaced after we've finished.'

'You're damned right you will!' Simmons replied.

He shook his head as more footsteps could be heard descending the spiralling wooden stairs. He looked through the gap in the curtains only to see officers carrying out two bagged and sealed computers.

'What the hell are you doing with my computer? I . . . I need that for work! There are confidential work files on there. The last thing I want is you idiots destroying them! And when exactly do I get them back, eh?' Simmons asked agitatedly as he ran his fingers through his short hair. 'Christ! You're a bunch of bloody idiots, all you're doing is wasting time! There's nothing on her computer or mine that's connected to . . . to . . .' Simmons faltered, unable to finish the sentence.

Brady didn't reply. There was nothing he could say that would ease Simmons' anger. Now wasn't the time to explain that paedophiles used the internet to get close to children. Most parents were completely unaware of the dangers. Brady knew the statistics and they weren't good. One out of every five children using chatrooms had been approached by a sexual predator unbeknown to their parents. Brady couldn't take a chance. The victim's computer had to be analysed. And as for Simmons' computer, it was simply protocol. He was after all the step-father and by default the first suspect in his step-daughter's murder. Regardless of whether or not he had appeared shaken when he identified her body.

'If you lot had done your job when I first reported her missing then she might still be alive,' Simmons stated through gritted teeth. His face was flushed, even his temples glowed a furious scarlet. He looked like a man who was about to have a heart attack.

'And don't take me for an idiot, Detective Inspector. I know you knew something when you first called round.'

Brady kept quiet. Simmons was looking for a fight and he wasn't up for accepting the challenge. He knew better than anyone the reason why the standard police procedure was to wait twenty-four hours before seriously acting on a missing persons report. If Sophie Washington had been under ten years old then the police would have acted immediately. However a missing child of Sophie's age was treated with a dose of cynical pragmatism.

Sophie Washington wasn't the first teenager to be reported missing and certainly wouldn't be the last. Typically, kids Sophie's age would disappear for a night, or at worst a few days. Arguments at home were the common cause for them absconding. However, sometimes parents weren't so fortunate, sometimes their children never returned home. Brady had dealt with missing kids as young as eleven running off to Manchester or London, only to be swallowed up by the rapidly growing child prostitution market.

Considering all the possible outcomes, Brady had had to

ask some awkward questions, unwelcome questions; ones that Paul Simmons didn't accept too readily. But what troubled Brady was the picture the Simmons were painting of their daughter. He was having difficulty swallowing it. She was perfect, too perfect. Yet they had waited until 3 am before reporting her missing? It didn't rest easy with Brady.

More so when Paul Simmons had no alibi; his wife had gone to bed at 10 pm, which left his actions unaccounted for. And then, six hours later his step-daughter is discovered brutally murdered yards from her own home. Simmons' lack of an alibi made Brady feel uncomfortable. Statistically, fathers were responsible for the majority of murdered children over the age of eight. Add to that the harsh reality that step-children were 100 times more likely to be murdered by their step-father.

The modus operandi suggested that Sophie knew her attacker well. The murderer had clearly left his signature; to spend time bludgeoning Sophie's face beyond recognition was an unnecessary addition to the murder. It reeked of emotional attachment to the victim. Brady had seen it numerous times when called to a murder scene where a woman had been beaten or stabbed to death by her spouse. It was always messy. The spouse would go into overdrive, which led to overkill. Unable to let go of whatever hatred they felt for the victim they would continue to rage long after the victim had stopped breathing.

'Maybe if you spent some time out there rather than in here asking us ridiculous questions you might get your answers!' snapped Simmons angrily.

'I understand your anger, sir. But as I've said these questions have to be asked.'

'What more do you want from us?' attacked Simmons.

125

'Can't you see the state my wife's in? This is damned ridiculous.'

'I'm sorry, but we need all the information you can give us, regardless of how small. Including anything else you can tell us about who Sophie socialised with, whether on the internet or in person,' replied Brady calmly.

'Why? Surely to God it was a random attack? I mean, why would anyone who knew her want to attack her?' questioned Simmons, his eyes fixed on Brady.

'I don't know, which is why I need to ask the questions I'm asking,' answered Brady.

Simmons didn't reply.

Brady decided to try another tactic; one that was guaranteed to get a reaction.

'Why would Sophie have a tattoo?'

Simmons froze.

Brady watched as his face paled.

'I . . . I don't know . . .' he muttered.

'If I'm getting this right, you're both telling me that Sophie was a grade A star pupil. That she tutored maths on a Saturday morning at school for Year 6 children and that she was also involved in quite a few extracurricular activities after school?'

'That's correct,' answered Simmons stiffly as he narrowed his cold eyes.

'Then why would such a bright, sociable fifteen-year-old decide to get something as rebellious as a tattoo? It just doesn't fit with the story you're giving me,' Brady challenged.

He could feel the temperature in the room drop as Simmons turned on him.

'You bastard! You have the audacity to question what we're telling you about our daughter when she's lying in a morgue because of you lot. If you idiots had taken me seriously when I reported her missing then she might not be dead. So don't you dare make out we're somehow guilty.'

It was a good move. So good Brady felt the punch. Simmons was clearly very adept at avoiding certain questions.

'I apologise if I've offended you and your wife. I just need to be absolutely sure that you're telling me everything you know about Sophie and not some edited version,' replied Brady, ignoring the fact that his BlackBerry was vibrating.

'I swear I'll kill you, you son of a bitch!' exploded Simmons.

'Paul?' Louise Simmons whispered.

'I mean it! No one comes into my house and disrespects Sophie. Get out! Go on! Get out before I throw you out!' shouted Simmons.

'All I'm trying to do is get a better understanding of who would do this to Sophie. And if that makes you uncomfortable, then I'm sorry,' Brady apologised.

'Detective Inspector Brady?' Louise Simmons tremulously said.

Simmons was staring at his wife, his face contorted with repressed anger.

'I . . . I didn't know that Sophie had . . . had that tattoo . . . but it doesn't surprise me,' nervously stated Louise Simmons, ignoring her husband's attempt to silence her.

'Why?' asked Brady.

'Her father, my ex-husband, died last September and . . . and Sophie never really got over his loss. She . . . she was never the same after that.'

'How so?'

Louise Simmons shrugged.

'It's hard to explain . . . she just seemed so distant and really angry most of the time . . . As if she was blaming me for her father's death somehow . . . Maybe she got the tattoo as a way of getting back at me? She knew I hated them . . . and . . . well . . .' She broke off as tears started to flow down her pale cheeks.

'Don't be ridiculous, Louise,' snapped Simmons. 'She was just a typical teenager who was talked into getting that tattoo by her friends, no doubt. You know what peer pressure is like amongst kids. You're reading too much into it. And if she was so affected by her father's death then her schoolwork would have suffered. And did it?'

Louise Simmons shook her head reluctantly.

'No . . .' she weakly muttered.

'Exactly! She was a straight-A student who excelled at everything she did. And yes, she could be moody and temperamental but you show me a teenager today who isn't,' asserted Simmons. 'So let's not waste police time talking about typical teenager behaviour. What counts now is finding out who did this monstrous thing to our Sophie. Yes?'

Louise Simmons looked up at her husband and nodded nervously.

'You're right,' she conceded.

She then looked at Brady.

'I'm sorry for wasting your time . . . I . . . I'm just not thinking straight . . .' she whispered.

'Come on,' said Simmons, calming down. 'How about I get you a refill?'

Louise Simmons looked down at the empty crystal glass cupped in her hands and nodded weakly.

Simmons took the glass and shot Brady a look which told him the interview was over.

Brady felt his phone vibrating again. He took it out of his inner jacket pocket and checked the caller.

'I'm really sorry but I'm going to have to take this,' he said as he looked at Louise Simmons.

He turned away, ignoring Simmons' furious glare.

'Of course. If you need privacy you can take it upstairs,' Louise Simmons weakly answered.

'Thanks,' Brady replied.

He headed out into the hallway before answering the call.

Chapter Twenty-Two

'About bloody time! I haven't got all day!' wheezed a familiar voice.

'Yeah, I was tied up,' Brady explained.

'Aren't we all, Jack? Aren't we all?' huskily wheezed Wolfe before succumbing to a coughing fit.

Brady patiently waited until the spluttering subsided to heavy wheezing. Wolfe had asthma. But that wasn't what caused his wheezing and gut-splitting coughing. He was a heavy smoker and drinker with a rather robust appetite; all combined it led to him being at least five stone overweight. He liked his vices, a little too much.

'What have you got?' Brady asked Wolfe.

'You'll have to wait. I'll be done by two. Meet me at the usual place. And lose the sidekick. He gives me indigestion,' Wolfe ordered before disconnecting the call.

Wolfe and Conrad had never seen eye to eye. Wolfe was the best Home Office pathologist in the force; everyone knew it, but everyone also knew he had a drink problem; one that began at lunchtime and could continue through to the next working day. Somehow, the old bugger had developed the tolerance of a rhinoceros. Brady didn't know how the hell he kept sober, but he did. Even Chief Superintendent O'Donnell was aware of Wolfe's indiscretion, but chose to ignore it, knowing that he would never be able to replace Wolfe's unerring skill.

Conrad on the other hand, found it difficult to listen to Wolfe's findings over a pie and a pint. He didn't have the stomach for it. Either for the food or Wolfe's autopsy reports and definitely not served together.

Brady looked out of the large window. Below him was the Simmons' long back garden. And just beyond it, the crime scene. Trees and overgrown bushes hid most of the farmhouse ruins but Brady could still make out the white-clad SOCOs. He sighed heavily and turned round. He was stood in one of the two double back bedrooms. But this wasn't just any room, Brady suddenly realised. This was Sophie's room. The room's heady aroma was claustrophobic; a sickly combination of perfume and deodorant, it was all that was left of Sophie Washington.

Brady had excused himself a few minutes earlier, stating that he needed to take a call. He wanted to be out of earshot of the Simmons and the other officers as soon as he realised it was Wolfe calling and had found his way upstairs into Sophie's room.

He looked around at the teenage chaos. Posters of bands and other crap covered the walls, reminding Brady that he was getting old. The double bed and the large chest of wooden drawers and bedside cabinets were covered in make-up, perfume, nail varnish, clothes, CDs; the sprawling paraphernalia was endless. The door to the walk-in closet had been left wide open and Brady could see from where he was standing that clothes and shoes lay scattered in much the same disarray as in her room. A large mirror stood in the corner, lost in a disarray of clothes, some of which were tossed over the mirror or dumped on the polished wooden floor. Wherever she was going last night, the last thing she had on her mind was homework.

He wasn't surprised that Sophie had a state-of-the-art forty-inch flat-screen HD television mounted on her wall or that she had every electronic gadget you could imagine scattered around. She was an only child after all, and one whose father had committed suicide and whose mother had remarried a man who Brady's gut feeling was telling him, she didn't actually like. The room smacked of guilt. Everywhere around him, from the fancy flat-screen TV to the expensive clothes, jewellery and make-up carelessly thrown about, suggested that Sophie's affections were being bought.

His eyes were soon drawn to the crammed notice board above the empty computer desk. He limped over to it. It was a colourful mosaic of different sized photographs. It took Brady a minute to realise that the girl staring back at him from most of the shots was the victim. But the girl he was looking at definitely didn't match the innocent girl her parents had just described. Nor the school photo they had first shown him.

In many of the photographs she was wearing heavy make-up and skimpy clothes; too skimpy in his opinion for an eighteen-year-old, never mind a fifteen-year-old girl. One group shot looked as if the victim and her friends were downing shots before heading out clubbing. What threw Brady was the fact that they all looked old enough to be knocking back spirits.

'Fuck me,' he muttered.

Brady swallowed hard. One photograph grabbed his attention. The victim was stood next to a man in his early twenties. Brady couldn't help but notice the way she was looking at him. That and the fact she had an arm wrapped around him while one hand playfully attempted to pull his face towards hers. Brady had had enough life experience to know that this looked far from innocent.

Without a second thought, he pulled it off the notice board and placed it in his pocket. As he did something fluttered to the floor. Wincing, he gingerly bent down and picked it up. It was flyer for a local band; The Clashed. He looked at the list of dates and the venues. They were due to play at The Fat Ox in Whitley Bay tonight. Why, Brady questioned, would a fifteen-year-old have a flyer advertising gigs held in pubs? And more importantly, why was tonight's gig circled in red?

Brady discreetly put the flyer in his pocket along with the photo.

'What do you think you're doing?'

Brady turned. It was Simmons.

'Just wanted to have a look at the view of the farmland from the back of the house,' Brady answered casually. He wondered just how long Simmons had been standing by the door.

'You might find it helpful if you actually looked out the window, Detective Inspector,' Simmons stated coldly.

'Sophie seemed like a popular girl,' Brady stated, as he jerked his head at the montage of photos.

'I thought I'd asked you to leave,' challenged Simmons, ignoring Brady's comment.

'Those photos of Sophie and her friends, didn't they bother you and your wife?'

'Get out! You hear me? Get out of her bedroom!'

'If I wasn't mistaken, I'd say you were obstructing this

investigation. You do want Sophie's murderer caught?' Brady questioned as he stared at Simmons' flushed face.

'What kind of question is that?'

'The kind that tells you I'm suspicious,' replied Brady evenly.

He then headed towards the panelled wooden door.

'Be warned, sir, sooner or later I'll find out whatever it is that you're not telling me.'

'Get out!' hissed Simmons.

Brady turned and left.

What he had seen was enough to worry him. The photographs of the victim and her murdered body blurred the fact that Sophie Washington was still only a fifteen-year-old schoolgirl. Even Brady would have found it difficult as a hardened copper to single her and her friends out as underage drinkers in any one of Whitley Bay's nightclubs. Something didn't add up.

Chapter Twenty-Three

Conrad started up the engine.

Brady waited until he had lit a cigarette before he said anything.

'I want you to see what you can dig up on Simmons,' instructed Brady.

'Yes sir,' answered Conrad.

The more he thought about it, the more the Simmons' statement about the victim didn't ring true. The evidence he'd taken from her notice board was testimony to that. Coupled with the tattoo, it wasn't looking good.

He slowly smoked his cigarette as he thought about Simmons' motive. Brady had a gut feeling about Simmons, one he couldn't shake. But he needed Wolfe's autopsy report to confirm if his hunch was right. Until then, he had no choice but to keep it to himself.

'What about the victim's mother?' Conrad asked.

Brady shook his head.

'No, we don't have to bother with her,' answered Brady.

He massaged his forehead as he thought over what she had said.

'She went to bed at 10 pm, the next thing she knew was

Paul Simmons waking her to say Sophie was missing,' Brady stated.

Conrad looked at him, surprised.

'Didn't you notice how many gins she knocked back while we were there?'

'Surely that's simply the ordeal of formally identifying her murdered daughter?' Conrad suggested.

'I take it you didn't see the amount of wine and gin bottles she had stacked in their recycling box then?' Brady stated.

Conrad shook his head as he concentrated on the traffic.

'If Sophie had come home after she had gone to bed she wouldn't have heard a thing. It seems that Louise Simmons had checked out of her daughter's life. The question is, why?' Brady asked.

Conrad shrugged.

'Louise Simmons knew something was going wrong in her daughter's life but she chose to hide behind a fog of alcohol,' Brady concluded.

'You think, sir?' Conrad asked, frowning.

'I guarantee it.'

Conrad drove along in silence for a minute before turning to Brady.

'Could Sophie have heard something when she got home? From her bedroom?'

'Like what? Kids messing about?'

Conrad nodded.

'It's possible. I checked out her bedroom and from the window you can make out the crime scene.'

'Could she have heard some of the kids who hang out down there screaming or something and she went down and checked it out, worried that someone was being attacked?' questioned Conrad.

'Maybe, but that's too easy, Conrad,' answered Brady. 'Whoever killed Sophie knew her. This wasn't a random attack, I'm certain of it.'

Conrad turned and looked at him curiously.

Brady shook his head.

'Overkill, Conrad. If she had just been sexually assaulted, then murdered, I agree it could be anyone. Whoever killed her, knew her. She met someone that night, Conrad. Our job is to find out who.'

'How can you be certain she met someone?'

'I guarantee that she returned home. When she got there, someone contacted her or maybe it was prearranged. Either way, she met this person at the bottom of the lane next to her house. There's an opening in the fence there which leads straight out onto the farmland.'

'How do you know?'

'Ainsworth, Conrad. The man's a genius. He found male hand and footprints at the fence matching prints found at the murder scene. He also found Sophie Washington's footprints leading from the lane out onto the farmland. So we know she went that way, our problem is finding out who met her.'

'Maybe Harvey and Jenkins will have come up with something?' Conrad suggested.

'Maybe,' muttered Brady as he thought over the likelihood of it being an ex-boyfriend or even a current one. The evidence Brady had found in her bedroom clearly showed that Sophie Washington, contrary to her parents' opinion, had a keen interest in underage drinking and boys.

'Maybe the kids who hang about on the farm are the ones we need to be talking to. Question is, how the hell do you get them to come forward? And even if they did, who's to say they witnessed anything? It's so dark there, that even stood by what was left of that bonfire, a body thirty feet away would have been impossible to see.'

Brady pulled out his mobile and checked to see if he had any messages. Nothing. He had secretly been hoping that Claudia might have tried to contact him. But she hadn't. What did he expect? he resignedly mused.

He reluctantly acknowledged that he now needed a statement from Jimmy Matthews' daughter. Only then could they start to build up a picture of the events that had led to the victim's attack.

'Thought you were giving up?' Conrad asked as he narrowed his eyes at the ash that had blown over what had started out at the beginning of the day as a spotless dashboard.

'Sorry,' Brady muttered as he attempted to appease Conrad's tense face by brushing the ash off the dashboard.

He turned and looked out of the passenger window while Conrad silently concentrated on the traffic ahead.

'So what do we do now?' Conrad asked.

'Talk to whoever knew the victim best and hope that they don't bullshit us.'

'I take it we're starting with Matthews' daughter then since the Simmons claimed she was Sophie's best friend?' Conrad asked as he turned to Brady.

'Seems we have no choice,' Brady answered quietly.

Chapter Twenty-Four

'Wait for me here,' Brady ordered as they pulled into the large, sprawling driveway.

But Conrad was too busy staring at the imposing eighteenth-century vicarage that was Matthews' home. Brady suddenly realised what Conrad must be thinking, more so since it was situated in Earsdon village. Ordinary people like them couldn't afford one of the huge sandstone houses that dominated the quiet, picturesque village, ironically only a few miles out from Whitley Bay. But Conrad wasn't the only one thinking it. Brady couldn't get the question out of his head. How the hell could a copper like Matthews afford this? Madley's name uncomfortably came to mind. But Brady knew Matthews well enough to know that he was straight when it really mattered. He certainly took liberties; didn't they all? However, Brady was certain that Matthews couldn't be bought; or he used to be.

His phone call earlier had left him with too many questions. So much so, he didn't want Conrad around when he talked to Matthews. He needed to get out of Matthews exactly what it was he had stolen from Madley. And to see if there was any way he could minimise what had happened by returning whatever it was he had taken. Brady's mind was literally spinning as to what it could be. Money, drugs or proof of overseas accounts. That was the real reason Brady was there. He very much doubted that Evie Matthews would be home; after all it was a school day. But someone was home, he was certain of that. The first thing he noted as they pulled into the driveway was that Matthews' car was missing. Instead a gleaming, new 4 x 4 Land Rover was parked outside the double garage.

'I reckon this is going to be difficult enough for Matthews' kid, without the two of us interviewing her,' Brady stated.

'That's fine, sir, I've got a few calls I need to follow up anyway,' answered Conrad. This was DI Matthews' home and the last thing Conrad wanted to do was poke around in his private life.

'Can you give Jenkins a call and see what they've got so far?'

'Yes sir,' answered Conrad as he took out his phone.

Brady reluctantly got out of the car. He'd not seen Matthews outside of work in over a year. Admittedly, they still drank together at the end of a shift but the conversation always revolved around the job. It wasn't personal. Whereas Brady's private life was a shambles, Matthews appeared to be doing very well for himself; new cars, designer Italian suits and now this big, fancy property in the exclusive village of Earsdon.

Brady hated to admit it, but he had a bad feeling about Matthews' sudden acquired wealth.

He wished he could have sent Conrad in, but knew it wasn't an option. This was his problem. Whatever trouble Matthews had got himself into, it was Brady's job to get him out of it. It was simple; he still owed him.

'What the fuck have you been getting up to, Jimmy?'

wondered Brady, as he limped up the white gravel driveway towards the double wooden front doors.

He steeled himself, before ringing the bell. He didn't know what to expect.

The door opened.

'Jack? What's going on? Where's Jimmy?'

'I was hoping you could tell me?'

He wasn't sure whether she would slam the door in his face or invite him in. She did neither. Brady followed her through the ornately tiled hallway to the large modern country kitchen at the back of the house. He couldn't help but notice the fashionable red Aga and the very sleek and very expensive kitchen units and appliances. Even the stone slabs on the floor looked as if they cost more than a couple of months' salary.

'That's right, you haven't seen this place?' she replied as casually as she could. But the strain in her voice was evident.

'Do you want some?' she asked, holding up a stainless steel coffee pot.

'Please,' Brady answered.

'Black, no sugar?'

'Yeah,' replied Brady as he pulled out a chair and sat down at the large farmhouse kitchen table.

'Nice car in the driveway. Yours?' Brady asked.

She nodded.

'Do you mind?' Brady asked as he took out his cigarettes and lighter and laid them on the table.

She shook her head as she placed Brady's coffee in front of him and then walked over and opened the French doors.

'Nice,' Brady commented as he nodded at the sizeable secluded walled garden.

'You get used to it after a while.'

'Yeah?' Brady questioned. That was something he was

certainly never going to be able to put to the test. He could barely afford the mortgage on his own place, especially now that Claudia had left.

'Directly behind the garden there's a field that we're renting for the horses,' Kate added.

'Yeah?' he answered, ignoring the creeping worry about where the money was coming from for the upkeep of horses.

He'd forgotten Kate's passion was horses. Always had been since he'd known her from the age of seventeen. Her mother lived in a sprawling country house outside of Morpeth and in the early seventies was a celebrated Olympic Show Jumper. She then married and had Kate, who had literally learned to ride before she could walk. Kate had been destined for greatness when it came to riding, even Badminton had been mooted. She was an all-rounder. Great at dressage, show-jumping and cross-country. That was until she met Brady.

She had been rebellious in her youth and had rejected her boarding school upbringing for the edgy, dangerous punks who frequented the carpet-sodden dive in Whitley Bay called Mingles on a Friday night. A regular occurrence was skinheads travelling down from Newcastle looking for trouble. They would force their way into the club, drunk and ready for a fight. It was during one of these blood-thirsty punch-ups that Brady had spotted Kate pinned against the wall looking on in horror as the wannabe punk next to her had a glass smashed into his face by a skinhead. Brady had grabbed her and managed to get her out before the same skinhead decided to rearrange her very privileged, pretty face.

As a rough-edged lad from the socially deprived Ridges, he wasn't great boyfriend material. But it was worse than that. Brady had introduced her to Matthews for which her mother had never forgiven him. With that came the end of her mother's dreams of her daughter competing at Badminton and ultimately, representing Britain in the Olympics.

Brady pulled out a cigarette from his packet and lit it. He had gone from trying to quit altogether to chain smoking. He decided to cut himself some slack; after all it had been one hell of a morning.

'Thanks,' Brady said as he gestured towards the makeshift ashtray.

His mouth felt dry. It didn't feel right being sat here in Matthews' kitchen.

'So, tell me what have you got out in the field then?' Brady asked, trying to make polite conversation.

She smiled at him. And as she did, he remembered what it was about her that had made him fall so deeply in love. In that smile shone her passion for life. She glowed with a zest that was contagious and addictive.

'They're thoroughbreds, both as crazy as one another. Melody's a chestnut mare, stunning at dressage, and Tico's a liver-chestnut gelding. He's fantastic at cross-country,' she enthused.

Brady watched as the glow on her face slowly faded.

Frowning, she reached over and took a cigarette from Brady's open packet and lit it.

'Thought you'd given up years ago?' Brady asked.

'I had,' she replied.

'Things that bad?' Brady asked.

She followed his eyes to the lily-white band on her left hand where her wedding ring should have been.

'Yeah, things are that bad.'

Brady's eyes slowly took in every inch of her face. He had forgotten just how striking her sculpted cheekbones were, let alone her haunting eyes. Needless to say she was too good for Matthews, as Brady had drunkenly told him on more than a few occasions. She was still only in her mid-thirties even though she had been married to Matthews for sixteen years.

She broke into a delicate, nervous smile as she caught Brady's eye.

'What about you? First day back that bad?'

Brady shrugged and looked down at the cigarette between his fingers. This was hard for both of them. They were trying their best to avoid talking about that night. A lot had happened since then. And a lot had happened before then.

'I heard about the shooting. I didn't think you'd be back at work so soon.'

Brady shrugged again.

'Jack?'

He dragged his eyes up to hers. Her elfish, short strawberry blonde hair fell in unruly waves across her forehead, partially covering her cheeks. She unconsciously tucked the stray locks behind her small ears as she held his gaze.

The last time he had seen Kate her hair had fallen in thick, tumultuous waves past her shoulders. In all the time he had known her he had never seen her with short hair. He resisted the temptation to reach out and gently move the stubborn lock that seductively fell again, partly obscuring her eye. Sitting so close to her hurt more than he wanted to admit.

But he wasn't sure it was real. He wasn't sure about anything any more. All he knew was that he had never felt so empty. Nothing he did seemed to fill the dark void in his life since Claudia had left.

He turned away and looked out at the garden. It was drizzling.

'Where's Jimmy, Jack?'

'I was hoping I would find him here,' Brady answered quietly.

When she didn't answer he turned to look at her.

'Kate?'

Her eyes were filled with tears.

'I'm sorry,' he said.

'Don't be,' she replied as she swallowed back the tears.

Brady had forgotten how her eye colour could suddenly change from a misty greyish green to a burnished emerald shade. She was angry. Who with, he wasn't sure. Maybe it was with the both of them; since Matthews wasn't the only one who had fucked with her head.

Brady held her gaze as she searched his eyes for confirmation that he had made the right decision. He couldn't give her an answer. He couldn't even give himself one.

He abruptly stood up and walked over to the open French doors. He kept his back to her as he slowly dragged on his cigarette.

'What's going on, Jack?'

He turned round.

'Jimmy hasn't told you?' Brady asked, unable to disguise his surprise.

'He hasn't been here for the past two days . . .' she bitterly stated.

'Didn't the Simmons call you?'

'The phone went at some godforsaken hour this morning. I was half-asleep and so didn't answer it, I didn't realise who it was until this morning when I saw the caller ID. I just presumed it was Sophie being silly trying to ring Evie. Believe me, those girls have done it in the past! I've lost count of the times Sophie would ring this house at some ridiculous hour asking for Evie. I've even caught Evie whispering on the phone in her bedroom to Sophie past two in the morning. The times I've wanted to strangle the pair of them! But . . . how did you know?' she faltered as she looked up at Brady's dark expression.

'Kate . . . Sophie was found murdered early this morning . . .'

She numbly shook her head at Brady as she tried to absorb what he had just told her. She didn't ask any questions. She was a copper's wife; she knew the score. Instead she slowly finished her cigarette then distractedly stubbed it out.

'Who did it?'

'We don't know yet,' Brady quietly replied. 'Is it right that Sophie was here last night?'

Kate numbly nodded.

'I take a yoga class on a Thursday night so I left the girls to it. That was just before six. When I got home after eleven, Sophie had already gone and Evie was in bed. Her lights were out so I presumed she was asleep.'

Brady resisted the urge to ask where Kate had been until eleven. He had no right, not any more.

'I'm sorry, Kate, but I'll have to take a statement from Evie.'

'Sure,' Kate mumbled as she bit her lip. 'Jack? Where did you find her?'

'Potter's Farm, opposite West Monkseaton Metro station.'

Kate covered her mouth as she shook her head.

Brady threw what was left of his cigarette out into the large, secluded walled garden. He then stared blankly at the miserable grey cloud smothering the North East of England.

He heard Kate stand up. He didn't need to look to know that she was now stood behind him. He could feel the closeness of her body.

He turned to face her.

Silent tears ran down her cheeks.

'There was nothing you could have done . . . Nothing.'

'No . . . if I'd come home earlier then . . . then . . . I could have given her a lift home . . .'

'Kate, if only life was that simple.'

She instinctively moved into his body and rested her damp face against his chest.

He stood still, not knowing what to do. He could feel her body trembling as she thought about what she hadn't been able to do. Brady knew better than anyone the 'what if' game. Masochistically going over an event again, and again, imagining making that vital difference. It was a point-less, painful exercise.

Before he had time to question it, he gently placed his arms around her fragile shoulders and pulled her in close. He held her tight and waited. He didn't want to think about how good it felt to have her pressed against him. He breathed in her smell and pretended for a moment that nothing had changed. That he still had her all to himself before Matthews had come between them.

They had had an argument about him needing to go away. His younger brother had suddenly upped and left the North East one night. Brady had heard rumours that he had got involved way over his head with a gang in Wallsend and that he had taken off. He had been told that his brother was in London, so that was where he was heading. Before he left, he had broken it off with Kate, angry that she had tried to prevent him from going, never dreaming that she would meet someone else before he got back. Worse than that, that it would be Matthews. He was Brady's closest friend and he had trusted Matthews, never questioning why he was always hanging around with them. Nor did he question the intimacy that was developing between Kate and Matthews. With hindsight he could see that Matthews had been biding his time with Kate. She was already pregnant with Evie when he returned. They were married within six months of Brady leaving for London and had a baby daughter three months later.

Brady had coped, but it had been hard. For a long time he wanted to get Matthews up against a wall and punch the hell out of him. But he didn't. He chose to walk away. If he hadn't needed to go to London, then it might have been him who had the big house in Earsdon and the teenage daughter. Life had a way of fucking you up when you least expected it. He had never asked Kate if she had turned to Matthews on the rebound. He didn't need to, it was obvious to both of them that she had used Matthews to hurt him. But then life had taken a momentum of its own and somehow that hurt had come back to haunt her.

'Oh God, Jack! What am I going to do?' she asked, bringing him back to the present moment.

He presumed she was talking about Matthews. He didn't answer.

'What's going on?'

Kate abruptly shook herself free from Brady's embrace.

'Evie? What are you doing? I thought you were in bed ill?' Kate asked guiltily as she moved away from him.

Brady was completely thrown. Not only had he banked on her being at school, but he no longer recognised her. He noticed that she looked tired; the dark patches of skin under her puffy, bloodshot eyes suggested that she hadn't slept too well.

Kate walked over to her and tentatively felt her forehead.

'Don't touch me!' Evie snapped as she pushed Kate's hand away.

'Evie, please don't be so rude,' Kate replied, embarrassed.

'What's he doing here?' she asked Kate accusingly.

He steadied himself as he looked at her. He couldn't believe how much she now looked like Matthews; especially her eyes. Sometimes Brady had wondered whether there was a possibility that Evie could have been his, but stood there, it was evident that she was Matthews' daughter.

Brady slowly took in what he had missed; her growing up. Her long, straightened, blonde hair was identical to the victim's and like the victim her fulsome body was more akin to an older girl's. Brady had to accept what Matthews had said, it would have been easy to have mistaken the victim for Evie.

Brady realised she was at least three inches taller than Kate and her build was wider, more powerful. He was still taken aback by how much older she looked, even without make-up she could have passed for eighteen. The happy little girl with gangly legs and scabby knees had been replaced by some petulant teenage Midwich Cuckoo. One who hated his very being. And considering what he had to tell her, he couldn't see matters really improving.

'I didn't recognise you, Evie,' Brady said, attempting a smile. 'You've changed a lot since the last time I saw you.'

'Yeah? Well, a lot of things have changed since I last saw you,' she replied. 'Uncle Jack!' she added contemptuously.

Brady knew she had good reason to hate him.

'Aunt Claudia not with you then?'

Brady didn't answer. It was pointless. He knew she was lashing out at him.

'Oh yeah, that's right, she's left you, hasn't she? Finally realised you couldn't keep your hands off my mother, was that it?'

'Evie, please!' cried out Kate. 'This is unacceptable.'

Evie turned to her mother.

'It's you that's unacceptable. What about you lying to me?'

'Evie, don't talk to me like that!' Kate retaliated, humiliated that Brady was witnessing their exchange. 'It's not what you think.'

'Yeah? How often does he come round when I'm at school and Dad's at work, eh?'

'Evie, stop it now! Apologise . . . I mean it! You apologise to Jack right now!' Kate demanded, her cheeks flushed.

'You're both as bad as each other, do you know that? You deserve Dad as much as he deserves you.'

Brady watched uncomfortably, feeling every bit the stranger he had become. He shifted uneasily. He knew why Evie was so angry with him. Brady had known Kate longer than she had known Matthews. It was no surprise that Kate had rung him, needing to talk when she had found out about yet another one of Matthews' casual affairs.

Admittedly, the last time Evie had sleepily stumbled in on them it hadn't looked good either. Kate, drunk and desperate for comfort, had suddenly kissed him. It was a kiss filled with regret for all those years she could have had with him. But what Evie had failed to notice was that he had resisted, despite wanting more. Loyalty to Claudia first had forced him to stop. That and the sobering fact that if Matthews had found out they had crossed the line, he would have killed Brady.

Since that night over a year ago he had kept his distance from Kate, realising he was getting too involved in Matthews' marriage, more than he was in his own.

Evie gave Brady a stabbing look of disdain before turning and walking out.

'Where are you going?' Kate called out, the panic apparent in her voice.

She didn't reply.

'Evie, wait. Jack needs to have a word with you . . . it's about . . .' Kate faltered.

Evie stopped and irritably turned round.

'Sophie, I need to talk to you about Sophie,' said Brady.

Evie's face paled as she looked from her mother's distraught expression to Brady's dark, foreboding countenance.

Chapter Twenty-Five

'Stop it! Stop it!' screamed Evie.

'Please Evie,' Brady persisted. 'I need to know who might have done this to Sophie.'

Kate grabbed Brady's arm.

'For God's sake, Jack, what the hell are you playing at?' she hissed. 'She's already told you she knows nothing!'

Brady pushed on.

'Evie? Do you understand how important this is? Do you? Someone did something terrible to Sophie. They hurt her, really hurt her and it's my job to find out who did that,' Brady doggedly continued, ignoring Kate.

He couldn't believe that Evie was refusing to talk to him. From the moment he had begun interviewing her she had been evasive. Refusing to even look at him, let alone answer any of his questions. She even had the audacity to take out her iPhone and start texting while he was asking questions. He couldn't understand her attitude given the gravity of the situation. She just seemed to have switched off from the reality of what had happened to her best friend.

She looked up at him, surprising Brady with the dark malice in her eyes.

'Jack? Come on, she's had enough,' Kate said, intervening.

Brady resisted the urge to shake her by her spoilt, selfish shoulders and wake her up to the cold, grim, brutal reality of what had happened to her alleged best friend.

'Evie? You must know something? For Chrissakes! You were her best friend!'

'Mum, make him stop! Please, make him stop!' cried Evie as she melodramatically dropped her phone and pressed her hands over her ears.

Brady watched powerless as she successfully played her mother off against him.

'Get out! Get out of my house now!' shouted Kate as she stood up. 'I mean it, Jack! Fucking get out!'

Brady immediately felt guilty as he looked at Evie as she now sat sobbing uncontrollably. This was Jimmy Matthews' daughter after all. Not only that, she was just a kid who had found out that her best friend had been brutally murdered. Why the hell was he giving her such a hard time?

*

Brady cradled his head in his hands as he waited in Kate's kitchen. It was fair to say it had gone worse than expected. Evie had fallen apart when she heard the news. It shouldn't have come as a surprise. But he had perilously pushed and pushed until she broke down.

He sighed heavily as he went over what he had managed to painfully extract; which wasn't much. Needless to say he'd have to come back and take another statement once she'd gotten over the shock. That was, if Kate would allow him back.

At least he knew that the victim was with Evie until around

ten. Then she left and walked back to West Monkseaton. Somewhere along that route Matthews must have stopped and given her a lift. After that, it was anyone's guess.

Brady lit a cigarette.

Matthews had dumped him in deep shit. There was no way he could tell anyone that Matthews had picked up Sophie. For starters, Brady didn't know the full story and secondly, Matthews going to ground made him look too damned suspicious; even in Brady's books.

'You bugger, Jimmy,' Brady said under his breath.

He looked up as Kate walked back into the kitchen.

Brady had never seen her look so worried.

'How is she?' he asked in a hoarse voice.

'She's much calmer. No thanks to you,' Kate replied abruptly.

He nodded, ashamed of how he had behaved.

'I'm sorry.'

Kate didn't reply.

Brady couldn't help but notice that she couldn't bring herself to look at him.

'Look, if I could have done it any other way I would have done. But you know the job, I had to ask her those questions . . .' Brady attempted, before giving up.

It was pointless, Kate wasn't listening.

He drew the cigarette up to his lips and inhaled deeply as he mulled over what little he knew about the hours leading up to the victim's death.

Evie had been evasive about how she and Sophie had spent the night. She was certainly clear on what time Sophie had left, but that was about it. When Brady had pushed Evie about where she and Sophie would go out to at night, she had reluctantly mentioned Whitley Bay Park. When

154

asked if that's where they'd gone last night, she had clammed up, refusing to answer any more questions.

'Are you sure that Evie should be going down to Whitley Bay Park at night?' Brady asked, breaking the silence. It had been plaguing him from the moment Evie had first let it slip. He knew the scum who hung around down there and Evie definitely didn't fit in.

Whitley Bay Park was part of Mayor Macmillan's regeneration programme for the rundown, shabby seaside resort. Built on one of the few green areas in Whitley Bay, it sat next to the local, sixties library and opposite The Avenue; a nineteenth-century dilapidated, boarded-up pub now left to rot. The park was sold to the council taxpayers at a staggering price of £350,000.

What the council failed to acknowledge was the nightmare it would cause for the police and the residents living opposite. During the day it fulfilled its function but at night it was a magnet for lowlifes who would travel from miles around. Word spread fast and kids aged from eight up to seventeen gathered there in the dark, shouting profanities, smoking, drinking cheap booze and getting high on whatever cocktail of drugs was available. The finale was either fighting or shagging whoever was off their face enough to be up for it.

Kate slowly turned to face him. 'Kids go to parks, Jack, where else are they meant to go? Maybe if you'd had some of your own you would have found that out!'

It was a cheap shot and she knew it. They both knew it was one of the reasons his relationship with Claudia had broken down. The other was down to him briefly forgetting he was still married.

Brady didn't reply.

He would check the park out for himself later. There was always the chance that some of the kids hanging around there could tell him something about last night; something that Evie couldn't bring herself to share. Not with her mother sat listening to every word.

'I'm sorry, Kate. I should go,' Brady said.

She nodded. He wanted her to say something. He didn't know what, but anything was better than ending it this way.

As he stood up he suddenly remembered the photo he had of Sophie.

'What do you make of this?' Brady asked, handing her the photograph that he had taken from Sophie's bedroom.

She couldn't disguise her surprise at the image of Sophie with her hand seductively pulling the twenty-something male's face towards her own. But Brady noted that she composed herself quickly.

'Look, Jack, I don't know what you expect me to say.'

Brady shrugged his shoulders.

'You tell me?' he replied.

'This . . . this is just . . .' Kate stopped and looked up at Brady shaking her head. 'They're still just silly girls, Jack. What don't you get?'

'That's precisely it. I don't get it,' answered Brady.

'I honestly don't know what you're trying to make out here. Someone killed her! She didn't go looking for it, so all those goddamn questions you asked Evie were inappropriate!'

Brady kept quiet.

The last person he was judging was the victim. All he was trying to understand was her background and what she did outside school. It was simple criminology to know the victim's history and then you can start to put together a profile of her murderer. There was something about Sophie Washington, something that made someone want to kill her with more fury and hatred than Brady had ever seen in his entire life as a copper.

'Just look at the photo,' Brady persisted.

'Christ, Jack, why the hell are you so cynical all the time?'

'Do you know who the bloke is?' Brady asked, ignoring Kate's jibe.

'He's their form tutor,' Kate replied shaking her head at Brady's expression. 'Like I said, it's innocent.'

'He looks too bloody young to be a teacher,' Brady replied. 'Are you sure?'

Kate gave him a withering look.

'I'm certain. This was probably taken on the school trip to the Black Forest a couple of months back. He was one of the teachers who organised the trip. Evie couldn't make it because she was ill at the time. She was absolutely gutted. Like most of the girls in her class she had a huge crush on Mr Ellison.'

Brady gave her a quizzical look.

'I'm her mother, Jack. You know these things. It's not rocket science; teenage hormones coupled with a young, handsome teacher like Mr Ellison, what do you think?'

Kate looked back at the photograph.

'When Sophie went without her she was beside herself. She hated me for not letting her go. Wouldn't talk to me for the whole week she was supposed to be away. It wasn't until Sophie got back that she started to calm down . . .' Kate faltered.

'Thanks,' muttered Brady as he took the photo back. He knew there was no point in mentioning the other photographs on the victim's notice board. Not now. He had to let Kate absorb what he'd told her and then later, when they were both feeling calmer, he'd come back and take another statement from Evie.

'Do you know the dates of the German trip?' Brady asked.

'Not off the top of my head but I can look them up for you,' answered Kate.

'That would be good. The sooner the better.'

Kate distractedly nodded.

'Jack?' Kate asked as he started to leave.

He turned back.

'I don't know what you think you're trying to prove,' she said.

'I'm just trying to get to the truth, that's all,' Brady answered in a heavy voice before heading towards the front door.

Chapter Twenty-Six

Brady walked back to Conrad's car. He couldn't help but notice that a dark silver BMW saloon was parked opposite the house. It didn't take much to recognise the passenger; he was easily discernible in daylight. He was six feet four and as wide as he was tall. Unfortunately it was all flexed muscle; glistening, powerful. Gibbs was one of Madley's henchmen. He covered as a bouncer at Madley's nightclub in Whitley Bay, but that was for pocket money; his day job paid the rent. Brady hadn't seen the driver before, a scrawny, dark-haired guy with a sneer for a face.

Brady got in and sighed wearily. His leg was playing up. He rummaged through his inside jacket pocket for some painkillers. His hand nudged against the set of house keys he'd discreetly lifted from Matthews' kitchen worktop. Matthews had left him no choice. Brady had to come back later to see if he had left any trace of where he'd gone.

He found the bottle and threw two tablets into his mouth and swallowed.

'Matthews' kid reckons that Sophie left here at ten last night and walked home. So, we need to widen our door to door enquiries to include the surrounding areas of

Wellfield as well as Earsdon. And, we definitely need to find out who was in The Beacon pub last night. For all we know, someone either leaving or entering the pub saw her as she walked past.'

'Right, sir,' Conrad answered as he concentrated on pulling out onto the main street.

Brady thought about organising a filmed reconstruction of the victim walking home from Earsdon village to jolt the public's memory. But what really worried him was Matthews' part in this. If someone had witnessed Matthews picking the victim up then it wasn't only Matthews who would be finished, it would be Brady too.

'Talked to Jenkins,' Conrad stated.

'Did she find out from her classmates whether Sophie had a boyfriend?' Brady asked, hoping for anything to take the heat off Matthews.

'Seemingly, Sophie had a reputation for being a party girl. There were some rumours about an older boyfriend, but no one could substantiate it. And as for ex-boyfriends, they only knew about her last boyfriend who was some kid named Shane McGuire. But, aside from that, she was exactly as her parents described, a straight-A student who was well-liked by everyone,' answered Conrad.

'Not everyone,' Brady replied in a low voice.

He looked at Gibbs and his companion as Conrad pulled past the idling Beamer.

'We've got company,' Brady stated.

Conrad looked in the rearview mirror. His jaw tightened.

Brady was aware that this was all the evidence Conrad needed to know that Matthews was in deep shit. Presumably, he mused, Madley's men were dumb enough to think that they would lead them straight to Matthews.

'Bloody idiots,' Brady muttered. But then again, that was why they had the day job they had with Madley.

Brady sighed as he rested his head back and closed his eyes. Worried didn't even come close; not any more. If Gibbs had been sent to find Matthews, then Brady knew that Madley was past talking. Gibbs had once been a heavy-weight boxer; successful in his time. Brady remembered when he used to do the boxing circuits throughout the North East. Since retiring from the ring, Madley had decided to keep him as a pet; a fierce, snarling, slathering Rottweiler at that, all bite and no bark.

Brady needed to find Matthews first. It was Matthews' only hope of coming out of this in one piece. Gibbs didn't talk and he certainly didn't let his opponent.

Brady pulled out his mobile and rang the station.

'Charlie? I want you to pass some information on to Rutherford for me. Yeah . . . yeah . . . I know he hates my guts. I know . . . yeah. Tell me something I don't know!'

Brady laughed as he listened to Turner's response. Rutherford was a traffic cop who had it in for Brady and would wait at certain junctions to catch Brady out. He knew Brady liked a drink and was adamant that one day he'd get him. There was no loyalty between Traffic and CID; at least not where Rutherford was concerned.

'Well, this will get him going . . . Tell the tight-arsed bugger that there's a dark silver BMW saloon, registration . . .'

'Y469 FGP,' put in Conrad.

He repeated the registration details to Turner and added a few embellishments for good measure.

Brady rested his head back against the headrest and smiled. 'That'll keep Gibbs busy for an hour or so. You know Rutherford's a tight-arsed git when he wants to be.

Let's see how Gibbs and his mate explain speeding in a stolen car.'

'Shall I put my foot down, sir?' Conrad asked.

'Does the Pope shit in the woods?' Brady answered.

He started dialling.

'Kate? It's me.'

'Now's not a good time, Jack,' she answered coolly.

'Look, throw whatever you need in a bag and leave.'

'You can't be serious?' answered Kate, incredulously.

'Kate, I wouldn't be telling you if I wasn't serious.'

'Tell me Jimmy's not behind this?'

Brady sighed wearily.

'He is, isn't he? What the hell has he got himself involved in now?'

'I don't know the details. Just trust me. Leave. Go to your mother's in Morpeth and wait there until everything's calmed down here.'

Kate sighed.

'I can't go there,' she quietly replied. 'Whatever trouble Jimmy's in I'll deal with it here.'

'Why can't you go to Evelyn's?' Brady asked.

'I just can't. She's sick of hearing me complain about Jimmy. This would be the last straw if she knew he'd just disappeared and left us to deal with whatever crap he's got himself involved in. Believe me, Jack, I don't want my family hearing about this. I . . . I don't know what I'm going to do yet about Jimmy but I do know I don't want Evelyn having another tirade at me about marrying him.'

Brady didn't say anything. He knew things were bad for Kate, but he just hadn't realised how bad.

Brady realised from her breathing that she was silently crying.

'What about friends? Surely there's someone you know who would put you up for a few days?' Brady quietly asked.

'No,' she mumbled. 'What Jimmy's done to me is embarrassing enough without the humiliation of having to share it. He's had too many affairs. Too many for my friends to have any sympathy left, not now. For years everybody I know, especially Evelyn, has been telling me to leave him. God, Jack, why did I get involved with him? Why?' she asked.

Brady couldn't answer her. Only Kate knew the answer to that question. All he could do was offer her a place to lie low until he had sorted out whatever mess Matthews had got himself involved in. The problem was he still cared too much about Kate to walk the other way.

'Go to my place. You should be safe there.'

'I . . . I don't know, Jack,' she answered. 'I don't think it's a good idea me staying at your place.'

'Just do as I say, please? Kate, you really haven't got much time.'

'On the condition you tell me what's going on?'

'I promise,' answered Brady. 'But not now. Later.'

'OK, but you'd better.'

'Don't answer the door to anyone. Understand?'

'I'm not an idiot!'

'And Kate?'

'Yeah?'

'I'm sorry about before . . . with Evie. I don't know what came over me,' Brady said.

Brady waited for an answer. He then realised that Kate had hung up.

'There's nothing to tell,' Brady replied, knowing what Conrad was thinking.

'Didn't say there was, sir,' Conrad answered evenly.

Chapter Twenty-Seven

Brady had no other option. He had to pay Madley a visit. He checked his watch. It was just after 2.40 pm. It would make him late for his meeting with Wolfe, the Home Office pathologist, but he had no other choice.

Madley's office was on the first floor above The Blue Lagoon nightclub and Brady was certain that was where he'd find him.

'This won't take long,' Brady said to Conrad before he got out of the car.

Brady walked up to the nightclub and banged on the locked glass doors.

A cleaner stopped wiping down the tables and timidly came over and mouthed in broken English that the place was closed.

Brady pulled out his ID and placed it against the glass.

The young woman nervously looked behind her and called out to someone.

Brady couldn't make out the words, but they sounded East European. He watched as two heavies appeared out of the shadows.

'What?' grunted one of the men as he unlocked the doors.

'I'm here to see Madley,' bluntly answered Brady.

'He's busy,' replied the same brutish hulk as he scowled at Brady.

'Detective Inspector Brady. You'll find he's expecting me.'

Before they had a chance to reply he pushed his way through the two men.

'Hey? Where the fuck do you think you're going?' shouted the shorter, uglier thug.

'To see Madley,' replied Brady as he made his way towards the emergency doors at the back of the club.

'You can't do that!' replied the shorter brute in surprise.

'Watch me,' muttered Brady as he pushed through the doors setting off the alarm.

Brady reached Madley's office door only to be greeted by two more loutish bouncer-types.

'DI Brady,' he stated holding out his ID card.

Brady knew the procedure and allowed himself to be frisked. The fact that he was a copper meant he couldn't be trusted. The police had been after Madley for years. Brady had to prove that he wasn't dangerous in any way before he'd be allowed in to 'talk' to the big boss.

'What took you so long, Jack?' greeted Madley as Brady limped into the huge room.

Brady would have recognised Madley's distinct Geordie twang anywhere, even with the rough edges gone. Madley was stood with his back to the impressive ceiling to floor window. He frowned as he watched Brady painfully make his way towards him.

'You sure you didn't start back too soon?'

'You know me, Martin, I can take it,' Brady answered as he limped across the polished oak floor towards the window.

It was hard not to notice what Madley's nefarious business dealings had paid for; his large office was kitted out

166

with the finest antiques. Brady didn't know much, but he recognised money. Not bad for a lad from the Ridges, he mused.

'Scotch?' Madley asked.

Brady shook his head.

'Not drinking? Things must be bad,' stated Madley.

'For Jimmy it seems,' Brady answered.

Madley's glinting brown eyes narrowed suspiciously.

He was the same age as Brady but three inches shorter with a smaller frame. However, his tanned, sharp features and menacing eyes warned the hardest nut not to mess with him. His dark brown hair was neatly cut and his clothes were expensive. He wore no jewellery, apart from an expensive watch, which cost more than Brady's annual salary. They had shared a childhood together; if it could be called that. Madley had always looked out for him, up until the point Brady and his younger brother had been put into a children's home. After that, Brady had considered himself lucky to even see anyone he recognised, including his brother, as he was shunted from one foster home to another throughout the North East. Both Brady and Madley had the same backgrounds, both had chosen a life of crime; Brady fighting it, Madley living it.

'What the fuck's going on, Martin? Why are you so interested in Jimmy?'

Madley turned and looked out of the window.

They stood in silence for a few moments watching the scavenging seagulls screeching over the remnants of a Thursday night in Whitley Bay. Curried chips and a half-eaten kebab were strewn across the pavement below, while pizza boxes and empty beer bottles littered the promenade.

'Because he's a copper. A bent copper at that,' Madley finally answered.

167

Brady looked uncertain as he thought it over.

'I would have thought a bent copper would be in your favour?'

Madley turned and looked Brady straight in the eye.

'You're right, up to the point he thought he could fuck me over,' Madley stated menacingly.

'Is it drugs?' Brady asked, worried for Matthews.

Madley was well-known for being one of the North East's major drug dealers, but still the police couldn't finger him. Anyone CID got close to always ended up dead before they had a chance to talk.

'Is that what Matthews has on you?' Brady questioned, unsure of whether he actually wanted to hear the answer.

Madley smiled, baring his perfectly straight white teeth.

'Do you really think I'm going to tell you, Jack? You're a copper and always will be.'

Brady looked out of the window. The horizon was a mute grey, matching the depressing sea.

'I need to find Jimmy, that's all. But I can't get hold of him. Seems he's trying to avoid you.'

'What makes you think Jimmy's hiding from me?'

'Gibbs and that new sidekick of his for starters. It's hard not to notice those two when they're sat outside Jimmy's house.'

Madley smiled as he shook his head.

'I'll leave it to Jimmy to fill you in on what he's done, Jack.'

Brady let it go.

'I see he's still with you then?' Madley said as he gestured towards Conrad's parked car.

'Yeah,' muttered Brady. 'He's a good bloke to have around.'

'Must be,' said Madley. 'What about Claudia?'

Brady shook his head dejectedly as he stared at the blackening horizon.

'No . . . nothing . . .'

Madley shrugged.

'Give her time, Jack.'

Brady nodded as he thought it over.

'Martin?'

'Yeah?'

'If you track him down, let me talk to him?' Brady asked.

Madley narrowed his glinting brown eyes as he weighed up what Brady was asking.

'I've got to find the bastard first.'

Brady waited until he was outside before calling Matthews. Still no answer.

'You stupid bugger, Jimmy,' Brady said under his breath.

The only thing he could do was keep his head down and get on with the investigation in the vain hope that Matthews would see sense and contact him before Gibbs and his sidekick got hold of him.

Chapter Twenty-Eight

'Pull over,' Brady instructed, suddenly realising they were already on Tynemouth Front Street. And he was late. It was after 3.44 pm.

He had been preoccupied with his conversation with Madley and his insight into Matthews, who still wasn't answering any of his calls, despite Brady leaving explicit messages to get back to him ASAP.

'Should have guessed,' Conrad said as he noted Wolfe's racing green vintage MG parked opposite The Turk's Head. 'I take it that Wolfe's expecting me as well?'

Brady raised his eyebrow at him. They both knew the score.

'Actually, I want you to attend this afternoon's press conference on my behalf, while I go over the post-mortem findings with Wolfe.'

The last place Brady wanted to be was sat before a room of journalists baying for blood. And he didn't want that blood to be Matthews', or his come to that. The journalist at the crime scene had unnerved him when she had asked outright if Matthews' suspension from the investigation was connected in any way to the murder. He definitely didn't want to be held to ransom by her at the press conference.

And given that it had only been six months since Brady himself had made the front pages when he had been shot, he didn't want his failed undercover drugs bust coming up either.

'There is only one slight problem, sir. Gates is expecting you,' Conrad reminded him.

Exactly, thought Brady. That in itself was a good enough reason. Gates was starting to get antsy about Matthews. Things were starting to turn from bad to worse. He now had confirmation that the victim had spent the hours leading up to her death with Matthews' daughter. This was news that he'd have to relay to the rest of the team at the briefing later. What worried him was that it made Matthews' behaviour at the crime scene, and now his sudden disappearance, all the more problematic. And right now, after his talk with Madley, Brady didn't want to be answering any awkward questions; either from the press or his boss.

'Tell Gates that I'll report back to him as soon as I've finished with Wolfe,' Brady instructed.

'Yes sir, but he won't be happy,' answered Conrad.

'He never bloody is where I'm concerned, so it won't make much difference, will it?'

'What about getting back to the station?'

'I'll get Wolfe to drive me. Maybe I'll even go home and pick up my own car,' Brady replied.

'I don't think you'd get very far. Do you, sir?'

Brady automatically looked down. Conrad was right. His leg was buggered and there was no way he could use it; every time he put pressure on it he felt as if someone was giving him electric shock treatment, straight up his left inner thigh to his balls. No, he'd have to make do with charity for now.

'I'm under orders from DCI Gates to be your chaperon for the next few weeks, sir. Until you settle back in, so to speak,' Conrad stated uncomfortably.

Bloody great, thought Brady. He needed to get back into Matthews' house later and the last person he wanted witnessing his break-in was Conrad. He didn't want to involve Conrad any more than he had to.

'Conrad? Not a word about my visit to Madley.'

'There's nothing to tell, sir,' answered Conrad.

Brady got out of the car. He steeled himself for his update with Wolfe. If his hunch was right, the post-mortem would have uncovered a darker side to Sophie's life.

Chapter Twenty-Nine

Brady breathed in the lingering stale smell of alcohol and furniture polish as he walked into the pub.

He nodded respectfully at the one-hundred-and-fifty-year-old collie dog, lying immortalised in a glass display box mounted against the wall. This was The Turk's Head, otherwise known affectionately by the locals as The Stuffed Dog for obvious reasons.

'You're late, laddie!'

Brady smiled to himself. He would recognise that wheezy gruff accent anywhere. Despite having worked in the North East for years he still hadn't lost the rough edges of his northern Scottish tongue. He turned to see Wolfe.

'It's been one of those days,' Brady apologised.

'Tell me about it!' Wolfe wheezed. 'Just finished with that girl of yours and they've already put someone else on bloody ice for me. And I've got three more before I get to him. It's like a damned conveyor belt.'

Brady raised his eyebrows.

'A floater. Dragged out the Tyne about two hours ago.'

'Jumped or pushed?'

Matthews' problem with Madley was still niggling him.

He knew what Madley was capable of and that worried him.

'Why are you so interested?' Wolfe asked. 'Haven't you already got your hands full with the murdered girl?'

'Just the copper in me.'

'I'd say suicide,' answered Wolfe. 'But can't say for sure until I've had a proper look.'

Relieved, Brady nodded. He was keenly aware that Matthews' disappearance was starting to make him paranoid. He tried to relax and put his concerns about Matthews to the back of his mind.

'Do you want another pint?' Brady asked, heading for the bar.

'I want a smoke. That's what I want. Bloody ridiculous, at my time of life I shouldn't have to freeze my bollocks off just to have a ciggy,' Wolfe wheezed.

Brady frowned as he watched Wolfe suddenly gasp for breath.

'Just need a ciggy, that's all,' he wheezed breathlessly as he bent forward and thumped his chest.

Wolfe shot Brady a questioning look when he returned with a soft drink.

'So, are you going to spit it out?' Wolfe asked, eyeing Brady suspiciously. 'I've known you a long time, laddie, and I've never seen you off your drink. Not a healthy sign if you want my medical opinion.'

Brady resisted the urge to tell Wolfe his medical opinion was worth shit. The only patients Wolfe dealt with were well past resuscitation. Coupled with the fact that Wolfe was a hard drinker, whose gut instincts made him deeply suspicious of any man who didn't drink. Sobriety wasn't a voluntary condition in his book.

'First day back and there's a lot of shit flying around,' said Brady.

'Matthews or your murder victim?'

'What have you heard about Matthews?' Brady questioned, trying not to look concerned.

'That the lad went a bit soft at the crime scene and ended up being pulled from the investigation. Why? Is there more to tell?'

'No, that's as much as I know.'

Wolfe shook his jowly head as he studied Brady.

'You look like shit. You need a proper drink in you, laddie.'

'Thanks!'

'How long have I known you?' Wolfe asked.

'Too bloody long.'

'Long enough to know that it's got to be something serious for you to be off your drink.'

Brady shrugged.

'Like I said, first day back and all.'

'The job's never gotten to you before, laddie.'

Brady casually shrugged.

'I should have known. Claudia, eh? You should have told me to keep my bloody mouth shut,' Wolfe stated.

'Well, seeing as you feel so bad about it you can take these off my hands then,' Brady said, suddenly remembering the concert tickets he'd stuffed in his coat pocket months ago. They had arrived a few days before he had been shot and he had grabbed the envelope off the hall floor, not wanting Claudia to see them. He had shoved them in his jacket and had forgotten about them until today.

He pulled out an envelope from the inside of his jacket.

He pushed it towards Wolfe.

175

'What's this?' Wolfe asked as he looked at the two tickets inside.

'I booked these for Claudia and I before . . .' Brady faltered, shrugging. 'Well, I've got no use for them now.'

'How did you get hold of these? I heard they'd sold out within a few days?'

'I have my contacts.'

'I can't,' answered Wolfe, as he ran a hand over his smooth, bald head. 'It wouldn't feel right. Why don't you give them to Claudia instead?'

Brady shook his head.

'She's in London and from what I've heard she's got no intention of coming back.'

Wolfe still looked unconvinced.

'Seriously, you'd be doing me a favour. Take a date with you,' Brady suggested.

John Tavener was one of the few contemporary British composers that Brady really liked. In particular, 'The Protecting Veil' was an evocative and haunting piece that had remained with Brady from the first moment he had heard it, more than a decade earlier. But, despite his appreciation of the piece, the last place he wanted to be was at The Sage in Gateshead, sat on his own, listening to music that would painfully remind him of everything that was wrong with his life. He could do that at home, sat in the dark holding on to a bottle of Scotch.

'When the hell have you ever known me have a date, laddie?' snorted Wolfe as he resignedly accepted the tickets.

For once Wolfe had him. Brady couldn't answer because he couldn't remember either. It was fair to say Wolfe was married first to his job and then to drink. Or maybe it was the other way round? Brady wasn't that sure any more.

Regardless of his relationship with alcohol, Wolfe was always impeccably dressed. He wore tailored suits, silk shirts and matching ties. And he always sported a silk hand-kerchief in his suit pocket. But his jowly face was starting to show the telltale signs of his affair with booze.

'Right!' blustered Wolfe, eager to leave his personal life behind. He ran his hand over his gleaming head before getting down to business.

'I'll obviously email you the report once it's been put together. But I thought you might be interested in some of the things I uncovered during the post-mortem.'

Brady bent forward, keen to hear what Wolfe had found out.

'Time of death was approximately between 12.30 am and 2.00 am.'

'Can you be more precise?'

'I thought I was being. I'm not the bloody detective here. All I've got to go on is the victim's body temperature, rigor and liver mortis and stomach contents. But if you can do better, laddie, then by all means!'

Brady kicked himself. He knew better than to tell Wolfe how to do his job.

'Can I continue?'

Brady nodded apologetically.

'There was no evidence of finger-shaped bruising or nail marks on or around the neck, but there were signs of swelling. Petechial haemorrhaging was present above and below a red ligature mark, and when I opened her up the hyoid bone had been fractured. All typically in keeping with ligature strangulation. Manner of death was without a doubt, homicide,' Wolfe concluded. 'However there were self-inflicted scratches at the front of the neck. They matched the skin tissue found under the victim's nails. Presumably the poor girl must have struggled to loosen the scarf from her neck while she was being choked.'

Brady had expected this. The scarf around Sophie's neck had turned out to be more than just a fashion statement. Someone had used it to strangle her to death.

'The skull was fractured and bone matter was present in the brain, but there was no bleeding between the skull and dura. Which means, as I'm sure you know, she was already dead before any trauma occurred to her face and head.'

Brady edged forward in his seat for what was coming next.

'The examination of her pelvic area indicated that the victim had not given birth and was not pregnant at the time of death. But,' Wolfe paused to get his breath, 'I found evidence of recent sexual activity but no indication that the sexual contact was forced. As you'd expect, I've had vaginal and anal fluid samples removed for analysis.'

'There's definitely no evidence that she might have been raped?'

'That's what I said. There was no indication of sexual aggression,' Wolfe repeated.

Brady nodded.

'How recent was the sexual intercourse?'

'Within the hour before she was killed,' answered Wolfe. 'But that's not all, there was also a significant amount of internal and external vaginal and perineum tissue scarring roughly dating back four years.'

'Suggestive of sexual abuse?'

'With that sort of severe trauma, I would say it was more than likely,' answered Wolfe.

Brady nodded, not surprised. He had had a gut feeling that there was a lot more to the victim's life than her parents would have him believe.

'Anything else?'

'Isn't that enough?' asked Wolfe, raising his eyebrow at Brady. 'We'll have a clearer idea of whether she was high on drugs or alcohol once the lab comes back with the samples I've submitted.'

'Sure,' Brady replied.

'They grow up damned fast nowadays, laddie,' Wolfe added as he picked up his glass.

Brady didn't disagree. Given what he already knew, it would come as no surprise if the toxicological reports found traces of drugs and alcohol in her blood and urine. But the fact was, she was just a kid; a kid who was having sex. Add to that forced sex from as young as eleven.

Paul Simmons immediately came to mind.

Statistically, step-fathers were not only more likely to kill a step-child than the biological father, but also four times more likely to sexually abuse a step-child. Brady couldn't shake the bad feeling he had about Simmons. It had been there from the moment he had met him. That coupled with the fact that Simmons had walked into Sophie's life over four years ago, around the same time that Wolfe suggested the sexual abuse had started.

But there were also the photographs of the victim that Brady needed to consider. Photographs which uncannily echoed Wolfe's sentiments that in today's society, kids grew up fast. Too damned fast.

'She was just fifteen,' Brady stated as he looked at Wolfe.

'Well, the evidence is there whether you like it or not,' Wolfe said as his sharp eyes scrutinised Brady. 'The question is what are you going to do with it, laddie?'

Chapter Thirty

Brady picked up the evening edition of *The Northern Echo*.

Someone had thoughtfully left it on his desk; along with an in-tray of emails he needed to answer and a pile of reports marked urgent. He noted that Rubenfeld had made the front page. Not only that, he had also got the newspaper to put up an award for any information leading to the apprehension of Sophie Washington's murderer. Brady knew it was a canny ploy at selling papers and gaining local respect. The cynic in him understood that the reward had nothing to do with helping the police but more to do with inflating the newspaper's profit margin.

Brady hated this kind of empty publicity stunt but he knew it had to be done. Sophie Washington's murder might last a few days in the headlines before the public got bored and circulation figures dropped. The public had an insatiable, even ghoulish appetite for murder and sex, sometimes in that order. Sophie Washington's life would be picked apart until there was nothing left. Then the scavengers, like Rubenfeld, would move on to sabotage someone else's life.

Still, Brady had to admire *The Northern Echo*'s cold-blooded attitude. It was clever; of all the rewards the paper had ever offered, he couldn't remember a single one being paid out. The paper couldn't lose, it was a win–win situation. And the credit was down to one man: Rubenfeld. No other paper would have that headline yet, so getting in first with a big reward was all the sweeter; it meant they had some kind of ownership on the story. And a reward of twenty-five grand would attract a lot of attention; this was the North East after all. Money was short and times were hard. There was a recession on, and unemployment was at a record high which meant people were desperate. Families had to be clothed and fed and the rent still had to be paid. In reality it meant a shed load of extra work for the police who would now have to screen thousands of bogus calls from people who would stitch their granny up if it meant they were better off by twenty-five grand.

He chucked the paper in the waste bin and reached over and picked up the photograph of the victim and her form tutor. Regardless of what Kate had said, it just didn't feel right.

Brady looked at his watch. It was just before 5 pm. He picked up his mobile phone and started dialling.

'Kate? It's me . . .'

'Have you heard from Jimmy?' she quickly asked.

'Not yet,' Brady said, trying his best to sound calm.

He looked over at the dusty, grey shafts of light stabbing through the Venetian blinds.

'What the hell is going on? Why isn't he answering his mobile?'

'I . . . I'm not sure, Kate.'

'You really don't expect me to believe that, do you? I know he tells you everything, so stop bullshitting me!'

'Honestly, I'm as much in the dark here as you. But

182

Jimmy's not the reason I rang. There have been some new developments regarding Sophie's murder.'

'What? Oh God, have you found out who did this to her?'

'No . . . But we've got some new leads which means I'll need to talk to Evie again.'

'I'm not sure that's a good idea. She's still in a really bad way.'

'Kate, I wouldn't ask you if I didn't have to, you know that. Believe me, if there was another way . . .'

Kate sighed.

'If you upset her, Jack . . .'

'I promise I won't. I'll call round in a couple of hours?' Brady suggested. 'I really appreciate this—'

Kate interrupted him before he could end the conversation and hang up.

'Thanks for the warning about your girlfriend. She didn't look too happy about meeting us either, not just after she crawled out of your bed wearing virtually nothing!'

'Oh shit,' muttered Brady.

Conrad had been right; Sleeping Beauty had still been in bed when Kate had let herself in. What the bloody hell had she been drinking last night? Brady wondered bitterly. More to the point, what the fuck had he been drinking?

He cursed inwardly as an image of a tousled Sleeping Beauty standing at the top of his stairs in skimpy knickers and a short, thin T-shirt came to mind.

'I'm sorry about that, Kate. Really I am,' Brady apologised, wincing. 'Really, she didn't mean anything . . .'

He buried his head in his hands. The last person he wanted to find out how low he'd sunk was Kate. He wasn't like Matthews, but she'd never believe that. Not now. Not after finding Sleeping Beauty half-naked in his bed. He was suddenly thrown back to the frantic, panic-stricken conversation he had had with Claudia over DC Simone Henderson. He had desperately tried to convince her that it had meant nothing. That he had made a foolish, idiotic mistake. But she hadn't listened. And after six painful months of going over it again and again, he now accepted that he had no right to expect her to. Claudia deserved better. He had always known it, but had somehow convinced himself that he had cheated fate.

'You're a shit, Jack, you know that? Since when did you start liking them so young? I'd be surprised if she's even sat her GCSEs.'

Kate's abrasive words suddenly hit him. He felt winded by the accusation.

'I'm sure she was over eighteen,' Brady hoarsely replied, the words choking in his throat.

'I seriously doubt it. Maybe if you'd been sober you would have realised she's just a kid.'

'What do you take me for?' he demanded, immediately regretting asking.

'A low-life bastard, that's what. Christ, of all the things I expected from you, this wasn't it.'

'Kate? It was just a one-off, that's all. I . . . I . . .'

He faltered as the line went dead. He held the phone in his hand unsure of what to do.

An assertive knock at the door shook him out of his reverie.

'Yes?'

Brady looked up distractedly as Conrad walked in.

'I reckon you should take a look at this,' Conrad said as he held out a file.

'What is it?' Brady asked.

'It's a log from the phone network of all the calls made to and from the victim's mobile over the past three months,' answered Conrad gravely.

'That's good isn't it?' asked Brady, concerned by Conrad's demeanour.

'The last call she made was at 1.31 am. Lasted less than a minute. Ten minutes later the phone was switched off.'

Brady felt sick. He knew from Conrad's expression what was coming next.

'Tell me it's not Matthews' mobile she called?'

Conrad's look said it all.

'Oh fuck! Who else has seen this?' Brady asked, his mouth dry.

'No one . . . I thought you'd want to see it first.'

'Keep it that way, will you? Just for now?'

Conrad looked uncomfortable.

'I know I'm asking a lot . . . but just give me some time?' Brady insisted. He couldn't imagine the day getting any worse.

'The victim also rang Evie Matthews' mobile at 12.51 am,' Conrad added.

Evie had failed to mention the call. But given the state she was in when he talked to her Brady wasn't surprised.

But it was Matthews' omission that was bothering him.

'Do you notice that other mobile number, sir? The unidentified one?'

Brady looked back down at the sheet.

'Can't trace it because it's a top-up phone,' Conrad explained. 'The number only started showing up two months ago, but the frequent number of calls and the duration suggests the victim was intimate with this person.'

Brady looked at the list of earlier calls and realised what Conrad meant. It seemed that this unidentified caller liked to phone Sophie. A lot. He momentarily forgot Matthews as he took in the fact that the caller had rung the victim on the night she was murdered. Once at 10.20 pm for 5 minutes and 27 seconds and then at 12.02 am for a further 3 minutes and 14 seconds.

Brady began to add up the numbers and didn't like the answer.

'Is it just coincidence?' Brady muttered.

'You've lost me, sir?'

'The victim and her form tutor,' explained Brady as he handed Conrad the photograph. 'I've checked the dates of a school trip to Germany the victim recently went on and those calls begin the same night Sophie and her teacher returned from that trip.'

'That's her teacher?' questioned Conrad sceptically.

Brady nodded.

'I think we need to ask him a few questions, don't you?'

Chapter Thirty-One

'I take it that you're here about Sophie?' asked Ben Ellison, politely standing aside to let Brady in, followed by Conrad and Jenkins.

Brady nodded. 'DS Conrad and DI Brady,' he flatly stated. 'And this is Dr Jenkins who is assisting us with the investigation.'

Jenkins moved towards him and shook his hand.

Brady couldn't help noticing Ellison turning on his boyish charm for Jenkins.

'Sorry for the mess,' he apologised as he cleared a pile of books from a chair for her benefit.

'Thanks,' said Jenkins as she sat down.

She slowly crossed her long, slender legs, forcing her skirt to ride further up than she had intended. Brady realised his weren't the only eyes on her. Embarrassed, Ellison quickly diverted his gaze.

Brady had asked Jenkins along to get a second opinion. He already had a gut feeling that there was something more than a teacher–student relationship between Ellison and the victim. But he wanted Jenkins' professional opinion before he started making any accusations.

'You're lucky you caught me. I normally leave by 5 pm,' Ellison said as he looked at Jenkins. 'Especially on a Friday.'

Brady ignored him as he quickly took in the pokey, cluttered, first-floor office. Two desks sat at either side of the room, strewn in papers, books and piles of folders. He then turned his attention to the victim's form tutor. He was the kind of guy you hated at school. Tall, athletically built and a natural on the sports field. He made ordinary guys feel like dicks. Which meant he was the kind that typically got the girls. Brady could see why. It wasn't just his boyish, chiselled good looks and messy, short blond hair. He had startlingly bright, compelling, azure-blue eyes. Altogether, it was a fatal combination; particularly around hormonal teenagers.

Ellison casually sat down on the edge of his desk. He followed Brady's eye to the sports posters on the wall behind him.

'Snowboarding, rock climbing and surfing . . . that's what I do. That is, when I'm not teaching,' Ellison modestly explained for Jenkins' benefit, rather than Brady's.

'I see,' Brady replied, disliking him even more.

He could understand the allure of surfing in the dazzling warm waters off Australia or the West coast of America, but the gripping, black North East waters that battered Tynemouth beach just didn't do it for him. There were better ways of spending your cold, drizzling weekends in Whitley Bay. And freezing your bollocks off in the sewage-strewn, icy waters of the North Sea didn't come close.

'Do you want a seat?' Ellison suddenly offered, realising that Brady and Conrad were still standing. 'Sorry it's so cramped in here,' he added as he moved an assortment of sports gear off one of the chairs and dumped it on the floor.

'Thanks,' Conrad said as he took a seat.

'I'm fine standing,' Brady answered.

His leg was really giving him some gyp and the last thing he wanted to do was to sit down and have it seize up on him in front of Surfer Boy. Not with Jenkins there.

'So, what can I do for you?' Ellison asked in a deferential tone as his boyish eyes rested on Jenkins.

'We were wondering what you could tell us about Sophie?' Brady began.

Ellison lifted his bright, azure-blue eyes up to Brady's as he thought about the question.

He shook his head and shrugged apologetically.

'I really don't know what I can tell you.'

Brady noticed that despite the relaxed voice, Ellison seemed slightly agitated. Brady couldn't specifically put his finger on it, but he felt it. He didn't need some fancy PhD in psychology to know when someone was lying or uneasy about something. It was simple: Ellison seemed too cool for Brady's liking, considering the circumstances.

'We were hoping that you might be able to tell us if she seemed worried at all? Perhaps preoccupied in lessons? That kind of thing,' Brady explained. 'We're just trying to get a clearer picture of what was going on in Sophie's life.'

'No . . . I can't think of anything . . .' Ellison answered. 'I mean . . . I still can't believe that this has happened . . . why would someone . . .?' His confused, hurt gaze returned to Jenkins.

'That's why we're here, sir,' Brady stated.

Ellison looked at Brady.

'I don't know what to say. She was a very popular girl.

189

Everyone liked her . . . I can't say she ever seemed distracted or worried to me. She was always such a hard-working, sociable student,' Ellison replied. 'I can't imagine anyone doing such a dreadful thing . . .'

'Someone did,' Brady pointed out. 'Someone who personally knew her.'

Ellison shrugged.

'I believe that Sophie had been teaching Year 6 maths on a Saturday morning for the past eight weeks?'

'Yes, that's right. She was gifted at maths and had already started her A-level module, even though she hadn't completed her GCSE,' answered Ellison.

Brady raised his eyebrow, intrigued that Ellison knew so much, given the fact he was just her form tutor.

'I was also her maths teacher. I teach Year 10 and 11 maths. And then A-level maths,' explained Ellison.

Brady was surprised. Ellison definitely didn't look like a maths teacher from his day. If Ellison had said that he was some jock who taught PE then Brady wouldn't have thought twice about it.

'What about the school trip to Germany?'

'What about it?' Ellison questioned as he distractedly ran a hand through his short, stylishly messy hair.

'We have reason to believe Sophie began a relationship with someone while on that trip.'

For a second, Brady swore that Ellison looked surprised.

'I'm afraid I still can't help you. I was just her teacher. Maybe one of her friends would know?'

'We've tried that, but no luck,' Brady answered. 'However they did say that she was allegedly seeing some older guy. You wouldn't have any ideas as to who that would be, do you?'

'No . . . no, like I said I'm just her maths teacher and form tutor.'

Brady waited for more.

Uncomfortable, Ellison turned to Jenkins.

'Maybe you got it wrong?' he suggested.

'I'm afraid not, Mr Ellison. Mobile phone records don't lie. They show that she started a relationship with someone directly after the German school trip. And then there's the autopsy report,' Jenkins calmly replied.

'I'm sorry?' replied Ellison uncomfortably. 'Are you saying what I think you are? That Sophie was . . .' Ellison faltered as he looked from Jenkins to Brady.

'Sexually active?' Jenkins asked.

Ellison nodded awkwardly.

'Yes,' answered Jenkins as she caught Brady's eye.

They both waited for Ellison to say something.

'I'm really sorry about all of this but there's nothing more I can tell you . . .' Ellison finally replied.

'A student of yours was found murdered in the early hours of this morning. I'm sure there's a lot more you can tell us, sir,' Brady firmly stated.

Ellison looked at him.

'I don't know what you're expecting from me. As I said, I was just her form tutor,' Ellison insisted with an edge of annoyance.

Brady took out the photograph he had and handed it to Ellison.

Ellison looked at it and then at Brady.

Something about the photo bothered Brady.

And it was clear that it also bothered Ellison.

'What exactly are you suggesting?' Ellison asked.

Brady shrugged.

Ellison's face muscles tensed up as he tried to figure out what to say next.

'Look, I can't help it if my students develop crushes on me. It sort of goes with the territory ... You know ...?' Ellison reasoned arrogantly.

'I'm sure it does, sir,' Brady cynically replied.

'I don't know what you're trying to imply, DI Brady,' Ellison repeated, as he dismissively handed the photograph back to Brady.

Brady noticed that Ellison's hand was trembling slightly. It seemed the photograph had triggered a nerve.

'I'm implying nothing, sir,' answered Brady.

'Most of the girls on that trip had a photo taken with me. You know what teenage girls are like? They're full of bravado,' Ellison said.

'But it wasn't bravado, was it? It was full-blown sex. Bit of a difference wouldn't you say?'

Jenkins suddenly cleared her throat.

Startled, Ellison looked at her.

'Do you mind if I ask a couple more questions?' Jenkins said, disarming Ellison with a seductive smile.

Brady looked at her. Ellison may have tried to make out he was an innocent teacher in all of this, but soon Jenkins was going to have him firmly by the balls.

'You see, I did some research on you,' began Jenkins slowly.

Ellison's face dropped.

Brady realised that Ellison had second-guessed what was coming.

'I'm just curious as to why you handed your notice in at the last school you worked at, Mr Ellison?'

He looked at Jenkins irritably, dropping the charming act.

'Why? There's no law against leaving one job for another?'

'No, there isn't,' calmly agreed Jenkins. 'But it is a little unusual, don't you think?'

Ellison didn't answer her.

'Particularly when you consider the rumour that you were having an inappropriate sexual relationship with a sixth former,' Jenkins said as she watched him.

Ellison shrugged nonchalantly.

'So what? It was just that. A rumour. And anyway, the girl was nearly eighteen so shoot me.'

Jenkins smiled at him.

'It just doesn't look that great from where I'm sat, now does it?' Jenkins continued.

'Meaning?' demanded Ellison, exasperated.

'Look, let's be straight here. Your fifteen-year-old student has turned up murdered. We have evidence that she was having a clandestine sexual relationship. One that started when she went on the Germany school trip, accompanied by yourself. You have a chequered past, shall we say, when it comes to becoming personally involved with your students—'

'That is a ridiculous assumption!' attacked Ellison.

'Really? It seems that your last employers suggested that you hand in your notice to avoid any damning publicity. Sixth former or not, it is still deemed unacceptable by most people.'

Ellison clenched his jaw as he looked at Jenkins.

Brady watched, impressed as she casually moved her sleek, black bob back from her face.

'Firstly, it was an unsubstantiated claim. The girl had a crush on me. When I refused to accept her advances, she turned into a malicious, hysterical liar and tried her utmost to make sure I lost my job. How about you open your eyes

193

and take a good look at the way these kids act nowadays? They're not the sweet innocent girls you're making them out to be. In fact, most of the sex talk I overhear in the corridors would make you blush.'

'Finished?' Jenkins asked.

He didn't answer, but his look said it all.

'Thank you for your time,' Jenkins politely concluded as she stood up.

Ellison didn't answer her. Instead he turned and busied himself packing his bag to leave.

'Sir?' Brady said, walking to the door. 'Don't disappear. It won't look good.'

'Why would I?' Ellison retaliated.

'That's what I'm trying to figure out, sir.'

*

'What did you make of Ellison?' Brady asked as Conrad drove them back to the station.

'I thought he was full of himself,' Conrad replied.

Brady nodded. He wasn't going to disagree. He didn't like Ellison. But it wasn't just the fact that he made Brady feel old. There was something about his manner that didn't rest easy with Brady. He thought about what Ellison had said. Or more to the point, what he hadn't.

Paul Simmons suddenly came to Brady's mind. His gut feeling was telling him that both the victim's step-father and teacher knew more about her life than they were letting on.

Brady turned to Jenkins who was sat in the back of the car.

'What did you make of him?'

Jenkins swept her hair back from her face as she thought about Ellison.

'He was very uncomfortable when you showed him the photograph, that much was clear. And he tried very hard to hide his surprise that you had it. Other than that, it's difficult to say,' offered Jenkins.

'Is that it?'

'What more do you want? Do you want me to tell you that I thought he was a jerk? Is that it?' Unlike him, she didn't react to hunches or gut feelings. Her job was to remain rational and impartial.

'His reaction to that photograph was understandable,' Jenkins stated.

'Maybe,' answered Brady.

His steady brown eyes penetrated hers, holding her gaze. She was surprised at how gentle his eyes were, realising she had never noticed before. There was something about Jack Brady that she found intriguing. Jenkins suddenly felt a flush of irritation as she tried to suppress the attraction she felt. She firmly reminded herself that he was an ex-patient and a colleague. Nothing could ever happen with him, more so given the fact that it was painfully obvious to her that he was still in love with his estranged wife.

Annoyed with herself, she shifted her gaze, breaking his hold over her.

'You have to think about how Ellison would have felt. A student of his has been found murdered. And then you turn up with a photograph of the two of them suggesting he was having an inappropriate relationship with her.'

'I didn't exactly say that,' retaliated Brady.

'You didn't have to. Subtlety isn't your strong point, Jack.'

'So what are you saying?'

'All I'm pointing out is that Ellison wouldn't be human if he didn't react guiltily when you handed him that photo.

Most people in his situation would. It's the ones who don't that you have to watch out for.'

'You mean like Simmons?'

'I didn't say that, Jack,' replied Jenkins.

'You didn't have to, I did,' stated Brady.

Jenkins sighed. Why, she questioned, had she ever allowed Gates to talk her into working with Jack Brady?

'Anyway, talk about me being heavy-handed. What about you with the accusation that he'd slept with a previous student?' Brady asked.

Jenkins smiled at him.

'I just wanted to see his reaction.'

'And?'

'And what?'

'Do you think he slept with her?'

Jenkins looked straight at Jack.

'I'm not paid to make assumptions. That's your job,' she answered, smiling lightly. 'But between you and me, there's no smoke without fire.'

'What about you? Do you believe that Ellison was nothing more than her teacher?' Brady asked as he turned to Conrad.

'Why not?' Conrad questioned.

'I don't know. It just seems to me that everyone's lying to save their own neck, while we have a victim who's turning cold. Very cold.'

Chapter Thirty-Two

Brady looked around the Incident Room. It was crammed with over thirty detectives and officers. They were tired and restless and he couldn't blame them. It was 7.10 pm on a Friday night and their shift still wasn't over. He had spent the last ten minutes briefing the team on what they had so far; which wasn't a lot. But what concerned him was what they were going to find if they kept digging. Matthews' name kept uncomfortably coming to mind.

'Harvey, Kodovesky: I want statements taken from all of the bar staff working in The Beacon last night,' Brady ordered. 'And I want you to scrutinise the security tape if they have one. The pub is right next to that abandoned farmland which means someone could have seen the victim before she was murdered. The person we're looking for might have been drinking in The Beacon for all we know.'

Harvey nodded.

'I thought we were looking for someone known to the victim? The modus operandi points to the murderer having a personal attachment to Sophie Washington, sir?' questioned Kodovesky.

'We still are,' Brady answered. 'Forensics found male hand and footprints at the opening in the fence leading out onto the back lane next to the victim's house. Prints that match ones found at the murder scene,' Brady replied. 'Someone was either waiting for her there, or she was already with them.'

Brady looked around the room.

'She then had sex, consensual sex an hour before she was murdered. So we can take it as read that this boyfriend her classmates talked about, who may be older, does exist. It's crucial that we find out his identity.'

'Are we sure she actually walked home?' asked Harvey.

'We know that the victim left Evie Matthews' house in Earsdon at around 10 pm on foot,' Brady answered.

But what Brady wasn't telling them was Jimmy Matthews' involvement after that. Given what Matthews had told him, he must have picked her up somewhere between Earsdon and West Monkseaton to have then dropped her off home. But what happened after that was lost on him. What worried him was a CCTV camera catching Matthews actually stopping to give her a lift.

'Our problem is we don't know what happened between the victim leaving her best friend's house in Earsdon at 10 pm and then being murdered yards from her own home between roughly 1.30 pm and 2.00 pm. That's between three and a half to four hours. Our job is to fill those hours in, minute by minute.'

Brady turned to Conrad.

'I need you to check out any CCTV footage we have between Earsdon and West Monkseaton. Anything, and I mean anything that looks suspicious you let me know.'

Conrad looked mildly surprised at the request but accepted the order without question.

It was simple. Brady trusted Conrad. He knew that if

Conrad found something on CCTV footage that implicated Matthews, he would bring it to him first. Not that he knew what he'd do about it, but at least he'd have time to figure something out. Whereas someone like Adamson would go over his head and take it straight to Gates.

Brady couldn't help but notice Adamson who was stood watching him against the wall to his right.

'After interviewing the victim's classmates we have one name to go on: Shane McGuire,' stated Brady.

A few hushed voices around the room proved he was well-known to police stations across North Tyneside.

'Seems he was an ex-boyfriend of the victim's. I want him found. He's not at his home address in North Shields and he's not at his nan's either. Adamson, I want you to pay a visit to The Sunken Ship and hassle his mother to see if she knows where he could be,' Brady instructed as his eyes rested on Adamson.

Adamson scowled at the prospect of Wallsend on a Friday night. Worse than that, The Sunken Ship on a Friday night.

Not that it bothered Brady. He was only too glad to give him something to keep him out of the way.

'I know it's a shit job, but someone's got to do it. And make sure you take someone with you for back-up.'

Brady knew the flak he would get; the place would be heaving with drunken thugs, ready to have a go at the police just for the hell of it. Whitley Bay had its problems all right, but Wallsend was the land that civilisation forgot. More so, where The Sunken Ship was concerned, known locally as the Hole. McGuire's mother worked there most nights. She had a habit to feed, never mind her son, and with a henchman for a husband serving time for some particularly nasty crimes, she had no choice but to offer all she had left; her body. It was the crassest of places where women with needle-riddled, fake-tan-smeared bodies danced in cages suspended from the ceiling.

The last time Brady was in the Hole, it wasn't money the men threw at the lap dancers, it was cigarette butts and whatever dregs of beer they had left. And spit wasn't the only body fluid the women found themselves being covered in. No, the Hole wasn't known for its refinement, it was what it sounded like; a hell hole.

'Can I take Dr Jenkins with me? From what I've heard of McGuire's mother it might be useful to have a woman of Dr Jenkins' skill on side to help question her,' Adamson asked as he looked across at Jenkins.

Brady knew from the look on Adamson's face that he was trying to wind Brady up. The problem was it was working.

Brady was about to say no, but Jenkins beat him to it.

'I've got no problem with it, unless you have?' Jenkins questioned as she looked at Brady.

He was thrown. He hadn't expected her to want to be within a mile of The Sunken Ship on a Friday night. He refrained from telling her that if she walked in there, the punters wouldn't let her walk out, that was a certainty.

'You haven't got a problem with that, have you, Jack?' asked Jenkins.

'I'm just not sure it's the sort of place you should be going,' Brady replied.

'And why is that?' quizzed Jenkins as she locked eyes with him.

'The punters there aren't exactly the kind of people you're used to dealing with,' replied Brady, aware that the whole room was watching. Including Adamson who was clearly enjoying the awkward situation he'd placed Brady in.

The last thing Brady wanted to be accused of was sexism. But even he wouldn't willingly go in there and that was saying something given his background.

'If I'm part of this investigation, then it means I get given the same crap meted out to everyone else. It might surprise you, but I can cope with a lot worse than a few drunken men in a strip bar,' coolly answered Jenkins.

Brady could tell from her expression that she wasn't going to back down.

'Fine, accompany DS Adamson,' he conceded. 'But just watch yourself.'

There was a reason this place was hidden down by Wallsend docks. And if Jenkins wanted to find out why, then who was he to stop her?

Brady turned and looked at the whiteboard behind him. He pointed at the photograph taken of the victim's tattoo.

'We need to know which tattoo parlour is responsible for this,' Brady said. 'Two reasons,' Brady added. 'The tattoo's fairly recent, so there's a chance she went with this older boyfriend. Also, we want to know which stupid buggers would tattoo a fifteen-year-old without checking for ID.'

'Whoever did it obviously didn't realise how young she was,' stated Jenkins.

Brady couldn't disagree. He had seen the body at the crime scene and had, as they all had, mistaken her for a young woman in her late teens to early twenties.

'Yeah, but I still think they should be shaken up a bit. There's a reason that you're meant to be over eighteen.'

Brady rested his eye on DSs Daniels and Kenny.

'Tomorrow you two check out all the tattoo shops in the

area. But right now your job is to find our missing lad, McGuire. Check out the local haunts in Whitley Bay and also do a round of the pubs down North Parade.'

Brady could see Daniels and Kenny both wincing at the thought of checking out the pubs in North Parade. Most of the drinkers in North Parade had travelled there for the weekend looking for trouble. And two plain-clothes coppers asking questions were easy targets.

'Can I say a few words, Jack?' asked Jenkins as she stood up.

Brady nodded and sat down. He knew what she wanted to say, having already briefed him earlier.

Jenkins moved over to the whiteboard.

'I know that we're looking for someone known to the victim,' Jenkins began as she turned from the board and faced the room.

'The modus operandi tells us that Sophie Washington knew her attacker. There was no struggle, at least not until she was being choked which suggests that she knew whoever did this to her and she trusted them.'

Jenkins paused as she looked back at the whiteboard.

'She either met her attacker at the crime scene or went willingly to the location with them. Forensics found no marks on the ground to indicate that she had been dragged or dumped there.'

She turned and briefly caught Brady's eye.

'The reason I'm going over what DI Brady has already effectively said is that the gravity of the attack to her face concerns me. And I think we can be blinded into thinking this is just overkill, which you'll all be familiar with, is any effort that goes beyond what is necessary to kill the victim. I'm presuming most of you will be surmising that it was this unidentified boyfriend of hers who killed her and then mutilated her face afterwards?' Jenkins asked.

The consenting grumbles around the room confirmed her suspicions.

'What I'm asking of you is to think out of the box for a moment. Think about why her murderer chose to specifically attack her face.'

The silence was heavy and awkward. Brady could see that no one was quite understanding Jenkins' point.

'Maybe he was the jealous sort? For all we know she could have been playing around and he'd found out?' suggested Adamson.

'Maybe. But why not mutilate her breasts and private parts? Why specifically her face and to such a degree of destruction?'

Adamson shrugged.

'You tell me, Doctor?' he said, smiling.

'That's the point, I can't. The attack to her face is definitely overkill, but not the kind I'd expect from a boyfriend. This is different. This hints of repressed anger and jealousy towards the victim. As we can see she was a very pretty young woman,' Jenkins pointed out as she looked at the photograph of Sophie Washington on the whiteboard.

'Someone hated her for that. So much so, that even when she was dead they couldn't bear to look at that face. Her murder wasn't enough to satisfy their anger and jealousy. Not until every identifiable trait was eradicated.'

'But isn't that the same as the jilted boyfriend or husband who throws acid in their ex-spouse's face? Or even slashes their face?' Adamson asked.

Jenkins looked at him and shook her head.

'No,' she simply answered.

'Why? It's the same mutilation surely?' Adamson queried, confused.

'No, the two couldn't be more different. In the cases you're referring to, the key distinction is that the victim is still alive. The point is to punish the victim. She has to live the rest of her life severely disfigured, satisfying the ex-spouse that if he can't have her, then no one else will want her.'

Jenkins paused as she looked around the room. She realised that most of them were on the same page as Adamson.

'The key difference with Sophie Washington is that she was already dead. The disfigurement to her face was never about punishment. It was about relieving the resentment and fury on the murderer's part,' Jenkins said, realising that she was talking to herself.

'I know I'm stating the obvious here, but we really want to be taking everything that's being left on the victim's wall on Facebook seriously. For all we know, the murderer has left a message. It's similar to the murderer feeling the compulsion to attend his victim's funeral, or even in some cases trying to get involved in the murder investigation. Same applies with the cyberworld,' Jenkins concluded.

The victim's blog and Facebook posts had thrown Brady, as much as they had thrown the rest of the team. There were some details that even he found unpalatable. Her entries had confirmed what they had already suspected. However, no photos were posted of her 'cyber boyfriend' and no name was given. Instead, his unsavoury sexual antics with her were graphically and immodestly blogged. At times it was too easy to forget that victim was only fifteen.

Jenkins looked at Brady as she stepped back and sat down.

'Thanks, Dr Jenkins,' Brady said as he stood up and took

over. 'All right people, we have our work cut out for us. So let's get started.'

The room grumbled in response as people started to get ready to leave.

'And Adamson,' Brady said, as he turned to the DS. 'You may have forgotten, but I haven't. I'm still waiting for Sophie Washington's medical records. I don't care who you wake up to get them but I want them before the night's out!' Brady ordered, fuming over the stunt he had pulled requesting that he be partnered with Jenkins. Brady wasn't sure whether Adamson thought he had a chance with Jenkins. But from what Brady knew of her, he didn't think she'd give him the time of day.

Adamson shot him a sour look.

'I don't give a fuck if you don't like it. I'm sure Sophie Washington didn't like the fact that someone was sexually abusing her from the age of eleven and then at fifteen she ends up dead with her face smashed beyond human recognition! It's our job to find out exactly what the hell was going on in that kid's life which led to someone fucking her and then murdering her. Someone, can I add, who that kid knew. This was personal. Someone hated that kid so much that even when she had stopped breathing they couldn't let go of the loathing they felt towards her. Were they connected to the sexual abuse that started when the victim was ten or eleven, who knows? Had she threatened to betray them and so they tried to silence her, again who knows? But it's our job to bloody find out. And if that means searching her medical records for some kind of clue as to what was happening to her then that's what we do.'

Brady suddenly caught Gates' eyes and wondered exactly how long he had been standing there.

'Can I have a word, Jack?'

Heads turned and looked at Gates.

Brady shot Conrad a questioning look. But Conrad seemed as unsure about Gates' sudden interruption as Brady.

'Now!' Gates ordered as he walked out, slamming the door shut.

Brady couldn't help but notice DS Adamson's self-satisfied smile. He clenched his fists in an attempt to resist the urge to wipe it off his face.

*

'What do you know about this?' Gates irritably demanded as he thrust a sheet of paper at Brady.

Brady quickly realised that it was the murder victim's toxicological report.

'I haven't had the opportunity to see it yet, sir,' Brady answered.

'Well here's your chance.'

Brady picked it up and quickly scanned through the information. He abruptly stopped.

The alcohol concentration in her blood sample was 3.9 grammes per litre, which meant she had been heavily intoxicated.

He read on. Traces of cannabis had also been detected.

Brady inwardly sighed. It was exactly as he had expected.

'What other unpleasant surprises are waiting to jump out?' Gates questioned angrily.

He stared at Brady as he waited for an answer.

It was a cold hard look. One that told Brady that Gates knew something.

'She was definitely with DI Matthews' daughter last night?'

'Yes sir,' Brady answered, realising that too many people were holding back on what they knew about the murder victim's lifestyle; Evie Matthews included.

'Then surely she must have had some idea about this?' Gates said, snatching back the toxicological report.

'Apparently not, sir. But I am due to re-interview her later,' answered Brady.

'And you don't think it's odd that DI Matthews didn't recognise the victim, given it was his daughter's friend?' Gates asked sceptically.

'I don't know, sir,' Brady slowly answered. 'You'd have to ask Matthews that question.'

'I wish I could but as I'm sure you're well aware, Matthews seems to have disappeared. And I think you know as well as I do the reason why. He recognised the body and kept the information to himself.'

Brady shifted uncomfortably under Gates' gaze.

'And what do you know about this?' Gates suddenly questioned as he held up *The Evening Chronicle*.

Brady shrugged, confused.

'It's about DI Matthews being suspended from the investigation. What I want to know is how this Harriet Jacobs woman got hold of that kind of information?'

'I don't know, sir.'

'Well, you should bloody know! This is your investigation. If someone's talking, it's your job to shut them up!'

Brady didn't respond.

'I'm warning you, Jack, don't make a fool of me!'

'No sir.'

'Is there anything else you want to tell me?' Gates asked as he scrutinised Brady.

Brady didn't answer. He couldn't without jeopardising his job.

'Have it your way for now,' Gates dispassionately replied. 'But if I find out you've been holding back on me, you'll live to regret it.'

'Yes sir,' answered Brady awkwardly.

'It's bad enough we've got a murdered fifteen-year-old girl. Let alone the implication that one of our own is involved. Sort it! And sort it fast! Before I'm forced to put an arrest warrant out for Matthews!'

Chapter Thirty-Three

Brady went back to his office to collect his coat.

He soon wished he hadn't when the phone rang.

'Yeah Charlie?'

'Better warn you, bonny lad, Harriet Jacobs from *The Evening Chronicle* has been doing a bit of digging and she's found out that Sophie Washington belonged to Facebook as well as some blogging site. Seems that she's got some unauthorised information on the victim from these sites that she's threatening to publish.'

'Shit!' Brady muttered as he logged onto his laptop. 'How the hell has she managed to get access to the victim's sites when we're meant to have removed them?'

'I don't know, Jack. But she did and she's wanting to publish it.'

He should have expected it. The scavenging rats had grown tired of the scraps thrown to them by the Press Office. Now they were starting to do their own kind of dirty detective work on the victim. Digital door-stepping showed just how low journalists would scrape for a scoop. Refused sordid information from the grieving victim's family or the police, journalists would take whatever material existed on the Web about the victim, regardless of the impact.

'It gets worse, Jack. This Jacobs woman is requesting an interview with you. If you don't then she's going to publish the girl's blog entries and some of those photos.'

Brady knew exactly which photos Turner was talking about. He sighed heavily. Harriet Jacobs was the same journalist who had shouted out questions at him about Matthews at the crime scene. She was also responsible for *The Evening Chronicle*'s front-page story suggesting DI Matthews' suspension somehow implicated him in the murder.

There was a knock at the door.

'Thanks for letting me know,' Brady said before putting the phone down.

He looked up to see Conrad walk in.

'I found nothing on the CCTV footage that's unusual, sir,' Conrad informed him.

'Go on,' Brady instructed.

'Well, you can see a young woman walking along the bottom road by Wellfield at roughly the time that the victim left Evie Matthews' house. From what I can make out it's her. She's wearing similar clothes, hairstyle etc. She's definitely alone and no one seems to be following her. But she does use her phone to call someone.'

'Thanks, Conrad,' Brady replied, not knowing whether to be relieved or disappointed.

Brady glanced down at his desk and suddenly remembered what had so riled him before Conrad had walked in.

'Maybe you can tell me what that bloody woman wants?' he asked looking up at Conrad.

'What woman?' Conrad asked, at a loss.

'The one who's intent on losing me my job!'

Conrad still looked puzzled.

Brady had to admit his description didn't exactly narrow it down; he'd pissed off quite a few people in his time.

'Some bloody journalist by the name of Harriet Jacobs.'

Conrad shook his head.

'Never heard of her, sir.'

'Works for *The Evening Chronicle*. Wrote that damned front-page story on Matthews being suspended from this murder investigation. What I want to know is who talked to her?'

Conrad looked uncomfortable.

'Do you know something?'

'No, just a suspicion,' Conrad answered.

Brady didn't have to ask, he already had his own reservations about Adamson.

'Do me a favour, Conrad, and talk to her will you? Find out exactly what she knows and who's feeding her this crap?'

'Yes sir,' answered Conrad, still at a loss as to why Brady was so uptight.

'The bugger's trying to blackmail me into talking to her,' Brady explained. 'But I reckon she'll be more than satisfied when you turn up. Especially after that press conference you did with Gates this afternoon,' Brady added, with a laconic smile.

Since the press conference, Conrad had been getting ribbed by everyone about his TV performance. But Brady had to admit Conrad had looked the part.

'I don't understand. What's she got over you?'

'This,' Brady said as he turned his laptop towards Conrad. 'She wants to publish everything, including the photos. Unless I talk to her.'

'I thought Jed had removed her Facebook page and blog?' Conrad asked, surprised.

'So did I,' said Brady.

He watched as Conrad scrolled down Sophie Washington's blog entries and photos.

Even Conrad seemed as surprised as Brady by the number of tributes posted on the victim's wall and on her blog. It seemed that bad news travelled fast in the cyberworld. Sophie Washington was now being hailed as a tragic heroine whose short life had been romanticised into something it wasn't. Brady had gleaned enough unpalatable facts about her life to know the picture these people were painting couldn't have been further from the truth. But she had nearly a thousand tributes posted on her wall. Brady doubted that most of these people even knew her. But he recognised that Jenkins was right; they'd have to look at every single one of them.

When Conrad had finished reading he looked the way Brady felt.

Brady shook his head.

'Why is nothing ever straightforward?' he asked as he stared at a photograph of the victim brazenly downing shots in one of Whitley Bay's nefarious bars.

The pub was easy to recognise; he'd been in it enough times himself, arresting underage drinkers. But what Brady hadn't banked on was seeing a photo of Jimmy Matthews' daughter with the victim, knocking back shots in the same damned bar. Worse than that, Evie Matthews had recently posted it as a tribute to her deceased best friend, Sophie Washington.

*

Brady had asked Conrad to get the car ready while he made a quick call.

He needed to talk to Jed, their forensic computer analyst. They only had one full-time computer geek. Money was short and Gates was tight which meant that Jed was always up to his knees in work.

Brady listened, unimpressed as Jed tried to bullshit him again with computer jargon.

'I don't give a shit about any of that! I want it taken off the net, regardless. I don't give a damn if the blog's on American Bloggers! I want it removed!' Brady insisted. 'I mean it, Jed, our jobs are on the line here. If any of this stuff gets published it's not only me who'll be answering to Gates. You know that don't you? So tell me why the hell it's taken so long to remove it?' he demanded.

'What do you mean it's not that easy?' Brady incredulously asked.

He sighed as Jed started again.

'Fuck civil liberties and privacy rights and all that crap!' Brady interrupted, losing his temper. 'This is a fifteen-year-old girl we're talking about here. What about her civil liberties and right to privacy now, huh? For fuck's sake! What about her family's rights in all of this?'

Brady took a deep breath as Jed kicked off. Brady knew he was one of the best forensic computer analysts around, but he was a pedant when it came to sticking to the rules.

'Damn it, Jed! Half the shit she posted on her blog is bloody illegal anyway! She was just a kid! And believe me, if those photographs of her getting off her face, never mind the bloody half-naked ones aren't removed from that site immediately then some bloody unscrupulous paper's going to have them covering their front page tomorrow. Not to mention Jimmy Matthews' kid!'

He rubbed his forehead as he listened to Jed's ever patient voice. Jed often got it in the neck; hazards of the job, Brady presumed. There was a whole cyberworld out there that facilitated the sick and twisted in every imaginable way. It was Jed's impossible job to nail them with whatever illicit and unsavoury material was stored on their hard drives.

'What about the victim's computer and her step-dad's? Found anything yet?' Brady asked in vain, hoping for some good news.

'Yeah, I know you're backed up,' he replied, wearily. 'I wouldn't ask this of you if it wasn't important. It's just that I'm waiting to see if anything shows up on Paul Simmons' computer. I've got a feeling about that guy if you get my drift?'

Brady nodded.

'Yeah, I know it's a Friday night. And yeah, I do appreciate it.'

He wasn't angry with Jed. He was angry at the immorality of it all. The fact that depraved journalists could make money out of someone else's misery was beyond him. Especially when it involved a fifteen-year-old murdered girl.

Brady grabbed his jacket and limped towards the door, reluctantly accepting that the worst was yet to come.

Chapter Thirty-Four

'Pull in here,' Brady demanded suddenly.

'What about Matthews' daughter?' Conrad questioned.

'There's something I need to do first.'

He still couldn't get hold of Matthews. But that wasn't his only concern.

He steeled himself before getting out of the car.

'Where are you going, sir?' Conrad called out, confused.

'To see what those little bastards know about the murder,' Brady replied before slamming the car door shut.

He wasn't in the mood for trouble. But the frenzied screaming and high-spirited jeers told him he'd come to the wrong place. He headed through the trees, away from the safety of the street lights towards the pitch-black area that was Whitley Bay Park. It was after 8 pm and no resident or dog walker in their right mind would go near the park at night. The raucous shouting and swearing started to get louder as Brady closed in.

'What the fuck do you want, mister? Looking for a fucking shag? Is that it?' shouted one lad before he cockily dragged on his cigarette.

He instinctively yanked his hood forward as Brady turned to look at him.

'It'll fucking cost you though. My lass ain't cheap!'

Brady couldn't help but smile. The scrawny little bugger looked no older than fourteen and here he was giving him lip.

Brady stood his ground, undeterred by the jeers and catcalls coming from the twenty or so teenagers who had now gathered around him. He realised that most of the kids were high; whether it was alcohol or drugs it didn't matter. The air was thick with the smell of cannabis while cans of cheap lager and bottles of wine clinked as they did the rounds. The outcome was still the same; kids too high to realise the consequences of being off their faces.

Adrenalin surged through Brady as he checked out Conrad's whereabouts.

He was relieved to see Conrad watching from a safe distance. It was reassuring to know that back-up could be called if things suddenly got out of hand.

'So, what's it to be, mister, eh? Twenty quid say?' leered the lad with the tab.

Brady could smell the cheap beer on the kid's breath.

'I just want to ask a couple of questions,' Brady answered firmly.

'Nah, mister. Don't work like that,' the lad replied with a cold glint in his eye.

He dragged on his tab before handing it to a giggling lass stood nearby.

'You give me forty quid and maybe I'll let you go,' he added menacingly as he pulled a knife out of his sleeve.

'You don't want to do that,' warned Brady.

'Don't I?'

'Fucking shaft the perv!' excitedly cried the lass as the lad suddenly jumped at Brady, knife outstretched.

Brady deftly grabbed the kid, twisting him into a dead-lock before he had a chance to realise what had happened.

'Ow . . . you're fucking psycho you are! Let me go or I'll fucking kill you!' rasped the lad as Brady restrained him under his right arm.

'Drop the knife or I'll fucking choke it out of you!' Brady threatened.

The kid limply dropped the blade to the ground. Brady stepped on it, aware that there were twenty more teenagers waiting to finish the job.

'Fucking let him go, mister!'

'That's fucking assault that is! And he's a fucking kid he is! I'm going to call the fucking police on you!'

'I am the fucking police! And if you don't want me nicking the lot of you, you'll bugger off!' Brady ordered as he gestured towards Conrad's waiting figure.

He watched as the kids belligerently dispersed, mouthing off as they went.

'Ahhh . . . you bastard! You're fucking choking me!' the lad hissed, as he struggled in vain to get free.

'What do you know about Sophie Washington?' Brady demanded.

'I don't fucking know nowt!'

'Try harder,' Brady suggested as he tightened his grip.

The kid started spluttering and kicking.

'Let him go, will you?' cried out the lass still holding his tab.

Brady ignored her.

'She used to come down here with her mate, all right?' he spluttered.

Brady already knew who the mate was without asking.

'Was she here last night?'

'Nah, haven't seen her around for a while.'

'Did she have any boyfriends that you know of?'

'Who knows? She was a right fucking slapper she was! Half of Whitley have shagged her!'

Brady relaxed his grip on the kid. He fell to the ground.

'You fucking need your head seeing you do!' screeched his lass.

'Tell me something I don't know.'

Brady turned to the kid as he started to get to his feet.

'You're coming with me,' Brady ordered.

'I'm going nowhere, you fucking pig!'

Brady suddenly felt something hard and jagged hit his forehead.

'You little shit!' Brady swore as he realised that the kid had got him good.

Before the kid had a chance to leg it, Brady grabbed him.

'Taken to beating up kids now have we, sir?' Conrad asked as Brady dragged the reluctant youth over to the car.

'Other way round. Little shit got me a good one,' Brady said as he pressed his shirt sleeve to his bleeding forehead.

'You want to get that seen to,' Conrad suggested as he took a look at the cut.

'It's nothing,' Brady muttered.

He had more to worry about than a wound.

'You sure about this, sir?' Conrad asked as he sceptically looked at the kid.

'Yeah, he knows something all right!'

'How can you be certain?' asked Conrad.

'Because that's bloody Shane McGuire.'

Chapter Thirty Five

'Bloody hell, Jack! What happened to you?' asked Turner as Brady limped into the station.

Brady shrugged.

'See if you can get hold of a social worker for me, will you?'

'Why would you—' Turner stopped short when Conrad came through the double doors with the lad.

'What the bloody hell have you done this time, McGuire?' Turner demanded as he raised his bushy, white eyebrows at the kid.

'Pissed me off,' muttered Brady.

'Aye, I can see that, bonny lad,' answered Turner as he shook his head at the nasty cut above Brady's left eye.

*

'Why the fuck should I talk to you? You fucking wanker,' growled Shane McGuire.

Brady casually leaned back against his chair.

'You wait till my fucking dad hears about this, then you'll fucking see!' McGuire threatened.

'Where is your old man again? That's right, he's banged

219

up. So tell me, what's he going to do to me from behind bars?'

The social worker that Turner had called in gave Brady a withering look.

Brady returned it with a lame smile. He'd worked with Linda Johnson on numerous occasions. She knew what hardened little buggers they were as much as Brady did. She was under no illusions; unlike some of the newly qualified bloody do-gooders.

'Can we cut straight to the point, DI Brady?' Linda asked as she raised a narrow pencilled eyebrow at him. 'It is a Friday night after all.'

'Sure, but I reckon you should be telling McGuire here that,' Brady replied.

McGuire responded by spitting a glob of phlegm at Brady. It missed and hit the table in front of him.

'So, let's go over last night again, shall we?' Brady repeated.

'Like I said, I was at home with my nan,' McGuire cockily replied. 'So you've got nowt on me!'

'Apart from your girlfriend's murder.'

McGuire sucked in air.

'She wasn't my fucking girlfriend . . .' he nervously replied.

'What was she then? Just some shag?'

'You fucking know nowt!' McGuire replied edgily.

Brady raised a sceptical eyebrow.

'What about these then?' Brady asked as he laid out photographs.

'Where the fuck did you get those?' McGuire spat as he snatched the photos.

Brady shrugged.

McGuire quickly flicked through the digital images of him and Sophie.

220

'So fucking what? It wasn't as if we were serious or nowt. We both just hung out sometimes. There was nowt in it!'

'But now's she dead,' Brady stated.

'Look, I haven't seen Sophie for a while now. All right?'

'What happened? Another schoolgirl catch your eye?' Brady asked laconically.

'It's none of your business. Anyhows, she and her mate always had booze on them, and weed. So don't fucking make out she was innocent. Cos she was far from fucking innocent!'

'That's what you say, McGuire. But who's going to believe a seventeen-year-old lad on remand caught out having sex with an underage girl?'

'Wasn't fucking like that! And anyhows, do you think I was the only lad that fucked her? Nah, fucking off her head most of the time. She was well mental,' McGuire retaliated.

'What do you mean?'

'She was mental like. You know? Always fucking extreme she was. That's why she stopped hanging out at the park cos it wasn't fucking good enough for her any more. Crazy fucking cow,' said McGuire resentfully.

'Where did she go then?'

'Soon as she realised she could get into the pubs in Whitley she was off,' muttered McGuire.

He slouched forward and held his head in his hands as he stared down at the table.

'Fucking knew she'd end up like this. It was only a matter of time. The stupid bitch!' McGuire's voice cracked and gave way.

'Why?' Brady asked, surprised that Sophie Washington had managed to get under Shane McGuire's thick skin. It was clear that he felt more for the victim than he was letting on.

'Cos she was fucking well mental! Ask that mate of hers, she'll tell you,' McGuire muttered.

'That's exactly what I plan on doing,' replied Brady evenly as he stood up to leave. 'Oh yeah, and Shane?'

He looked up at Brady resentfully.

'Tell your mam I was asking after her.'

'Fuck you!' McGuire replied scornfully as he kicked out at the table.

Chapter Thirty-Six

Brady barely recognised his kitchen. Gone were the pizza boxes and Chinese and Indian take-out cartons. Also, the two months' worth of empty Peroni lager bottles and whisky quarts had disappeared, leaving behind an unrecognisable, clean granite work surface. The Belfast sink had been emptied of all its debris, as had the dishwasher. The place smelled clean for a change.

Brady felt uneasy. It was no longer his home.

He quickly turned as Kate walked into the kitchen.

'Your girlfriend left her number for you,' she said coldly before he had a chance to talk.

'Oh fuck . . .' Brady mumbled.

She looked at him, expecting a better answer. She caught sight of the gash above his eye and resisted the temptation to ask if he was all right.

'Kate . . . I want to apologise for—'

'I'd rather you got on with what you came here for,' she interrupted.

'Yeah, sure . . .' mumbled Brady.

*

When Claudia had left she had pretty much stripped the house while he had lain in hospital recovering from his gunshot wound. He had made do with a beat-up leather sofa and a scuffed, worn-out armchair and the other bits of crap Claudia had seen as unworthy of taking. Including his eclectic vinyl collection which included original recordings of Bessie Smith and Jelly Roll Morton.

He looked around the living room. It certainly looked different from the chaos he'd left it in this morning. The empty bottles and ashtrays that had littered the place had been removed. The wooden floor had been washed and the fireplace had been cleaned out. Logs of damp wood had been replaced by a lazily burning fire.

Brady had never known Kate to be remotely interested in cleaning and put her nervous energy down to recent events. Like him, she still hadn't heard from Matthews. But she knew enough to realise that this time Matthews was in over his head. And then there was the unthinkable; the murder of her daughter's best friend.

He sighed wearily and rubbed his tired face. He hated the way things were between them. He wondered if she would even tell him if Matthews were to contact her?

A lot had changed.

Brady heard footsteps and turned to see Evie standing in the doorway looking apprehensive. Kate stood behind her.

'I'll be in the kitchen if you want me,' Kate stated, not giving Brady a chance to object.

He watched as she disappeared leaving him with Evie.

Brady noticed that she looked worse than she did this morning. Her hair was uncombed and her face hadn't been washed. Old mascara was smudged and embedded around her distrustful eyes. When had she started wearing make-up, Brady wondered, let alone drinking and smoking? He didn't want to think about the sex.

He ran a hand over his stubble as he watched Evie sit down.

'Look . . . Evie . . . I know this is difficult but I really do need to ask you a few more questions about Sophie,' Brady tentatively began.

She stared down at her iPhone, avoiding his gaze.

'Why didn't you tell me she had a boyfriend?' Brady asked gently.

He waited a few moments.

'Evie?'

'I . . . I . . . didn't think,' she mumbled as she distractedly touched the screen of her phone.

'What did she tell you about him?'

'Nothing . . .' she muttered.

'Come on, Evie, she must have told you something about him? His age, what he looked like, even what music he was into? Something?' Brady lightly prompted, desperate for the slightest clue.

Evie slowly shook her head.

'He'd made her swear to keep quiet.'

'But you were her best friend? Surely she would tell you?'

She bit her lip as she concentrated on bringing up some music on her iPhone.

'Evie, you must know something. I mean, even your class-mates knew that Sophie was seeing an older guy?'

'Yeah? So? Sophie saw a lot of guys,' she casually stated as she continued to play with her iPhone.

Brady patiently watched her.

'Evie?' Brady questioned, trying to get her attention.

She purposely ignored him and continued to mess around with her phone.

'For fuck's sake, Evie! This isn't a game. Someone murdered Sophie for Christ's sake! And there's a good chance it was this man she was seeing! So put the bloody phone down will you?'

Brady's gut instinct had told him this was no Shane McGuire they were dealing with; it was definitely a man. The sexual acts detailed on her blog told him as much.

Hot, salty tears trickled down Evie's mascara-smudged cheeks.

He immediately kicked himself realising that he'd upset her. But he'd wanted to shake her until she understood that drinking and having sex at fifteen wasn't a laugh. Depending on the roll of the die, the price could be higher than you ever anticipated.

'Look, I'm sorry . . . I didn't mean it,' Brady apologised.

She didn't answer him. Instead she continued to stare at her phone.

He waited, giving her time to calm down.

'Did you know about the tattoo she had?'

Evie nodded, refusing to look at him.

'When did she get it done?'

''Bout a month ago. I thought she was stupid doing it,' she whispered.

'Why?' asked Brady, surprised she wouldn't have thought it was cool.

'Cos she did it because of him.'

'What do you mean?'

'He had one,' Evie answered reluctantly. 'She told me her tattoo was identical to his but a smaller version. Apparently his covers most of his back.'

Brady shifted forward in his seat. This was the most detail they had so far on the victim's boyfriend.

'Do you know where she went to get it done?'

Evie shook her head.

'Some place in town was all she said.'

Brady nodded. It wouldn't take them long to track down the tattoo parlour now that he knew where to start looking.

'Why did Sophie ring you?' he eventually asked.

She looked at him, startled.

'We know from a record of the calls she made that she rang you at 12.51 am?'

More tears flowed down her cheeks.

'She . . . she rang me because she'd lost her keys. She thought she'd left them in my bedroom. But she hadn't . . .'

He watched as she wiped her face roughly with her dressing gown. As she did, Brady suddenly caught sight of her wrists. They were covered in neatly wrapped bandages.

She caught him staring and abruptly pulled her sleeves down over her hands.

'Evie?'

'She . . . she asked if she could sleep at my house . . .' she stuttered, trying to ignore his penetrating gaze.

Brady was concerned. It was more than clear that she wasn't really coping with Sophie's murder.

'She was scared of him . . .'

'Who? Who was Sophie scared of?' Brady asked, suddenly realising the significance of what was being said.

'Her step-dad . . . Paul.'

'Why?'

Evie shook her head as more tears trailed down her face.

'Evie?'

'He used to touch her . . . You know?' she conceded reluctantly.

The allegation matched his gut feeling about Simmons. Together with the autopsy findings and Evie's evidence, Simmons' problems had only just begun.

'I . . . I promised I would never say anything. Sophie didn't want anyone to know . . .' Evie mumbled, scared.

'Things have changed, Evie,' Brady reassured her. 'Sophie would understand.'

Evie looked at him with eyes filled with distrust.

'What did she tell you?' he asked gently.

'She never talked about it. Only when she was really pissed . . .' She suddenly faltered, remembering. 'Then . . . then she'd go crazy. Didn't care what she did. Didn't worry about getting hurt or even . . .'

Brady waited for her to continue.

'He knew about the tattoo . . .' she suddenly stated. 'Went off it when he saw it but he couldn't do anything about it, you know?'

Brady nodded, realising what she meant. With clothes on no one would ever have known Sophie had the tattoo.

'He was still . . .?' Brady gently asked.

'What do you think? She was desperate to get away from him. That's why she would stay out so late, you know? Just to avoid him. And she'd stay behind at school just in case he'd got back from work early. She'd wait until she knew her mum was definitely home.'

Brady nodded.

'Thanks for telling me that, Evie. I know it must have been really difficult for you.'

Brady mentally prepared himself for asking the question that had been plaguing him.

'Evie? Why would Sophie have your father's mobile number?'

She looked at him blankly.

'Why?' he repeated.

She shook her head numbly as fresh tears welled up in her eyes.

'I . . . I . . . said that she could ring Dad if she got scared. So . . . so he could go pick her up. I knew he was at work last night and . . . and that he could stop, you know . . .?' Evie faltered as more tears fell down her cheeks.

Brady breathed a sigh of relief.

He had needed to hear that. He had to admit that he'd been thrown when Conrad had shown him the logged calls and Matthews' number had shown up as the last number called by the victim. It hadn't made any sense then. But now it did.

'You see she was up a height when she rang me. She was really worried about going home without her keys . . . He used to get angry with her . . . I mean really angry and then if she didn't . . . you know?'

Brady nodded in response.

'It's my fault,' muttered Evie.

'No, Evie—' Brady began.

She turned and stared at him.

'You don't understand. If it hadn't been for me it would never have happened. Instead of just letting her come back to mine I . . . I told her to stand up to him . . . to tell him . . .' She shook her head as tears licked their way down her cheeks.

'Evie, believe me, what happened to Sophie had nothing to do with you or what you said. It would have happened regardless,' Brady reassured her.

Brady looked at her, waiting for an acknowledgement. But she had already forgotten him and had her earphones on, listening to music as she wrote a text.

*

He walked into the kitchen and saw Kate standing by the window, arms folded, blankly staring out into the darkness.

'She told you then?' she asked without turning.

'Yes,' answered Brady.

'She's scared, Jack. She's still just a little girl . . .'

'I know.'

Brady waited, not knowing how to say it.

'I saw her wrists,' he finally said.

Kate kept her back to him as she nodded.

'She didn't realise I'd come back. I walked in on her . . .' Kate said, her voice trembling. 'That's when I forced her to talk. To tell me what would frighten her so much that she'd harm herself.'

Brady didn't answer.

'I mean, Christ? Can it get any worse?'

'Do you want me to organise someone to talk to Evie? To help her with . . . well, you know?' Brady gently suggested.

Kate spun round and looked him at him with blazing green eyes. She was angry, but he didn't know if it was with him or the situation.

'What's going on, Jack?'

'What?'

'All of this?' She theatrically gestured to the room. 'For fuck's sake! What's really going on here? Why am I hiding out in your house for Christ's sake?'

'You know why. Jimmy's got himself into a bit of trouble

230

and I'm just looking out for you until he sorts it,' Brady answered.

'At what price? Or is this just you on another Jack Brady crusade?'

Brady looked at her, thrown.

'No,' he muttered, hurt. 'Jimmy and I go back. You know that.'

'I know Jimmy's in it up to his neck, that's what I do know. And that DCI Gates is desperate to find him. But what I can't figure out is what part you play in all of this?'

'I owe Jimmy, that's all,' Brady quietly replied.

'How?'

'He got rid of someone for me.'

Kate looked at him, surprised.

'What did Jimmy do?' she asked after some deliberation.

'I never asked,' muttered Brady. 'He just dealt with it.'

Kate looked at Brady questioningly. They both knew what Matthews was capable of.

*

'Problem?' Conrad asked as Brady climbed into the car.

'For Paul Simmons,' Brady answered.

'Why?' Conrad asked, realising from Brady's expression that something was wrong.

'He needs to be brought into the station for questioning.'

Conrad looked at him.

'I know. I know, I'm going to look like a real fucking bastard but I don't give a damn.'

'Nothing new there then, sir,' Conrad stated.

Chapter Thirty-Seven

Brady leaned across the table and looked Simmons straight in the eye.

'So, what's it going to be? Are you going to tell me the truth or are you going to keep feeding me the same bullshit?'

'I'm not taking this any more!' Simmons snapped as he stood up.

'I'm not done with you yet,' Brady answered as he pushed him back down.

'I'll have you done for assault, Detective!'

'It's Detective Inspector, sir,' Brady pointed out.

'You've got nothing on me,' Simmons stated defiantly.

'I wouldn't be so sure, sir,' replied Brady.

'I'll make damned sure Chief Superintendent O'Donnell and the press hear about this!' he threatened.

He turned accusingly to Conrad.

'You got me in here on the grounds that this was just an informal chat. Do you even know what time it is? It's nearly 11 pm for God's sake!'

'I'm afraid that the situation has changed somewhat, sir,' Conrad replied.

'I've already been here an hour. How long are you planning on holding me?'

'Given the gravity of the investigation, we have the right to detain you for up to twenty-four hours without legal representation,' Conrad answered.

'I came here in good faith. If I had known that I was going to be treated as a suspect then I would have brought a lawyer,' Simmons objected.

Simmons then turned to Brady.

'And you,' he said as he narrowed his eyes. 'Whatever you've got better be bloody good or you'll find yourself out of a job.'

Brady opened the file beside him and pulled out sheets containing printed downloads of the victim's blog.

'Doesn't quite match what you told me this morning. Does it, sir?'

Simmons froze.

He looked at the words and the photographs as he shook his head in dismay.

'Not only did she drink, she took drugs and had casual sex repeatedly. But then, you'd know all about that, wouldn't you, sir?'

'You bastard,' Simmons muttered thickly.

'So what happened then, sir? It's late, the door bell goes; it's her. She's drunk and she's lost her keys. You start raging and she gets scared?'

'You're one fucking sick bastard.'

Brady leaned towards him.

'What happened next?' he asked slowly and clearly. 'What did you do to her to make her run from you?'

Brady paused as he stared at Simmons' contorted face.

'And then you found her, didn't you? Hiding in the farm-house ruins behind your house? And then . . . well, we know the rest.'

'Goddamn you, you sick son of a bitch!'

'Did she threaten to tell? Was that it?'

Simmons shook his head.

'No . . . no . . . I don't know what you're talking about.'

'Or had you found out that she was having sex with her new boyfriend?' Brady questioned. 'I imagine that must have made you furious? Enough to—'

'I didn't do it!'

'No?' Brady asked, unconvinced. 'We've found the stone that was used in the attack, sir. It's only a matter of time until the lab finds your fingerprints and DNA.'

Brady scrutinised him.

'Maybe you will be needing that lawyer after all?'

'I'm telling you I didn't murder her!'

'You were fucking her though, weren't you?' Brady asked quietly.

Simmons' lip trembled.

'I have a witness, sir, whose statement supports the autopsy findings.'

Simmons' face drained as his jaw hung slack.

Brady nodded.

'Extreme trauma and scarring was found in and around the victim's vagina and perineum. The autopsy states that the trauma is suggestive of sexual abuse presumed to have started as far back as when the victim was eleven.'

Simmons didn't move.

'How old was Sophie when you and her mother got together?'

Simmons remained deathly silent, his face pale.

'Let me remind you, shall I?' questioned Brady. 'She was eleven, sir.'

Simmons shook his head.

'No . . . no . . . this is a mistake. I want to see my solicitor.'

'Interview terminated at 11.07 pm,' Brady instructed.

Chapter Thirty-Eight

It was giro day in The Fat Ox. Every second Friday of the month and the pub would be heaving from lunchtime straight through to chucking-out time.

'What'll it be, Jack?' a small blonde woman in her late forties yelled over to him.

'Pint of the usual.'

After the interview with Simmons he needed a drink. He'd left Simmons in one of the holding cells waiting for his solicitor to turn up. Given the fact it was eleven-thirty on a Friday night, Brady reckoned Simmons could find himself sweating for quite a few hours.

He looked around for Conrad but couldn't see him. They had come to see The Clashed. Not that Brady had particularly wanted to, but he knew they had to check out exactly why the victim had the band's flyer for the gig that night.

'Make that two pints and a double Scotch,' a deep voice grunted from behind.

'You sleazy bugger! How do you always manage to turn up when I'm at the bar?' Brady asked, smiling as he turned round. 'It better be worth it.'

'Isn't it always?' Rubenfeld said as he wiped his sweaty forehead with his fat, sausage fingers.

'Ahh! You don't know how much I need this. It's been a bloody hell of a day!' Rubenfeld grunted as he knocked back the short.

'Tell me about it,' Brady agreed as he took a much-needed drink of his own cold, dripping pint before settling the bill.

'One for yourself,' he added as he handed a twenty over. Nowadays a tenner wouldn't even cover it.

Rubenfeld rubbed his two days' worth of scraggy stubble as he scowled at Brady.

'That bitch Harriet Jacobs is after your blood. What have you done to piss her off, Jack? You haven't tried to shag her, have you? Bloody hell, Jack, when will you learn to keep it in your pants?' Rubenfeld goaded with a sleazy smile.

'I don't know her,' Brady answered uncomfortably, accepting that his brief affair with DC Simone Henderson would follow him for the rest of his career. That and his infamous days before Claudia as a bit of a player.

Ordinarily Rubenfeld's comment wouldn't have bothered him, but this time it had hit a nerve. He still felt disgusted with himself over Sleeping Beauty.

Rubenfeld ran his fat fingers through his short, receding black hair.

'Well, someone wants you and Jimmy off the force, Jack. If I was you, I'd bloody find out who before it's too late. I did hear something that might interest you,' Rubenfeld throatily offered.

'Yeah?'

'Word is Madley wants Matthews as good as dead. That's why he's disappeared. Matthews may be one hard nut but this time he's gone too far.'

Brady didn't react.

Rubenfeld shook his head, aware that Brady knew more than he was letting on.

'Be careful, Jack. You don't know who you're dealing with here.'

Brady didn't answer.

'Got to go, people to see and all that crap!' Rubenfeld swiftly concluded as he drained his pint.

Brady watched as Rubenfeld pushed his way through the crowded pub towards the doors. The Clashed suddenly kicked off, filling the place with angry lyrics. His face darkened as he listened to the singer's anarchistic words. Why, he questioned, would a fifteen-year-old schoolgirl be interested in a seventies punk tribute band?

'I fought the law and the law won, I fought the law and the law won,' screamed the lead singer.

He was no Joe Strummer, but he had energy concluded Brady as he twisted his neck to get a look. But all he could make out was the drummer and bass guitarist through the throbbing crowd.

'Jack!' a high-pitched voice trilled out, followed by a burst of excited giggles.

Brady's stomach turned. That voice was bad news.

'Jack?'

He turned to see Sleeping Beauty stood before him, self-conscious and girlish. He felt sick as he tried to remember what they had gotten up to in the early hours of that morning.

'Why didn't you ring me?' she asked, a hint of vulnerability in her voice.

Brady cursed himself. In the cold light of sobriety she was definitely only about twenty, if that.

'Look, something's come up and . . .' Brady began.

He broke off when he saw the disbelief spread across her face.

'You bastard!' she replied angrily. 'That was your wife and daughter, wasn't it?'

Stunned, Brady shook his head.

'I told you my wife's left me.'

He had never considered how Kate and Evie turning up would have looked to Sleeping Beauty.

'I thought that . . . last night?' she faltered as her deep, brown eyes searched his for confirmation.

'The timing isn't good right now,' Brady lamely answered.

She bit her bottom lip. 'Maybe I'll see you around then?'

He could hear the hurt in her voice but knew there was nothing else he could say.

She turned and walked back to her friends.

He knew she would think he was a bastard and she was right. He decided to make himself scarce and pushed his way through to the front of the crowd.

Brady suddenly forgot all about Sleeping Beauty as he stared in disbelief at The Clashed's lead singer.

Ben Ellison uneasily caught Brady's eye as he screamed to an enraptured crowd:

'*Should I stay or should I go now?*'

Brady leaned against the wall, deciding that maybe it was worth sticking around to watch the band after all.

Chapter Thirty-Nine

'What did you think then?' Ellison asked hoarsely as Brady approached him.

He had just finished for the night and his pores were oozing a mixture of sweat and adrenalin.

'Surprised you went ahead with the gig,' Brady replied, ignoring his question. 'Considering Sophie was one of your students.'

Ellison ran his hand through his stylishly messy blond hair as he considered Brady's remark.

'Had no choice. Couldn't let the band down, could I?' he replied with a casual shrug.

Brady realised that he wasn't the only one interested in Ellison. A group of girls were excitedly and drunkenly talking with the other band members while they waited for the lead singer. He couldn't help but notice that Sleeping Beauty was one of them.

'Why do you think Sophie had a flyer for tonight's gig?'

For a moment Ellison seemed thrown.

'Don't know. She could have got it from anywhere,' he answered, shrugging. 'I leave them lying around. In the staff room, sixth form, even the cafeteria. Anywhere where I think they'll get noticed. It's no secret that I play in a band, Detective Inspector,' Ellison replied.

Yeah, I bet it's not, Brady mused as he watched Ellison's pretty boy face.

Something just didn't feel right about him.

'So, do you get a lot of your students coming to watch you perform then?' Brady asked as he gestured over at the giggling groupies desperate to catch Ellison's eye.

'Mainly sixth formers,' Ellison answered. 'Sometimes Year Twelves come along.'

Brady's expression conveyed his disapproval.

'It's not my problem to police them, that's up to you lot,' Ellison pointed out.

'Don't you have some moral duty as their teacher?'

'Come on, Detective Inspector, what sixteen-year-old doesn't drink? I'd rather have them getting pissed in a pub than in one of the local parks. I've heard what goes on down at Whitley Park at the weekend. Believe me, a pub's a much safer environment.'

Brady didn't say anything. He knew Ellison had a point.

'Anyway, you lot know all about underage drinking. How often do you carry out raids on The Grapevine?' Ellison questioned.

Brady shrugged. Again he had a point.

The Grapevine had become a constant headache for Whitley Bay Police. The pub was part of the line-up of sleazy, garish bars that made up North Parade. The Grapevine attracted the men who wanted easy sex with very young girls. The average underage drinker regularly picked up during police raids was aged between thirteen and fifteen.

Brady blamed Councillor Macmillan for the dive that Whitley Bay had taken; empty promises of regeneration were constantly doled out to the residents while the council lined their pockets with beer money from underage drinkers. Most of the local residents wanted the pubs and nightclubs in Whitley Bay closed down. But Brady knew that would never happen; the council wasn't interested in serving the local residents, only making sure the revenue from the pubs and clubs kept rolling in.

'Did Sophie ever come to one of your gigs?' Brady suddenly asked.

'Maybe? As a teacher you hear things. Things you'd rather not know if you get my drift?'

Brady didn't and his expression said as much.

'Look, I know most of the kids over the age of fourteen are regularly drinking and having sex. It's just the way things are now. They grow up faster and with that comes a price,' Ellison suggested. 'Come on, Detective, you're a man of the world. You can't tell me you don't know what's going on out there.'

'Are you saying that was what Sophie was?'

Ellison looked at Brady.

'What do you think? The girl had a reputation. Let's say I heard a lot concerning Sophie Washington.'

'Like what exactly?'

'That she drank, took a bit of dope and had sex. That was her thing, sex. And from what I heard she was shit hot, if you know what I mean?' Ellison said as he raised his eyebrows at Brady.

Brady felt sickened by Ellison's comments.

'Why didn't you mention this when I saw you this afternoon?'

Ellison shrugged. 'There was a lady present,' he said, winking.

Brady couldn't shake the hunch he had about Ellison.

The guy was a jerk. But the fact that Brady wanted to floor him wasn't enough to bring him in for questioning. He had no evidence to substantiate his feeling about Ellison, other than a flyer and a school holiday photograph. Brady had no choice but to let it go.

He turned and walked towards the doors. As he pushed past the group of girls he caught Sleeping Beauty's arm. She turned, surprised, and very drunk.

'Steer clear of the lead singer. He's just looking for an easy lay,' Brady warned.

She gave him an incredulous look before throwing back her thick, dark head of hair and laughing.

'I'm just looking out for you, that's all.'

'Yeah? Like you did last night?' she asked with a contemptuous smile.

'I'm sorry,' Brady apologised.

'Don't be,' she stated acerbically.

'Look . . . I'm really—' Brady uneasily began.

'I get it!' she interrupted. 'You're not interested, so why don't you just fuck off?'

Brady made his way out of the pub awkwardly, ignoring the shrill laughter directed at him.

He waited outside for Conrad to join him. He needed some fresh air to clear his head. He slowly dragged on a cigarette, grateful to be alone. Things were winding down inside. Last orders had been called and the punters were more desperate for that last pint than they were for a tab.

He turned as he heard the doors of The Fat Ox open behind him. Conrad's reserved figure appeared.

'Where were you?' Brady questioned.

'Looking for you,' Conrad replied. 'Saw your girlfriend in there,' he added.

'She's not my girlfriend.'

'That explains why she's all over the lead singer then.'

Conrad's words hung heavy in the cold night air. Brady stood for a moment as he dragged deeply on his cigarette. It helped ground him. Otherwise, he would have found himself going back inside and rearranging pretty boy's face.

'When we get back to the station I want you to run every check you can on Ben Ellison. I don't trust that bastard.'

'Sir? We're already holding Simmons for questioning!'

'But that doesn't mean we stop looking for the boyfriend the victim wrote about on her blog. Does it?'

'You don't seriously believe her form tutor was having sex with her, do you?'

'Why not? Some bastard was.'

Chapter Forty

A loud rap at his office door forced Brady to snap out of his maudlin mood.

His run-in with Sleeping Beauty had made him take a long hard look at his life. The end result wasn't good. He hated what he'd become and couldn't quite figure out how he'd ended up at such a low point in his life.

'Simmons, sir,' Conrad began as he entered the room.

Brady looked at him.

'The lab results have come back . . . we've got nothing on him.'

'You what?'

'No legible prints could be found on the stone that was used on the victim. And as for the other DNA evidence Forensics found at the crime scene and on the victim . . . well . . . nothing matches with Simmons' DNA. Same with the hand and footprints.'

'Shit!' cursed Brady.

'The upshot is he's been released.'

'On whose bloody orders?' Brady demanded.

'Gates.'

'Shit,' said Brady. 'I take it Gates has read Evie Matthews' statement and the autopsy report?'

'Yes sir. But Simmons' solicitor pointed out it's her word against his client's. We have no other evidence against Simmons to substantiate her claim.'

'Apart from the autopsy report.'

'Yes, but as Simmons' solicitor stated, we have no proof that Simmons was responsible for that.'

'But what about the fact that he has no alibi?'

Conrad shook his head.

'Simmons' solicitor is good and Gates knows it. I don't know what she said but she's backed Gates into a corner.'

Brady sighed wearily, exhausted.

He didn't like the way this day was starting out. They were less than an hour into it and already he wanted it to end.

'Why the bloody hell has it taken so long to get hold of those?' Brady asked as he gestured at the files Conrad was holding.

'Adamson, sir,' Conrad answered simply as he laid them on Brady's desk. 'Bureaucracy I think he said.'

'I should have expected as much from him,' muttered Brady.

He shook his head as he picked up the top file. It was after one-thirty in the morning and he still had a lot of reading to get through before he could even consider catching up on some sleep.

*

Brady closed the final medical file on Sophie Washington and reached for his BlackBerry.

'Conrad? My office.'

He massaged his pounding forehead as he waited for Conrad. It was well after two and he was running on empty.

Brady held up the files for Conrad as he walked into the office.

'If you see Adamson before I do, tell him I'll shove bureaucracy up his arse. I should have had these hours ago.'

'What did you find out?' Conrad asked.

'Nothing that I didn't expect to find. Seems that from about the age of eleven Sophie Washington suffered from migraines. But the doctor diagnosed them as "emotional migraines",' Brady explained.

Conrad frowned.

'Meaning that something was really stressing her. She'd been having them on and off for the past four years and not surprisingly, she suffered a serious bout of them around the time her father committed suicide.'

'Do you think the migraines were connected to Simmons?' Conrad asked.

'Does the Pope shit in the woods?' questioned Brady. 'Bloody useless sods!' Brady muttered as he gestured to the files. 'If they'd done their job then I wouldn't be sat here now.'

Conrad looked at him.

'She was offered counselling when her father died,' explained Brady. 'Which she started, but from the files here it seems she was signed off after the third session. The counsellor noted that Sophie's home life was causing her a lot of anxiety, but she put that down to her father's suicide and her mother's recent marriage to Simmons, who Sophie openly admitted she hated. The counsellor took that admission at face value and presumed that it was because her mother was seen to be replacing her father, who she idealised, with Simmons.'

Brady shook his head.

'All too bloody middle-class, that's the problem here. You know if she'd been dragged up on the Ridges the counsellor would have had a whole different approach to Sophie. But no, instead she sat back and heard what she wanted to hear. Nice middle-class family, straight-A student with a few emotional problems. Fairly typical given her father's suicide. Add in that she doesn't get on with her mum's new husband, and there you go. Nothing to really worry about. Just a case of typical middle-class teenage angst.'

'Yes sir,' agreed Conrad, knowing not to question Brady in the middle of a tirade.

'She was crying out for help, but no one was listening to her, Conrad. Her father bailed out on her by committing suicide, her mother chose to drown out her suspicions with alcohol and finally her doctor and counsellor literally accepted what she told them. She was a smart girl. She told them what they wanted to hear, too ashamed, too guilt-ridden and scared to admit to them what was really going on in her life,' Brady explained. 'When she really needed help, there was no one around. Surely if they had made that extra effort with her, then maybe she wouldn't have ended up in the morgue.'

Sophie's short, tragic life had really got to him.

'No one really listened to her.'

Conrad nodded.

'All it would have taken was one person in her life to notice . . . to really notice what was going on . . .'

He looked up at Conrad who was stood, patiently waiting for Brady to finish his diatribe.

'I'll get him, Conrad. Mark my words, I'll get the bastard that did this to her,' Brady threatened, as he looked at her medical files. 'He may be roaming free but I'm not done looking for him yet.'

Brady took a mouthful of lukewarm coffee before he realised that Conrad was waiting to tell him something.

'Go on then?'

'You know you wanted me to run some checks on Ben Ellison?' Conrad questioned.

Brady nodded, still distracted by the victim's medical files.

'He actually lives five minutes from The Beacon and a few minutes from Potter's Farm.'

'You're kidding me?' Brady spluttered.

'Gets better,' Conrad added. 'We received a call that might interest you.'

'Go on,' Brady instructed with a degree of cynicism. Since *The Northern Echo* had increased the reward money to £50,000 they had had hundreds of crank calls.

'Caller works at The Beacon pub and was in on Thursday night. She said that she was certain she saw a girl come in who looked similar to the victim.'

'Didn't Harvey and Kodovesky take statements from everyone who worked that shift?'

'Yes sir. But what threw her were the victim's clothes and make-up. They made her look much older than the school photo we put out. So she kept quiet. But the more she's thought about it afterwards, the more she became convinced it was her.'

'What time?'

'She said it was definitely after 10.30 pm.'

'Did she meet anyone in there?'

Conrad nodded.

'Yes sir, this is the part that will interest you.'

'Go on?'

'The man described matches Ben Ellison.'

Brady felt a rush of blood as he digested the words. Nothing could have prepared him for this.

'You can tell me the rest later. Go get the car. I'll meet you outside,' ordered Brady as he grabbed his coat.

*

As Brady came out of the station his eyes were fixed on the trouble at the top of the street. A group of drunken louts were aggressively mouthing off at one another.

So much so he didn't see the lingering, dishevelled figure until it was too late.

'You got a tab on ye, son? For old time sakes?' asked the old drunk as he staggered towards him.

Brady felt his body tense up as he instinctively clenched his fists. He mutely shook his head, unable to even look at him.

'What about giving me some money for a drink then, eh?' the short shabby figure rasped holding out his grime-encrusted, gnarled hand.

Repulsed, Brady backed away towards Conrad's waiting car.

'What's yer fuckin' problem? Too good to talk to me, eh? Is that it? Think yer better than me now, do ye? I've been waiting for ye to show!'

Brady yanked open the car door keeping his back to the old man.

'Fuckin' look at me, will ye? Ye bastard I'm talking to you!' the old drunk shouted.

Brady slammed the door shut just as an empty vodka bottle exploded against the passenger window.

Conrad picked up the car radio.

'Just drive. We haven't got time to piss about with this.'

'Easy to say when it's not your car, sir,' Conrad stated as he revved the engine.

'Fuckin' bastard! I'm not going away! You hear me?' shouted the staggering old man at they drove away.

'You all right, sir?' asked Conrad as he turned and looked at him.

Brady realised he was covered in a cold, clammy sweat. He looked at his hands and saw that they were trembling uncontrollably.

'Yeah, it's nothing,' answered Brady.

The last thing he could tell Conrad was the truth. He shook his head, trying to get rid of the old man's ravaged face. It was a face that he recognised from years ago. One he had never expected to see again.

Chapter Forty-One

'Why am I not surprised that he's not home?' Brady cynically asked.

Conrad didn't risk stating the obvious.

They both knew whose bed Ellison was sleeping in.

'Can't we just leave, sir?' Conrad asked. 'Let that lot bring Ellison in when he shows,' he suggested, gesturing towards the four plain-clothes coppers parked nearby. 'We both could do with a few hours' sleep.'

Brady shook his head.

'No, I want to be here to greet the bugger!'

Conrad reluctantly turned the car engine on in an attempt to defy the bitter northern November wind whipping up outside.

'Look, sir. It's highly probable he's gone back with your . . .' Conrad was about to say it and stopped himself. 'The girl who was at your place yesterday morning,' Conrad corrected.

'So?'

A heavy, awkward silence filled the car.

They had already checked out the other band members' whereabouts. Ellison wasn't with them. The only information they had was that he had gone on with a girl fitting Sleeping Beauty's description.

Brady felt sick at the thought of him with Sleeping Beauty. Not to mention the danger that she could be in right now. And there was nothing he could do about it.

'We could try and find him,' Conrad suggested.

'No,' muttered Brady.

'But we both know where he's likely to be. Surely anything's better than being sat waiting in the freezing cold for him to show? The sooner we bring him in for questioning, the better for all concerned.'

'We wait here,' Brady firmly repeated.

Conrad turned and looked at him. Brady's face was unrelenting.

'What about if we send someone else to check whether he's at her address?'

Brady shook his head as he stared daggers at Ellison's house.

'Why not, sir?' Conrad asked.

'I don't know it,' Brady muttered, refusing to look at Conrad. 'I don't know where she lives.'

Conrad considered this.

'We can run a check on her name then, sir? That will bring her address up.'

Brady remained silent. His eyes now locked on the two unmarked police cars parked outside Ellison's house.

Conrad waited awkwardly.

'Oh shit,' he murmured, suddenly aware of why Brady wasn't forthcoming. He realised that Brady didn't even know her name.

'Do you really think I would be sat here if I knew where I could get hold of that son of a bitch? Do you?'

'I'm sorry, sir, I didn't realise. I just presumed that you would know her . . .' Conrad faltered.

Brady tensed up. The last thing he needed was Conrad's pity.

'Yeah? Well, now you know what kind of a bastard I am.'

He sighed heavily as he realised how much he'd fucked up his life. What made it worse was having Conrad sat next to him, presumably thinking exactly the same thing.

Brady fumbled in his jacket for cigarettes. His head was thumping again. He needed something to calm him down and take the edge off the pain. He shakily lit one.

Conrad automatically buzzed Brady's electric window down, sucking damp, chilling air into the car.

The stinging cold air slapped him hard in the face making him feel even more wretched.

He checked his watch; 3.30 am. He turned and looked at Conrad's tired, taut face. Conrad was right. it was point-less waiting for Ellison, the others could handle it. And if Ellison did show up, there was a chance that Brady would end up killing him. Better to put some distance between his fists and Ellison's pretty boy face. After a few hours' sleep he'd be able to think straight and forget about Sleeping Beauty. Just now, he couldn't stop torturing himself with thoughts about what Ellison could be doing to her and there was nothing he could do to protect her. Add to that that he was sleep-deprived, in pain and freezing. Not a good combination.

'All right, Conrad. Let's go.'

'Yes sir,' answered Conrad, relieved.

'Drop me back at the station and then go home and get some sleep. You look like crap.'

'You don't look so great yourself, sir.'

Brady sighed with a combination of exhaustion and defeat as Conrad pulled out from Thorntree Drive onto Earsdon Road. He needed to get his head down for a few hours and the battered couch in his office was starting to look inviting.

He closed his eyes just as his phone buzzed.

'Yeah?' he mumbled. 'Amelia?' Brady forced himself awake.

'Have you got him?'

'No,' muttered Brady. 'It seems he's sleeping in someone else's bed tonight. But we'll get him when he returns home in the morning.'

'Damn,' cursed Jenkins.

'My sentiments exactly,' replied Brady.

'I'm sorry, Jack. I feel really bad about this . . .'

'About what?' asked Brady.

'When we interviewed Ellison. I didn't see it . . .'

'Don't worry about it. You're just not as cynical about the world as I am. Anyway, we had nothing on him then,' Brady replied.

'But if I had taken you more seriously rather than thinking it was just your male ego being threatened, then another girl's life wouldn't be at risk,' admitted Jenkins.

Brady remained silent. He'd been thinking about nothing else. But to hear it verbalised made him feel sick.

'Jack? Are you still there?'

'Listen, Amelia, if anyone's to blame it's me. I left him in The Fat Ox chatting the girl up. If I'd only known . . .' Brady said, trying to ignore the horrible images going through his head.

*

When he got back to his office Jenkins was waiting for him.

'Here you go,' she offered as she handed him a mug with a generous measure of malt. 'You look like you need it.'

'Thanks,' he muttered, surprised but grateful for her company.

He drained his mug and then walked over to the couch. Jenkins carried the bottle of Scotch over and joined him.

'Refill?'

'What the hell, it's been a shit day,' he relented, holding out his mug for her.

He watched as Jenkins then poured herself a liberal measure.

'What kind of good time did Adamson show you then?' Brady asked.

'Don't,' replied Jenkins as she rested her head back against the couch.

Brady couldn't help but look at her. She was striking; even at 3.50 am. He watched as she closed her almond-shaped, dark brown eyes, sighing wearily. He was trying to ignore the fact that he was starting to enjoy her company and more than he wanted to admit.

'Remind me never to work with that man again!' she said.

'I tried to tell you,' Brady stated.

'Yeah, yeah . . . Don't fool yourself. You just didn't think I could handle myself in that stinking strip club. It had nothing to do with Adamson,' pointed out Jenkins.

Brady didn't reply. There was nothing he could say. Instead he watched her relaxing on his couch, in his office, drinking his Scotch. He wanted to ask why she was there, but knew if he did, she'd leave.

She opened her eyes and turned to him.

'Thank you.'

'What for?' Brady asked.

'For not being an arsehole like your colleague, DS Adamson,' she answered.

'Is that what you expect of me?'

'From what I know of you, Jack, what else should I expect?'

She was right; most of the time he had been an arsehole, at least where she was concerned. As his psychologist he hadn't given her a chance. He had been too scared that if she took him apart she would never be able to put him back together again.

'I take it Adamson must have really pissed you off?'

'You could say that. Well, technically, he didn't piss me off, as you say, but he did offend Trina McGuire.'

'What did he do to upset Shane's mam then? From what I remember of Trina it's normally the other way round,' Brady replied.

'Let's just say Adamson was asking a bit too much from her.'

'How so?'

'He treated her like a piece of shit,' Jenkins explained. 'Thought because of what she did he owned her. We asked her about the whereabouts of her son Shane, but she had no clue. Genuinely had no clue, you could tell. But Adamson wasn't having any of it. I don't know who he thought he was, but it wasn't acceptable.'

Brady took a drink. He knew he wasn't going to like whatever it was that Jenkins was about to tell him.

'After we'd finished questioning her about Shane's whereabouts, Adamson said he wanted a private word with Trina and told me to go wait in the car. So, I left the office and headed back through the bar. But you know when you have a bad feeling that something isn't right?' she asked as she looked at Brady.

He nodded.

'So, I went back to the office and opened the door which he'd closed behind me and there he was with Trina pinned against the wall, pants round his ankles, demanding that she suck him off or he'd start to make life difficult for her.'

Brady sighed. He wasn't surprised by what Jenkins had just told him. He'd heard the rumours that Adamson liked to play dirty which was why Brady wanted nothing to do with him.

'Adamson doesn't realise who he's dealing with when it comes to Trina McGuire. She'll make sure he pays for that stunt. And believe me, Amelia, if you walked in a few minutes later, either Adamson would have been rolling around in agony on the floor after Trina had kneed him in the balls or if he had forced her head down on him, then he would now be missing a big part of his manhood.'

Jenkins looked at Brady quizzically.

'I know Trina from old, and when a punter gets a bit too heavy, like Adamson, she's been known to fight back. And when she fights, it's dirty. One guy nearly lost half his dick by shoving it down her throat,' Brady stated. 'Trina has a shit life, but at least the sleazy bastards who go into the Hole know not to touch her, unlike that idiot Adamson. She's a pretty little thing, and so she's had to learn to handle herself.'

'If you like that kind of thing, I suppose,' Jenkins uncomfortably answered.

'She's not as hot as she used to be. The drugs and booze have had their effect. But in a shit place like the Hole, she

258

still turns heads. Like I said though, she has a reputation, so everyone knows they can look but they can't touch. And until now, no one's dared.'

Brady looked at Jenkins.

'I wish you'd waited a couple more minutes, then Adamson would have got what he deserved.'

'I'll be sure to remember that the next time I think a woman's in trouble,' answered Jenkins stiffly.

Brady shook his head at Jenkins.

'Trina isn't like other women. She can't afford to be,' Brady stated. 'So, what did Adamson do when you caught him with his trousers down?' he asked.

'What do you think? He went limp with embarrassment, pulled his trousers up and stormed out the office.'

'Bet the drive back to the station was fun,' Brady replied.

'Not really, the arrogant son of a bitch completely blanked what had happened and started talking about bringing Trina McGuire in for withholding information.'

'Yeah, that sounds like Adamson,' Brady said, sighing. 'What are you going to do? Report him?'

'I don't know yet,' she quietly answered.

Brady nodded. There was an unspoken code of loyalty in the force. And if you were going to report a colleague for misconduct then you had to be absolutely certain that you were prepared to pay the price. Brady knew that Jenkins would be uncomfortably aware of the fact that Adamson was well-liked, particularly by Gates.

He drained his mug and then leaned back against the couch. He shut his eyes, enjoying the closeness of Jenkins' body as she relaxed into him.

He felt her hand brush against his leg as she moved closer

into him. Even though he had his eyes shut, he could feel her staring at him.

'Are you sure you're going to be all right today?' Jenkins asked gently.

'Why not?' he asked as he opened his eyes.

She was staring at him intently.

'You know why,' she answered.

Brady shook his head, refusing to even acknowledge what she was talking about.

She had read the files from his childhood, files that had lain untouched for years. Jenkins knew more about his past than anyone else, aside from two people, one of whom was Jimmy Matthews. Even Claudia wasn't fully aware of his background.

'Come on, Jack, this is me you're talking to. Thirty years ago to this exact day you witnessed your mother being murdered. It's obvious it's had an effect on you—'

'Isn't that meant to be confidential? Doctor–patient crap?' Brady abruptly interrupted.

'It's still confidential,' answered Jenkins quietly.

'Yeah, but you're not my shrink any more,' Brady replied coldly.

His mouth was dry and he was starting to feel caught out. She had lured him into a false sense of security and then trapped him.

'I'm not asking as your doctor, I'm asking as your friend.'

'Is that what you are? A friend?' Brady sceptically asked.

'I don't know . . .' she whispered as she stared into his troubled, dark brown eyes.

She searched his eyes, wanting an answer.

Brady suddenly came to his senses and stood up.

She looked at him, confused.

He didn't say anything. He couldn't. All he knew was that he needed some fresh air. He resisted the urge to grab his coat and just walk out.

'Jack?' Jenkins questioned, startled by his sudden reaction.

Brady looked at her and shook his head.

'I can't do this,' he stated, gesturing at the Scotch on the floor beside her.

Jenkins nodded. She knew exactly what Brady was referring to, she didn't need him to point it out.

'I need to get some sleep,' Brady reasoned.

Jenkins stood up and smoothed down her dress.

'Thanks for the drink,' she said as she picked up her coat and bag.

Brady watched silently as she put her coat on, wishing there was something more he could say.

'You sure you'll be all right on your own?'

He shrugged.

'Why wouldn't I be?'

She didn't answer. She didn't need to. As Brady's psychologist, she knew that because of his past he couldn't handle emotional intimacy. Her dark brown eyes said it all, they both knew that their professional relationship had just crossed the line.

Chapter Forty-Two

Brady pushed his plate away. Ordinarily, a bacon and egg stottie was the only way to kick-start a bad day. But today wasn't like any other bad day. It was worse, much worse.

He took a mouthful of black, bitter coffee as he looked around the decrepit basement cafeteria. It was long due an overhaul. The red, chipped laminated sixties tables had seen better times, as had Brady. He looked at the barred windows. The grey, drizzling day bleakly called out to him to make a move.

It was only 8.36 am and he felt exhausted. He had had less than three hours' sleep. Disturbed sleep at that. The old drunk who had accosted him earlier had troubled him more than he wanted to admit. And when he finally did fall into a restless slumber, it was only to be beset by nightmares about the old drunk.

Brady rubbed his tired face. His rough stubble caught him by surprise. He needed to straighten himself out. He knew that at some point he'd be facing Gates, if not the press, and he needed to look halfway decent.

But he couldn't go home. Not with Kate there.

He had arranged for a patrol car to drive by every half

hour during the night to ward off Madley's henchmen. But when he had called Kate earlier, she had made it clear that she couldn't be bought off with a patrol car. She wanted Matthews and was convinced that Brady was protecting him. Brady had tried his best to persuade her that he was as much in the dark about Matthews' whereabouts as she was, but she wasn't accepting it.

The conversation had ended badly. Enough for him to want to keep out of her way for a while. He couldn't blame her for being angry; a lot had happened in the last twenty-four hours and he still had no answers.

Brady always kept a razor and clean clothes at work for unexpected situations like this. As soon as he had finished his coffee his next visit would be to the dilapidated shower rooms hidden in the basement. He had no choice; he stank from the crap he'd been dealing with for the past thirty hours. And there was still more crap to deal with before the day really got going.

But at least they had Ellison in custody, albeit still drunk. He had rolled home at 7 am. From what Brady had heard Ellison had got quite a shock when CID showed up.

But Brady was painfully aware that Sleeping Beauty spending the night with Ellison hadn't exactly helped his judgement. And in the cold light of day he was now wondering whether he had been over-zealous in dragging Ellison in? He already had Gates questioning his decision to bring Simmons in. But Brady knew it was more than male pride where Ellison was concerned. He had a photo and a flyer with his gig circled in red. That and a barmaid stating that she had seen someone of his description with the victim hours before she was murdered.

Brady was now waiting for news on Ellison's DNA and

prints to see whether they matched the forensic evidence found at the crime scene. And he also had Jed, their computer forensics officer, searching Ellison's laptop and desktop computers that would tie him to the victim.

Brady's phone rang.

'Yeah?' he answered.

'It's him all right,' answered Conrad.

'Are you sure?'

'Yes, sir. He definitely has the same tattoo as the victim covering his back.'

'Thank fuck,' said Brady, relieved. 'All right Conrad, as soon as the bugger's sober let me know.'

Brady disconnected the call. He forced himself to move, aware that it wouldn't be long before Ellison was clear-headed enough to interview.

*

'Who are you trying to impress?' Harvey laughed as he took in Brady's clean-shaven face and change of clothes.

For once, Brady was wearing a shirt and a suit. It was the only change of clothes he had at the station in case he suddenly had to give a press conference.

Brady gave him the finger before going into his office.

He knew Harvey was talking about Jenkins. He was sure half the station would have been talking about them by now. It wouldn't have gone undetected that she had been in his office with him until well after four in the morning.

'Touched a nerve have I, Jack?' Harvey called out after him jovially. 'By the way, you don't happen to know where Dr Jenkins is, do you?' he laughed.

Brady slammed his office door shut.

He pulled out his BlackBerry as he limped over to his desk.

He sat down and waited for her to pick up.

'Amelia?'

'Yes?' answered Jenkins.

'It's Jack,' added Brady.

'I know,' she answered.

'Where are you?' Brady asked.

'At work,' she evenly replied.

'I haven't seen you around,' Brady stated.

'You wouldn't. I'm in my own office dealing with my own backlog of work.'

'Is that it? You're off the investigation?' Brady asked, trying to hide his disappointment.

'I wouldn't have thought you needed me any more. You've got Ben Ellison, so there's nothing more I can do. Anyway, I've got a pile of work I need to catch up on.'

'I see,' said Brady.

'Look, Jack . . . this is . . . well . . . it's becoming difficult . . . for both of us,' Jenkins attempted. 'I think it's better this way.'

'Sure, you're the doctor,' answered Brady lamely.

Someone knocked at the door.

'Got to go,' Brady said.

'I'm sure you do,' answered Jenkins before she disconnected the call.

'What!' Brady called out as he eyed yet more paperwork that had surreptitiously made its way to his in-tray.

Conrad walked in.

Brady noted that Conrad looked more refreshed than he did. He presumed Conrad hadn't tried sleeping three hours on a lumpy, old sofa.

'Trina McGuire rang wanting a word with you, sir.'

'Yeah?' asked Brady, surprised. 'Why the bloody hell would she want to talk to me? Oh, don't tell me,' he muttered. 'She wants to make an official complaint about bloody Adamson.'

'Shane McGuire's in hospital, sir.'

'What happened?' Brady asked.

'That's what she wants to know,' answered Conrad.

*

'Yeah?' Brady said as he answered his mobile.

He looked over at the hospital's main entrance.

Numerous patients were stood outside the revolving door tabbing away. One old guy with gaunt, sunken cheeks and sagging yellowing skin even had a drip attached to his large, bony hand. In between his skeletal fingers he tremulously held a cigarette. His other bony hand was gnarled around a portable oxygen tank. His blue lips sucked greedily at the cigarette, oblivious to the people walking past. He then yanked at the oxygen mask flaccidly hanging around his scrawny, chicken neck before taking another puff.

Brady hoped for his sake that the portable oxygen tank was switched off. Otherwise, the daft old bugger might end up going a damned sight quicker than he expected.

Fuck, Brady thought. Life can't get worse than that.

'Got a message for you, Jack,' Turner, the desk sergeant, said hesitantly.

'Spit it out then,' replied Brady.

'It's from Claudia,' Turner began.

Brady immediately stiffened.

'And?'

'She wants you to call her as soon as you can.'

'Why not call my mobile if she wanted to talk to me?' questioned Brady.

'I don't know, all she wanted me to do was pass the message on,' Turner explained uncomfortably.

'I see,' Brady stiffly replied. 'Thanks for letting me know, Charlie.'

He sighed heavily as he disconnected the call.

'Bad news?' Conrad asked as he set the alarm on his car.

'I don't know,' reflected Brady.

He decided to worry about it later. If it had been that important she would have rung him rather than going through the station.

First he had to see exactly what had happened to Shane McGuire.

Chapter Forty-Three

Someone had done a good job, Brady had to concede.

Shane McGuire was an ugly sight. His face was so swollen and disfigured it was difficult to know whether it was really him.

Tubes protruded from his scrawny arms while multiple wires fed back to various bleeping machines.

Brady wasn't surprised. He had read McGuire's medical report and even though he wasn't a doctor, he recognised enough to know it didn't look good.

McGuire had four broken ribs, one of which had punctured his right lung. His nose, left arm and right leg were broken, as was his back in two places. His spleen had also been ruptured and he had suffered significant internal bleeding.

McGuire moaned as he tried to open his swollen eyes.

'Shane pet, Jack Brady's here. I want you to tell him who did this to you,' Trina gently asked.

'Tell him to fuck off. I told you there's nothing to tell,' whispered McGuire hoarsely.

'For fuck's sake, Shane! Whoever did this tried to kill you!'

'I told ye, Mam, I didn't see 'em,' moaned McGuire.

'This is your fault!' accused Trina McGuire as she spun round on her four-inch stilettos.

'Look . . . I'm really sorry about Shane but I don't see how—'

Trina McGuire cut Brady off.

'Of course you don't cos you lot think you can throw your weight around wherever you want, regardless of the consequences for people like me and my Shane!'

'I'm really sorry that this has happened, but I don't see the connection,' Brady replied firmly.

'Then maybe you should think twice about dragging him off in front of his mates to the police station for questioning, eh? Makes him look like a fuckin' grass or someit! No surprise he then gets given a beating if they think he's been talking to you lot!'

'Look, Mrs McGuire—'

'Fuck me! Listen to you! Detective Inspector Jack Brady! You wouldn't think he'd grown up with the likes of me? Would you?' she asked sarcastically as she turned to Conrad.

Conrad stepped back.

Brady couldn't blame him. She may have only been five feet four and six stone if that, but she was dangerous.

Trina McGuire threw back her long, glossy blonde hair as she turned her attention back to Brady.

He was unfortunate enough to have known her from a previous life. She had caught his eye, just as she had caught many men's roving eyes at the time. Growing up she had blossomed into a remarkable beauty, somehow avoiding absorbing the ugly harshness of the Ridges. But now, years later, she epitomised it. She still had a 'heroin chic' beauty about her, but even with the liberal make-up, it was fading fast. A poverty-stricken, desperate junkie, who didn't have a hope in hell of getting out. The best thing she had ever done in her life was lying in a hospital bed with the shit kicked out of him.

'You're bloody lucky your brother's not still around. He'd soon sort you out.'

Brady kept quiet. He knew they had once been an item and that she blamed Brady for him leaving the North East and ultimately her, behind. But that was years ago. He had gone to London to get away from the fact that Brady was a copper. Not that Brady could blame him. He was secretly relieved that his brother had made that decision, otherwise it would have been Brady who would have had to put some distance between them.

'Shane?' Brady said, deciding it was time to leave.

The last thing he wanted was Trina McGuire bringing up the past: his past. Not in front of Conrad.

'Listen, if you decide you want to talk, just let me know. Here's my number, yeah?'

'Fuck off will ye? And take yer fuckin' number with ye?' said McGuire, thickly.

Brady ignored him and left his business card on the kid's bedside table.

'Take care,' Brady said, looking at Trina McGuire.

'Save it, Jack. We both know you don't mean it,' she replied. 'And you tell that little shit Adamson that his days are numbered. No one treats me like a piece of fuckin' shit. Especially not a copper!'

Chapter Forty-Four

'Who's the lucky woman then?' asked Conrad as he pulled out of the hospital car park.

'No one you know,' Brady replied quietly.

He looked down at the wilting bunch. The hospital gift shop wasn't exactly Interflora, but it was the best he could do considering the circumstances.

'Do you mind driving to Whitley Bay Cemetery first? There's something I need to do,' Brady asked softly as he avoided looking at Conrad.

'Sure,' answered Conrad, suddenly feeling like an idiot.

They drove along in concentrated silence.

Conrad felt too uncomfortable to make small talk. Not that it mattered. Brady was too preoccupied to even realise.

Brady looked out at the bleak, depressing coastline. The brooding, dirty-grey sea looked as unwelcoming as ever. He watched as dog walkers braved the constant drizzle and the North East winds whipping in from the Arctic.

Conrad pulled in behind the row of solemn cars parked outside the cemetery gates.

'I'll wait here, shall I?' suggested Conrad.

'Yeah, I won't be long,' answered Brady.

'Take as long as you like, sir,' replied Conrad.

'Thanks,' Brady said appreciatively before closing the car door.

He pulled his beat-up leather jacket tight around his body in a miserable attempt to ward off the sub-zero freezing wind and rain. He looked across towards St Mary's lighthouse. The tall, white Victorian structure bleakly held out against the blackening sky while the sea raged at the battered rock on which it stood.

He let his gaze drift over to Feather's caravan site which sat on the remote edge of Whitley Bay with unblemished views of the lighthouse and the sea on one side and wild fields and open countryside on the other. Who in their right mind would come to blustery, miserable Whitley Bay? questioned Brady. But the caravan site was popular. Who with, Brady had no idea, but it was the last standing testimony that Whitley Bay had once been a lively family holiday resort and not the binge drinking paradise and gang fighting haven it had now become.

The caravan park and the miniature golf course were all that was left, everything else had gone. The bucket and spade shops with lettered rock and candy floss had long since been boarded up. As had the amusement arcades and finally, the Spanish City fairground. A primary school had ironically replaced the 'Corkscrew' roller coaster, along with the ghost train and waltzers that had lurched and twisted as kids, himself included, had shrieked in stomach-churning delight.

Brady turned the collar of his jacket up against the stabbing rain and headed through the black wrought-iron gates of the cemetery. He nodded dolefully at the undertaker sat grim and irritable behind the wheel of his loaded hearse. Ahead of him a funeral had overrun. Like life, even in death nothing was ever straightforward, Brady mused as he walked past, head down.

He turned off, avoiding the straggling mourners coming out of the chapel, and limped along the familiar row of headstones and cherubs. Brady counted his steps as he had done as a child. He reached twenty and stopped dead. Someone had got there before him.

An extravagant bouquet of white orchid lilies stood out amidst the sea of grey stone. Brady sucked in. He knew who had beaten him to it and had at the same time unwittingly outdone him. Embarrassed, Brady looked down at the cheerless hospital flowers in his hand. He thought the better of chucking them and instead, painfully knelt down and placed them on the ground in front of the headstone.

He clenched his jaw as he tried to hold back the overwhelming emotion he felt.

Brady closed his eyes as he tried to block out the noise from his past.

'Expected to find you here,' mumbled a hoarse, thick Geordie voice.

Brady quickly stood up, inwardly wincing as his leg kicked off at the strain. He turned round shakily.

'What the fuck do you want?' he muttered in a low, strained voice.

'That's no way to talk,' replied the shabbily dressed old man sarcastically.

Brady stepped back in repulsion as he took in the pathetic drunk in front of him. The same drunk who had accosted him the previous night outside the station. In daylight he looked worse. What was left of his sandy-coloured, curly hair hung in matted, grey wispy clumps. His yellowing, sagging skin was covered in angry patches of burst blood

273

vessels and crusted sores. His stocky body had become swollen with whatever spirits and cheap beer he could lay his gnarled, liver-spotted hands on.

Brady looked with disgust at his bloated, drunken face.

'What? Don't recognise me then?' he asked gruffly before taking a swig from the bottle clutched in his blackened hand, his venomous eyes never leaving Brady.

Brady stared at him, unable to answer.

The drunk staggered backwards as he took another swig from the half-full bottle of vodka.

'What are you after?' Brady asked menacingly as he narrowed his dark brown eyes.

'Come on, Jackie lad, there's no need to be unpleasant,' the man slurred.

'Get to the point.'

'I'm a bit strapped for cash right now,' he said, shrugging his shoulders.

'I've already given you enough.'

He smiled at Brady crookedly as he drunkenly shook his head.

'Well obviously it wasn't, was it? Or I wouldn't be back.'

'I told you the last time, that was it.'

'Come on, Jackie? I came to offer you a deal,' the old drunk pleaded. He smiled repulsively baring the few blackened teeth he had left.

Brady turned and walked away.

'I'll give you till Monday then?' he called out after him. 'Monday, yeah?'

Brady stuffed his clenched fists into his jacket and lowered his head, ignoring the looks he was getting from the group of people waiting to go into the chapel. His face was stinging from the salty rain blowing in from the North

274

Sea. All he cared about was getting back to the car before he lost it.

'Sir?' asked Conrad, startled as Brady's ashen-faced figure climbed into the car.

Brady didn't react. Instead he closed his eyes and rested his head back against the seat.

'Are you all right?' Conrad asked, concerned.

'I'm fine.'

He realised he was still trembling. The cold, damp North East air had seeped through his clothes. But he knew that wasn't the reason he couldn't stop shaking.

'Conrad?' said Brady. 'Drive, will you? Just get me the hell out of this place.'

He pulled himself together. There was only one person now who could help him. He took out his mobile and started punching the number.

'Yeah, it's me,' Brady said as he massaged his aching forehead.

'I need to talk.'

Chapter Forty-Five

Brady limped into Antonelli's restaurant and deeply breathed in the heady aroma of freshly ground Italian coffee. He'd left Conrad parked up watching what was left of the North East's fishing trawlers as they docked into North Shields quayside.

'Better be good, Jack,' warned Madley as Brady approached his table.

'You know me better than that,' said Brady.

He grimly nodded at the thirty-something, smart-looking, dark-haired man sat next to Madley.

The dark-haired man smiled laconically at Brady.

'What is it with you coppers? Always turning up just before the deal's on the table,' laughed Paulie Knickerbocker.

Brady attempted to casually return the smile.

It was enough for Paulie to know something was wrong.

Brady and Madley had both known Paulie since St Joseph's Primary School. As soon as word got out amongst the kids that his parents were Italian and ran the ice-cream vans parked up in all weathers outside St Mary's lighthouse, Tynemouth Sands and Tynemouth Priory, the nickname 'Knickerbocker' came about. And for some reason it had stuck, regardless of the years and Paulie's two Italian restaurants known by his family name, Antonelli.

But running two restaurants and the family ice-cream business wasn't all Paulie was known for; he was also the local fence. The vans and the restaurants acted as the ideal cover for such an operation. Paulie had contacts that Brady could only dream of and was always Brady's first unofficial line of enquiry if a violent burglary had taken place.

Paulie had a strong sense of moral duty which generously extended beyond family and friends. He had an unerring sense of right and wrong when it came to crime. He was happy to fence stolen goods as long as no unnecessary violence was exacted during the robbery. Brady had often laughed about the irony of being a fence with a conscience, but Paulie didn't see the incongruity of it. His attitude was you should always act civilised, regardless of what you did for a living. Brady put Paulie's morality down to being raised a devout Roman Catholic combined with growing up in the Ridges, where the brute reality of surviving the streets meant that at times, Catholic morals had to be temporarily put on hold.

Brady pulled out a chair and wearily sat down directly across from Madley.

'You look like you need a coffee,' suggested Paulie as he nodded at the waitress busy arranging the tables for the expected lunchtime rush.

'Same as Martin would be good,' accepted Brady as he gestured towards Madley's espresso.

Brady was still trembling. He couldn't get rid of the image of the shabby drunk who had threatened to destroy what was left of his life. He dragged a shaky hand through his hair as he caught Madley's concerned gaze.

'Paulie? Give us a minute will you?' Madley suggested.

Paulie respectfully nodded as he looked at Brady's hunched figure.

'Good to see you, Jack. Don't leave it too long,' he said, patting him on the back before leaving.

'Yeah, same goes, Paulie.'

Brady watched as Paulie disappeared behind the double doors that led into the busy kitchen.

'Cheers,' Brady said as he took his coffee from the attractive, dark-haired waitress.

Brady took a sip of scalding black coffee as he turned his attention to Madley.

'Thanks for the flowers.'

Madley nodded.

'She was always good to me.'

Brady looked at him. He was right, his mam had always treated Madley like another son. He sometimes forgot that he wasn't the only one who had taken her death badly.

'So, what's this all about?' Madley questioned as his glinting brown eyes searched Brady's pale face.

'He's back,' replied Brady.

'I thought you'd already taken care of him?'

'Jimmy had. He'd scared him off. But he must have heard that Jimmy's in it up to his neck and so the bastard reckons he can try and blackmail me again,' explained Brady.

Madley waited patiently for Brady to say more, but he didn't.

'You should have let me take care of him like I said.'

Brady couldn't bring himself to disagree. He knew Madley was right.

'Question is, Jack, what are you expecting from me?'

'I don't know.'

He sighed heavily as he stared down at his espresso.

'Until you do, I can't help you. You understand that, don't you?'

Brady nodded.

'I know . . .' he said. 'All I want is for the old bastard to disappear for good.'

Madley narrowed his menacing eyes as he stared at him.

'There's only one way to guarantee that,' Madley said, lowering his voice. 'But it has to be your decision, not mine.'

'I know . . .'

Chapter Forty-Six

Brady breathed in the salty, decaying stench of North Shields quayside. It may have gone upmarket with all the fancy Italian restaurants and café bars, not to mention the expensive new apartments that now dominated the harbour backdrop. But one thing hadn't changed and that was the nauseating smell of rotting fish.

Brady stood and watched the sailing boats as they passed by, heading out to sea. He could see a ferry docked further up the Tyne. He turned and stared across at South Shields and the row of brightly-painted Victorian houses that looked out over the river. Even he had to admit it was a beautiful spot to just stand and watch life moving around you.

In the seventies and eighties and even as late as the nineties the harbour and the pubs lining it were notorious for crime and prostitution. If you were looking to have your throat slit, then a night visit to North Shields harbour would do the trick. The no-go area was frequented by hardened, bloodthirsty sailors from all corners of the world, prepared to kill a man if the mood took them. By the time the police were called, the sailors in question would have long since set sail for other nefarious quarters while the victim lay turning very cold.

He walked over to Conrad's car which was parked up facing the bleak, swirling waters of the Tyne. Seagulls screeched and dive bombed one another as fishing trawlers dredged up whatever crap filled the frothing black water. Brady climbed into the car and helped himself to one of Conrad's hot, greasy chips. The quayside had the best fish and chips in the North East which explained why it was always so damned busy regardless of the bitter weather.

'Do you want me to get you some, sir?' asked Conrad.

'Nah, not hungry,' answered Brady as he took a few more.

He looked out the windscreen and thought about what he was going to do about the old drunk. He was trouble, always had been. Maybe now was the time to put an end to it, once and for all.

'Ready?' Brady queried, as he turned to Conrad.

He checked his watch. It was just before 2 pm and they still had a hell of a lot to do before the day was over.

'Yes sir,' answered Conrad as he scrunched up his vinegar-soaked remains.

He buzzed his window down and threw the scraps out for the birds.

'Better watch you don't get done for littering,' noted Brady as he watched as scavenging seagulls descended upon the offering.

'By who, sir? This is North Shields.'

'You're lucky this time. Come on then. We're needed back at the station.'

*

Gates had requested to see him. Immediately. It was now 1.33 pm and Gates had been expecting him since 1.15 pm.

281

Brady was under no illusions what it was about. But he had other things on his mind. He had just returned to the station and the first thing he needed to do was to call the lab. He was still waiting for the results on Ellison's DNA and prints. He wanted to be able to walk into the interview room with as much evidence against Ellison as possible.

Brady punched in the relevant numbers and waited as his eyes drifted over to his office window. Grey shafts of dusty light stabbed through the Venetian blinds. He still couldn't shake the shabby, old drunk from his mind. He didn't know which way to turn and bitterly wished that he could talk to Matthews.

'How can I help you?' answered a female voice.

'DI Brady here. I'm waiting for some results?'

'Can you hold please, sir?'

'Sure,' he answered absentmindedly as he waited.

'Just the man I've been wanting to talk to.'

'Ainsworth?' Brady questioned.

'You're not going to like this but you've got a problem.'

'Go on?'

'We've got the lab results from the murder victim's body and Jimmy Matthews' DNA was all over her.'

'No, that can't be right. Are you certain?'

'Hundred per cent. And I don't just mean the kind of contamination that happens when you lot turn up at a crime scene. I would have expected some from Matthews since he was the first one there, but not to this level.'

Brady shook his head.

'You do know he put his coat over her body?' questioned Brady in an attempt to explain Matthews' DNA on the victim.

282

'Yes I know. Silly sod, what the hell was he playing at, eh?'

'I don't know,' answered Brady.

'But even that still doesn't explain the degree of contamination, Jack. And then there's his handprints at the bloody crime scene. I mean, a man of Matthews' rank knows the protocol at a murder scene. Bloody hell, Jack, he's not some wet-behind-the-ears DC here.'

'Does Gates know?' Brady asked.

'What do you think?' replied Ainsworth.

'Bugger. Why didn't you let me know first?'

'Why do you think? You're bloody lucky I'm warning you,' replied Ainsworth.

'I realise that. Thanks,' apologised Brady quickly.

'I should bloody think so.'

'As soon the lab has the DNA results on Ellison you'll let me know, yeah?'

'Yes, yes. I'll give you a call,' concluded Ainsworth before cutting the line.

Brady contemplated the news. It was no surprise then that Gates wanted to see him ASAP. Matthews' inexplicable DNA evidence all over the murder victim who was also his daughter's best friend explained Gates' urgency.

'Shit!' he cursed as he realised the enormity of the situation.

His leg kicked off again; a constant reminder of why he shouldn't be there.

He limped over to the window and peered through the Venetian blinds. Police cars and vans blocked most of the street. He looked up at the black, ominous clouds overhead and wondered if the day could get any worse.

*

Brady tried his best to look relaxed in front of Gates.

'Do you want to tell me what's going on?' Gates asked.

The problem was, he didn't know where to start. He could feel the sweat breaking out on his forehead as he thought about his conversation with Ainsworth.

'Then start by explaining to me why they found Matthews' DNA all over the victim's body?'

'I can only assume it's because he covered the victim's body with his overcoat, sir,' Brady replied.

'And how do you explain his handprints?'

Even Brady had to admit that it didn't look good, a man of Matthews' rank contaminating a murder scene.

'He knelt down to look at the body, placing his hands on the ground?' surmised Brady as casually as he could.

But he knew he was fooling nobody.

'Without gloves? For God's sake, Matthews is one of my most experienced DIs!'

Brady remained silent. There was nothing he could say. Matthews had recognised the victim, and had, understandably, lost it.

'No, I'm having trouble explaining it myself,' stated Gates in response to Brady's awkward silence.

'How do you account for the call the victim made to his mobile?'

'Evie Matthews' statement clearly explains why, sir. Evie gave Sophie the number so she could call Matthews if she felt things were getting out of hand at home with Simmons. I presume that's what happened, sir.'

Gates deliberated for a moment.

'What troubles me is that it should be Matthews sat in front of me explaining this, not you.'

Brady didn't answer.

'What's he hiding?'

'I know as much as you, sir.'

'You expect me to believe that?'

He sighed as he stared at Brady.

'We both know Matthews recognised the victim. His erratic behaviour gave him away. What I want to know is why he didn't come forward with her identity as soon as he realised it was her?'

'I don't know, sir,' answered Brady uncomfortably, reluctant to explain that Matthews was worried about the implication of driving the victim home the night she was murdered.

Gates slowly weighed Brady up.

'And Evie Matthews' traces of DNA? The hair samples that were found? How do you explain that?' Gates asked.

'Sophie left the Matthews' house wearing Evie's jacket. So it's no surprise her DNA was found on the victim's body.'

'And the other DNA evidence found on the victim?'

'I'm hoping it's Ellison's, sir. I'm just waiting for word back from the lab.'

'I hope for your sake, and Matthews', that you're right. Even if it is just coincidence and poor judgement on Matthews' part, it still doesn't look good.'

'Yes sir,' replied Brady doing his utmost to maintain Gates' unnerving eye contact.

'You have heard the insinuations the press are making about Matthews' suspension?'

Brady nodded as Harriet Jacobs came to mind.

'This is the last thing this force needs. I want an arrest and I want one fast!' ordered Gates.

'Yes sir. My next move is to interview Ellison,' answered Brady quickly.

'Actually, I'd rather you weren't involved in the interview.'

'Sir?' Brady asked, confused.

'I think Adamson would be better suited.'

Brady sat back stunned.

'I've enough of a headache trying to deal with Paul Simmons after the way you handled his interview to risk any more of your unorthodox methods.'

Brady understood why Gates was so pissed at him. Simmons was considering suing Northumbria Police Force on the grounds that Brady had roughed him up. Brady had shrugged it off when he had first heard, knowing that all he was responsible for was forcibly making Simmons sit back down. In his opinion, Simmons had too much to hide to want to go public. However, Brady accepted that Gates didn't necessarily share his opinion.

'With all due respect, sir, Adamson doesn't have the experience to deal with this,' Brady objected.

'I beg to differ. He's already passed his Inspector exams. It's only a matter of time before he gets promoted.'

Brady felt winded. He hadn't been expecting to have to stand back and watch someone else take over. Let alone Adamson.

'I've talked to Ellison twice now. I know what I'm up against. Adamson doesn't,' Brady insisted. 'We're too close to have someone new come in and mess this up, sir.'

Gates contemplated Brady; his emotionless, cold, intelligent eyes weighing up what was before him.

'You screw up and that's it. No second chances. And don't think Chief Superintendent O'Donnell will bail you out. Not this time.'

Brady shifted in his seat.

Gates' eyes remained fixed on Brady.

'Sir . . .' attempted Brady, but Gates held up his hand.

'Save it for the report you'll be writing up. I get any more complaints about you, Jack, and you're not only off the case, I will do my utmost to get you off this force!'

*

Brady looked up at the dark gloom that was the sky. The air felt heavy and damp from the sea fret. It had been drizzling on and off for days now. Then again, mused Brady, what else did he expect from the North East of England? He threw his cigarette butt away and took out his phone.

He tried Matthews again. It cut straight to voice mail.

'Jimmy? I really need to talk to you. Fuck it, Jimmy! Just ring me, will you?'

Chapter Forty-Seven

Brady held his head in his hands as he mulled over his next move; interviewing Ellison.

A loud knock at his office door broke through his thoughts.

'Yeah?' said Brady distractedly.

Harvey walked in.

'I've got Tracy Hamilton's statement here.'

Brady took the file from him.

'She understands that if we charge him, she'll be called as a witness?'

Harvey nodded.

'And there's no doubt in her mind that it was Ellison?'

'She picked him out from Christ knows how many photos.'

Brady sighed with relief.

They had him; they had Ellison firmly by the balls. Whether or not he had murdered Sophie Washington, he was clearly having a relationship with the victim; one that criminally transcended the pupil–teacher norm.

He quickly read through the barmaid's statement. She had served him in The Beacon pub, accompanied by the victim. She had then passed him on her way home to

Seatonville Road climbing over the gate into Potter's Farm.
He paused on the last page.

'Says here that a taxi was called from The Beacon for
Sophie Washington?'

'That's what she said,' replied Harvey.

'Which explains why Ellison was later seen on his own
by the barmaid going into Potter's Farm.'

Harvey nodded.

'Find out which taxi company they use and then find
the driver. I need to talk to him. We need to know where
Sophie was going and why.'

*

Ben Ellison looked like crap.

Hung over and sleep deprived, he looked worse than
Brady had imagined. His confident, relaxed veneer had long
gone, replaced by raw, animal fear.

Ellison dragged a shaking hand through his messy hair.

'Look . . . I've already told you. I didn't have anything to
do with her murder.'

'But you were having a sexual relationship with her.'

'I don't know what you're talking about.'

'I think you do,' Brady answered.

Ellison's red-rimmed, bloodshot eyes darted between
Conrad and Brady, trying to figure out what was going on.

'I have a reliable witness,' Brady informed him.

'How do I know that you're not making this up?' Ellison
demanded edgily.

He looked and smelled like he needed a hot shower and
a change of clothes. The windowless interview room was
heavy with a dank, acrid smell. Brady had smelled it before;

289

it was the stench of guilt. It sweated its way out of the suspect's pores, regardless.

'Our witness saw you in The Beacon having a drink with your fifteen-year-old pupil, Sophie Washington. She then said that as she was making her way home past Monkseaton Metro towards Seatonville Road she passed you as you climbed over the gate into Potter's Farm.'

'So?' Ellison questioned.

'Do you know what time Sophie was murdered?' Brady asked.

Ellison didn't answer.

'Between 12.30 and 2 am. And,' Brady paused, giving Ellison enough time to absorb this information, 'as she looked back you were seen by our witness walking down the farm's dirt track towards the crime scene at 12.15 am. I wouldn't describe that as circumstantial, sir.'

'For fuck's sake! I didn't do it! What kind of guy do you take me for?'

'One who gets off on buggering and fucking his fifteen-year-old pupils,' quietly answered Brady.

Ellison shot Brady a 'fuck you' look.

'The autopsy report,' Brady flatly explained.

'You've still got nothing on me,' Ellison stated with false confidence.

Brady folded his arms as he stared at Ellison. He knew they had him; the stench of sweat was overpowering.

'I have rights! You can't do this to me!'

'Actually, where you're sat you've got no rights,' Brady evenly replied.

He shrugged apologetically as Ellison looked at him in bewilderment.

'We can keep you without legal representation for the

next twenty-four hours. So I'd get used to it if I were you.'

Ellison's face paled as he stared at Brady. His healthy, rugged complexion had waned to a jaundiced colour.

Brady wanted Ellison to sweat. And a few more hours in the cell might loosen his tongue.

'Interview terminated at 2.37 pm.'

Brady turned to the officer stood by the door.

'Take him back to his cell.'

'I've done nothing wrong! I want a solicitor! This is a police set-up! Do you hear me? It's a set-up! I want a solicitor,' he shouted desperately.

Brady slowly shook his head.

'You've been watching too many films, sir,' he stated as he stood up.

Brady limped out of the oppressive, dank interview room, ignoring Ellison's increasingly desperate yelling.

Chapter Forty-Eight

The station was buzzing. Less than two hours after the interview with Ellison and the lab reports had come back, as had the computer forensic findings. Brady had been waiting for enough evidence against Ellison to charge him and now they had it, and more. The anal and vaginal fluid that Wolfe had sent for forensic analysis had found traces of Ellison's DNA; in both samples. Ellison was screwed; literally, Brady darkly mused.

And that was before they even considered Jed's findings. He had uncovered emails that the victim had deleted. Sexually explicit emails. And Jed being Jed had managed to source them back to Ellison's laptop. Ellison had done a good job of opening an email account with false registration details, but it wasn't good enough to get past Jed's computing forensics skill. They now had incriminating evidence tying Ellison to the victim. Evidence that also included an email suggesting a drink in The Beacon the night she was murdered.

The evidence was so damning that Brady had granted Ellison legal representation. He had word that the lawyer had already arrived and was currently briefing his client. Not that there was a lot a lawyer could do with the evidence the police had against Ellison. It was damning, so damning he'd be banged up for years.

Gates already had a press conference arranged. It was all about PR and being seen to be making the right noises; especially in front of the media. It was a coup for Northumbria Police. But things had been shaken up since then and now they were about to make a very public arrest.

It had taken less than thirty-six hours from the discovery of the murder to arresting the suspect. Gates had every right to brag, Brady mused. Such a tight timeframe was unprecedented, apart from cases of spousal homicide. But those kinds of murders rarely made the news, despite the staggering homicide rates. Brady had been involved with enough investigations where the woman had been killed by her current or previous partner, not to be surprised at the Home Office statistic that every three days a woman in the UK was murdered. However, the public interest didn't stretch to domestic homicides; it was too close to home. The media had it sussed; they knew that the public gleaned vicarious pleasure from their insatiable appetite for lurid sleaze and horrific murders, just as long as it wasn't on their doorstep.

Sophie Washington's murder had all the right ingredients; an illicit pupil–teacher relationship that had ended in murder. It was sordid and disturbing enough to make it newsworthy. The end of this investigation could be the making of Gates' career, Brady concluded.

He ignored the triumphant voices behind him as he made his way to tell Ellison the good news.

*

293

Brady walked into the interview room but it wasn't Ellison who caught his attention; it was the lawyer representing him. Brady caught her eye, turned round and walked straight back out.

Conrad followed suit.

'Sir?'

'Did you know that she was in there? Did you?' Brady asked, trying to keep his voice steady.

Conrad shook his head.

'No sir, no one told me. I just assumed Michael Travers would be representing Ellison,' Conrad answered uneasily.

'But you knew she was back?'

Conrad gave a lame shrug.

'I heard things . . .'

'And you didn't think to tell me?' Brady questioned incredulously, unable to disguise his hurt.

'I presumed she would have told you,' Conrad answered uncomfortably. 'Look sir, after everything that's happened I didn't want to get involved.'

Brady suddenly remembered that she had tried to contact him. She had left a message with Charlie Turner the desk sergeant asking him to return her call. But he had got so caught up in the investigation that it had slipped his mind. He dragged an unsteady hand through his hair as he tried to get a handle on the situation.

'Problem, Jack?' facetiously asked an all too familiar, well-educated voice.

Brady turned as Claudia firmly closed the door of the interview room behind her.

Shaken, he watched as she irritably swept her luxuriously long, wild curly red hair off her face. The first time he had met her she had literally stood out from the crowd. Before she had even turned round, he had known that she was perfect; too perfect for him.

'Maybe you should check your messages? After all, I did my level best to warn you that I was helping Michael out. He's tied up with a client at North Shields so I did him a favour by coming here.' Her provocative green eyes flashed at him in annoyance.

'Michael?' asked Brady uneasily. He knew Michael Travers well enough not to trust him. He was a senior partner at the law firm where Claudia worked, or had worked. Even a fool could tell that Michael was desperate about Claudia.

'Yes, he's been an absolute rock throughout all of this,' she replied cuttingly.

'I bet he has.'

'I'd expect that pathetic egotistical response from you. That's where Michael's different. He's more than happy to let me stay at his place while I'm back up here, with no strings attached.'

Brady bit his tongue, resisting the urge to warn her not to be so damned naive.

'I know that's something you could never understand,' Claudia replied in response to Brady's cynical expression.

'I thought you were in London?' Brady questioned, changing the subject.

'I am. I'm just tying up loose ends here. Works both ways, Jack. I'd heard you weren't due back until Monday. Otherwise if I'd known in advance you were going to be here I wouldn't have agreed to help Michael out.'

'Maybe if you'd asked around then you would have found out I started back yesterday.'

'I might have done if I had been interested. But I'm not,' she stated acerbically.

'We need to talk,' Brady stated, ignoring her jibe.

'Bit late for that don't you think?'

'You know what I mean,' muttered Brady.

'Do I?' challenged Claudia. 'And what about my client? Surely your personal life can wait? From what I remember you were only ever interested in work?'

It took Brady all his strength not to fall apart. She was as beautiful as he last remembered. Damn it, he thought as he tried to get his head together.

'I'll wait for you in the interview room, shall I, sir?' offered Conrad.

'Yeah . . . I won't be long,' replied Brady awkwardly, unable to take his eyes off her.

'My office?' he suggested as calmly as he could.

'This better be about work,' Claudia threatened as she angrily tossed her hair back.

Chapter Forty-Nine

Brady limped over to his desk and sat down. He gestured for Claudia to take the seat opposite.

'I'd rather stand,' she answered abruptly.

She then folded her arms and looked him straight in the eye.

'Look, let's get something straight, shall we? This isn't some cosy little chat reminiscing about what we once had, this is about work. So get to the point while I can still stomach being in the same room as you.'

Brady didn't know what to say or even what to do. He'd gone over this scene a hundred times in his head, but now that it was actually happening he felt numb.

He noticed that she looked taller than her usual five feet four and realised with gut-wrenching clarity that she was wearing heels. Since when did she wear heels to work? His eyes drifted up her pale legs to her well-defined body. Her clothes were as expensive and tasteful as ever. But the dress was also shorter and tighter, emphasising her curvaceous body.

It was enough to make him sweat.

'I . . . I didn't realise you were back . . .' Brady muttered. 'Or I would have kept out of your way.'

'Really?' questioned Claudia scornfully. 'Doesn't sound like you, Jack.'

'Maybe I've changed,' he replied quietly.

She contemptuously flashed her green eyes at him.

'Please Claudia . . . take a seat? Yeah? Just so we can talk?' asked Brady, desperate for the atmosphere in the room to change.

'You expect me to talk to you! For fuck's sake, Jack! Remember, you were the bastard in all of this! If I hadn't walked in on you screwing that young, dark-haired slut in our bed then none of this would have happened,' she angrily pointed out.

She was still furious, enough to want to hurt him badly. And she had succeeded. Brady felt the punch straight to his gut. It was just a desperate, drunken shag. A pointless, senseless, empty, pathetic act that had cost him everything. Even his reputation at the station was destroyed because of it. Admittedly, before he got together with Claudia he had been known for playing around. But there was something so unique and unattainable about Claudia that when they had got together he had never imagined cheating on her. Yet he did with DC Simone Henderson. It was no more than a drunken, egotistical shag, but it had led to the end of his marriage. He couldn't even remember much about it. Fuelled by a lethal cocktail of alcohol and self-pity it resulted in him destroying the best thing that had ever happened to him.

'I didn't know that you'd walked in . . .' Brady said un-comfortably, hating himself.

'Believe me, I could tell!' she replied sharply.

Disgusted with himself, Brady looked away.

'Let's just say that little acrobatic stunt with your junior colleague finally did it for me. I always promised myself the day you brought your work home would be the day I walked out!' Claudia scornfully replied.

Brady kept his mouth shut. There was nothing he could say in his defence.

To know that he had hurt her was more painful than even her most cutting words. She was the only person he had ever felt comfortable with, and yet when she had needed his unfailing support he had bailed. He had supported her as she built her career as a respected lawyer, but it wasn't enough for her. She wanted more despite the detrimental effect on their relationship. When he argued with her that the only time he ever saw her was when she was acting Duty Solicitor at the station, she promised to cut back on the hours. But if anything she became more resolute about focusing all her energy on her career, resulting in him looking for comfort elsewhere.

But he knew the obsession with her career was her way of coping with the fact that they couldn't have children. Or more specifically, she couldn't. They had tried for a year before being referred to fertility specialists. His results had come back normal, whereas Claudia's showed that it was highly unlikely she would ever conceive naturally.

Then they went down the IVF route. But after the second and third attempt had resulted in early miscarriages, Brady refused to try again. He couldn't live with the devastating effect that the fertility treatment was having on their relationship, or more to the point, on Claudia. She couldn't understand his decision and had made it clear she could never forgive him. His punishment was to be excluded from her life as she dedicated every hour she could to her work.

He looked at her and wondered what would have happened if he had let her continue torturing herself with the IVF. How many attempts would it have taken for her to realise it just wasn't going to happen? Not only had they found out that Claudia could not conceive naturally, but an investigation into the two miscarriages had shown that her body's immune system was attacking the embryos. Yet, despite being one of the cleverest people he knew, she had convinced herself that if they just kept trying she would eventually have their baby. He didn't know what was worse, her leaving him or the alternative which was to watch as Claudia slowly drove herself insane fighting for something that just wasn't possible.

Claudia shot him a scornful look.

'What? Got nothing to say after all this time? I'm surprised that you still haven't thought of some lame excuse by now for sleeping with a junior colleague in our bed!'

Ashamed, Brady lowered his eyes.

'When you got shot the following night I couldn't help but smile at the fact that you had got what you deserved.'

'Bet you did,' Brady stated quietly as he met her disdainful eyes.

'Oh come on, Jack! When the hell are you going to take some responsibility for your own actions? You fucked up! You, not me. On both accounts. With that girl you screwed and with the drugs case you were working on,' she pointed out as her eyes sparkled with emblazoned fury.

Brady slowly swallowed. He looked at her as she stood with her hands defiantly on her hips waiting for him to respond. But he couldn't. All he could think about was how much his body ached to take hold of her and remind her of why she had been so attracted to him in the first place.

But more than that, he ached to touch her again. To breathe in the delicate scent of her soft skin and bury his face in her unruly red hair. He wanted her now more than he had ever wanted any woman.

Before he had a chance to act, a knock at the door broke the spell.

Brady cleared his throat.

'Come in,' he ordered.

The door opened and Jenkins walked in.

She stopped when she saw Claudia, stood with her arms folded, clearly annoyed at the interruption.

'I'm sorry, I didn't realise you were busy. Conrad told me I could find you here,' Jenkins apologised.

Brady couldn't help but feel embarrassed by Jenkins' intrusion. He didn't know what she was playing at. The last time he talked to her she had said she was no longer part of the investigation.

'It's all right, Dr Jenkins, we're done here, aren't we?' Brady said awkwardly as he looked at Claudia.

'Are we?' asked Claudia caustically.

Self-conscious, Brady stood up.

Claudia turned round to face Jenkins and then turned back to Brady, making a play of sweeping her red hair back off her face.

'Well, aren't you going to introduce us?'

She didn't wait for an answer. Instead she turned round and walked slowly and seductively towards the door.

'I must apologise for Jack. He can be so rude at times,' she said as she held her hand out. 'Claudia.'

'I've heard a lot about you, Claudia. It's good to finally meet you,' Jenkins answered, smiling. 'Amelia Jenkins.'

Claudia shook Jenkins' hand, returning the smile.

'Yes, good to meet you, Amelia. I've heard a lot about you too,' Claudia replied.

She then turned to Brady.

'Don't keep me waiting, Jack,' warned Claudia. 'I think you've messed me around enough already. Don't you?'

Embarrassed, Brady watched as she turned and left the room.

*

'So, what brings you down to the station then?' he asked, getting straight to the point. He wasn't in the mood for small talk. Especially with his ex-shrink.

'Shane McGuire,' Jenkins answered, sitting down.

Brady sat back and tried to focus. His head was still reeling from the shock of Claudia's unexpected appearance in his life.

'His mother, Trina McGuire, rang me,' Jenkins explained.

Brady frowned, curious as to why Trina would be calling Jenkins.

'I gave her my number just before I left The Sunken Ship. I realised Adamson had blown any chances of her coming forward with Shane's whereabouts and so I thought I'd leave my contact details with her. And it's just as well that I did. She said Shane knows something that could be crucial to the murder investigation.'

'Then why didn't she call me?' Brady asked sceptically.

'Because of that tone that you're using on me now,' Jenkins pointed out.

'What tone?'

'That cynical tone you use with people.'

Brady frowned. He didn't have time to argue with Jenkins.

He was still trying to figure out Claudia. Added to the fact that the last time he had seen Jenkins was in his office and he had thought better of finishing the bottle of Scotch they had been sharing. If Claudia hadn't been in his life, then maybe that night would have ended differently. She was a very attractive woman after all; something Brady had found hard to ignore.

'What did she tell you?' he asked, trying to sound interested.

'Are you sure you want to know?' replied Jenkins.

'Of course I do.'

'Then I think it's better you hear this from her. Or should I say, from Shane,' Jenkins said standing up.

'Yeah, sure,' Brady replied. He stood up and grabbed his jacket off the back of his chair.

'Oh shit,' he muttered.

'Problem?' asked Jenkins as she opened the door.

'No . . . it's nothing,' lied Brady as he thought about Claudia.

'Give me a minute will you?' Brady asked.

Jenkins nodded. 'I'll meet you downstairs.'

Brady sighed as he watched Jenkins leave. The last thing Claudia was going to want was to be left waiting indefinitely for him to continue the interview with Ellison. He pulled out his BlackBerry.

'Conrad?'

'Yes sir,' answered Conrad.

'Is Claudia there with you?'

'I've just left her in the interview room with Ellison, why?'

'I need you to meet me out front. Shane McGuire reckons he knows something connected to Sophie's murder so we need to talk to him. I want you to make some excuse to Claudia. I don't care what it is but just make it sound convincing, yeah?'

'Easier said than done, sir,' replied Conrad.

'Look, just think of something, quick! And if she asks you, it's got nothing to do with the woman she met in my office.'

'I'm sorry, sir?' questioned Conrad.

'Just do as I say,' ordered Brady.

He cut the call and wearily rubbed his tired face. Why the hell was his life so damned complicated?

Chapter Fifty

'Are you sure that's what she heard?' Brady questioned.

Shane McGuire nodded painfully.

He noted that Shane's injuries looked worse than yesterday. And that he was still on a morphine drip twenty-four hours later. There was one thing he was certain about, McGuire and his family would get the bastards who had done this to him. That was the way it worked. The lads who had organised McGuire's beating had overstepped the mark. It was one thing to warn him to keep quiet, it was another thing to actually very nearly silence him for good.

Brady also had to accept the rules. McGuire was talking off the record. The information he was giving Brady was second-hand. And he had made it clear that Brady would never be able to get it straight from the source. Kids like them didn't talk to the police; more so when it was a murder enquiry. But Brady was grateful for anything connected to that night. And he trusted McGuire. He knew the lad had been deeply affected by Sophie Washington's murder, to the extent that he had asked too many questions. He should have kept quiet when they gave him the answers he was searching for; instead he did the wrong thing. He put pressure on them to talk to the police.

Brady knew that a group of kids must have been hanging about the abandoned farmland that Thursday night. The smouldering bonfire was evidence enough; that and the empty cider and Lambrusco wine bottles. But what Brady hadn't banked on was McGuire being mates with them.

'Look, the lass may have been pissed, yeah? But she was certain she heard them.'

'Run it by me again. What exactly did she hear?'

McGuire thought about it slowly.

'She reckoned she heard these two lasses arguing and then later, one of the lasses was talking with this guy . . .'

'What time was this?' asked Brady.

'I dunno, she reckoned about one-ish, if not a bit after. But you know she was off her face and like, so she's not that sure.'

Brady nodded. The time seemed pretty accurate to him. He glanced briefly at Conrad. If McGuire was right then this could be the breakthrough they needed.

'She reckoned it sounded like they were an item, you know? She said she heard her mention the two of them going off to London together but he was having none of it. So she started to get upset and began threatening to tell people about them.'

Brady stiffened.

'And?' he pushed, trying to keep calm.

'She said the next thing she heard was him getting angry and threatening her that if she did she'd regret it. But that just made her mad. She started screaming that she didn't care what he was going to do to her, she was going to go ahead and tell everyone about their relationship anyway. And then she heard her shout out the name "Jimmy" and then . . . then she started screaming . . .' McGuire faltered and stared up at Brady.

'That's when my mate's lass got scared and legged it.'

Brady realised that Sophie must have desperately tried to call Matthews when Ellison had turned violent. It explained the phone call to Matthews, but after what he had just heard it didn't make him feel any better. He then thought about the time of the call to Matthews which was at 1.31am.

'Did you say this witness was there about 1 am? Could it have been slightly later?'

'Could have been. Like I said she was off her face.'

Brady nodded.

'It was Sophie, wasn't it?' asked McGuire.

'I believe so,' answered Brady.

McGuire attempted to reach out for a drink causing him to moan in pain.

'Here, let me help,' said Brady as he picked up the tumbler of lukewarm water. He inserted the straw between McGuire's swollen, split lips and held it there until he'd had enough.

'Thanks,' he muttered as Brady put the tumbler back.

'Did she hear anything else?' Brady asked.

'No,' mumbled McGuire as he turned his head away from Brady. 'You'll get him? The bastard who did this to her?'

Brady nodded.

'Believe me, Shane, we'll get him with what you've just told us.'

'She didn't deserve to die . . . not like that . . .' said McGuire, softly.

'I know she didn't,' he quietly agreed.

Brady turned to Trina who was stood with her arms folded at the back of the room.

'Thanks,' Brady said.

'Don't thank me. If it had been up to me you wouldn't be here,' Trina coldly replied. 'But he's a good kid. Too bloody good,' she said, worried.

Brady nodded. He understood her fear. McGuire, despite his hard-ass act, didn't belong to her world. But the problem was, there was no way out for his sort and Trina McGuire knew it.

Brady turned and looked back at Shane McGuire. They'd finish off what they'd started if they knew what he'd just told him. It didn't matter that a fifteen-year-old girl had been murdered. There were two rules; you don't ask questions and you don't talk to coppers. Shane McGuire had broken both of those rules. Brady was certain about one thing; if McGuire was summoned to reveal the source of the evidence he'd disclosed to Brady, he would most certainly end up dead.

Brady tried not to think about what would happen to McGuire. He had other things to worry about now.

*

'Was it helpful?' Jenkins asked as they left McGuire's room.

'Let's say I owe you a drink,' Brady replied.

He absentmindedly rubbed his pulsating left thigh as he thought about his next move. Interviewing Ellison. Conrad had gone to get the car while he stayed behind to thank Jenkins. She had made it perfectly clear that she had to get back to work.

Not that it bothered Brady, he was equally keen to get back to the station.

'Conrad will fill you in on the details, but it looks fairly certain that a group of us will be having a few stiff drinks in The Fat Ox later,' Brady said.

'Are you sure you won't be sharing that drink with your wife?' Jenkins asked.

'Ex-wife,' Brady quietly pointed out.

'Didn't look that way to me in your office,' Jenkins replied.

Brady didn't answer; he couldn't.

Jenkins made a move to leave.

'Thanks,' Brady said, unable to look her in the eye.

Jenkins waited, expecting more. Neither of them had mentioned what had happened between them in his office in the early hours of that morning. But she realised there that even if he did find her attractive, he had so much to contend with from his past that the likelihood of anything developing between them was low.

'Seriously, Jack. If you need to offload onto someone, you know my number.'

He watched as she turned and left, knowing that he could never take her up on her offer. No matter how much he would have liked to, it was never going to happen. If there was one thing he had learned from his relationship with Claudia, that was never to mix business with pleasure.

He pulled out his vibrating phone.

'Look, I'll be there soon,' Brady answered.

'You better be, Jack. I've got better things to do with my time than wait around for you,' replied Claudia curtly.

Before Brady could speak she had cut the call.

'Fuck!' he grumbled to himself wondering how the hell he had ended up working with Claudia again.

Chapter Fifty-One

Ellison stared at Brady numbly.

'I need some time to think,' he said anxiously.

'The facts don't lie,' Brady stated, ignoring him. 'Like I said we've found your hand and footprints at the murder scene and at the opening in the fence where the victim entered the farmland.'

Ellison shot Claudia a desperate look.

Claudia signalled for Ellison to relax.

Brady presumed that Claudia had done what she was paid to do and advised Ellison to keep his mouth shut; the right to silence and all that legal spiel. Ellison had already been given his rights when he had first been detained, but Brady was sure it wouldn't have sunk in.

'Humour me, will you?' Brady suddenly said.

Claudia shot him a look which warned him not to do anything crazy.

'Show me your back?'

'What?' said Ellison.

'DI Brady, I must object,' interrupted Claudia.

Brady opened up a folder in front of him and laid out various photographs of the victim's tattoo.

'Just for the record I'm showing Mr Ellison photographs of the deceased's tattoo,' Brady said.

He looked at Ellison. His face had paled.

'Recognise it, sir?'

Ellison didn't answer.

'Now can you please stand up and show me your back?' Brady repeated.

'What on earth is all this about, DI Brady?' questioned Claudia.

'If I'm right, your client has exactly the same tattoo as the victim, but his covers most of his back,' Brady explained. 'Isn't that right, sir?'

Ellison didn't know what to do.

'Five weeks ago you took the victim to a place off Westgate Road called Tattoozed. Eddie who owns the place remembers you. Do you know why?' Brady asked.

Ellison narrowed his eyes as he stared at him.

'Sure you do,' encouraged Brady. 'He said you came back from a trip to Thailand a year ago wanting a jade dragon tattooed across your back. Reckoned it took three days to do, but it was worth every minute. In fact, he even had a photograph of it,' Brady said as he took the photo out of the folder and laid it on the table.

'Reckons it was one of the best tattoos he's ever done,' Brady added. 'So go on. Let's see if it's as good as Eddie says it is?'

Ellison looked at Claudia, unsure of what to do.

She shot Brady an unimpressed look before nodding at her client to do as Brady requested.

Ellison shakily stood up and turned round. He then lifted his T-shirt over his head.

'Just for the record the suspect is showing us the tattoo on his back. Identical, apart from size to the victim's tattoo,' Brady stated.

'Have to admit it's a beauty,' Brady said, admiring the intricate artwork.

'Have you quite finished, DI Brady?' asked Claudia.

Brady shot her a grin.

'What do you reckon? Should I get one?'

'Do I look like I'd be remotely interested in anything you did?' she abruptly replied. 'Now can we please get back to interviewing my client?'

Brady folded his arms and sat back and waited for Ellison to sit back down.

'So, do you recognise the tattoo on the victim in the photographs in front of you?' Brady asked as he looked at Ellison.

Ellison ran a shaking hand through his messy hair as he looked down at what Brady had laid out in front of him.

'Can you say yes or no?' Brady prompted, ignoring the fact that Ellison looked as if he was going to puke.

'Yeah,' muttered Ellison, unable to look at the photographs. 'I recognise the tattoo . . . but I . . . I . . .' His voice trailed off as he shook his head. 'It doesn't mean I hurt her.'

Brady coolly watched him.

'That remains to be seen, sir,' stated Brady.

Ellison looked at Brady, distraught.

'We've traced the emails you sent to the victim.'

Ellison turned to his solicitor.

Claudia motioned for him to keep calm.

'Computer forensics found them. In spite of the fact that you deleted them, as did the victim, presumably under your instruction. It seems you're not as clever as you thought.'

Ellison anxiously ran his hand over his patchy blond stubble.

'So, do you email all your pupils or just the ones that you shag? From the emails you sent Sophie, you were doing more than just shagging her though, weren't you?'

Brady looked down at the emails Jed had sent him until he found the one he wanted.

'You wanted to "fuck her so hard until she screamed for you to stop". Well, I'm sure she did that. Right at the moment when she realised you were killing her. Is that what happened? You fucked her and then buggered her up the arse? But it wasn't enough for you, was it? Is that how you get turned on? Fucking a minor and choking her to death at the same time?'

'DI Brady, can I remind you that you still have presented no evidence that my client murdered Sophie Washington,' Claudia interrupted.

Brady looked at her and nodded.

'I'll get to that part in a minute,' he replied evenly.

Claudia shot him a look which asked what the hell was going on.

Brady knew that he should have disclosed the vital information that Shane McGuire had told him. But he had been so thrown by Claudia's sudden appearance that he had barely had a chance to get his head together for the interview. As it was, he was grateful he could string two words together with her sat opposite him.

He turned his attention back to Ellison, deciding that he'd worry about Claudia later.

'So what happened? Got carried away in the moment? And then before you realised it, she had stopped breathing?'

Brady leaned forward.

'You must have panicked? After all, it was just an accident. You didn't really mean to kill her, did you?'

Ellison stared hard at Brady as he shook his head.

'I didn't kill her . . .' he said.

Brady ignored him.

'You put her clothes back on first. After all, she was just fifteen years old. No one would have expected her to have been having sex, let alone with her teacher,' Brady slowly said, shaking his head. 'But you were certain that no one knew about you and Sophie, weren't you? So confident that you thought you were going to get away with it. You realised then that you had to make her death look like a random attack. So you picked up a chunk of stone and smashed her face beyond recognition.'

'Someone actually did that to her?' Ellison questioned, surprised.

'You should know,' Brady replied in a low voice.

'I . . . I would never have harmed her . . .' Ellison replied.

Claudia gripped Ellison's arm; a firm reminder to keep his mouth shut.

'No, you just fucked her, didn't you?' Brady questioned.

Ellison narrowed his blue eyes and gave Brady a 'so what?' look.

'We got some lab results back. Results that I think will interest you, sir,' Brady said as he held Ellison's stare.

Ellison shook his head, confused.

'I'm afraid so, sir.'

Ellison turned to his solicitor.

'My client would now like to make a statement,' Claudia interrupted.

Brady realised Claudia had presumably told Ellison to keep quiet until he had no choice. It was time for Ellison to set the record straight. Ellison definitely didn't want to be charged with murder, which meant he had to try to convince Brady otherwise. Whether Brady believed him or not didn't matter, that was up to the courts now.

Ellison looked at Claudia.

'Remember, stick to exactly what we discussed,' she instructed reassuringly.

Ellison looked from Claudia back to Brady, his face fraught with panic.

'I didn't do it. I didn't murder her . . . It's not what you think . . . I swear I didn't murder her!' Ellison panted.

'Prove it,' coolly demanded Brady.

'All right . . . I was seeing Sophie,' Ellison reluctantly confessed.

He dragged a hand through his hair as he looked at Brady.

'But it's not the way you're making it out. I know it was wrong . . . but . . . it just happened. We were on the school trip to Germany and she just kept throwing herself at me . . . you know?' Ellison said, shaking his head.

Brady did his best to keep his cynical comments to himself. He'd heard it all before. He'd interviewed enough men like Ellison over the years to recognise their delusional thinking.

'She . . . she looked much older than fifteen. You saw her,' Ellison said, turning to Brady. 'And so, I thought why not? She was more than up for it.'

Brady fought to hold his thoughts in.

Ellison's eyes dropped to his fidgeting hands as he uneasily continued.

'Any man would have done what I did . . . even you,' Ellison said, as he challenged Brady.

315

'All I know is that she was your fifteen-year-old pupil and you crossed the line,' Brady stated. 'And she wasn't the first, was she? Dr Jenkins already established that you have a history of seducing your underage students. But this time you got caught out. This time she wasn't going to put up and shut up like the other kids. Not Sophie, she wanted more than what you were giving her. And when she realised you were just using her, like you'd used the others, then she wanted to make you pay. Didn't she?'

'No, it wasn't like that,' Ellison replied cagily.

Ellison stared at Brady's unyielding expression.

'I don't expect you to understand . . .'

'No, I don't understand,' Brady coolly answered.

Ellison didn't reply. Instead he looked at Conrad who was sat, tight-lipped with unmoving, cold, steel-grey eyes. Ellison nervously cleared his throat.

'I never once forced her. It wasn't like that. She came on to me. Sophie would tell you . . .' Ellison faltered, lost for words.

'But that's the problem. Isn't it? Because Sophie can't tell us, can she? All we have is your word,' Brady pointed out evenly.

'I didn't murder her. I swear to you!' cried Ellison anxiously.

'Then tell me what happened that night,' Brady calmly suggested as he leaned forward.

Ellison swallowed as he ran a shaky hand through his hair.

'I . . . I met her at The Beacon for a couple of drinks. But then . . . then we had an argument. You see, she was always pushing me to tell people about us. I tried to explain to her that I'd lose my job, even go to prison if it came out. But, she wouldn't listen,' Ellison said slowly.

316

What more did he expect? Brady thought cynically. He resisted the temptation to state the obvious to Ellison. Brady tried to look sympathetic as he nodded for Ellison to continue. But it was hard.

'She was desperate to leave home. She said she hated her step-father and that she had to get out. She suggested that we move to London and start a new life there. I would get another teaching job . . . no one would know . . . But she didn't realise it wasn't that simple. The band was starting to get some local recognition . . . I couldn't move. Not after all the hard work I'd put in. And . . . and whatever it was that was between us had gone. You know? The relationship was over whether she wanted to believe it or not.'

Brady realised then that Sophie needed Ellison more than he had needed her. She had wanted an out from home, from Simmons and that was where Ellison came in.

'And then what happened?'

Ellison dropped his eyes as he thought it over.

He shrugged. 'I don't know where she went. She asked one of the bar staff to ring her a taxi and then she left in a strop. She was really mad with me,' Ellison quietly said.

He looked back up at Brady.

'That was just after eleven and then . . . I didn't see her until later. I rang her about midnight to try to talk to her. I don't know where she was, but there was a lot of noise in the background. I presume it was another pub. But she showed up twenty minutes later where we used to meet, which was by the gap in the fence next to her house. Where . . . where I presume you found my handprint,' Ellison uneasily explained. 'She was threatening to tell the school about what had happened so I agreed to meet her to talk her out of it.'

Brady nodded.

'We had sex first and then we talked for a while afterwards. I tried to reason with her that it was best if we finished it.'

'Where? Where did you have sex?' Brady asked, resisting the urge to point out that buggering and fucking a fifteen-year-old kid wasn't classed as just having sex.

Ellison looked at him, surprised that it mattered.

'In the ruins of the farmhouse. It's secluded there. It's where we used to go when we met.'

'Was anyone else there?' Brady questioned, wondering if Ellison had seen the girl that Shane McGuire had talked about.

Ellison shook his head. 'Not that I saw. It was dark and I wasn't really looking. At that time of night it's not the kind of place you expect to see someone,' he answered.

'And?' Brady prompted.

Ellison looked at him. 'Like I said I tried to explain to her that maybe we should be cooling things. That's when she lost it. She got really mad and started shouting and making these crazy demands. Then she started threatening that she would tell everyone anyway as a way of forcing me to stay with her. I tried to reason with her, but nothing was working. So, I left.'

'What happened before you left?' Brady calmly asked, fighting the adrenalin coursing through him as he thought about Shane McGuire's evidence.

'Like I said, we were arguing and so I decided to go home. It was pointless talking to her when she was like that,' Ellison replied as he anxiously ran a hand through his hair.

'What? Pissed?' Brady asked.

Ellison dropped his eyes, refusing to look at Brady.

'What time did you leave her?'

'I . . . I don't know . . . I can't be sure . . . maybe around one? Oh Christ . . . I . . . I'm not sure . . .'

Brady sat back and contemplated everything Ellison had said. He turned and looked at Conrad who had sat poker-faced throughout the interview.

'I don't get it. How did your lab results show my sperm in . . . in . . .' Ellison looked at Brady, confused. 'I . . . I was wearing a condom.'

'I recommend that next time you read the back of a condom packet. At best they are only 98 per cent effective,' Brady coolly answered.

Ellison numbly shook his head as he absorbed the evidence against him.

'I didn't murder her . . . you've got to believe me . . .' Ellison muttered.

'Well . . . this is the problem, sir, I have a witness who says otherwise,' Brady confided as he leaned in towards Ellison.

'Enough, DI Brady,' Claudia interrupted. 'I think it's time we had a chat.'

Brady nodded. As he terminated the interview he couldn't help noticing that Claudia looked angry with him.

Brady got up and walked out of the interview room followed by Claudia.

He heard the door slam behind him.

'I should bust your balls for that!'

'Someone's already tried, remember? Oh, yeah I forgot, you left as soon as you found out that I'd been shot! Maybe you didn't realise how bloody serious it was!'

Claudia furiously swept her red hair back off her face as she shot Brady a 'don't fuck with me' look. It was a look he'd seen often.

'You know the rules!' she stated furiously.

'And what about you? You're back? Just like that? No word for six bloody months and then you just turn up at work?' angrily questioned Brady.

'Why? Does it bother you?'

'You know the answer to that.'

'Do I, Jack?' Claudia bitterly questioned. 'I don't know you any more. I don't even think you know yourself! And anyway, it's a bit rich you acting all aggrieved that I'm back. What's the problem? Am I cramping your style? Is that it?'

'I'm sorry?' questioned Brady, confused.

'Amelia Jenkins? But then again why am I surprised given your history, Jack?'

Before Brady could say anything, Claudia abruptly changed the subject.

'So, what exactly do you have on my client?'

Chapter Fifty-Two

Brady watched Ellison.

He was speechless.

Brady had just informed him that he had been charged with the murder of his pupil, Sophie Washington. It was to be expected; the evidence was damning. Even Claudia didn't put up a fight when she'd added it all together.

'But I didn't kill her . . . I swear I didn't,' Ellison desperately pleaded.

But no one was listening.

'Do you hear me? You can't do this to me! You've got the wrong man,' Ellison repeated frantically.

Brady sceptically looked at Ellison.

'They all say that.'

'But I'm telling the truth . . . I didn't hurt her,' Ellison pleaded.

'That's a matter for the courts to decide,' Brady coolly replied.

'But . . . but why? It doesn't make sense! She was just an easy shag, that's all. She was the one who complicated things by trying to make it something more than what it was!' Ellison shouted. 'She was just a fucking slapper! Why would I murder her?'

Brady stared, unmoved at Ellison's contorted, angry figure.

'Our witness overheard the victim threaten to reveal your sordid relationship. If she did, then that would have been the end of your profession as a teacher, let alone your band, and the beginning of an indeterminate prison sentence.'

Ellison frantically shook his head. 'It wasn't like that.'

'No?' Brady questioned. 'You yourself said that the victim had threatened to expose your relationship. When she wouldn't listen to reason, I believe you lost your control and attempted to silence her by whatever means necessary. She started screaming. So you choked her until she stopped screaming and finally, stopped breathing.'

'No!' Ellison yelled. 'No!' He stared at Brady with wild desperation.

'Why would I do that terrible thing to her face? She meant nothing to me. I wanted to end the relationship for fuck's sake!' Ellison retaliated.

'Exactly,' Brady answered evenly. 'The attack on her face was such an act of fury that it could only have been committed by someone emotionally involved with the victim. Someone who had a motive to want her dead.'

Ellison shook his head, his bright, blue eyes fiercely rejecting what Brady had said.

'You see, a stranger would have just murdered Sophie and then left,' Brady quietly explained, shaking his head. 'But you were still filled with anger and hatred at what she had threatened to do to you. After all, she had threatened to take everything you'd worked so hard for from you, sir,' Brady stated. 'Your band is all you're interested in. Being a teacher pays the bills, but what you really want to do is make it big in the music business. What would have happened to your music career if word got out that you were having a sexual relationship with your fifteen-year-old student? One that you had tired of. Wouldn't exactly be a great PR stunt, now would it?'

Brady turned and nodded at Conrad to signal the close of the interview.

'You bastard! This has got nothing to do with Sophie!' Ellison shouted as he stood up. 'You're trying to set me up. Don't think I don't know what's going on. This has more to do with me spending the night with your girl-friend!' Ellison asserted as he aggressively shoved the table at Brady.

Brady didn't react. He was too aware of the fact that Claudia was taking note.

Not to mention Conrad.

'I saw the way you looked at her when she was talking to me. Couldn't handle the fact that she moved on to me? She told me all about the other night. Fuck! You're old enough to be her dad, you sick bastard!'

Brady instinctively clenched his fists.

'It's not my private life that's under scrutiny here,' Brady stated.

'Yeah? Well it bloody should be!'

He saw Conrad motion to the officer by the door to get help to remove Ellison.

The officer did as he was instructed and left.

'What's wrong? You don't want your colleagues knowing that their boss likes to shag seventeen-year-old girls? Is that it?' Ellison demanded of Conrad.

'You know something? You're not that different from me! You can pretend you're better than me. But you and I, we're very alike!' Ellison stated with bitter satisfaction. 'And just for the record, your girlfriend was a really good shag. But then, you'd know that, wouldn't you?'

Brady felt as if he had been punched in the abdomen. He could feel the nausea rising to the back of his throat. He couldn't look at Ellison, let alone Conrad. And he certainly couldn't bring himself to look at Claudia. He could feel her burning green eyes weighing him up for the low-life he had become. He couldn't even face himself without a Scotch.

'I'm sorry you heard that,' he muttered in Claudia's direction as he turned and walked out.

'Call yourself a copper? You're a fucking hypocrite, that's what you are!' Ellison shouted after him. 'You're the one who needs locking up! Not me!'

Brady heard Conrad use some choice words directed at Ellison. He couldn't look at the two officers who had returned to handle Ellison. He just kept his head down and headed back to his office. Sure, he'd nailed him, but at what price? If there had been any chance of Claudia taking him back Ellison had ruined it. Or if he was honest, he had ruined it. No one else. He swallowed back the pain as he thought of what he'd lost, again.

Chapter Fifty-Three

Brady looked up from his desk distractedly.

'Good job, Jack,' Gates congratulated as he stood in the doorway.

'Thank you, sir,' replied Brady, accepting that there was a first time for everything.

'I'm surprised that you're not with the others,' Gates said, frowning.

Brady shrugged. 'Six months of paperwork,' he lamely offered.

That and he wanted to make sure he kept out of the way of Claudia. He hadn't seen her since Ellison's arrest and decided it was best left that way; at least until things had cooled down.

Gates accepted his excuse. Brady knew he had other things on his mind. He had a press conference to attend at headquarters. An arrest had been made and the public had to be told. Conrad had been invited to accompany Gates. Brady was pleased for him. He deserved it. And he looked the part, more than Brady ever would.

'Make sure you join them. You should be there. It's just after nine, so I reckon you should be calling it a day, don't you?' Gates added firmly before closing the door.

Brady presumed it was Gates' guilty conscience kicking in. That was, if he had one. It should have been Brady sat with Gates during the press conference; he was after all Gates' next-in-command, not Conrad.

Brady had left the rest of the team congratulating one another in the Incident Room. Soon they would be moving on to The Fat Ox where they would no doubt get hammered. Brady wasn't sure if he was in the mood for joining them; he still felt uneasy about Matthews. And then there was Claudia.

He picked up the note Harvey had left on his desk. Harvey's barely legible scribble gave the name of the taxi driver and the cab company that had picked Sophie up from The Beacon. Brady fingered the yellow square of paper. Harvey had already talked to the driver. All he remembered was dropping Sophie off in the centre of Whitley Bay. From there she could have wandered into any number of the crass pubs that lined the seaside resort's streets. The Bedroom pub in the middle of the small town might have been the first stop; aptly named for the scum that drank there. Ironically, once legless, they would end up shagging whatever came their way, but it wouldn't be in the comfort of a bedroom. A back lane or the beach would do; regardless of the freezing North East conditions.

Brady had already flagged up with Gates that they didn't know what Sophie had gotten up to in Whitley Bay before she had met up again with Ellison. But Gates wasn't that bothered, he was more interested in how she had ended the night in Ellison's hands; literally. Gates had reminded Brady that the investigation was officially closed. Ellison had been arrested; end of story. Again, it was about meeting targets for Gates and an arrest was money in the bank. His performance-related pay guaranteed that.

But it didn't rest easy with Brady. Ellison's insistence that he hadn't murdered her disturbed him. Then again, Brady mused, how often did criminals insist they were innocent, even when caught with blood on their hands?

Brady contemplated what his next move should be. There was still a piece missing from the jigsaw, whether or not it mattered any more was irrelevant. Brady presumed it was the copper in him. He didn't like loose ends. If he was honest, what he really wanted was to get rid of the niggling doubt he had about Matthews. He still couldn't get hold of him. He had left God knows how many phone messages on his mobile. He had at least expected him to return his last call. But Matthews hadn't, despite the news that Ellison had been charged with Sophie Washington's murder.

Brady sighed wearily as he scrunched the paper up and threw it into the wastepaper bin.

Gates was right; it was over.

He pulled out his phone and before he had a chance to think about it, he made the call.

'It's me,' he said.

'I've got nothing to say,' Claudia answered.

Brady could hear glasses clinking in the background.

'Where are you?' he asked.

'That's not your concern, not any more,' she coldly answered.

Brady heard a man's voice talking to her. He realised it was Michael Travers. Bastard, thought Brady.

'Claudia?' he attempted again.

'Not now, Jack. This isn't a good time,' she replied, cutting him off.

'I bet it's not.'

'Meaning?' asked Claudia.

'Nothing . . . Look, forget I rang, OK?' Brady said.

'Bye Jack.'

He heard Michael Travers' distinctive laugh before she disconnected the call.

*

Brady stood alone at the bar and looked on as the team got hammered. He still couldn't place all the faces; not that it mattered. After today everyone who had been called in to help with the investigation would be returning to their own Area Commands, including DS Adamson.

'Not joining us?' Harvey asked as he came up to the bar.

'No. Don't really feel up to it,' Brady answered.

'Matthews still bothering you?' Harvey asked as he placed his empty glass down. He signalled to the barmaid. 'Same again, pet. And one for Jack.'

She nodded and began pouring the pints.

Brady turned and faced Harvey.

'I need to find him, Tom.'

'All I know is what I've already told you,' Harvey answered. He shrugged apologetically. 'I'm not certain, but she might have said she lived in North Shields, if that's any help.'

Brady shrugged. It didn't help; North Shields was a big place.

'What?' Harvey questioned.

'I just want to make sure Jimmy's all right. I heard some talk that Madley's after him. So . . . you understand,' Brady replied.

'Shit! Why didn't you say before?'

'Because Jimmy didn't want anyone to know. He thought he could handle it himself,' Brady answered.

Harvey shook his head.

'Fuck, I had no idea that Jimmy had pissed Madley off. What's the stupid sod done?'

'I wish I knew,' replied Brady.

He picked up his pint and drained it as he thought it over. He was tired. Too tired to think straight. What he needed was a good few drinks and then at least twelve hours' sleep. After that everything would seem clearer.

'Listen, keep it quiet, yeah? I'm sure Jimmy's fine. He can handle himself, even against the likes of Madley. Anyway, what's Madley going to do to him, eh? He's a copper for fuck's sake!'

Harvey nodded.

'Yeah, you're right. Bloody Jimmy though. Silly bugger. Knowing him he's shagged Madley's girlfriend or something. You know what a daft sod he is where women are concerned!'

Brady smiled and shook his head. 'Can't disagree with you there, Tom.'

'You sure you don't want to join us?' asked Harvey.

'Maybe later? I just need some time on my own.'

Brady watched as Harvey joined the rest of the team. He knew he had done the right thing by keeping away. Especially since Adamson was sat with them. But he wasn't just sat with them, he had his arm around Fielding, the young SOCO he'd met the other day at the crime scene. He'd seen her when he'd walked in earlier, and since then, like the rest of them she had got more and more drunk. She had somehow ended up with Adamson draped over her.

He looked up to see why Harvey and the rest were shouting and cheering as Fielding slapped Adamson. Brady was certain Adamson had it coming, but he knew the type of guy he was, and he wouldn't take that kind of humiliation from a woman lying down. The cheering and whooping continued as Fielding moved away from Adamson and sat down with some other female colleagues. If the bar staff hadn't known they were coppers, Brady was sure they would have been told to get out.

Brady just wanted to keep his head down and just finish the day. He remained hunched over a couple more pints. It was only when he saw Adamson making his way to the toilets that he decided he'd order his fourth pint after he'd had a few private words with the sleaze ball.

He pushed his way into the toilets and saw Adamson with his back to him, relieving himself at the urinal. Brady leaned against the door, blocking anyone from coming in.

Finished, Adamson zipped up his trousers and turned around.

'What the fuck do you want?' he snapped irritably when he saw Brady.

Brady gave him a relaxed smile.

'That's no way to talk to a senior officer,' he answered.

'Yeah? Well the investigation's closed and as of Monday I'm back at North Shields. So you can go fuck yourself!'

'She really got to you, didn't she?' laughed Brady.

'Fielding's just a fucking tease. The bitch better be careful because one day she'll go too far,' threatened Adamson.

Brady resisted the urge to floor him there and then, realising it wouldn't be a great way to end the investigation.

'And that would be you who would teach her a lesson I take it?' asked Brady.

'Did I say that?' answered Adamson.

'You didn't have to,' replied Brady.

'Fuck you!' cursed Adamson as he tried to push past Brady.

Brady shoved him back.

'What the fuck's got into you? I just want to finish having a drink with the lads, all right?'

Brady realised he had Adamson worried.

'Word of warning, watch your back!'

'What? Are you threatening me?'

Brady shook his head.

'No, that's a threat from Trina McGuire. Remember the stripper from the Hole whose mouth you tried to shove round your cock?' Brady stated.

Adamson looked surprised, but quickly composed himself.

'She was gagging for it, the bitch. If it hadn't been for Jenkins then no one would have been the wiser,' Adamson replied, clearly pissed off that Jenkins had told Brady.

'Anyway, what's your problem? Wanted some of her yourself?'

Brady slowly smiled at him.

'Just watch your back, Adamson. If you ever go near her again, it'll be me you're dealing with. Same applies to Fielding. I hear of anything happening to her and you'll find that you'll never be able to play with that limp dick of yours again,' Brady warned.

'Fuck you!' swore Adamson as Brady moved out of the way to let him pass.

Brady headed back to the bar to order that fourth pint. But when he saw Conrad coming through the pub's doors with Jenkins, he decided he'd had enough. It was time to leave. He wasn't in the mood for talking, especially to a shrink. And one that he found too damned attractive for his own good. He couldn't trust himself to continue drinking with her, not after what had nearly happened in his office. It was better to leave and avoid the awkward small talk.

He looked over at Harvey and the rest of the team and considered going over and letting them know he was off, but then decided the better of it. They wouldn't notice either way; too busy swapping complaints and anecdotes about their seniors – Brady included.

He made an attempt to go out the back door before Conrad and Jenkins spotted him. He was too late.

'Sir?' Conrad called out. 'You're not leaving already?'

Brady turned round wearily. 'Yeah . . . things to do and all that crap. You know how it is,' he replied, shrugging.

Conrad realised Brady's run-in with Claudia earlier had understandably dampened his mood. He nodded.

'See you Monday then, sir,' Conrad replied.

'Yeah, see you Monday,' Brady answered.

'Didn't you promise me a drink for all my hard work, Jack Brady?' Jenkins pointedly interrupted as a smile played on her red lips.

Jenkins' arrival was as good a reason as any to leave. Brady didn't want to give Claudia the satisfaction of proving yet again that she was right about him. He shrugged apologetically.

'It's been a long day.'

She looked unconvinced.

'Make sure you get the drinks on me, will you?' Brady asked as he handed over a fifty to Conrad.

'Are you sure you're not just avoiding me?' uncomfortably asked Jenkins.

'I've got a mountain of paperwork to catch up on, after

being off for so long,' Brady unconvincingly answered, before turning and leaving.

'Jack?' she called out after him.

He pretended he hadn't heard. Instead, let the door swing shut behind him and sighed, relieved to be out in the cold, November night. He fumbled in his jacket for his cigarettes as he tried to decide where to go. The station seemed tempting. It would be quiet and he was guaranteed to run into no one he gave a damn about. They were all getting plastered inside The Fat Ox. Apart from Claudia. He had tried ringing her again, to explain about Sleeping Beauty, but her phone was switched off. Consequently Brady had left a hesitant, awkward message and not surprisingly, she hadn't returned the call. And he'd be damned if he gave Michael Travers the satisfaction of turning up at his £900k place in Jesmond looking for his wife.

He lit a cigarette and leaned back against the wall and listened to the celebratory, muffled voices inside. He looked across the road at St Paul's church. It stood wrapped in a comforting silence; the church and graveyard temptingly lifeless. If the church wasn't guaranteed to be locked against drunken bums like himself, he might have considered taking time out inside.

Brady slowly breathed out.

He decided to walk. It didn't matter where, he just needed to walk to clear his head.

Chapter Fifty-Four

He somehow found himself walking along the coast from Whitley Bay to Tynemouth. The sea was having the desired effect on him and was taking the edge off his uneasiness. That, and there was no one around to bother him. Not even dog walkers. It was after well after 10 pm which meant it was too late, and too cold. In the distance he could see the Grand Hotel, one of the most luxurious hotels in the area. An imposing Victorian building, originally built by the Duke of Northumberland in 1872 as a summer residence and then later converted into a hotel. It was dramatically lit up against the blackness of the night. It was not only a stunning landmark out at sea, but from where Brady was stood, it was a proud architectural example of a bygone age of luxury and elegance.

Before he knew what he was doing he was already walking up the stone steps of the Grand Hotel. He nodded at the doorman who politely held the door open for him as he walked through into the impressive elegant hallway. An ornate, sweeping marble staircase spiralled up to the first floor, hinting of an opulent era of aristocratic balls. Brady smiled at the receptionist who had looked up to greet him and turned right through the double glass doors into the bar.

He walked over to the barman.

'A Scotch. Make it a double,' Brady ordered as he placed a tenner on the bar.

He was tired, but not tired enough to be able to fall asleep on the couch at his office. His head was still spinning and he needed a drink to try to switch off. For some reason he couldn't accept the outcome of the investigation. Something was niggling at him, something he didn't want to acknowledge. He kept remembering what Jenkins had said about the overkill aspect of the murder. She had clearly stated that the murderer had destroyed Sophie's face out of pure, vengeful jealousy. So, why would Ellison do it? It didn't make sense. Brady could understand why he would murder Sophie. She had become a liability to him. But, why mutilate her face beyond recognition? Brady had initially assumed that Ellison was still emotionally involved with the victim. So even murdering her wouldn't have satisfied his rage. But it was clear from his interviews with Ellison that the man had no emotional attachment to the victim. She was just another underage conquest that he had used and abused for his ego's sake. One that he needed to get rid of, without drawing attention to himself.

The bartender handed Brady his drink. He took a deep, long gulp before turning to look out of the majestic windows that faced directly out onto the sea. He took another much needed sip and savoured the view. The walk along the coast was worth it for the relaxed ambiance in the bar. A stark contrast to what he'd left behind in The Fat Ox.

Someone's deep voice caught his attention. Brady realised the distinctive voice belonged to Chief Superintendent

O'Donnell. He turned round and caught O'Donnell's eye as he made his way to the bar.

Brady was surprised to see him in black tie, and presumed he was at some social function.

O'Donnell beamed at him.

Brady smiled back.

'Jack? What are you doing here? If I'd known I would have asked you to join us for dinner,' O'Donnell greeted.

He came up to Brady and warmly embraced him.

'You know me, sir, I don't do formal dinners,' Brady replied.

'I know, I know and I daresay you never will,' O'Donnell replied as he smiled at him paternally.

Brady felt a pang of regret as he looked at O'Donnell. He was still a huge bear of a man with enough presence to scare most people. But he was getting old. His black curly hair was more silver than black and his heavily-lined green eyes looked watery and tired. Brady knew the word was out that he would be retiring soon, but Brady wasn't ready for that. Not yet, even if O'Donnell looked more than ready to step down.

Brady watched as they were joined by another man dressed in the same formal attire as O'Donnell.

'Jack Brady, Mayor Macmillan,' O'Donnell said as he introduced Brady to his dinner companion.

But Brady didn't need any introduction. He knew Macmillan well enough.

Macmillan shot him a slick, oily smile as he bared his perfectly whitened and straightened teeth at Brady. It was a politician's smile; soulless.

Macmillan was a slender five feet ten, in his early forties with sharp, penetrating blue eyes. This, coupled

336

with his blond hair and smooth, tanned skin were his charm arsenal. The public and the press couldn't get enough of him. But to Brady, Macmillan's handsome face lacked compassion and empathy. And there was always a coldness in his eyes, even when he was smiling directly at you.

'Good to finally meet you, DI Brady,' Macmillan said as he offered his hand.

Brady reluctantly accepted his overly firm grip. Word had clearly got back to Macmillan that Brady wasn't his biggest supporter.

'And congratulations are in order I hear? Well done!' he said, as he gave Brady an insincere smile. 'Bill here has only the highest praise for you,' he added as he playfully thumped O'Donnell on the back.

Brady didn't reply. He had a feeling that Macmillan was being disingenuous. Add to that the fact he was feeling very uncomfortable about the relationship between O'Donnell and Macmillan. It seemed that they were very familiar with one another; too familiar. Brady tried to ignore what Matthews had said to him earlier about O'Donnell being in Macmillan's pocket.

Brady looked at O'Donnell and couldn't bring himself to believe it. The man had too much integrity, surely? He couldn't be bought. Not by a sleaze bag like Macmillan.

'What's it to be then, Bill?' Macmillan asked as the bartender dutifully waited on them.

'The usual,' answered O'Donnell. 'Jack? Another?' he asked.

Brady shook his head.

'Sorry, can't stay. I need to go back to the office.'

'Surely you're done for the night?' O'Donnell asked, disappointed.

'You know me,' Brady answered apologetically.

He caught Macmillan's eye. It was a cold, penetrating look that told him he was making the right decision to leave.

Brady turned and swiftly downed what was left of his malt. He decided it was better to leave before he ended up saying something to Macmillan and jeopardising not only his job, but his friendship with O'Donnell.

*

He had intended to go back to the station, but instead found himself outside Madley's nightclub – The Blue Lagoon. Running into O'Donnell and Macmillan had really screwed with his head and the last place he wanted to be was sat in his office. His mobile rang as he stood outside debating whether to go in.

'Yeah?' Brady abruptly answered.

'Jack?'

'What's wrong? Has something happened?' he asked when he realised it was Kate.

'No . . . no. I just wanted to talk . . .'

Brady sighed, relieved.

'Sure, but I'm still caught up with something right now . . .'

'Oh . . . OK . . .' Kate said hesitating. 'Jack, is it true? The news has reported that it was her teacher?'

He slowly breathed out.

'Yeah . . . The news is right, we've just charged him with her murder.'

'Oh God! I . . . I never would have thought he was capable of doing something like that. Are you definitely sure?'

'Yeah, we're certain.'

'I can tell Evie that it's over with then?'

'Yeah, I think that would be a good idea,' answered Brady.

'Jack? You haven't heard from Jimmy have you?'

'No . . . I'm sorry, Kate, but I've heard nothing from him.'

'Oh . . . Just . . . it's just that I feel like I'm going mad . . . I need . . . I need someone to talk to . . . you know? What with Jimmy still gone and . . . and . . . Jack? I really need you right now . . . could you . . .' she faltered.

Brady was sure she was crying.

'Give me an hour, then I'll come back. Yeah?' Brady offered.

'Promise?'

'You've got my word,' assured Brady before cutting the call.

He quickly shook off any concerns he had about Kate when he looked back up at the nightclub. He was certain he could see Madley's figure silhouetted in the first-floor office window expecting him.

*

He attempted to limp past the two meatheads guarding the door.

'Oi, mate! We're not open till eleven,' a fat, thuggish, bald man grunted.

Brady looked at him aware that it was well after eleven. He was dressed in the required black suit and bow tie. His fat fingers were covered in chunky gold rings. Brady presumed they came in handy when he had to throw a few

339

punches. He fixed his dark brown eyes on the bouncer's threatening glare.

'I'm here to see Madley,' Brady gruffly replied. He knew there was no point in being polite; these thugs were bred for violence, it was the only language they understood.

'He's not here,' the bald man gutturally said. 'So piss off.'

'I'll wait until he shows then,' Brady asserted.

'Are you thick or what? I said piss off!' The bouncer grunted as he started to flex his fat, porky fingers.

Brady knew he didn't stand a chance. He pulled out his wallet and showed his ID.

The bouncer glared at Brady in disgust before jerking his head for him to go through the doors.

Brady limped in. The place stank of stale sweat and sweet, sticky alcohol. Music was pulsating throughout, too loud and too crap for Brady's liking. He made his way towards the bar where the staff were setting up for the night.

'I need to speak to Madley,' Brady shouted to a young girl behind the bar.

He didn't recognise her and presumed she was new.

She eyed him suspiciously. 'What's it about?'

'I'll tell him when I see him,' Brady answered.

She reluctantly sighed. 'Name?'

'Detective Inspector Brady.'

'I'll see if he's around,' she replied irritably.

She put the mixers in her hand down and walked to the end of the bar. She picked up the phone and dialled.

Brady watched as she spoke to someone, presumably explaining that there was a copper looking for Madley. Brady saw her mouth his name. She then nodded and put the phone down.

She walked back to him.

'He's expecting you,' she said. 'Through the emergency door there and then up the stairs. First door on the right.'

'Yeah, I know where,' Brady answered as he made his way to the door.

He couldn't shake the feeling that he was making a mistake.

Brady allowed himself to be frisked by the same two henchmen from his visit on Friday.

'You're bleedin' popular!' grunted one of them.

'It's my good looks. Madley can't resist,' replied Brady.

The brute scrunched his face into a frown as he tried to figure out whether to deck Brady or not.

'Wouldn't if I were you,' Brady dryly commented, noting the readied fist.

He walked into the office, leaving the henchman confused and frustrated.

'I heard the good news,' Madley coolly stated.

He was stood with his back to Brady looking out the ceiling-to-floor window.

Brady joined Madley and looked out at the scene below and immediately regretted it. The promenade was full of Saturday night drinkers. A group of pissed, raucous girls in knicker-high skirts and bra tops zigzagged their way across the road followed by leering lads. Taxi cars beeped at them as they tottered across the road, gesturing and mouthing obscenities at the cars.

'Scotch?' Madley asked as he headed over to the drinks cabinet.

Brady nodded. He knew he'd already had enough to drink, but he had a feeling he was really going to need this one. He turned and looked out at the rowdy gathering below.

'Business seems good, Martin.'

'I do all right out of it,' Madley answered.

'Yeah.'

Madley joined Brady with the drinks.

'I was surprised that you got someone for that girl's murder,' Madley stated. 'A convenient open and shut case,' he added with a tinge of cynicism.

Brady looked at him. He had his face turned to the window, seemingly intent on the people below. Brady knew better; Madley was always on his guard.

Brady shrugged.

'I didn't think you were like the rest of them.'

'What do you mean?' Brady asked, confused.

'Don't take the piss with me, Jack. We go too far back for that.'

Brady took a drink and thought about it. He savoured the Scotch as it slid down the back of his throat. If he wasn't mistaken it was a Talisker malt, flown in from the Isle of Skye. Madley had expensive tastes; he had a lot to make up for given his childhood.

'I don't know what the fuck you're talking about,' Brady answered.

Madley questioningly looked at Brady, his glinting brown eyes narrowed.

Brady held his gaze.

'You know as well as I do that that poor sod didn't kill the girl,' Madley quietly stated.

'What the fuck are you saying, Martin?' Brady demanded.

'You know exactly what I'm saying. You lot tied that case up so damned fast that it has to be a set-up. You didn't want anyone spending too much time on it because you knew it would eventually lead back to Jimmy.'

'What do you mean?' Brady asked nervously.

Madley turned and looked back out of the window.

They stood in silence watching the drunks in the street below.

Brady kept quiet. He was scared shitless of what he was about to hear. He knew he could turn and walk out, leaving things as they were: Ellison arrested for the murder of his pupil. Did it really matter if he hadn't actually killed her; hadn't he already done enough with his sordid hands to warrant life in prison?

Brady knew most would turn a blind eye, but not him. Madley knew that, as did Matthews. Brady had an unfailing sense of duty.

'You've got the wrong man, Jack, and you know it,' Madley quietly stated, as he kept his eyes fixed on the black, tumultuous sea.

Brady didn't say a word.

He took a drink and waited for the malt to slowly numb him.

'Why else would you have turned up?' Madley questioned.

'I . . . I don't know . . .' muttered Brady.

'He was here with the girl,' Madley stated.

Brady felt sick.

He hadn't expected this; he had been certain that Matthews must have had some sort of run-in with Madley the night of the murder. But that was it.

'Thursday night, she was here with Jimmy. He was all over her. I just took it she was another one of his slappers. I thought she was a bit young, but then again, it was Jimmy. You know better than anyone what he's like. The bastard can't keep his dick in his trousers.'

Brady gripped his whisky glass to steady himself.

'I've got it all on security tape if you don't believe me,' Madley added.

'Why? Why are you doing this?'

'Whose money do you think paid for that big house of his in Earsdon? A copper's salary couldn't pay for that kind of lifestyle, Jack, and you know it,' Madley asserted. 'Why else did you turn up yesterday? You knew, but you didn't have the balls to ask me outright.'

Brady couldn't disagree with Madley. He was right, he had known. Matthews' lifestyle couldn't be maintained on a copper's salary. And he had known all along that was where Madley came in.

Brady looked out of the window. The horizon was as black as the sea.

'You've got no choice, Jack,' Madley said, breaking the heavy silence. 'Not now you know.'

'You've still got to convince me first,' Brady evenly replied.

Madley smiled. 'Yeah, still the same old Jack.'

Madley took Brady's empty glass and walked back over to the drinks cabinet.

'I take it you'll be needing another?'

Brady nodded. 'When can I see the tape?'

'The package on my desk is your copy.'

Brady looked over at the desk. Two identical large, padded brown envelopes lay unopened.

'Who's the other one for?' Brady asked, feeling his leg starting to flare up.

'Let's say it's my insurance. I don't know if I trust you to make the right decision. If I was in your position I don't know what I'd do. So, in case you decide to put your friendship first, then I'll have to take matters into my own hands.

I'm sure your boss will be interested in Jimmy's little problem.'

Brady felt his throat tighten as he looked at the sealed packages. He knew it was pointless grabbing them and making a run for it; not that he could with his leg. He knew Madley would still have the original and no doubt, multiple copies.

Madley returned with two refilled glasses.

'You look like shit, Jack,' Madley stated.

'I feel it,' Brady muttered as he took the glass. He then took a deep gulp.

'Go on, I'm listening.'

'As I said, Jimmy was all over her. She didn't seem to mind though, but then again she did look pissed.'

Brady wasn't surprised, given the amount of alcohol the lab results found in her.

'Jimmy then asked me for the use of one of my private rooms,' Madley said as he gestured towards the ceiling.

Brady knew that Madley had luxurious living quarters on the third and fourth floor, despite having a six-bedroom house on Marine Avenue. Not to mention the farmhouse in the wilds of Northumbria.

'Why not use your hotel next door?' Brady asked. Madley also owned the Royal Hotel as well as the two clubs in town.

'Exactly what I said, but he claimed he didn't want to be seen checking in with her. Never bothered him before, but I understand why now,' Madley answered.

Brady thought it over. It didn't sound like Matthews.

'Are you sure he didn't just want to take her upstairs so she could sober up before he took her home?' Brady asked.

'No,' Madley firmly answered.

'But why not use his car if he just wanted to shag her? Why use one of your rooms?' Brady asked, puzzled.

Madley didn't answer.

Brady knew he was holding back on him but he expected no less from Madley.

'Then what happened?'

'I refused to let him use any of my private rooms so he left with her,' answered Madley.

'What time?'

'Sometime before twelve.'

Brady took a slug from his glass of whisky as he thought about it.

'That means he couldn't have done it. She was murdered by Ellison after Jimmy dropped her off,' Brady said as a surge of relief rushed through him.

Madley continued to look out at the black sea.

'Where's the copper in you, Jack? You know that that dumb sod you've arrested didn't murder her. Otherwise you wouldn't be stood here now.'

'Why wait until now? Why didn't you call me as soon as you knew about the murder?' Brady asked, doubting Madley's good citizen act. 'Yesterday when I came to you about Jimmy? Or even when I saw you this morning. Why didn't you say something?'

'This morning you had something else on your mind, Jack. Remember? And, as for yesterday, let's say I was giving Jimmy some time to come forward.'

'You know if he ends up inside, they'll kill him because he's a copper?' Brady asked.

'My heart bleeds,' Madley answered.

'And if he's innocent? Something like this will ruin his career, his marriage, everything he's ever worked for.'

Madley remained unmoved.

'All he had to do was give me back what was mine. Instead,

he goes into hiding. So what am I meant to think? He's done this to himself, Jack. He's a liability now. You of all people know the score. If word got out that I was a soft touch then what would happen to my business? No one steals from me, Jack. No one.'

Brady drained his glass and handed it back.

'Thanks.' Brady wasn't sure whether he meant for the malt or for telling him about Matthews before telling Gates.

'Still on for poker on Monday night?'

'Why wouldn't I be?'

'See you there, then,' Madley replied as he turned back to the window.

'Yeah,' Brady replied quietly.

'Oh and Jack, have you had time to consider your other problem?'

Brady turned and looked at Madley.

'Yeah,' he muttered. 'Sort it, will you?'

Madley nodded.

'Consider it already done.'

'Thanks,' muttered Brady.

'You sure you've got no doubts? After all, he's still your dad,' Madley added.

Brady turned and looked at him.

'He was never my dad,' Brady answered as he tried to get rid of the image of the shabby, drunken tramp in his head.

Brady waited until he was outside before calling Matthews. Still no answer.

'You stupid bugger, Jimmy,' Brady said under his breath.

He lit a cigarette as he weighed up his options. He had none. The only thing he could do was go back to the station and watch the tape. After that, he could decide whether what Madley had was bad enough for Matthews' career to be over.

Chapter Fifty-Five

Fuck, thought Brady as he tried to think straight.

Madley had been right, the tape was incriminating. Matthews' career as a copper was finished. Brady felt his stomach lurch as he thought about what he'd seen.

Matthews seemed to be all over Sophie Washington; as much as she was all over him. He tried to swallow down the acidic bile that had forced its way to the back of his throat. No matter how hard he tried, he couldn't ignore the fact that Sophie was the same age as Matthews' own daughter. Brady shook his head. This was Jimmy he was talking about; Jimmy. The betrayal he felt was beyond words.

Brady poured himself another Scotch as he sat in the heavy darkness. An orange glow from the street lights outside stabbed through the blinds. His phone vibrated again. He knew it would be Kate. But right now he couldn't face anyone. And certainly not Matthews' wife. He rested back in his chair and closed his eyes as he listened to the CD of Samuel Barber's *Adagio for Strings* in an attempt to drown out his torturous thoughts. He took another mind-numbing mouthful of Scotch and waited. For what, he didn't know. But wait was all he could do.

*

Minutes slowly passed as Brady sat in the dark accepting he had no choice. He was aware that as soon as Gates saw the tape questions would be asked. Matthews had withheld crucial information and to make matters worse, he had disappeared. Add to that the allegation that he had been taking backhanders from Madley, the local mafia boss. Right now things couldn't get any worse.

Brady reluctantly picked up his phone and dialled.

Conrad's voice answered. In the background Brady could hear shouting and cheering. It sounded like the team were still celebrating the case being closed. Brady slowly breathed out as he prepared himself.

'Conrad?'

'Sir, is that you?'

'Yeah it's me. I'm still at the station,' Brady answered softly. 'I need to talk to you. It's important. And Conrad? Keep this to yourself. Whatever you do, don't tell Jenkins.'

'I thought the investigation was closed,' replied Conrad.

'I wish it was,' muttered Brady. 'Conrad, how much have you had to drink?'

'Just a couple, sir. Why?'

'I might need you to drive me somewhere,' answered Brady.

He disconnected the call and waited.

*

Conrad parked opposite Matthews' house in Earsdon. He cut his lights and switched off the engine.

'Wait here. If Matthews turns up call me,' Brady ordered reluctantly.

'Are you sure about this?' Conrad asked.

Brady turned and stared at him.

'You saw the tape. What do you think?'

Conrad didn't reply. He couldn't.

'It's better this way. I need to have a look around and see if I can get any leads on where he's gone. I need to talk to him before Gates gets hold of that tape. Madley was serious about giving a copy to Gates. Once he sees it . . .' Brady stopped, unable to finish.

They both knew what the outcome would be. Matthews' career would be over. At least this way Brady might be able to convince Matthews to come forward and explain how the bloody hell he had got himself involved with Madley, not to mention his involvement with the victim. Maybe if Matthews came clean then the outcome wouldn't include prison.

'Conrad? If I'm not back out in ten minutes . . . well just bugger off. I don't want you caught up in all of this. Understand?' Brady instructed.

It wasn't worth ringing the doorbell to see if anyone was home, he already knew the answer. He took out the set of keys he'd lifted when he'd first come to see Matthews.

'Shit!' he cursed as an alarm started its countdown. Brady had to think fast or he'd have uniform pulling up outside, or worse some security guards believing they were the law. This was Earsdon after all; expensive houses with lots of fancy goods inside.

He followed the noise to an alarm control unit under

350

the stairs. Steadying himself he keyed in the code from Matthews' old house and inwardly prayed. It went silent.

'Shit,' he muttered uneasily as he pulled himself together.

He didn't have long. He looked around until he found what he presumed was Matthews' study. The drawers to his desk had been ransacked. Matthews had obviously been in a hurry when he had left and grabbed whatever he could. However, a spare set of car keys had been left in one of the drawers.

Brady picked them up and headed towards the garage. Being a copper, Brady knew Matthews was aware of the likelihood of being traced. CCTV cameras were everywhere and once the police had a report on a vehicle it wouldn't take long to track it down.

When Brady reached the utility room he tried the door which connected the garage to the house, expecting it to be locked. It wasn't. It swung open into a large, dark space. He stepped down into the garage and waited for his eyes to adjust to the dense blackness. Matthews' car was parked against the opposite wall. Brady felt himself trembling and knew it wasn't just the cold.

Instinct made him try the boot first. It opened. There was a half-full black bin liner. Without thinking Brady shone his torch into it. He stepped back in disbelief at the sight of Matthews' clothes; the exact same clothes he had worn to Madley's nightclub the night of the murder. The pale shirt and tie were splattered in indiscriminate patches of rust-coloured blood. Brady had seen enough. He didn't have the stomach to search through the rest of the bag and decided it was better left for the lab.

He ran a trembling hand through his hair as he remembered Matthews' coat draped over the victim's body. The same coat he was filmed wearing as he left Madley's night-club with Sophie. Brady had accepted Matthews' lame excuse that he had been worried that the victim might have traces of his DNA from when he drove her home and that he had covered her body with his coat as a convenient ruse for explaining why any of his DNA might be on her.

Brady now realised the truth was much darker.

He steeled himself as he walked round to the passenger's side. He shakily opened the car door and shone the torch across the front and back seats; nothing. At least nothing that the naked eye could see. He was sure that something would show up under a forensic ultraviolet light. He opened up the glove compartment. Again nothing. Brady sighed as he bent down to have a look at the floor. He shone his flashlight under the passenger's seat and caught a glimpse of something. He reached under and pulled out a mobile phone. At first he wondered whether Matthews had left his phone behind, but realised that was highly improbable.

Brady opened the phone; it was an expensive Motorola. The exact type that the Simmons had said their daughter owned. It was switched off. Brady knew that after the call to Matthews' mobile the phone had shortly lost its network connection; meaning someone had turned it off.

Brady pulled out a small plastic bag from his jacket pocket and deposited the phone inside. He took another look inside and saw something sticking out from under the seat. It was an empty condom wrapper. He picked it up and placed it in an evidence bag.

Brady closed his eyes for a moment as he thought about what he was about to do. His head was pounding; too much Scotch and not enough sleep. He reluctantly opened his eyes and started to call Conrad.

'There's no need for that,' a hoarse voice suddenly threatened.

Brady froze.

He looked up. Matthews was stood in the doorway.

'Jimmy?'

Chapter Fifty-Six

Matthews slowly walked towards Brady, his eyes glinting dangerously like a rabid dog in the dark.

Brady felt himself tense up. Matthews was desperate and Brady had witnessed his brutish temper when threatened.

'I can help you,' Brady offered, aware he wouldn't stand a chance against him. Not with the state of his leg.

'You want to help? Then give me her phone and leave,' Matthews quietly suggested.

Brady clenched his hands as he prepared himself.

'I can't do that.'

'You owe me, Jack,' Matthews threatened.

'It's too late.'

'Why? No one's looking for me.'

Brady tried his best to sound in control. He swallowed hard.

'Not yet, but the evidence is there in your car, Jimmy,' Brady slowly stated. 'And there's a surveillance tape of you and Sophie at Madley's nightclub the night she was murdered.'

'You fucking bastard!' Matthews shouted as he lunged at him. 'You really believe I'm capable of doing that? You think I could murder her?' he questioned as he delivered a hard and fast blow to Brady's stomach.

Brady doubled over in agony, unable to breathe.

Matthews yanked him up by his hair so he could see his contorted expression.

'And I didn't fuck her if that's what you're thinking!'

'I didn't say you did!'

'No? But that's what you think,' accused Matthews.

'I don't think that, but others will when they've watched the tape. You were all over her,' Brady panted, as he tried to get his breath back.

'She was pissed. So pissed she didn't even realise who I was. She kept throwing her arms around me and trying to kiss me. For fuck's sake! I was trying to persuade her to go home to sober up. Only a sick bastard like you would think something else. I was just trying to keep her from getting picked up by the other perverted bastards who go to Madley's nightclub.'

Brady gasped in air as he tried to steady his erratic breathing.

'I won't be the only one looking for you,' he breathlessly wheezed. 'Soon Gates will know about the tape and then you'll have no choice but to come in. Gates is clever, he'll put two and two together and—'

'You bastard! You've fucking opened your mouth!'

'I haven't told anyone!'

'You fucking liar!'

'Madley gave me the surveillance tape. You fucking stole from him, Jimmy. Fuck! The last person you steal from is Madley. He wants to make sure he gets even with you. He's using the tape of you and the victim to incriminate you and destroy your career for good,' Brady explained as he tried not to breathe in Matthews' sour breath.

'That fucking bastard! Did he tell you how he's making his filthy money? Did he?' Matthews spat in his face.

'He just gave me the surveillance tape, Jimmy. It was enough. It shows you with her. It shows you leaving with Sophie.'

'Give me the tape then!'

Brady shook his head.

Matthews shoved Brady hard against the car.

'For fuck's sake, Jimmy!' shouted Brady. 'Don't you get it? No one steals from Madley, Jimmy. Christ! Surely you know that much about him!'

Matthews lodged his arm under Brady's neck, pinning him even further back against the car.

'He gave me a copy of the surveillance tape and he's also giving a copy to Gates. It's over with,' Brady croaked.

'I don't believe you,' he said as his eyes stared wildly at Brady.

'Why would I lie? You know me,' Brady replied.

'I thought I did. But not any more.'

He rammed his arm hard against Brady's neck forcing him to gasp for air.

'And where's my fucking wife, you bastard? I disappear and you fucking move her into your place! Is that what you've been waiting for all this time? Me to clear off so you could have her? Well, I'm not going to let it happen. Not while I can still do something about it!' Matthews growled as he watched Brady struggle to breathe.

'No . . . Jimmy . . . you're not thinking straight!' gasped Brady.

'Maybe you and Madley are in this together. I wouldn't be surprised since you both come from the same shit hole. You've set me up, you bastard! What the fuck else has Madley told you?'

'I only know what I've seen, Jimmy. The tape . . . and then . . . oh fuck . . . your clothes in the car and Sophie's phone . . .' Brady cut off, trying desperately to think of something to calm Matthews down.

'Let's talk about this? Before it's too late,' Brady attempted.

'It's already too late.'

'Don't be a fucking fool!' Brady spluttered as Matthews pulled out a handgun.

Matthews steadily aimed the gun at Brady's head.

'Shit, Jimmy! You won't get away with this,' Brady reasoned nervously.

'You broke into my house making some crazy accusations. Then you threatened me with this gun. I struggled with you and the gun went off. Simple,' explained Matthews chillingly as his gloved hand released the safety trigger.

'Put the gun down!' ordered a loud, stern voice.

'Put the gun down!' repeated the voice. 'That's an order, Jimmy.'

It was Gates' voice. Behind him stood Conrad. Outside, Brady could hear the reassuring wail and screech of sirens as back-up arrived. He slumped back against the car realising that Conrad had disobeyed his order to abandon him if he didn't return after ten minutes.

He closed his eyes and rested his head back against the cold metal as armed officers surrounded Matthews. He shakily breathed out, unsure of how he could ever thank Conrad for what he had just done.

Chapter Fifty-Seven

'They'll crucify him if he goes inside. You know that, don't you?' questioned Gates.

Brady didn't know what to say.

They both knew the reality for coppers who found themselves on the wrong side of the bars. He'd tried for the past hour to get Matthews to open up. But he wouldn't. He had decided on his right to silence until convicted. And with the amount of evidence they had stacked up against him, his conviction looked an absolute certainty. Forensics had pulled out all the stops since Matthews' arrest. Gates had called the whole team back in, regardless of hangovers and sleep deprivation. There was an eerie disquiet around the station. Everyone found it hard to believe that Matthews could have murdered the girl but the evidence looked indisputable. Ainsworth's team had found DNA from the victim in Matthews' car on both the passenger and the driver's seat. The victim's hair, tissue and blood had been scraped up, presumably contaminated by Matthews when he had left the murder scene. It was no surprise when the blood on his shirt matched the victim's.

'Tell me one thing. Did you know? Had Jimmy confided in you?' asked Gates.

'No sir,' answered Brady.

'If I find out that you're lying to me, Jack, you'll be facing more than just a disciplinary hearing,' Gates threatened as his cold, detached eyes bored into him.

Brady hazarded a guess that Matthews' sudden role in the murder had managed to scupper Gates' newfound chances of promotion.

Brady held Gates' scrutinising stare.

'Get out of my sight, Jack. I don't want to see your face in front of me again until you've succeeded in getting Jimmy to talk. Understand?' Gates demanded.

'Perfectly, sir,' Brady replied.

He turned and limped towards the door.

He couldn't shake his instinct that Matthews was hiding something from him. Worse, he couldn't shift the nagging doubt that he was innocent. But then, why wasn't he talking? The only answer that came to mind was that he was protecting someone. And it definitely wasn't Ellison. Matthews had made it quite clear that he would have been prepared to let Ellison go down for murder; regardless of whether he actually killed her.

The question Brady had to figure out was who? He already had an idea who it might be, but as of yet, he couldn't bring himself to seriously consider it.

'And Simmons?' called out Gates before Brady walked through the door.

'About to interview him now, sir.'

'Just make sure you nail the bastard!' Gates added.

Simmons' solicitor had kicked off big-time and had threatened to publicly humiliate Northumbria Police over their treatment of his client. Problem for Brady was that Simmons' solicitor was Claudia.

To add to his problems Gates had been dragged in front of the Chief Constable to explain why Simmons was planning on suing the force for inappropriate handling of his step-daughter's murder. The fact that he had been treated as a prime suspect hadn't helped. Brady knew it was his fault that Gates' integrity had been called into question. It was down to his dealings with Simmons, and it was his dealings alone that would clear Gates' name with the Chief Constable.

'The evidence alone will do that, sir,' Brady quietly replied.

He had repeatedly pushed Jed to continue searching Simmons' hard drive, refusing to accept defeat. He had had a gut feeling that Simmons was sexually abusing his step-daughter and had been since she was eleven years old. Forty-eight hours later and with the murder investigation coming to a close, he had finally received a call from Jed giving him the ammunition to bring Simmons back in. Brady had been certain that once his hunch about Paul Simmons had been vindicated he would rest easy. But the sickening reality couldn't have been further from the truth.

Chapter Fifty-Eight

'You bastard! This better be good or you'll find yourself out of a job!' threatened Simmons as Brady walked into the interview room.

'Do you know what bloody time it is? I was dragged out of my bed at seven on a Sunday morning and forced to sit for nearly three hours in one of your holding cells like a criminal waiting for you to bloody roll into work!'

Brady ignored him and instead turned to Simmons' solicitor. He was expecting Claudia and was both surprised and equally disappointed to find Michael Travers in her place. He realised this was her way of saying it was over. And what better way of delivering that message than through Travers? She knew he hated the uptight, arrogant bugger. And Claudia knew he had every reason to, especially when Travers was trying his damned best to seduce her.

Brady resisted the urge to wipe the arrogant smile off Travers' tanned, almost triumphant face.

'I hope for your sake, DI Brady, that you've brought my client in to apologise!' Travers stated abruptly.

'For?' asked Brady.

'Oh for goodness sake! Don't play the idiot with me. I've already put in an official complaint about your unfounded allegations against my client and his step-daughter,' Michael Travers said irritably. 'So don't push me.'

Brady couldn't help but smile.

'Aren't you forgetting the claim for damages that you've lodged? How much exactly is it that your client's suing Northumbria Police for?' asked Brady.

'I don't expect to sit here and be insulted. Be warned, DI Brady, if this is some cheap stunt of yours then mark my words, I'll have you.'

'Oh we can do better than some cheap stunt, can't we, DS Conrad?' said Brady as Conrad sat down beside him.

'Yes sir,' replied Conrad as he placed a file on the table.

'What's this?' demanded Travers, his voice losing its self-assured edge.

'This,' Brady said gesturing at the file, 'shows what kind of a man you're representing.'

'Get to the point,' demanded Travers impatiently.

Brady looked at Simmons.

'I accept that you didn't murder your step-daughter, sir,' Brady began. 'But I'm sure a jury will agree that what you did to her over a period of four years is worse than what she suffered in those last moments before she died.'

'This is ridiculous! What kind of unfounded allegation is that?' spluttered Travers.

'It's not unfounded as you'll find out soon enough,' Brady answered as he turned to Travers.

Brady could see that the solicitor was worried. His voice had lost its slick, arrogant Oxbridge edge.

'Let me see that,' ordered Travers as he gestured towards the file.

'Be my guest,' offered Brady as he picked up the file.

But instead of handing the file over, Brady opened it and

started to carefully place the contents in front of Simmons and his solicitor.

'What exactly is this, DI Brady?' demanded Travers as he quickly took in the stark photographs.

Taken aback, he turned and looked at his client whose face had turned white.

'Don't say a word. Understand?' Travers quickly instructed.

Simmons stared at the photos incredulously, not believing what was in front of him.

'But . . . it was—'

'Encrypted?' finished off Brady. 'Message from our computer forensic officer – if you are going to encrypt something, don't use anything based on dictionary words.'

Simmons stared at Brady numbly.

'It took a while but our forensic officer's password cracker got it in the end,' added Brady. 'One thing I can say about Jed is, he doesn't give up easily.'

Brady smiled as he looked at Simmons.

'Suddenly you've gone very quiet, sir. Maybe you've decided that suing us for wrongful arrest isn't such a lucrative prospect any more?'

'I . . . I can't see what you're getting at here, DI Brady?' interrupted Travers uncomfortably.

'Take another look then,' suggested Brady.

'What I mean is there is no proof that the man in these photographs is my client,' replied Travers stiffly.

'Admittedly, it's easy to see that the girl, dating from as young as eleven up to fifteen, is Sophie Washington, Mr Simmons' step-daughter,' agreed Brady. 'This latest photograph here even shows the victim's distinctive tattoo.'

'I . . . I can't dispute that. But as to the man in the

photographs with her, well . . . it's inconclusive as to whether it's my client or not,' pointed out Travers.

'So it seems,' replied Brady. He then looked straight at Simmons. 'But you're not as clever as you think you are, sir.'

Brady pulled out a handful of disks from the file in front of him.

'These are films that you made over the period of the four years you were in Sophie Washington's life. Unlike the photographs here where you've selected the image to exclude your face, these films do contain images of your face. Images that we were able to digitally enhance to prove 100 per cent that you are the male actively engaged in these extremely pornographic images involving your step-daughter.'

Brady watched as Simmons now stared straight ahead, refusing to look at the photos on the table.

'I . . . I would like to see the evidence that proves that the man in these photographs is my client,' demanded Travers.

'Of course,' obliged Brady as he pulled out more photographs.

He laid them on top of the other photographs.

'There's no denying that the man in these film images is Paul Simmons,' Brady flatly stated.

Travers cleared his throat as he looked at them.

'Not very tasteful are they?' said Brady, noticing Travers' bronzed face flush an unhealthy colour. 'Some of the acts of sexual abuse committed on the victim by your client in these shots are the worst acts of child sexual abuse I've ever seen. So extreme that the majority of them fall into the category of Level 5,' Brady pointed out. 'Add to that the knowledge that some of these extreme acts of child sexual abuse were filmed live on the internet on virtually a daily basis for other like-minded men.'

Not that Brady had needed to add that. He could see from Travers' taut, sickened expression that he had got the message.

'Given the severity of the child pornography that we're dealing with here, the Serious and Organised Crime Agency will be taking over this investigation. And, as you can see from the photographs before you, which is only a fraction of Mr Simmons' disturbing collection of his step-daughter, they have enough evidence to put your client away for an indefinite period of time.'

Satisfied, Brady watched as Travers, lost for words, tried to regain some composure.

'Yes . . . well, I think I need some time to confer with my client . . .' Travers replied, as he turned to Simmons.

'Take as long as you want,' suggested Brady. 'He's going nowhere.'

He looked at Conrad and nodded. They were finished with Simmons.

'Interview terminated at 10.27 am,' he stated as he shoved his chair back and stood up.

Brady gave Simmons one last cursory glance.

'I only wish that it hadn't taken Sophie's murder for your sick abuse of her to be exposed. Whatever happens to you will never make up for the horrific sexual acts you did to that eleven-year-old girl,' Brady said as he picked up one of the photos. He shoved it in front of Simmons' face. 'See? See that? That ripped the victim's eleven-year-old body apart. The damage was so brutal that the scars and trauma were still painfully evident in her autopsy.'

Simmons turned away.

'Look at what you did to her, you sick son of a bitch!' demanded Brady as he pushed the photograph into Simmons' face. 'I should make you choke on it, you bastard!'

'DI Brady, I wish to remind you that this threatening behaviour is completely unacceptable,' complained Travers.

'Yeah?' snarled Brady, refusing to take his eyes off Simmons. 'So sue me!'

'And you, you sick son of a bitch. I swear you'll live to regret every act of sexual abuse you committed on her so help me God!' threatened Brady as he scrunched up the photograph in his hand and threw it at Simmons' rigid face.

'Come on, Conrad, the air in here is turning my stomach!' Brady said as he turned and left.

Chapter Fifty-Nine

Brady was on his third coffee as he sat in the depressing basement canteen. He couldn't digest anything after his interview with Simmons. The Serious and Organised Crime Agency were on their way which meant that Brady would have no further dealings with him. Not that he was bothered. He just wanted the assurance that the bastard would get everything he deserved.

He looked up at the barred windows and wondered what was going through Matthews' head right now. Brady couldn't figure him out; this wasn't Matthews. Sure he may have had a hard job keeping his dick in his trousers, but shagging a fifteen-year-old girl and then murdering her? That wasn't the Matthews Brady had known for sixteen years. Brady watched the miserable drizzle steadily trickle down the barred windows, blurring the outside world. He didn't know why he was sat there. He just knew he needed somewhere familiar to get his head around what had happened in the past twelve hours.

He couldn't help going over the events that had led to Matthews' arrest. He wished he'd stayed with the others in The Fat Ox instead of tracking down Madley. Brady accepted that he had been looking for trouble and that's what he'd got. But he had never expected it to turn out this way. He couldn't shake the feeling that he had set Matthews up; that Matthews had walked into Brady's trap. But it wasn't like that. Not that Matthews would believe him. Brady had had no idea that he would end up finding incriminating evidence against Matthews when he searched his house. Let alone that Conrad would call Gates while he was in there. But then again, if Conrad hadn't then maybe Brady wouldn't be sat in the miserable police canteen on his third coffee. He'd be dead and Matthews would be long gone.

Brady stared at the grey dusty shafts of light stabbing through the barred windows. Matthews was scared to talk; scared shitless of the consequences. Brady tried to ignore the thought that kept going through his mind. It was too horrific to even contemplate.

He took a sip of burnt, bitter tasting coffee.

His phone rang. He picked it up off the table and answered it.

'What?' he muttered thickly.

'I heard about Jimmy,' she explained.

'Yeah?' said Brady, not in the mood for talking.

'Conrad told me,' she added.

'So?'

'You look like you need someone to talk to, that's all.'

Brady suddenly realised that she was standing a few tables away from him.

'I'm not in the mood for small talk,' he warned.

'Good, that makes two of us,' Jenkins concluded as she walked over to him.

She pulled out a chair and joined him.

They sat in silence for a few minutes while Brady mulled over everything that had happened.

'I need to get him to talk,' Brady eventually stated. 'But he thinks I set him up.'

'And did you?' Jenkins asked.

'What do you think?' replied Brady edgily.

He wearily sighed as he ran his hand over his stubble. He hadn't had time to shower this morning. Not that it mattered.

'Shit, Amelia! Matthews thinks I was behind his arrest. That I had it planned and had arranged for an armed response team to be there, along with Gates. How the hell was I to know he was going to be at the house? He'd gone to ground for the past few days not answering my calls. And then he turns up when I least expect.'

'You're being too hard on yourself,' Jenkins reasoned.

'Am I?' he questioned.

Jenkins nodded.

'I know it wasn't Jimmy,' Brady eventually said.

She looked at him questioningly.

'And . . . I reckon I know who did it . . . but . . .' Brady's voice trailed off.

He shook his head, not wanting to believe it.

'I hope to God that I'm wrong. Because if I'm not . . . Fuck!' Brady hoarsely said as he stared at Jenkins. He kept going over in his head what she had said about the significance of the attack on the deceased victim's face. And he didn't like the answer that kept coming to mind.

Chapter Sixty

'I know,' Brady conceded reluctantly.

Matthews ignored him.

'I know who you're protecting.'

'Keep your fucking mouth shut,' hissed Matthews.

'I can't let you go down for something you didn't do.'

'Shut the fuck up! You don't know what you're saying. I did it! Me! Nobody else! You get that? I murdered her!'

'You drove her back home, but what you didn't realise was that Ellison had already rung Sophie at 12.02 am, arranging to meet her on the abandoned farm behind her house.'

'Don't do this, Jack. For fuck's sake, don't do this to me!' pleaded Matthews.

Brady did his best to ignore him but it was the hardest thing he'd ever had to do. Every word coming out of his mouth tasted bitter.

'She had sex with him, followed by an argument. We have a witness who overheard that part. When Ellison had gone, she realised she couldn't find her keys. So she rang Evie, believing she'd left them there.'

'No!'

'We've got a record of the call, Jimmy,' Brady said quietly.

'Evie brought the keys. She knew what Simmons was like

and didn't want her best friend hurt. So she sneaked out of the house and ran down to the farmland. She knew exactly where to find Sophie,' Brady carefully explained.

'Jack . . . no don't . . . don't . . .'

Brady ignored him. He had to, otherwise he wouldn't be able to finish.

'You see, Jimmy, the witness said that she overheard two girls arguing. I didn't think much of it at the time but now I realise that it was Evie and Sophie. She even heard the victim shout out your name. I had presumed that was because Sophie had been ringing you in a desperate attempt to stop Ellison from hurting her. But I couldn't have been further from the truth. Instead, Sophie was drunkenly taunting Evie with the fact that she had been at Madley's nightclub with you and that you had driven her home. She might have been Evie's best friend but it didn't mean that they weren't jealous of one another. Maybe that was the trigger, because Evie believed she was telling the truth,' Brady said, shaking his head. 'They'd both had too much to drink, too much to see sense.'

'I mean it, Jack. I'll fucking kill you if you don't stop!' Matthews sobbed.

Brady paused for a moment, caught off guard by Matthews. He breathed in and forced himself to continue, ignoring the tears of desperation in Matthews' eyes.

'You were back before Evie left to find Sophie. Your car was parked in the driveway. Evie couldn't find the keys in her bedroom so she did what Sophie had suggested when she called. She searched your car. Evie found them, but she also found the condom wrapper and put two and two together.'

Matthews suddenly lunged for Brady.

Conrad scrambled to his feet just in time to pull Matthews back.

'Come on, Jimmy. Calm down!' Conrad advised through gritted teeth as he did his best to restrain him.

'You don't know what you're talking about!' Matthews grunted.

'The condom wrapper has Evie's prints all over it. As has Sophie's phone. Initially it would be easy to rationalise her fingerprints on the victim's phone, as she was her best friend. You see, that's what we did when we found Evie's DNA at the crime scene and on the victim's body. We eliminated her because she was the victim's best friend and they shared clothes as teenage girls do. But that wasn't what happened, was it?'

Matthews struggled in vain to get to him.

'Evie knew you were seeing someone, Jimmy. She didn't know it was this Tania woman, she presumed it was Sophie. And why wouldn't she after the evidence she found in your car? And Sophie was more than happy to mislead her, to pretend she was having an affair with you. She was viciously drunk and Ellison walking off had left her furious. So she took her vindictiveness out on Evie. And what better way of hurting Evie than by destroying the image she had of her father? The man Evie idealised? Sophie wanted what Evie had – a "normal" family life and if she couldn't get it, she would make Evie equally miserable.'

'No . . . you don't know what you're talking about,' Matthews said shaking his head in desperation.

'You weren't there, Jimmy, not until it was too late,' replied Brady.

Matthews turned his sickened face away.

Brady inwardly winced as he realised that his hunch had

372

been right. Matthews had just shown as much. Up until that moment he had been hoping against the odds that Matthews would somehow prove to him that Evie had nothing to do with Sophie's murder.

Brady swallowed hard before continuing.

'The witness heard Evie and Sophie's argument over Ellison. We just assumed it was Ellison, not Evie. You see Ellison and Sophie argued about him ending their relationship. He left and Sophie then rang Evie. We know that Evie left her home to meet Sophie.'

Matthews questioningly looked at Brady.

'We have CCTV footage at that time of a girl who we presume to be Evie walking past Wellfield towards West Monkseaton. We know Sophie rang Evie at 12.51 am. It would have then taken Evie less than thirty minutes to walk from Earsdon to Potter's Farm. Which means she would have met Sophie at roughly 1.20 am, and then . . . well, we know the rest, don't we?'

Matthews dropped his head in defeat.

'When Evie couldn't bear to hear Sophie's taunts any longer, she attacked her, grabbing Sophie's scarf and knotting it around her neck in a desperate, drunken attempt to silence her. Which she succeeded in doing.'

Brady ran a shaky hand over his chin as he thought about walking out of the interview room. He had had enough. But he knew he had no choice, he had to see it through to the end. He shifted his gaze, unable to watch Matthews' anguish.

'Strangling her wasn't enough for Evie. She wanted to destroy the very face that had laughed and taunted her with sexually explicit details of what she claimed she had done with Ellison. Evie was so riddled with jealousy that Sophie was having a relationship with the same teacher she had a huge crush on. And then there was you. Sophie presumably bragged about being in a nightclub with you and you dropping her home. The idea that not only was Sophie sleeping with her teacher, she was now seducing her dad would have been enough to send her over the edge. So she picked up the object closest to her, a heavy jagged stone, and exacted her blind rage on Sophie's lifeless face. She hated Sophie's face because it was her prettiness that had attracted Ellison and even you. Not Evie's face, but hers. Everyone noticed how pretty Sophie was, didn't they? Who could help but notice? No wonder Evie hated Sophie. And it comes as no surprise that she destroyed the very thing she hated so much.'

Brady breathed out slowly, steeling himself.

'When she finally came to her senses, she panicked,' Brady whispered hoarsely.

He felt the words choking him but knew he had to finish.

'So, she rang you, Jimmy. Not because you were a copper. No, because you were her father and she believed you would know what to do. She didn't have her phone on her. In the rush she'd left it at home, so without thinking she used Sophie's phone. That's why Sophie's phone showed a call to your mobile just after 1.31 am.'

He took a drink of water to get rid of the dryness in his mouth.

'The jacket the victim was wearing,' Brady said shaking his head. 'That's what didn't make sense, Jimmy. You see, I talked with Ellison again this morning and when Sophie met him she wasn't wearing a jacket. Then when I checked the security tape, again no jacket. But when she was discovered murdered she was wearing a jacket,' Brady slowly stated. 'Evie's jacket,' he added.

He stood up wanting to stretch his leg. It had flared up again.

'Evie was the one wearing the jacket. I double-checked the CCTV footage and she was definitely wearing a jacket similar to the one found on the victim. Sophie was only wearing a scarf the way girls do with just T-shirts, despite the weather. But the jacket was your idea, wasn't it?' Brady paused as he waited for Matthews to object.

Matthews didn't. Instead he mutely stared at Brady.

'That's why you left the jacket open so it could explain the blood and tissue sprayed over the victim's T-shirt.'

Matthews turned his head away, unable to look at Brady.

'You knew that Evie would be charged with Sophie's manslaughter, if not murder. So you decided to try and hide the evidence by leaving Evie's jacket, which was covered in blood, on the victim. You told me that first morning that Sophie had borrowed Evie's jacket. You said you recognised the jacket at the crime scene and your first reaction was to think that it was Evie lying there. I suppose it was the copper in you that made you decide to hide the evidence on the victim. You put the jacket on Sophie, didn't you?' Brady asked.

Matthews didn't say anything.

'That's why your own shirt got covered in blood because you handled the body, didn't you?'

Matthews continued to stare with mute desperation at Brady.

'After the copper in you had seen to the body, you then drove Evie home. You told her not to breathe a word to anyone, not even Kate. You told her to get showered to get rid of any evidence and then you told her to wash her clothes. Didn't you? But even you know that that wouldn't be good enough. You can't get rid of blood stains that easily, Jimmy. We've just searched your house and found her clothes . . . Evie's clothes, the ones she was wearing that night.'

Matthews looked at Brady, surprised.

Brady nodded.

'I didn't expect to find her clothes there either. I take it that you told her to get rid of them?'

Matthews didn't answer. But Brady could see from his reaction that that was exactly what he had done. Brady expected no less; Matthews was a copper after all.

'She's just a kid, Jimmy. She was no doubt still in shock and just stuck them in the washing machine. And like I said, blood stains don't wash out that easily. They're being forensically examined to see if they match with Sophie's DNA. But we both know the results will be positive, don't we?'

Matthews raised his head and looked disconsolately at Brady.

'Then you waited for the call to come in from the station that a girl's body had been found.'

Matthews stared at Brady. His eyes were cold and empty.

'Evie wasn't really ill on Friday morning, was she? You told her to pretend that she felt ill because you didn't want her to suddenly crack. You wanted her to wait it out at home until the news about Sophie's death became public.'

'Why, Jack?' muttered Matthews. 'Why couldn't you have just left it? She's just a kid . . .'

'So was Sophie. That's what you're forgetting here. Sophie was just a kid too. A kid that everybody used. Including you, Jimmy.'

Chapter Sixty-One

'Let him go,' Brady told Conrad.

Conrad did as he was told.

Matthews collapsed into his chair and sank his head into his large trembling hands.

'You don't understand what you've done,' he rasped.

'I'm not letting you go down for murder when you're not responsible.'

'Don't you realise this is all my fault? Don't you?'

Brady didn't reply.

'Maybe if I'd been around more, then this would never have happened . . .'

Brady looked away. He didn't have the stomach to look Matthews in the eye because he knew that at some level he was right. If Matthews had only taken more of an interest at home, then maybe none of this would ever have happened.

'When I'd dropped Sophie home after Madley's night-club Tania rang me. Evie must have overheard the conversation but it wasn't until later that she made the assumption that I'd been talking to Sophie. Soon after my call Sophie rang Evie to fetch her house keys from my car saying that I'd taken her to a nightclub and had dropped her home afterwards. And you were right, Evie found Sophie's keys on the floor next to the empty condom wrapper,' Matthews disconsolately conceded. 'I hadn't even realised it had been there.'

He despairingly shook his head as he thought it over.

'Evie presumed the worst. That's the kind of shit dad I've been. My own daughter thinks I'm so immoral that I'd have sex with her fifteen-year-old friend.

'But then, what else did she have to go on?' Matthews rhetorically questioned.

Brady shrugged.

'She'd started drinking . . . fifteen and drinking. I had no idea . . . What bloody kind of father does that make me?'

Brady could have added that drinking wasn't all she was doing but knew that Matthews was suffering enough. And what did it matter now? he mused.

'If only I hadn't gone to The Blue Lagoon . . . if only . . .' Matthews' voice trailed off.

'But I was so close to getting on the inside of Madley's sex business in underage Eastern European girls. That's why I went,' Matthews explained as he despairingly looked at Brady.

'You've lost me,' he muttered.

But Matthews didn't hear him. Or if he did, he acted as if he hadn't.

'Honestly Jack, it made me sick when I realised what he was doing . . . I . . . I couldn't continue working for him. Not when I knew where the money was coming from . . . So I thought I could redeem myself somehow. Have Madley sent down and then he'd have no hold over me. You believe me, don't you?'

Brady numbly shook his head.

'Punters are paying big money to get into Madley's nightclubs,' Matthews explained.

He stopped for a moment, suddenly registering Brady's incredulous expression.

'You don't know about this? Come on, you two are like brothers! Surely you were aware of what he's up to?'

Brady didn't answer him. He couldn't. He had no idea what Matthews was talking about.

'Madley's running a sex trafficking racket from his nightclubs. He brings them in from Eastern Europe. He then hires them out as sex slaves in those private rooms of his above the clubs, girls as young as fourteen. Or, if the price is right he'll sell them. But it's not just Madley. Macmillan's behind this. He's the one pulling the strings.'

Brady sat back, stunned. If he was honest, he found it hard to believe Madley would get his hands that dirty. He could readily accept Macmillan being involved in something as depraved as that, but not Madley. Dealing drugs was one thing, but trafficking and selling underage girls as sex slaves was an entirely different level of corruption.

'All right, convince me. What have you got to substantiate this?'

Matthews looked at him and dejectedly shook his head.

'That's my problem, it was all rumours and hearsay. Jack, I have nothing . . .'

Brady didn't react. But inwardly, he breathed a sigh of relief. This was Madley Matthews was talking about. Brady shared too much history with Madley not to know what he was involved in. And sex trafficking and sex slavery definitely wasn't Madley's style.

'Then I see Sophie stagger into the club on some sick bastard's arm,' continued Matthews. 'I did what any father would have done and prised her away from him and tried to persuade her to let me take her home,' Matthews explained.

'But when she wouldn't leave I was stupid enough to think of it as the perfect opportunity to see Madley's set-up for myself. I'd seen the businessmen coming and going upstairs for the sex trade he had going on. So I pretended I wanted to use one of Madley's private rooms I'd heard about on the third and fourth floor for sex with her. I . . . I used her. I used Sophie as a cover . . .'

He shook his head as he looked at Brady.

'But Madley didn't trust me. He'd cleared my debts. All of them, and more,' Matthews mused bitterly.

'He obviously realised that I had a lot to gain if I could get something over him. And I was still a copper at the end of the day . . . one who would be indebted to him for years unless . . .' Matthews faltered. 'And then, there I am in his office, begging him for a private room upstairs so I could have something over him for a change. And he knew it. He knew he had me just where he wanted. I realised in that moment that I couldn't do it any more. I hated myself for what I'd become and I knew then that I had to get out from under Madley. I had already noticed that the safe had been left open. So when someone came to the office door saying there was a problem downstairs I took my chance at getting my life back. I waited until he'd gone and stuffed as much money as I could down my shirt. I then fastened my suit jacket and put on my overcoat. I went back down into the nightclub and grabbed Sophie and disappeared before Madley realised what I'd done.'

'You've lost me again,' Brady said.

Matthews looked at him.

'How were you indebted to Madley?' Brady asked, confused.

'Shit, Jack! You must have known. You saw the way I played poker. Didn't you notice my losing streak?'

Brady nodded.

'Yeah, but it wasn't my business to ask where you were getting the money from to continue playing. You're a grown man, Jimmy,' Brady defensively answered.

Brady had seen enough men lose everything they owned in the name of poker; himself included. He wasn't a fool. He'd noticed Matthews' losing streak; even a blind man would have noticed. But Brady had chosen to ignore the fact that no matter how badly Matthews lost, he always had money for the next game.

'Yeah? Well, Madley was more compassionate than you. He loaned me money to cover my debts. More than I could ever pay back,' said Matthews.

'How much?'

'Six hundred thousand,' answered Matthews as he looked Brady in the eye.

'How the fuck were you going to pay that back?' asked Brady, stunned.

'Exactly. Madley had me by the balls!'

'Oh fuck, Jimmy! Why didn't you come to me?'

'And what would you have done?' asked Matthews bitterly. 'That's why I stole that money from him. I wanted to start a new life abroad. I already had my plane ticket bought. I was going to start a new life. As far away from Madley as possible.'

'Exactly how much did you take?' Brady asked, not sure if he wanted the answer.

'Nearly a million. Would you believe it was just sat there

in his safe?' replied Matthews coolly. 'And there was more. A lot more. I just didn't want to be greedy.'

He laughed at Brady's reaction.

'Now do you believe me about the sex trafficking? Drugs money is nothing compared to what people will pay for illicit sex.'

Brady swallowed hard. He still couldn't get his head around what Matthews was telling him.

'Where were you going to go?' Brady finally asked.

'Where else? Spain,' answered Matthews. 'Tania was going to come with me. She knew exactly what was going on with Madley and she'd suggested that I should steal enough money to get us out of the country, so we could start a new life together.'

'Did she hide you?' Brady asked.

Matthews nodded.

'She has a caravan up by Rothbury. She held on to the money. She exchanged as much as she could into Euros and traveller's cheques and sorted out the plane tickets while I lay low. We were going to take the rest of the cash and buy a place over in Spain and start again. But the one thing she couldn't get me was my passport which was in my house.'

Brady looked at him.

'Initially I panicked. Sophie's murder threw me. So, I had to do what I could to protect Evie first. Then, when things had calmed down I was going to return to get my passport and get rid of the evidence in my car.'

'Why didn't you get rid of the evidence and take it with you when Tania picked you up? I presume she picked you up because you knew at some point we'd be looking for your car?'

'I just didn't think straight. I honestly believed I'd be able to get back in the house. I didn't realise Madley's men would be watching it. And I definitely didn't think I'd find you there.'

Brady sat back and absorbed what Matthews had just told him. He couldn't figure out how he could just up and leave his family for a new start.

'What about Kate?'

'What about her?' Matthews asked. 'It's over with, has been for a long time. But then, you already knew that, didn't you?'

Brady didn't answer.

'If I had only taken Sophie straight home when she had first come into the nightclub, then maybe none of this would have happened.'

Matthews looked at Brady.

'Oh God, Jack. What have I done?' he muttered as he held his head in his hands.

Chapter Sixty-Two

Brady stood in the damp drizzling early evening air, too numb to feel the cold. He put a cigarette to his lips as he thought about his next move. Soon, very soon the scavenging rats would be crawling all over the place, wanting photographs, interviews, sordid details. The Press Office at headquarters had already been alerted and damage control was rapidly being set up. Whether it would be enough, Brady wasn't sure; there was a lot he wasn't sure about any more.

Brady knew that the press would crucify Louise Simmons. Britain was a blame culture, one very much facilitated by the media. Once Sophie's pitiful, squalid life had been picked over, fingers would sure enough start pointing at the mother. Brady had seen it before on other child murder cases, where they would find reasons to blame the parents, ignoring the murderer's part in all of it. But this was different, Paul Simmons had played a big part in Sophie's demise, as had Louise Simmons. A step-father, who from the moment he had entered her life at the age of eleven had started sexually abusing her, and a mother who had chosen to look the other way. It was easier to knock back a gin and tonic than accept your husband was sexually abusing your eleven-year-old daughter. But it was worse than that, he was sharing his abuse with the world. Years of photographs and films of his sexual exploits had been posted on endless encrypted paedophilic websites, egotistical evidence that had led to his downfall.

Footsteps approached from behind him. Brady didn't turn round, there was no need; he knew who would be there.

He slowly breathed out. Now all he had to do was wait.

Conrad's silver Saab slowly turned into the street. Brady threw away his cigarette and resisted the urge to walk back inside.

Instead he watched as Conrad opened the passenger door and gently helped Evie out. She looked a mess; hair uncombed, clothes dishevelled. But it was her face that got to Brady. It was a child's face. Gone were the smudged tell-tale signs of make-up and the petulant, defiant hardness of the teenager he'd interviewed, replaced by red, swollen, vulnerable eyes and unnaturally pale cheeks. Brady held his breath; she could have been that skinny kid again with long, dangling pig tails and bleeding, scuffed knees. She was crying, hot, salty tears of remorse. They flowed down her pale face as, trembling, she looked up at the police station. He resisted the urge to go to her and put his arm around her petrified body and tell her it was all going to be all right. But he couldn't, because he knew it wouldn't be the truth.

He swallowed hard. Where had it all gone wrong for her? he thought, as he questioned the enormity of what he had just done.

He had been playing the 'what if' game from the moment Conrad had gone to bring her in. Maybe he should have kept his mouth shut and let Matthews go down for it? Worse still, should he have let Ellison take the blame? As Matthews had pointedly said, Ellison deserved a hell of a lot more than the courts would mete out; a sexual relationship with his fifteen-year-old student didn't warrant much punishment. Not in today's world. So maybe he should have let him take the bullet? These were questions that he couldn't get out of his head. If he had had his way, he would have let Simmons go down for it. Brady had seen the sick material he had filmed of his step-daughter, disturbing evidence that would have turned most people's stomachs. But Brady was a realist. he knew the judicial system well enough to know that Simmons would go down for a good few years, given the horrific nature of his sexual abuse.

But it was all a moot point now. Whether he had made the right choice, he couldn't say. All he knew was that he had done his job.

Ashamed, Brady turned away as Conrad and Claudia accompanied Evie, now crying uncontrollably, up the ramp. Distraught, Kate followed behind.

'I . . . I . . . didn't mean it to happen . . .' sobbed Evie as she stopped in front of Brady.

Her pale face was filled with regret; genuine, raw regret.

'I know,' he quietly acknowledged, wishing there was more he could say.

'I . . . I . . . don't know why I did it . . . I honestly didn't want to hurt her . . . not Sophie . . .' she faltered as tears choked her words. 'But . . . but she just got to me. Made me so mad that I . . . I just saw red and then . . . I didn't realise what I'd done until it was too late.'

'I know you didn't,' gently replied Brady.

She looked up at him with surprise as tears streamed down her face, realising that he believed her.

'We were both drunk and we started arguing and then . . . she said some horrible things about . . . about me . . . and about

her and Mr Ellison and and then my dad and her so I . . . I
. . .' she faltered as her words were replaced by choking sobs.

Brady watched as Conrad took Evie firmly by her
convulsing shoulders and walked her through the double,
wooden doors of the station.

Brady looked at Claudia.

'Thanks for doing this.'

'I'm not doing this for you, Jack. I'm doing this for Evie,'
Claudia replied.

'I know . . .' muttered Brady looking away.

'Jack?'

He looked at her.

They were both hurting. They had known Evie from when
she had been a little girl. Neither one could believe life had
turned out like this for her, or for them come to that.

He suddenly took hold of her hands.

'Claudia . . .' he gently said. He didn't know what more
to say to keep her there.

She looked up at him, not resisting his hold over her.

'Maybe I should take that job offer?' she said.

He searched her face, surprised.

He didn't need to ask what had changed her mind. He
knew that what had happened with Evie Matthews had
somehow forced them back together. Whether it meant that
she would consider being a part of his life again didn't
matter, not yet. What counted was that she was going to
be back in the North East. It was a start.

'I've got to go,' she said. 'Later, OK?'

Brady nodded and let her hands go. He watched,
impotent, as she disappeared.

A few seconds later he realised that Kate was stood beside
him.

'What's going to happen to her?' she asked.

Brady numbly shook his head, unable to look her in the eye. It was a closed case. The evidence was conclusive; more so after Matthews' statement.

'I can't say. At least Claudia is representing Evie . . . she's really good. She'll . . . she'll figure something out. She knows people,' Brady replied unconvincingly.

Brady forced himself to look at Kate. He apologetically shrugged. He was at a loss himself.

Dazed, she mutely accepted this and walked on.

'Kate?' he called out after her.

Whether she heard him or not, he would never know.

Brady closed his eyes and shakily leaned back against the station's red brick wall and shallowly breathed out as the wooden doors slammed shut behind her.

'I can't do this . . . Conrad will have to take my place.'

'You have no choice in the matter. This is your investigation. You finish it.'

Brady turned to face Gates.

Gates waited, forcing his hand.

'All right. Just give me a minute to clear my head.'

'As soon as you can, Jack. This is your shit, you clear it up.'

'I know it is. But it doesn't end here. I owe it to Matthews to do what I can to substantiate his allegations.'

'What? Against Madley?'

Brady looked Gates straight in the eye. He knew Madley too well. Enough to know he wouldn't dirty his hands with anything to do with sex trafficking. Drugs, maybe. But sex trafficking was a different league.

'Macmillan, sir. Mayor Macmillan. And if that means upsetting a few people, then that's what I'll have to do. After all, isn't that what I'm good at? '

Read on for an exclusive extract from Danielle Ramsay's next novel Broken Bodies, coming in 2011.

Chapter One

'*Nachui! Nachui!*'

'*Kales vaikas!*' Irritably replied another man.

'Oh God . . . no . . .' she desperately panted, too scared to look behind her.

Exhausted, she started running again. She didn't hear the foghorn forlornly bleating in the distance, or feel the wet sea fret as it wrapped itself around her painfully thin body. All she heard was the threatening footsteps of her pursuers.

Somewhere down by the promenade muffled, drunken shouts were followed by the roar of a car's engine. Seconds later a hazy orange glow appeared at the bottom of the dark street as a car turned up from the promenade. Shallowly panting, she ran as fast as she could towards the glare of the oncoming car, grazing her bare feet against the jagged, uneven pavements. Her long, dark hair clung to her waxen, ghostly face as she ran out into the middle of the road.

'Stop! Stop!' She shouted frantically waving her bare white arms at the approaching headlights.

The car suddenly slammed its brakes on barely avoiding hitting her.

'Help me, please . . . help . . .' She gasped in short breaths.

She hunched over, gulping in air as the driver aggressively punched his horn to make her move out of the way.

She straightened up, wildly shaking her head.

'No! You've got to help me!' She implored as the driver banged his fist on the horn again.

Desperate, she ran round to the driver's door and frantically tried to open it.

The doors were locked. She hysterically started pounding at the window.

The driver, a dark-haired man in his late twenties looked at her with contempt.

'Please . . .' she stuttered, panicking. 'You've got to help me . . . please . . .' She begged. 'These men . . . they're trying to take me . . . they want to . . .'

'Piss off you drunken cow!' He spat in disgust as he scowled at her dishevelled appearance.

Her face was covered in a sheen of cold sweat as smudged, black eye-liner and mascara trailed down her cheeks. Her short, strapless black dress was ripped halfway down the side, immodestly showing her naked body underneath.

'No, you can't leave me here! You don't understand! They'll kill me!' She screamed, banging furiously on the window.

'Fucking right I can, you slapper!' He answered before revving the engine and then screeching off up the street.

'No!' She yelled, feeling physically sick as the car disappeared.

She stood alone, feeling utterly helpless.

Panicking, she looked at the Victorian terraced row of houses on either side of her.

Realising that there was a light coming from the second

floor of a three storey house further down the street, she ran as fast as she could towards it. She pushed the ornate cast iron gate open and ran up the pathway towards the heavy, red panelled door. She repeatedly pressed the old fashioned doorbell. There was no answer. She then started to bang furiously on the door.

'Please . . . Anyone . . . Help me!' She desperately called out.

She waited a moment, but nothing happened.

'Come on! Someone! You've got to hear me! Please . . . anyone . . .' She shouted.

'*Kikite su manimi shliundra!*' Ordered a deep, guttural voice.

She froze, recognising the voice. She knew it was over. She had tried her best to outrun them, but they wouldn't give up, not until they had her.

Trembling, she slowly turned around. His six foot two, threatening body was stood by the gate. The shorter one was stood behind him, waiting with his muscular arms folded.

'No . . .' She whispered.

Seconds later a car idled down the street, coming to a stop behind the two men.

'*Ateiti cia kale!*' The taller man ordered as he stared straight at her, ignoring the car.

'No . . . please . . .' She begged.

'*As tai dabar apskretele!*' He barked, gesturing for her to come to him.

She shook her head as tears started to trickle down her face.

'No . . . no . . .' She muttered.

'Fucking bitch!' He cursed in a thick accent as he strode over to her.

She turned and started pounding hysterically on the door.

'Help me! Someone! Help me!' She screamed as loud as she could.

He brutally grabbed her from behind. She attempted to struggle, but it was pointless.

He covered her mouth with a leather- gloved hand and dragged her backwards down the path. Her heels scraped, ripping the skin as she tried her best to resist.

Still with his hand over her mouth, he took her to the idling silver Mercedes. The passenger window buzzed down and a heavily set man in his late forties looked at her.

He roughly tilted her face towards the passenger window.

Tears trailed down her cheeks as she realised that the drunken voices on the promenade had faded into the blackness of the night. She was completely alone with them.

She waited, hardly daring to breathe as the man in the car decided what to do.

Seconds later he nodded at the man holding her. Then, without a word the electric window buzzed shut.

She was unsure of what it meant.

'Please . . . please . . . let me go . . . I promise I won't talk . . .' She begged.

Her captor seemed to relax his grip on her.

'I promise I won't say anything.' She continued, hoping that he would let her go.

'*Nusishypsosi shaltais dantimis shliundra!*' He hoarsely whispered, brushing his lips against her cold, glistening cheek.

The pungent smell of strong, stale tobacco lingered on his sour breath.

His hands gently encircled her throat and slowly started to squeeze.

'No . . . no . . . please?' She begged as her fingers tried to prise his hands from her neck.

She questioningly looked towards the dark tainted glass of the Mercedes' passenger window. But she couldn't see anything. She then looked at the other man who was silently stood by the car with his arms folded, impassively watching.

She caught his eye, but he looked past her, as if she didn't exist.

Terrified, she struggled, clawing and scratching at the hands around her throat.

But he pressed deeper into her malleable flesh.

'I . . . I . . . can't breathe . . .' she gasped, suddenly realising what was about to happen.

He grunted with satisfaction.

She frantically tore with bloodied, broken nails at his unrelenting hands as her lungs began to burn. As the exploding pain became unbearable she suddenly thought of her sister and her mother, realising that she would never see them again.

Ten seconds later she felt the fight leave her body.

'*Kekshe* . . .' He softly grunted as her body began to spasm.

Chapter Two

Shivering, a woman in her late-thirties hid behind the heavy curtains as she tentatively looked out of the bedroom window. It was eerily quiet now. She had been startled awake by someone banging on the front door. Followed by hysterical, drunken screaming.

She watched, relieved as a car disappeared down the road and presumed that the girl who had been drunkenly screaming a few minutes earlier had been picked up. She looked down at the street below. It was empty. She thought about calling the police again and thought better of it. Whoever it was had gone now. And what could she say? That some drunken girl had been banging on her door at 3AM, ranting and raving? To the police that was a normal occurrence in Whitley Bay on a Friday or Saturday night.

And sadly for her, and the other residents in the street, this was becoming a regular problem. The street had set up a resident's association to combat the drunken intimidation they encountered at weekends and in particular, Bank Holidays. But the association had hit a brick wall with the council. It was simple; the councillors didn't live there, so consequently it wasn't high on their agenda. That, and the fact that the pubs and clubs in Whitley Bay brought in easy revenue.

Every weekend she was guaranteed to be woken by some disturbance caused by the pubs in South Parade. Either taxi cars speeding up and down the street, or police helicopters hovering overhead as they tried to catch some drunk who'd gone too far. And then there were the revellers, too high and too smashed to make their way home quietly.

The amount of times she would wake up to vomit outside her gate, empty, smashed vodka bottles or beer cans indiscriminately left behind. And then there were the half-eaten Indian's or pizzas' from the restaurants lining the promenade at the bottom of the street, all dumped outside.

She yawned, and decided to go back to bed. Whoever it was had gone.

'What's wrong now?' Sleepily muttered her husband as she climbed into bed.

'Nothing,' She answered.

Not that he cared, she thought. He somehow blocked all the noise out. Even when someone was banging and screaming at their front door he never budged.

'Just a drunk,' he had flatly stated when she had woken him.

And as soon as he had said it the commotion had stopped.

'See? What did I tell you?' He had groaned as he turned and buried his face into his pillow.

Resentful, she watched him now as he rolled over and fell immediately into a deep slumber. It would take her hours to get back to sleep, she bitterly thought. She could still feel the adrenalin and anger coursing through her tense body. She hated hearing drunks in the early hours of the morning, shouting and cursing outside. But that girl's screaming had really gotten to her. She felt on edge, fearful that something wasn't quite right. Maybe she should have done something. Frustrated, she turned and stared at the orange glow of the street lamp as it shone through the window, wishing that the house wasn't in negative equity so they could get as far away from Whitley Bay as possible.

Chapter Three

Jack Brady turned over and groaned. His head was thumping and the relentless buzzing wasn't helping.

'Buggering bugger!' He cursed.

He blindly stretched his hand out and reached for his BlackBerry.

'What?' He irritably demanded, wincing with pain at the exertion.

He listened to the caller between the pulsating thumping.

'Conrad? What the bloody hell are you playing at?' Grunted Brady, affecting a rough, hard-edged Geordie accent for Conrad's benefit. 'It's Sunday for bloody hell's sake!'

Conrad's words always had the uncanny knack of sobering him up.

Brady slowly sat up and ran a shaking hand over his narrowed bloodshot eyes.

'Run that by me again!' He huskily ordered.

He looked over at the alarm clock and cursed when he saw that it was only five am.

'Yeah . . . yes, I hear you Conrad. Yeah . . . I'll be ready . . . No . . . you're not interrupting anything . . .' said Brady before cutting Conrad off.

*

Not a lot had happened to him in the last six months. He still had the same hard-nosed boss, Detective Chief Inspector Gates and the same obtuse, career chasing side-kick – Detective Sergeant Harry Conrad. And he still had the same old job as Detective Inspector. Simply put, he wasn't the kind to get promoted.

But he was still a hell of a lot better off than his long-standing friend and now ex-colleague, Detective Inspector Jimmy Matthews. He had found himself inside Durham Prison, slumming it with the very scum he had risked his neck, and at times career, to put away. Matthews had ended up doing time for conspiring to pervert the course of justice. Instead of acting as a copper, he used everything he had ever gleaned from the job to fool the investigative team. And it worked, right up to the point that Brady couldn't accept that her teacher, who had been charged with the murder, had actually killed her. Brady had no doubts over the fact that the teacher had had sex with his fifteen year old pupil; repeatedly and in every way imaginable. But a hunch had led to him digging up more than he had bargained for. While the rest of the investigative team celebrated in the Fat Ox, he had followed a trail that led him led circuitously back to Jimmy Matthews.

Brady had tried to go and see Matthews in Durham prison, but Matthews had refused to see him. Not that Brady could blame him.

Brady bent over the bathroom sink threw cold water over his face. He had no choice but to get himself straightened out, and fast. Conrad was already at the crime scene, as was half the force by the sounds of it. And given the crap Gates had been doling out to him recently, who was he to argue about it being his day off? Brady smacked of the old school, which meant he didn't fit in any more. Coppers like Brady were being squeezed out, replaced by the likes of Conrad; graduate material whose eye was on fast-tracking his way to the top. No getting their hands dirty, no bending the rules and definitely no going out on a limb because of gut feeling.

Brady stared hard at the dark, heavily-hooded eyes reflected back in the mirror. He still looked the same; handsomely rugged with a permanent five o'clock shadow and long dark brown hair that he still hadn't gotten round to getting cut.

It had been eight months since Claudia, now officially his ex-wife had left him. He'd be the first to admit that both his personal and professional life was shot to hell, which included the bullet in his thigh. He was still single, living in the hope that Claudia would want him back. But he still had a long way to go to convince her he was worth the risk. She was still of the opinion that he was a cheating son of a bitch. Not that he could disagree. But things had changed since he'd screwed up big time. Whether she had noticed was another matter. At least she had stayed around which was more than he had expected. She had taken up the job offered by Chief Superintendent O'Donnell and was now heading the North East's first Sex Trafficking centre. Not that Brady ever got to see her, either professionally or personally. She claimed she was too busy and kept him hanging by promising that she would get together with him soon. Whether soon would ever come was questionable.

And as for Amelia Jenkins, the police psychologist, Brady hadn't seen her since she had worked alongside him six months ago on the Sophie Washington case. He had often thought about contacting her, but realised it wasn't a good idea. First, he had to figure out exactly what was going on between him and Claudia.

He ran a long slender, olive-skinned hand over his stubble as he stared hard at his reflection, wondering exactly what had washed up onto the shores of Whitley Bay beach. Or to be more precise, exactly who had floated to the surface of the cold, grey murky waters of the North Sea.

Chapter Four

Police cars, vans and tape blocked off a good stretch of the promenade. Brady pulled up and nodded at the two uniformed officers who automatically let him through. As he slowly drove along the sea front he couldn't help noticing the countless boarded up, dilapidated Victorian buildings that had become the scourge of the seaside resort.

He parked up by the old Avenue pub; yet another abandoned eyesore. Originally built as a hotel, it was a dominating three-storey building dating back to a Victorian era of afternoon teas and brass bands. Decades later, when the holidaymakers opted for the sunshine in Majorca instead of the drizzle and biting winds of Whitley Bay, the hotel had been turned into a pub for the locals. Eventually, even the locals stopped coming, driven away by the heavy influx of weekend and Bank Holiday binge drinkers who travelled from Glasgow and Newcastle for a couple of nights of debauchery in Whitley Bay's nirvana of pubs and clubs. Now the old, sprawling building stood abandoned and in disarray with its state of the art security steel sheets covering the windows and doors while its sign creaked and moaned in protest at the bitter, North East winds.

Noise drifted up from the beach, distracting Brady from

his morose brooding about what a shit hole Whitley Bay had become. Soon enough the scavengers would be here, Brady mused, pointing their microphones and cameras, trying to get an inside story. Rubenfeld, a hard-nosed local hack, would be one of the first of the many rats scrambling over whatever sordid scraps they could find. Sick, twisted murders sold newspapers and increased circulation figures big-time.

He limped along the bleak, rubbish-strewn promenade. His leg was playing up; some days it was fine, at other times like this morning, it would give him jip. It was clear enough where he was heading; it wasn't difficult to spot uniform on the sectioned off beach below him. They were stood around trying to look official while head to foot white-clad SOCOs diligently moved in and out of a large white forensics tent.

Brady kicked a broken vodka bottle out of the way, scattering the screeching seagulls from their fight over dumped curried chips. Beside it a deflated, limp condom lay abandoned. Both a testament that despite the credit crunch scum always found money from somewhere to get trashed and then shag and gorge on whatever; regardless. Whitley Bay hadn't suffered because of the global economic crisis; at least the owners of the pubs and clubs hadn't, unlike the residents. Property prices had crashed, but unlike the rest of Britain, it wasn't the global recession that had sunk prices to an all-time low, it was the scum that travelled from miles around to get off their face and into someone else's knickers just to briefly forget how pointless their lives were.

What more did he expect from Whitley Bay at six am on a Sunday morning?, questioned Brady as he looked around at the debris from the night before. The place was a dump.

A half-eaten takeaway was strewn across one of the seats that faced the sea. Beside it empty beer bottles lay discarded. Even the air around him stank of stale piss, spilt beer and take-away food. Brady looked over at the unnaturally still waters of the sewage-strewn North Sea. He stopped for a moment and watched a small fishing boat drift over the eerily calm surface as he wondered how a girl's body had come to be washed up onto the shores of Whitley Bay?

Brady turned and headed in the direction of the steps down to the beach, ignoring a group of four bleary-eyed men languishing against the railings, opposite The Royal Hotel and The Blue Lagoon nightclub. He presumed they were residents of the hotel, visiting for the weekend to get off their faces and pick up whatever woman was pissed enough to let them.

Both the hotel and the nightclub belonged to Martin Madley, reputed to be the boss of the local mafia. Not that the police could ever finger Madley. It was rumoured that his main business was drugs, but Madley was meticulous about covering his tracks and so far, the police had failed to get him. Brady knew Madley well; too well. They both shared a childhood in the riot-fuelled, car burning streets of the Ridges until Brady was lifted off the streets and dumped in countless foster homes across North Tyneside. Neither had escaped their crime-ridden, violent background. It was in their blood; but Madley chose to work with it, and Brady against it.

Brady cast a quick glance over towards The Blue Lagoon nightclub, his eyes automatically looking up towards Madley's generous first floor office. He was half-expecting to see Madley there, watching him, but the impressive ceiling to floor window was empty.

Brady turned back to the four hung-over revellers slumped against the promenade railings idly watching the proceedings unfolding on the beach below. They had a couple of six packs between them which they were casually slugging. A no-drinking zone operated along the promenade and on the beach, but that did little to deter the scum.

'Hey, mate? Do you know what the fuck's going on down there?' One of the four men asked in a fast, thick Scottish accent.

Brady automatically dropped his gaze to the activity on the beach below and mutely shook his head.

'Heard some lass was found fucking dead . . . fucking washed up on the beach!' Slurred a second Scottish voice as he respectfully slugged from his can of lager.

'Aye, fucking can't believe it would happen here would you?' Added his mate as he morosely shook his head.

Brady resisted the temptation to spoil their illusion about Whitley Bay and instead shrugged them off and headed towards the two officers standing guard at the sealed off steps leading down to the lower promenade.

'What the fuck was his fucking problem then, eh?' Jeered one the men in a razor sharp, Scottish accent.

'Fuck if I know.! Fucking miserable bastard!' Sourly replied one of his friends.

Brady smiled as a half-empty lager tin flew past him.

'Sir,' promptly addressed one of the uniforms.

'Get rid of them will you?' Brady said jerking his head towards the four spectators. 'It's bad for business.'

'Yes sir,' answered PC Hamilton as he uncomfortably weighed up the drunken men.

The other uniform dropped his eyes, safely fixing them on the ground.

For a brief second Brady felt for the red-faced constable. Even he wouldn't want to try to break them up; not when they'd been up drinking all night. Brady could still remember the days when the public were respectful, if not fearful of the police. Nowadays the police were treated with contempt; both by law abiding citizens who were frustrated by how little jurisdiction the police had when it came to actually dealing with the scum who made their lives a misery; scum who knew their rights better than the solicitors called into represent them. Instead of the police reading them their rights when arrested, it was now the other way round.

'What do you fucking mean we can't fucking stand here? Eh? It's a fucking free country isn't it?' Shouted one of the four drunken revellers, aggressively.

Brady couldn't make out Hamilton's reply only that his delivery was calm and to the point.

'Hey, don't you fucking tell me I can't drink where the fuck I want to!' Angrily garbled another of the men as he threw a scrunched up lager can at the officer.

'I'll fucking give you a Glaswegian smile if you're not careful you wee shite!'

Brady didn't know which members of the group were giving PC Hamilton grief and didn't want to know, he had other things to worry about now. He bent under the police tape and started making his way down the steps looking for what his guts were already telling him was going to be trouble.

Brady caught sight of Conrad. His deputy's erect, stiff figure stood out from the crowd; for all the right reasons. Unlike Brady, he had the makings of a Chief Superintendent and soon enough it would be Conrad kicking Brady around. But for now, it was Brady's job to do the kicking.

Conrad had already noticed Brady heading down the steps. He promptly finished talking to one of the white-clad SOCOS and made his way across the beach to meet him.

Brady nodded in response as the young, clean-cut figure of Conrad approached him.

'I take it this isn't an accidental drowning then?'

Conrad stiffly shook his head.

'No sir. This definitely was no accident.'

'Explains the amount of coppers we've got crawling all over the beach then,' Brady said.

'We're still looking for the rest of her, sir,' Conrad quietly answered.

Brady questioningly looked at him.

'Better you see this for yourself sir,' replied Conrad.

Brady followed Conrad's eyes as he uneasily looked towards the large, white forensics tent.